DISCARD

THE
ROCK

also by

KANAN MAKIYA

Republic of Fear

Post-Islamic Classicism

The Monument

Cruelty and Silence

THE
ROCK

A Tale of Seventh-Century Jerusalem

KANAN MAKIYA

Pantheon Books ~ New York

Library of Congress Cataloging-in-Publication Data

Makiya, Kanan.
The rock : a tale of seventh-century Jerusalem / Kanan Makiya.
p. cm.
Includes bibliographical references.
ISBN 0-375-40087-7
1. Qubbat al-ṣakhrah (Mosque : Jerusalem)–Fiction.
2. Islam–Relations–Christianity–Fiction.
3. Islam–Relations–Judaism–Fiction.
4. Jerusalem–Fiction. I. Title.

PR6113.A58R64 2001   823'.92–dc21   2001031400

www.pantheonbooks.com

Book design by Fearn Cutler de Vicq de Cumptich

Printed in the United States of America

FIRST EDITION
2 4 6 8 9 7 5 3 1

for Sara, Naseem, and Bushra

Now this religion happens to prevail

Until by that one it is overthrown,

Because men dare not live with men alone

But always with another fairy tale.

Abu al-'Alaa al-Ma'arri
Born in Syria. Died 1057

Contents

Contents

THE
ROCK

In the Name of God the Merciful
the Compassionate

Praise be to Him, before Whom bow all who are in the heavens and the earth, willingly or unwillingly, as do their shadows in the mornings and the evenings. There is no God but He whose subtle proofs triumph in disputes created by anxious minds, whose work, which is creation in all its splendor, reduces to nothing the justifications put forward by the tongues of Unbelievers.

In the Book whose every word bears witness to Him, the story is told of the creation of the waters and the mountains, the heavens and the earth, truth and falsehood. Things sensible and insensible were created out of nothing to look and sound the way they do for no other reason than to serve as proof of Him. Their every shade of color was painted with a single hair. The nymphs and satyrs of the desert were created from smokeless fire; man, from a single drop of sperm. Every separate thing, heartless or otherwise, found its place in the scheme of God.

Surely in that are signs for a people who consider.

∾

The Rock was the first sign. From its surface, God issued the first ray of light. The ray pierced the darkness to fill His chosen land. Then the light spread, to cover the rest of the world without discrimination.

3

On the third hour of the sixth day of creation, the Lord of Creation gathered dry black clay with which to make the body of the first man. He gathered it from the Rock for the head, from the site of the Ka'ba for the breast and back, and from the land of the Yemen for the limbs. He worked and kneaded the clay with water until it became sticky and slimy.

By the fourth hour of the sixth day of creation, a body had been formed. It was hairy, as tall as a palm tree, and was given the name Adam, because, like Allah, the Arabic name for God, it begins with the first letter of the alphabet.

In the seventh hour, the angel Iblis was ordered to enter Adam's mouth and emerge from his anus, following which he was obliged to retrace his steps and emerge from his mouth. Then God blew a spirit into the body of His Prince. It entered Adam's brain through his mouth, from which it went to his eyes and nose and further through the whole body, whereafter the body turned into flesh, blood, bone, veins, and sinews. And the first man was clothed in a fiery Garment of Light.

The dimensions and splendor of our angel ancestor awed and frightened the other angels.

"Bow yourselves to Adam," God said to the angels.

And they fell down, bowing all together, save Iblis. He was not among the bowing, which angered God.

"Go forth! Thou art henceforth the Accursed One," God said to Iblis.

∽

While Adam was in the Garden, the life of the Creator pulsated within him. God and His Creation were as One.

Adam's Fall changed everything.

He enjoyed the splendors of the Garden for less than two hours before being tempted to eat of the forbidden fruit.

And so in the twelfth hour of the sixth day of creation, he was stripped of his Garment of Light and clothed instead in a layer of

skin. He was cast out of the Garden, and set down upon the Rock of
Foundation, thenceforth known also as the Rock of Atonement.

"Thou shalt be the prototype of thy children" were the last
words of God before placing His foot on the Rock to ascend back to
Heaven.

Banished from the Garden, the father of mankind descended on
a stone, the first station of a new world, an exile's world—bleak and
brooding, with harsh sunlight and deep shadows, desolate rocky
peaks and steep ravines, dry burning heat and cold luminous
nights. Adam, whom God had appointed His deputy on Earth, had
landed in the elemental landscape of his Creator's imagination.

On a mountain that happened to be the closest to Heaven of all
the mountains of the Earth, he landed—so close that, when Adam's
feet were planted on its summit, his head poked into the Garden out
of which he had been cast.

The sight terrified the angels. They had not wanted Adam in
their presence in the first place. "Wilt Thou place upon the Earth
one who will corrupt it and shed blood, while we proclaim Thy
praise and call Thee Holy?" they asked the Lord. Unable to stand
the sight of the fallen man any longer, they begged God to do something about him. And so it came to pass that Adam was cut down to
sixty cubits.

The first man whined and complained at his fate.

"My Lord! I was Your protégé in Your house, having no Lord
but You and no one to watch over me except You. There, I had much
to eat and could dwell wherever I wanted. I used to hear the voices
of the angels and see them crowd around Your Throne, and I
enjoyed the sweet smell of Paradise. But then you cast me out and
cut me down."

Like Iblis, the rest of God's creatures now refused to pay him
their respect.

The Eagle was the first to see Adam on the mountain. He flew
down to the sea and said to the Fish: "I have seen a creature walking on its hind feet. It has two hands to attack with, and on each
hand are five fingers."

"I think," the Fish replied, *"that you describe a creature that will neither leave you alone in the height of the air nor leave me alone in the depth of the sea."*

~

*A*nd Adam ruled the Earth and all its creatures, which he named according to what God had taught him in the Garden. While he slept, God rubbed his back, making all Adam's future offspring appear before him. When Adam learned that David would live only a short time, he gave him fifty of the thousand years that were alloted to himself. And the number of Adam's offspring was forty thousand as his nine-hundred-and-fiftieth year approached, and Iblis and the angels gathered round him for the last time.

"Why did you not bow down before me, Iblis, when God commanded it?" asked Adam.

"Because I believe that only One is to be adored. And of all the dwellers in the Garden, there was no stricter champion of His Unity than I."

"You disregard God's Command?" asked Adam.

"That was trial," said Iblis, "not Command."

"Do you still remember what He looked like?"

"O Adam," Iblis said, "pure thought needs no memory, and thought is His memorial with me. I serve Him now with a purer purpose, in a present emptiness of self-purpose. In the Garden I served Him for my own well-being, but now I serve for the sake of His."

When she who had been made from Adam's shortest and most crooked rib heard the words of Iblis, she feared the worst, and tried to go in to see her husband alone. He had become an irritable and angry old man, and said to her, "Go away from me and these messengers of my Lord. I would not have encountered what I did except for you, and what happened to me would not have happened except for you."

And Adam died, and the angels washed his body with the

leaves of the lote soaked in water. They wrapped the corpse in a single garment, dug a grave, and buried it. Then they said, "This is the precedent for all Adam's children after him." And the first man was buried under the Rock of Zion, the same Rock from which he was made, that hulk of craggy limestone that stood for a hardness of resolve and clarity of purpose that our angel ancestor always lacked.

Prologue

Ishaq son of Ka'b, a bookbinder by training, shall record in this seventy-second year of the Prophet's Exodus from Mecca, in the City of the Temple, all that is worthy of being known about the summit of the mountain known to the Jews as Zion, or Moriah. My account is based on stories passed down to me by my father, Ka'b al-Ahbar, and on my own experience as an advisor to Abd al-Malik, the ninth Caliph of Islam.

Ka'b was born Jacob of the ancient tribe of Judah. Prompted by Jeremiah's prophecy of doom, his distant ancestors left the Holy City forty-two years before the destruction of Solomon's Temple and crossed the Jordan River in the hope of reaching the land where their father Abraham was born. They lost their way in the desert. After years of wandering, seventy thousand men, women, and children, priests and slaves, settled in the Yemen. In the course of time, they became both the most Jewish and the most Arab of all Jews.

My father, the grandson of a widely respected rabbi, advisor to the last Jewish king of the Yemen, was trained in the Law and Hebrew scripture. Ka'b al-Ahbar is the name he adopted after his migration to Medina and his acknowledgment of Muhammad as the Messenger of God.

I was born at the moment of that acknowledgment in Medina. But I grew up in Jerusalem, in a house located on the eastern offshoot of the main street known to the Christians as the Cardo. The

Christians favor the western offshoot because it is wider and colonnaded on both sides. Both streets run due south from the Gate of the Column, Jerusalem's main entrance from the north. Thus is Mount Golgotha to the west separated from Mount Zion to the east. The eastern branch of the Cardo follows the low road into the valley separating the Christian and Jewish holy mountains until it reaches the large esplanade built by the Jews in ancient times.

In the first weeks after the Muslim conquest of the city, Ka'b found the time to buy a house. "I was the first!" he would say to anyone who cared to listen, meaning that he had been the first follower of Muhammad to buy property on a Jewish mountain near the site of the old Temple where the prophet David fell down, bowing, and sought forgiveness of his Lord. It mattered little to him that the house and its immediate surrounds were filthy when we moved in. My Arab stepmother soon cleaned them up, turning the place into a home. I was brought up a Muslim in this house by this good woman, to whom I became deeply attached and because of whom I have no memory of any Jewishness in my upbringing.

Our two-story abode sat between a tiny paved courtyard bordering the street and the huge flat expanse of the platform built by Solomon, which rests like a giant tabletop on Mount Zion. Emerging from that tabletop, eighty-six paces from the boundary wall between it and our house, rose the gently suppurating mass of the mountain's summit.

Ka'b's stories knitted around that extension of stone were like pieces of unused furniture in our house. I lived constantly with them, rarely noticing they were there. From the day that Jerusalem entered the Muslim fold, they held together the scattered remembrances of my father's life. The most interesting had changed ownership more than once, like the holy mountain that shaped their content.

Those who live on such a mountain are unable to see it, even as they are unable to form a single thought of which it is not a part. Its shape and colors, the sounds of children scrambling over it, sparrows in the springtime, the howling wind—these are the mountain, a place that bears down on its residents, gradually appropriating their memories. Thus did the mountain's hold upon me grow tighter and tighter with the passage of time. And yet fifty-five years passed before I picked up the pen to tell all that I know about it, which is all that my father knew, which is more than any other man has ever known about the most sacred spot in the cosmos.

~

Only the tip of the original Rock that I grew up with remains visible today. By far the greater bulk lies dormant and unseen, tucked away beneath new flagstones. This is all that is left of a mountain whose slopes have been hacked, tunnelled, and terraced since the beginning of time, a landscape beaten into its present shape through endless cycles of construction and destruction—a dozen in all, beginning with Solomon's great Temple. And this is to say nothing of ruinous sieges, intervals of total desolation, bloody transitions from one religion to another.

The last bit of the Rock that can be seen today, having weathered all these storms, exudes the aura of an ancient face. A face that does not talk about what it has seen, a face that does not even know it has seen anything.

Nothing competed with that face's impassive presence after all the rubble and refuse that had accumulated upon the sanctuary was cleared away. As children, we used to scramble and play on it. That stopped after a little girl fell down from its highest point and cracked open her skull.

Surface and texture gave no sign that the Rock had been levelled to create a usable surface, or cut into and chipped away at by builders, pilgrims, men who wished it ill. The natural slopes and furrows, I recall, were well preserved. Traces of yellow earth could be found tucked away inside cracks and crevices; they must have sat there undisturbed for centuries, resistant even to the regular washing down to which the Rock has been subjected from the time of the conquest. The ring of stone hidden beneath the polished marble floor is naturally flat, until the point at which the outer walls supporting the new building begin. Here, the stone's profile takes a sharp dip, sloping downward. The mountain, key to the Rock's secrets, has begun its descent.

Before the Christians and the Romans, before even King Solomon and his miracle of engineering, when the Earth was without form and void, and darkness was upon the face of the deep, the Rock and the mountain were one. Or so my father used to say. Zion would then have looked no different from the other mountains upon which this city is built; it was not distinguished from its neighbors by size or height. In fact, Zion is not a mountain at all; it is more of a hill, a bump in the landscape. Neighboring Golgotha is higher.

Today, the mountain and its summit look separate, and people say that the Rock is suspended by an invisible force between Heaven and Earth. But that is an illusion created by the fact that the Rock is attached to the mountain in only one place. Below the Rock, underneath its highest point, is a low-ceilinged cave. The cave is small, less than five paces square, and barely a man's height. Eleven crudely carved steps lead to the cave from the summit. Why eleven? I remember asking my father. Because, he said, eleven is the first act of transgression over ten, the number of God's Commandments.

The cave is pierced by two holes. The first bores through solid stone for the length of a man and is round and smooth, just large enough for a child on a rope to slither through and drop down on the floor below. Not even my father knew who cut this hole or why.

The smaller second hole pierces the floor of the cave below. For as long as I can remember, it has been covered with a large, round slab that has a hoop set into it, which I was never able to shift. Ka'b said that on the slab's underside there is another hoop protruding downward with a chain attached onto which Solomon used to hang the keys of his Temple. The slab conceals an underground cavern that drops like a giant waterskin into the belly of the mountain. People call it the Well of Souls. They say that, if you listen very carefully at certain times of the year, you will hear muffled mumblings emanating from deep within the mountain.

*We shall show them Our signs
in the horizons and in themselves.*

Those who know what a great seducer the desert is understand how the faith of its sons gets tested daily simply by their being condemned to live in it. Amid sands and dunes that shift and undulate like loose women, rocks stand out, omnipotent and steadfast, commanders of presence, demarcators of boundaries, bearers of witness—visible presences in place of invisible ones, the known in place of the unknown and the unknowable. And when such signs of God's work cannot be found because the terrain is too flat, too muddy, too monotonous, and unresistant, they have to be made up. A building then takes the place of a mountain.

In the Holy Land, such signs did not have to be invented as they were in Babylon and Egypt with their sacred assemblages of brick and stone aping the kind of permanence that nature itself had eschewed. They were already there. But they had to be identified and their relation to God interpreted correctly. Sinai, Horeb, Zaphon, Carmel, Hermon, Tabor, all pointed to the attributes of

Him who created them—the Fixed and the Unalterable, the Great and the Illimitable. These are among His names. Not that mountains are God. They are merely signs of Him from whom revelation and knowledge pour into the mind like water into a valley.

Only He whom the eye cannot attain knows why Zion was chosen above all other mountains, and why its summit was blessed with a share in His majesty.

Is a stone thus singled out still a stone? The Rock will always be itself, a plain and humble piece of limestone no different from the other stones upon which this Holy City is built, but in what ways does it partake in the nature and mystery of God? Rediscovering those ways, which began long before they could be told, and which sprang from the source from which all religion springs, was Ka'b al-Ahbar's most important contribution to the religion of Muhammad.

The Rock of Foundation

A name, my father used to say, "*is* the thing it names. Did not God teach Adam the names of all things so that he might know them?" Ka'b refused to call the Rock by anything other than its oldest name, the Rock of Foundation.

"You are like a superstitious midwife," my stepmother would joke, "who blesses the child she has just delivered with a name at exactly the moment she cuts its umbilical cord, and is then afraid to call him by any other name."

Precious Stone. Rock of Atonement. Adam's Sepulchre. Navel of the Universe. Stone of Stumbling. Rock of Sacrifice. David's Rock. Holy Rock. Rock of the Holy of Holies. Zion's Rock. Rock of Calvary. Rock of the Ages. Jacob's Rock. Peter's Rock. Rock of the Church. Rock of Salvation. Stone of Consolation. Rock of Fear and Trembling. Rock of Judgment. The Rock has many names.

So many names. So many carriers of blessing. So many proofs of excellence. Are they a sign of confusion? Perhaps the Rock has been delivered too many times into the world. Perhaps a thing encumbered with this many names has turned into a kind of fetish.

The names troubled Ka'b.

"Is the Rock one thing, or is it many things at once?" he asked me one day by way of a challenge.

"I have no idea, Father."

"God, who makes the tongues of the eloquent fall short of

praising His beauty unless they use the means by which He praises Himself, has at least ninety-nine names. Does that mean God is ninety-nine different things, because He has ninety-nine names?"

"I suppose not."

"You suppose! You don't know! What is that worthless Shaikh teaching you every day?" he exclaimed, referring to the old man who had come with Umar's army and now held classes for the children of settlers in a room on the sanctuary.

Ka'b meant to say that, even if a name is the thing it names, it is not that thing's whole essence. Each name reveals an aspect of essence, one meaning among many. The elucidation of meaning requires a story, the stuff of religion, a story that lies at the origin of a particular name.

How much is unquestionably authentic about these stories? Justifications of conquests, apologias of defeats, tales of victory and of woe, rituals of worship, all mixtures of lies and truths have become wondrous stories accumulating around Moriah's weather-beaten face since men first fixed their eyes upon it. Women weep for themselves beside the Rock, suffering infinitely, only to leave it transformed in heart and soul, light shining from their faces; brash young men lift their faces to Heaven, guffawing, only to leave the Rock they have seated themselves upon terrified, their bodies twisted and trembling. Sifting through all the debris in search of the Rock's essence is an unreliable exercise at the best of times.

But not so for the Rock's first name, Ka'b said, its most important name, following which all the other names came, in the order of the prophets and the strange and wondrous things that happened to them on or near the Rock.

∼

"Father, I asked Shaikh Abdallah at school today where God was during creation."

"And what did he say?"

"He said that God was in a watery mist without shape or form.

There was no Heaven, no Earth, no height, no depth, no name. Just a milky-white mist the pallor of a dead man's face. He created the sky and the waters out of that mist. He sat his throne upon the water. Still, there were no separate things with or around Him. Then, the Shaikh said, God dried up the original water upon which His throne sat, thus forming the Earth. Mountains were pushed into place by the froth left on the surface of the water as it was drying up."

"Something troubles you about what the Shaikh said?"

"The fact that water comes first, before mountains and rocks. He didn't mention rocks." I needed to know how Ka'b accounted for the holiness of the Rock, if Shaikh Abdallah was right.

Instead of answering the question, Ka'b began solemnly to recite words handed down by Solomon:

> *The Lord made me the beginning of his work,*
> *the first of his acts of old.*
> *Ages ago I was formed,*
> *before the establishment of the Earth.*
> *When He made the Heavens, I was already there,*
> *when He drew a circle on the face of the deep.*

"Father, who is speaking?" I said, interrupting him before it was too late.

"Wisdom."

"Are you saying wisdom came first in the order of creation, before water?"

"Yes," he replied, "according to the great Solomon himself."

"But the Holy Book opens with: In the beginning God created the Heavens and the Earth. Wisdom is not even mentioned."

"The beginning is not necessarily the *very* beginning. In the very beginning, God did not create things like the Heavens or the Earth, and certainly not men or demons. He created wisdom, by which He founded the Earth."

"What is this wisdom?"

"It is the great underlying plan according to which the Heavens and the Earth and all that lies in between are laid out."

"What does that have to do with the Rock?"

"Everything."

"I don't understand."

"Does not the idea of a circle precede its drawing?"

"It does."

"And to execute that idea on the face of the deep, does one not need a point upon which to stand?"

"You mean like the stone tied to the end of Shaikh Abdallah's piece of string when he is drawing a circle for us in class?"

"Exactly. The Rock was that fixed point in relation to which the Lord laid out the rest of creation. Just as Shaikh Abdallah's circle would not have appeared without the fixed end of his compass, so wisdom would not have become manifested in the world without the Rock."

"But I *see* his circle. I cannot see wisdom."

"Can you see good or evil? The Rock is to wisdom what the body is to knowledge of good and evil."

"What did God make the Rock from?"

"He plucked a jewel from underneath his throne and plunged it into the abyss. One end of it remained fastened there, while the other stood out above. Upon this end He stood while He went about the rest of creation, spreading the earth to the right and to the left and into all directions until it became as you see it today."

"I don't see a jewel," I said, pointing in the direction of the esplanade. "What happened to the jewel?"

"It was tarnished by our sins until it metamorphosed into the thing you see before you. The People of the Torah call it the Rock of Foundation, because this was where God began his work on the first day of creation. We call it simply the Rock. But the two are one and the same."

"Jerusalem is littered with rocks. How can you tell which one of them is the Rock?"

"Just as the navel is the center of the human body, so the land of Palestine is the center of the world. Jerusalem is the center of Palestine. The Mountain is the center of Jerusalem. Upon its summit, Solomon built the Temple. The innermost precinct of that Temple, the Holy of Holies, is the center of the Temple, and at the center of the Holy of Holies is the Rock of Foundation."

Locusts and Christians

Until he reached puberty, my father once told me, he thought Jerusalem was a place in Heaven, not on Earth. "Rabbi Salih taught me otherwise."

Rabbi Salih taught my father that Mount Zion was a real place that had not been destroyed by the Romans. He taught him that the Rock of Foundation was the last remaining vestige of Solomon's Temple, that it was the highest point of the mountain, and that it used to project three fingerbreadths above the floor of the Holy of Holies in Solomon's Temple. He taught him that the Ark was situated at the center of the Rock, facing east toward the Mount of Olives.

These teachings instilled in my father the desire to see that which Rabbi Salih had described.

Every young Yemeni Jew with aspirations to scholarship yearned to go to the Holy City and see the capstone of creation. But the city was in Christian hands. And Ka'b had to feed and clothe his newly acquired wife, who was but twelve years old and had been betrothed to him since childhood. Under such circumstances, yearnings were not enough.

It was fear that eventually drove my father out of the Yemen.

Attacking in swarms like flies on the Day of Resurrection, locusts ate up the fruits and vegetables, and then made their way into unshuttered houses and shops. They left carcasses of men lying scattered in the streets like dung on an open field. My mother, nevertheless, thought of them as a source of food, even a delicacy. She could count eight kinds of kosher locust, and whenever she was in one of her nostalgic moods, I am told, she would say, "A locust in my mouth is better than a fattened lamb. And it is kosher!"

She ate her fear, but my father never could because he said locusts caused epilepsy. As soon as anyone but mentioned "locust," he would begin a painstaking description of what the body of a man consumed by famine looked like, his skin shrivelled upon the bones, or swollen and transparent like glass. His words left the impression that he had run away from the Yemen, not because there was nothing to eat, but because of his horror of locusts.

Ka'b was by then already an old man, and the star of the Yemen had long since been on the wane. The land was tired, its spirit broken; agriculture was in ruins, the population beset by famine. Christian ships sailed the Red Sea. Why had my father waited for the knife to cut through to the bone before tearing up his roots and dragging my unwilling mother along, going to Medina?

First, there were the locusts. And then there was the fear that, once he left and was far away from the land he knew well, he might become so filled with anxiety about what lay ahead as to want to go back. Travelling was a test that he imposed upon himself—an ordeal not all that different from the one pilgrims undergo as they travel further and further away from all they know in order to get closer to God.

By contrast with the Yemen, Arabia's star was on the rise. Mecca had become the religious center of the Hijaz, and people increasingly travelled there for trade. And there was news of a desert prophet who lingered in the surrounding mountains, who heard voices coming forth from the rocks. His name was Muhammad.

∾

Ka'b began taking an active interest in the Prophet, God's Blessings Be Upon Him, after he heard that he had sent an envoy to the people of the nearby town of Najran, inviting them to accept Islam and guaranteeing their safety if they did so.

The pork-eating people of Najran had heard this before when, thirty years prior to the birth of Muhammad, Dhu Nuwas, the last Jewish king to rule the Yemen, sought to convert them. Ka'b's father and uncles had believed that Dhu Nuwas was the Messiah, and had fought by his side like wild lions. But the Christians of Najran would have nothing to do with Dhu Nuwas. They said that it was Jesus who raised the dead. It was Jesus who healed the sick. It was Jesus who declared the unseen. It was Jesus who was the Son of God. Therefore it had to be Jesus who was the Messiah. This reply angered the Jewish king. He put a choice before the people of Najran: convert or die. The town chose death.

After the fighting, Dhu Nuwas had his men dig pits and threw all the survivors into them; some he slew with the sword before tossing their bodies into the fire; others he burnt alive in pits, as the Holy Book bears witness.

Slain were the Men of the Pit,
the fire abounding in fuel,
when they were seated over it
and were themselves witnesses of what they did with the believers.
They took revenge on them only because they believed in God
the All-mighty, the All-laudable,
to whom belongs the Kingdom of the Heavens and the Earth.
God is Witness over everything.

They say the king killed twenty thousand Christians that day. Two of Ka'b's uncles died in the fighting. But later the Byzantines got their revenge. Dhu Nuwas was last seen fleeing an army of Christians come from Abyssinia. As the enemy approached, he drove his horse into the sea, spurring it on through the shallow waters into the deep, where horse and rider vanished.

∾

But after Muhammad's envoy had spoken, the town, convinced that great benefits would accrue to it, accepted Muhammad's offer, whereupon they were taught how and in which direction to pray to the Lord of Creation.

What drove Ka'b to visit Najran? After all, he hated the People of the Cross even more than he feared locusts. "If you fatten your dog, will he not eat you?" he would say about their converts. Was it curiosity about the Prophet, whose followers used to pray in the direction of Solomon's Temple and fast on the Jewish Day of Atonement? Perhaps Ka'b's visit was an act of defiance, or a family pilgrimage—his way of paying respect to the memory of his dead uncles.

I don't know what happened in Najran on the day of his visit. But afterward, he began to believe that the distance between Judaism and Islam was not very great.

My father despised the state of weakness that the Jews had fallen into after the vanishing of Dhu Nuwas. "Like goats they take to the rocks for fear of the wolves," he would say of his own kin. He spoke wistfully of the succession of hopeless rebellions against Byzantine overlords, always followed by unrelenting repression. It was a time when false Messiahs declared themselves all over southern Arabia, and Ka'b's tale of the madman who proclaimed himself a second Moses left a deep impression on me as a boy.

The tale was brief. The would-be savior promised his disciples a miraculous journey to the Promised Land. He told them that redemption was imminent, and then he walked them over a cliff to a horrible death on the rocks below.

"At least he ventured forth," Ka'b said.

But my father ached to leave a land whose self-esteem had sunk so low, and nothing angered him as much as hearing a fellow Jew justify his downtrodden position by reference to the curse of Ezra. Travelling all the way from Palestine to the Yemen, Ezra the Scribe had come to plead with his brethren to return to Jerusalem and help in the rebuilding of the Temple.

"Why should we suffer afflictions once again?" Ka'b's ancestors had said in response. "It is better for us to stay where we are and worship God." An angry exchange had taken place, after which Ezra had put a curse on all Jewish heads in the Yemen, forever depriving them of peace.

~

Ka'b yearned for a savior in the warrior tradition of his uncles, someone like Jabbar, the noble Jewish opponent of the Arab hero Antar. Jabbar is said to have foretold that a Savior would appear to the Jews of Arabia from across a river of sand. He would come riding a white ass followed by a sea of warriors seated on camels and lions. Every fortress besieged by them would collapse; every army would be annihilated. He would make all other religions disappear and renew the Law that God gave to Moses on Mount Sinai. Thus would the glory of the Sons of Israel become more dazzling than ever before.

Hope is a medicine that needs continual administration. God, in His infinite wisdom, presses down on us when we breathe. Then He expands and fills our chests by releasing us from pressure. His mystery is present in both motions.

"A prophet has appeared among the Arabs," Ka'b said, testing the waters with an old friend. "They say that he is proclaiming the coming of the annointed one. What say you, dear Abraham?"

"That he is an impostor," Abraham replied, groaning at the prospect of the conversation he knew was about to transpire. "Do the prophets come with sword and chariot? There is no truth to be found in this so-called prophet, only bloodshed. It is written of his ancestor, Ishmael, that his hand will be against every man, and every man's hand against him. Mark my words, Ka'b: Should those sons of locusts become a swarm covering the surface of the earth, their only purpose will be plunder."

"What if the Holy One is raising them up in order to save us from the Kingdom of the Cross? Have you thought of that, Abraham? God puts a prophet in their midst to bring them to greatness, following which a great terror will be unleashed between this prophet's followers and the Christians."

"How can we know that these happenings in Arabia are our salvation and not harbingers of even greater hardship?" replied Abraham. "You are talking about a people who give the large and oddly shaped rocks they see around them names! They are rock-worshippers, my friend!"

"Hardship," said Ka'b, "is the nurse of salvation. Did not Isaiah hear in a vision, come to him while his loins were racked with pain, that the deliverance of Israel would come from a man mounted on a camel followed by a man mounted on an ass?"

"He did."

"And was it not the habit of the prophet Elijah to appear in the guise of a desert Arab?"

"It was."

"The rider on the camel is a prophet whose coming heralds that of the rider on the ass, the Messiah. Did not Isaiah hear our Lord Yahweh say,

> *Now I shall lay a stone in Zion,*
> *a granite-stone, a precious corner-stone,*
> *a firm foundation-stone:*
> *No one who relies on this will stumble.*
> *And I will make fair judgment the measure,*
> *and uprightness the plumb-line.*

"Enough, Ka'b! My patience is at an end. You will bring a terrible retribution on all our heads. Do not force me to repudiate you. I will hear no more of this talk." And with that, Abraham turned his back on my father and stalked out of the room.

Medina

On a night that had dropped over the Yemen like a stone, my father, with my unhappy mother in tow, left for the city of Medina. They arrived shortly after the unification of Arabia, in what became known as the Year of the Delegations, a momentous year in the annals of Believers. As tribes from all over Arabia were streaming in to swear allegiance to Muhammad, an air of excitement and unfulfilled promise hung over the dusty streets. It had taken Ka'b a long time to overcome his fears and leave; time had crawled like a worm. In Medina, it began to fly like a flushed bird.

The beardless, fiery Syrians who live on my street and grew up under Caliphs from Abd al-Malik's House think they know everything about those early years in Medina. They are like experts on the desert who have never seen a valley bare as an ass's belly, much less lived in one. They cannot imagine that a man might bear witness to Muhammad's prophecy and remain a Jew at the same time. But that was the practice in Medina when Ka'b, then known as Jacob, first arrived. He remained a Jew in that he prayed, observed the Sabbath, dressed, and in all other respects behaved and looked like a Jew. His friends thought him one. And even the rabbis I have consulted, however much they disapprove of calling Muhammad a prophet, say there is nothing un-Jewish about thinking it.

The Prophet himself looked for Jewish recruits after the Exodus. He needed them. Disappointment showed on his face when so few of them believed in the revelation that descended upon him. In the end, Muhammad understood their unbelief as God's will:

> *When there has come to them a Messenger from God*
> *confirming what was with them, a party of them*
> *that was given the Book of God rejects it.*

The Jews of Medina said Muhammad didn't know enough to be a prophet. Since when has knowledge of scripture become a precondition for knowing God? Why, Ka'b may even have been attracted to the Arabs of the Hijaz because they knew nothing. These rough warriors of the desert were everything Ka'b's downtrodden compatriots in the Yemen were not. Perhaps they leapt too fast to their swords. But the tumult and messiness of their lives was compensated by the openness of their hearts and the directness of their ways. The poetic impulse ran deep in their veins. And Ka'b, too, was a certain kind of poet, but his poetic streak, unlike that of the Arabs, derived from an anguish he was unwilling to talk about during his sojourn in Medina.

~

Ka'b made a living teaching stories about the Creation and the Prophets. My mother would complain there was no one to talk to her. "Death is better than this," she would say to her husband, complaining also of the harshness of the sun and the smells in the streets.

"Seek the welfare of the city to which God has exiled you, and pray to Him on its behalf, for in its prosperity you shall prosper," he would reply before going out to other people's houses, where he would tell the same stories over and over again.

At the time of Ka'b's arrival in Medina, Muhammad was too weak to climb the pulpit or even stand upright. Yet even in sickness, he was handsome. He had beautiful curly hair, neither short nor woolly; and his white face radiated sweetness and was as luminous as the moon. Ka'b was present at his last sermon, which Muhammad delivered seated; it was the closest he ever got to the person of the Prophet.

Muhammad began with greetings to all the prophets who had gone before him. Then he said:

"There is after death a Day of Doom and Reparation, and there will be no more favor shown of me on that Day than of any man. Therefore, if I have struck any man among you an unrequited blow, let him strike me now. If I have offended any man, let him do as much now to me. If I have taken any man's goods, let him now receive them again. Make me clean of guilt, so that I may come before God guiltless to man."

"No, God's Apostle!" the crowd cried out, weeping and tearing their hair in grief, "your wrongs are wiped clean. We are the guilty ones before you!"

One man, Ka'b recalled, stood up and reminded Muhammad of a trifling sum he had given to some beggar at his bidding.

"Better to blush in this world than the Other!" the Prophet said, and paid him what he owed. Then he got up on his feet, shuffled to his favorite wife's hut, and lay down on his pallet, where he died with the heat of noon on the following day.

Anxiety oppressed Ka'b in the weeks that followed Muhammad's death. He had left everything behind and travelled far. Was it to no avail? Joy shriveled up in him like drought-stricken grass. He moved around, I am told, like a drunken man, overpowered by the desire to sleep, afflicted by a listlessness that the monks of the desert call "the noonday demon."

All Medina had become afflicted with the same.

Certain clans of the city reacted to the Prophet's death by pulling away from the faith, confusing it with its Messenger. To the collectors of the poor-tax, they said: "Pray we will, but pay this tax we will not."

The congregation had sworn allegiance to Abu Bakr, Muhammad's closest Companion, as Muhammad's successor, he of the deep-set eyes and fleshless hands who dyed his hair with henna.

Abu Bakr would not court the renegades, and said: "God's Apostle is dead, and Revelation comes down no more. But while I can grip a sword in my fist, I'll fight them, as long as they deny me even so little as the price of a camel halter. He who makes a distinction between prayer and the poor-tax, him will I surely fight, for the poor-tax is a duty of faith."

Ka'b blamed himself for coming, for subjecting my mother to the indignities of being uprooted from home and children. He had, after all, been trained to seek in every setback reasons for his own guilt.

"Better than holy war is war against self," he said to her by way of expressing his remorse and how deeply he had been summoned into the consequences of his own confusion. The words were a saying of the Prophet, but he did not tell her that; it would not have helped. She searched his face eagerly to see if he were remorseful enough. Not that anything my father could have said would have softened my mother toward him. She would not forgive him for dragging her along on a journey that she never wanted to make.

My father came out of his inwardness after Abu Bakr prevailed against the renegades and returned the Holy Cities of Arabia to Muhammad's religion. Medina had begun to recover from the news

of the Prophet's death. It was a miraculous recovery, a new beginning that showed how far Ka'b had already travelled from the ways
of his ancestors. He started to read holy scripture as it had not been
read before. Dimly recalled passages were culled from the less-
penetrable recesses of his great storehouse of memories. Jumbled
images were magically teased up to the surface; they were coming at
Ka'b like waves, just as God wanted them to, fresh from the depths.

"What inspired you?" I asked my father in later years.

"The words of the Prophet: Believe in the Torah, in the Psalms
and the Gospel, even though the Quran should suffice you."

Inspiration descends upon a prophet from the angels, my father
would tell an audience; it is communicated easily, as from one man
to another. But to Muhammad inspiration had arrived ringing like a
bell, penetrating his very heart and stilling every other sound. My
father's listeners would raptly nod their heads and rock their bodies slowly in assent. Then Ka'b would startle them by saying that
the coming of Muhammad had been foretold.

"By whom?" his astounded audience would want to know.

"By the prophet Isaiah," Ka'b would reply, citing this passage
of the Torah:

> *Behold My servant whom I shall uphold;*
> *My chosen one, whom My soul desired;*
> *I have placed My spirit upon him*
> *So he can bring forth justice to the nations.*
> *He will not shout nor raise his voice,*
> *Nor make his voice heard in the street.*
> *He will not break even a bruised reed,*
> *Nor extinguish even flickering flax;*
> *But he will administer justice in truth.*
> *He will not slacken nor tire until he sets justice in the land,*
> *And islands will long for his teaching.*

God's messenger to the Arabs possessed these qualities prophesied by Isaiah, Ka'b would say. After all, did not everyone who had

known Muhammad personally—which was, of course, the whole town—attest to his gentleness and self-control? Had he ever raised his voice or been rude or interrupted anyone in mid-speech? Yes, he was critical of his followers if necessary, but he was always careful not to push them too far, or to expose a man's faults in public. When a Companion started to beat a man for letting a camel stray from the road during the pilgrimage, what did Muhammad do? Did he berate or stop him? No. He just smiled and said, "Look at what this pilgrim is doing."

Only a prophet knows how to shame a man by appealing to the best, not the worst, in his nature.

Ka'b was everything the Arabs were not—a scholar; an expert in Scripture and Oral Law; a quiet, apparently moderate man in whom the spirit of blind obedience to authority had been carefully inculcated. By temperament and family history, however, Ka'b was drawn to fiercely opinionated men who unsheathed their swords first and asked questions later. Was it the memory of his uncles who had served a fighting king that made the Arabs attractive to him? Or was it Ka'b's inspired vision of how things ought to be, nourished by the impulse of all great teachers to project their past upon the future?

My father's knowledge and mesmeric delivery became the talk of Medina. His command of the Arabic language, the first speaker of which was King Ya'rub of the Yemen, was greatly admired. Young men desirous to learn thronged around him. Many became his disciples and students. Prominent among these was Abdallah, the fourteen-year-old son of the Prophet's uncle, Abbas, destined to become the most distinguished scholar of his generation.

"Abdallah was forever writing notes while I was talking," my father would say of the boy who rose to preeminence because of the blood ties that he had renounced. "He wanted to know if the angels who praise God by day and by night ever got bored."

The son of Abbas would be the first to understand the importance of gathering accurate information about the Prophet. He began the task of questioning Muhammad's closest Companions, a task made easier by the fact that he was the Prophet's cousin. By the time I came of age in Jerusalem, Abdallah had grown into the most important teacher and interpreter of scripture among Muhammad's People. His glittering career he owed entirely to Ka'b and those first years in Medina.

Soon, my father was moving in influential circles. Abdallah's family connections helped. In the eyes of the Prophet's closest Companions, he began to look less like a Jew and more like a Muslim. Or at least the men around him didn't seem to care one way or the other, with one exception: Umar the son of Khattab, he whom the Prophet himself had once called the Separator of Right from Wrong.

Umar was a tall and impulsive man with fiery red hair. Out of zeal for Mecca's stone idols, he had in his youth set out to kill the very Prophet whom he now revered. On his way to do the terrible deed, he heard his sister reciting to herself from the Holy Book. Awestruck by the beauty of the words, this hard and unbending man changed his religion on the spot. Umar became as zealous a Muslim as he had been an unbeliever. That same passionate intensity led him to criticize Muhammad on occasion. No one else among the Prophet's Companions would do so, not in public at any rate. Umar's uprightness and strictness in matters of faith were never in doubt; they were of a piece with the angularity and hardness of his features, with the long, gaunt body that carried not an iota of extra flesh. This was a man who would not soften, not even when he was lying comfortably on the ground, one leg under the other, a habit he took up after the Prophet, who knew how to enjoy himself. No one could remember when they had last seen Umar smile. Levity and lightness, which were tolerated in the Prophet's own presence, had to be suppressed whenever Umar was around. It was not as if he was unaware of the seductiveness of the pleasures of the world; if anything, he felt them more keenly than most.

This is the man who now insisted upon a public confession of faith by my father.

Yet not even Umar asked Ka'b to do so by repudiating Judaism.

And my father did not. He continued to call the Torah "God's Book." And afterward, Khattab's son honored my father with a new surname: Al-Ahbar, meaning the most learned of the learned. Thus was my father set apart from peddlers of dubious tales by one whose own daughter had been married to Muhammad, to enter Arab society under the sponsorship and protection of the Prophet's most distinguished and loyal Companion.

It was then that my father changed his name from Jacob to Ka'b, his authority and learning having been publicly affirmed. Umar now took to saying that Ka'b had been reborn the first Jewish follower of the Messenger of God. I am not sure that he was the first. But if there were others, Believers have forgotten them. Certainly Ka'b was the oldest sage in Medina and first in his knowledge of the Holy Books.

∾

Like so many turning points in Ka'b's life, his presence in Umar's circle was confirmed with a story.

"What do we owe to Adam?" Umar asked Ka'b shortly after my father had changed his name.

"Our salvation," Ka'b answered in the blink of an eye. "If we have been afforded even a glimpse into the secrets of Heaven, in spite of the silt of time that has covered us in doubt, it is because we are descended from Adam's body. All the people who have ever lived, including all those still alive today, and those yet to be born tomorrow, owe, not only their existence, but their reason for existence, their validation as created beings, to him who was created first."

"But Adam was stripped of his Garment of Light and saw his nakedness."

"His imperfections have also chased us over the ages like a demon. If we are forever striving to defeat Adam's demons, it is in order to restore us to the state of perfection that was initially breathed into him."

"And the rest of the prophets? Were they also being chased by Adam's demons?"

"Certainly. And none more so than David, conqueror of the City of the Temple."

"What did the great warrior-Prophet do?"

"He upset the peace by attempting to dislodge the keystone of creation."

"Tell us the story, O Ka'b," said Umar, not knowing that the story he was about to hear was destined to become the kindling of his zeal for another Holy City.

The Fundaments of the Universe

Wisdom and pain, the fundaments of the universe, Ka'b told Umar, are memories of Heaven and Hell. "Think," he said, "of two symmetrical cones balanced apex to apex. God's design is such that the ever-expanding cone of wisdom meets the bottomless abyss of pain at a singular point, the fulcrum of the cosmos. The Rock keeps the peace by holding the burden of memory in balance. Which is why David positively ached to build a Palace of Peace upon it."

"A peace that was disturbed."

"Yes, many times, beginning with Solomon's father."

"What did David do?"

"He tried to move the Rock."

"Move the Rock! How could anyone dream of such a thing?"

"It had become covered in refuse and dirt. The king was hopelessly entangled in the family troubles that plagued his last years. He spent all his time in prayer and neglected the affairs of state. The people of Israel began to complain that he was not doing anything for them. David was obliged to come out of seclusion. How could he do so and repent for his sins at the same time? Suddenly, he remembered the Rock he had purchased from Araunah the Jebusite as a young man, and he went in search of it."

"What did he want to do with it?"

"Turn it into the cornerstone of God's House. But Mount Zion had been soiled by the idolatry of the Jebusites and, it must be said, by David's own sins. Accompanied by Ahithophel, a prophet blessed with unnatural wisdom, David set out to seek repentance by clearing the summit of all that had sullied its sanctity over the ages."

"The king removed the refuse with his own hands?"

"He dug up the top layers of dirt that had accumulated around Moriah's summit. Then he threw the soiled earth over the side of the mountain. David kept on digging away at the dirt until he hit the Rock. A piece broke off, and, not knowing what it was, he started to throw it away.

But the Rock said, "You cannot lift me."

"Why not?" David asked.

"Because I am here to hold back the Waters of the Deep."

"Since when?"

"Since the hour in which the voice of God was heard to utter the words, 'I am the Lord thy God.' As the earth trembled, split asunder, and began to sink into the abyss, I was put here to hold it back!"

David persisted in his efforts to remove the piece of Rock. When it finally broke off, the Waters of the Deep, the enemies of order, began to rise, threatening a deluge far worse than that which had engulfed the Earth in the time of Noah, a deluge so powerful as to completely undo the work of creation and sink the world into primordial chaos.

Terrified by what he saw, David cried out: "Whosoever knows how to stem the tide of waters and does not do so will one day throttle himself!"

Ahithophel acted swiftly. He inscribed the divine name upon the piece of the Rock that David had dislodged, and pushed it back into place, chanting:

This is the spell and the seal
By which the Earth is bound
By which the Heavens are bound

> *The Earth flees from it*
> *All tremble before it*
> *It opens the mouth of the sea*
> *And closes the waters*
> *It opens the firmament*
> *It waters the world*
> *It uproots the earth*
> *And confounds the Universe.*

The raging seas were stilled, the waters subsided, their rebellion suppressed through the agency of the terrible, glorious, ineffable Name. The Rock had been saved, and was thenceforth called the House of the Lord God.

But the waters had sunk so low that David feared that the earth was about to lose all her moisture. So he began singing and strumming his harp, a magical instrument whose strings were made from the guts of the ram sacrificed by Abraham years before. And the Waters of the Deep rose again to their rightful place.

The Conquest Foretold

One day Abu Bakr went into a beautiful garden and saw a ringdove in the shady leafage of a tree. "You must be as happy as Adam in such a garden!" he sighed, "to find your shelter inside the green leaves of such a bountiful tree, and your food close at hand, and never to be called to account. Ah! Would to God that I had lived such a life!" Then he came down with a fever and died, but not before writing a testament appointing Umar, the son of Khattab, Caliph after him.

On the morning after Abu Bakr's burial, Umar mounted the Prophet's pulpit, around which the Believers had assembled. The pulpit had three steps. The Apostle of God always stood on the top one, but when Abu Bakr was Caliph, he had taken to addressing the congregation from the second step. Everyone waited to see what Umar would do.

Umar stood on the first step, gave praise and thanks to God, and swore to do justice. His first act after he stepped down was to write a letter appointing a new chief commander of the host in Syria. His second act was to appoint Ka'b his counselor and to call upon him to explain the extraordinary visitation which had come upon Ka'b in his sleep.

~

The outline of my father's vision or dream, I know not what to call it, was recorded immediately upon waking, while still fresh in his mind. I treasure his record of it, written in his own hand on a small brown papyrus sheet whose edges had gone ragged.

It is devoid of ornament if you discount the long upstrokes lilting to the right, even though he wrote from right to left, and you can see how meticulously Ka'b has scripted the letters *ain, ghain, fa'* and *qaf.* Why, the ink has not run into a single eye. That takes painstakingly careful execution of each letter's head, no mean achievement for a man who wrote so little, preferring to commit things to memory.

What is on this sheet of papyrus, I hasten to add, is not everything my father saw that night, for a vision is a sudden wider view of past and present realities, a form of illumination issued by God in the shape of images, not words. Impetuously, it drives the soul upon which it has been visited to fuse with the larger sweep of His intentions, moving toward a grander goal than the mere contingencies of an individual life. The words I have before me are Ka'b's poor substitute for all that, hastily scribbled down after the searing clarity of what he saw in the darkness had already begun to recede with the light of dawn:

> *On that day when the Redeemer will come*
> *To the downtrodden,*
> *Signs will be seen in the world:*
> *Earth and heaven will wither,*
> *The sun and the moon will be struck,*
> *The dwellers in the Holy City will fall silent.*
> *The kings of Byzantium and Persia*
> *Will be ground against one another,*
> *Until only the armies of Byzantium hold firm.*
> *Then will a rising star go forth from Arabia*
> *Whose followers will seize the Holy City,*
> *And the dwellers of the world will be judged.*
> *The heavens will rain dust on the earth.*

Terrible winds will spread throughout the Land.
Gog and Magog will incite one another,
Kindling fear in the hearts of the Christians.
Christians and Arabs will fight in the valley of the Jordan;
They will fight until their horses sink in blood and panic.
Some people will make peace
While others will be terror-stricken.
Some people will be shown mercy
While others will have their daughters stoned,
Until the Kings of Christendom will be no more.
Then shall the sons of Sara and Hagar be freed of all sins.
No more shall they be kept from David's Sanctuary.
Blessings will shower on Abraham's children,
Whose deeds will live forever, engraved in the Book of Life.

After his conversation with Umar, Ka'b was invited to tell Believers what he had seen that night. Word of it spread through the city like a spring wind.

I would give ten years of my life to have witnessed my father's performance that day. But I was still a growing seed in my mother's belly. Ka'b, I am told, was dressed in a long black cloak that sat well on him in spite of its rough homespun cloth. In his right hand he carried a staff upon which he appeared to lean and sway from time to time. Inside a square enclosure, whose sun-dried brick walls had been assembled by the Prophet himself, God's Blessings Be Upon Him, my father stood beside a column cut from the trunk of a palm tree, under the shade of a roof made from palm fronds. He stood not twenty paces from where God's Messenger lay buried, his grave covered with freshly cut fronds. In that blessed house, the first mosque of Muhammad's People, forty or so of the Prophet's closest Companions were present, along with many of the young men who were shortly to bridle their horses and set off on the road to glory.

The Arabs did not know it at the time, but they were standing on the threshold of great conquests. Place and timing were crucial to understanding the extraordinary reception my father received that day. Heraclius, the Byzantine emperor, had just evicted his Persian rival, Khusraw, from Jerusalem and restored the cross of Jesus stolen by the Persians. That part of what my father had to say was already known to his audience. But Ka'b was saying much more: with cool, refreshed eyes that could see that for which they longed, he was telling the followers of Muhammad that the City of the Temple, held hostage by Byzantium, was a pomegranate ripe for the picking, and that they were going to be thanked for taking it by the People of the Torah.

Overnight his words reached Muhammad's followers all over the Hijaz. It helped that he was among the finest speakers of Arabic of his generation. Young men lined up in droves just to talk with the new seer of Arabia. Established traditionists like Abu Hurayra, whose knowledge of the Torah was not in doubt, came all the way from Mecca just to meet with my father.

∾

Dreams are the measure of a man's age. Like the wind, they are in the air that everyone breathes. Just as men don't know anything is in the air until it brushes past their face, so they don't know what is in their dreams until it is pointed out to them.

Ka'b's words meant something to everyone. But they meant one thing to Believers who were there when he spoke them, and they meant something else entirely to those who heard them exaggerated a hundredfold off the lips of other men. Then they meant yet a different thing to those who heard them after the Holy City had fallen to the armies of Khattab's son, he whom men, following in Ka'b's lead, now took to calling "the Redeemer."

The greatest excitement was caused by Ka'b's prediction that the first holy axis of Islam, the city that David had brought to True Belief, was going to fall into the hands of the sons of Ishmael. Fighting bands of stalwarts raised in the desert had been probing the Byzantine defenses for years. Raiding parties had sacked many a village and town. But Ka'b was predicting the fall of Syria and the defeat of the most powerful empire the world had ever known. He was saying these things at a time when not a soul in the length and breadth of Arabia had yet dared to dream them.

Much later, after the death of Umar, my father's enemies accused him of being just another oracle-mongerer who happened to strike it lucky. All of his prophesying was a ruse, they said; Ka'b was pretending to be a Believer in order to get into Umar's good graces and accompany the Caliph to Jerusalem. What evidence was there that he was no longer a Jew? If the tribe that provided him protection was Muslim, not Jewish, that only showed how duplicitous the man was. Ka'b knew, they claimed, that the Prophet had expelled two Jewish clans from Medina, and that he had ordered the heads of hundreds of men from the tribe of Qurayza cut off because of their treachery during the Battle of the Trench. How could a Jew come to Medina after such an event without an Arab cover? Especially one who by his own admission was intent on using Arabs to liberate the City of the Temple to absolve Jews of their own sins!

Ka'b's detractors made no headway in the early years because of the circles into which my father had been drawn. Respect and affection had developed between him and Umar the son of Khattab. But there was another, more important, reason why mud would not stick to Ka'b in the early days. He was performing a service by showing how the Prophet was completing the work of the entire line of prophets who had come before him, beginning with Adam. The story of the salvation of the world had reached its terminus in Muhammad's revelation. Ka'b was providing Believers with the tools they needed for understanding themselves as inheritors of the mantle of past revelations. Umar, who dared to follow in the path opened by Muhammad, understood that this was what Ka'b was saying.

In those days, there was no agreement about the content of the Holy Book. The first Muslim sages were accustomed to granting authority to the Torah and the Christian Bible as long as those texts did not contradict what, in their opinion, was the revelation made to Muhammad. Many of Muhammad's closest Companions—great Muslims like Ali the son of Abu Talib, Salman the Persian, the son of Abbas, and Abu Hurayra—ardently sought stories from Jews and Christians that amplified or explained God's words to Muhammad. Zayd the son of Thabit was instructed to learn Hebrew in order to read scrolls about Abraham to Muhammad. Later, the Prophet himself, often in the company of Abu Bakr and Umar, made visits to the Hebrew Temple in Medina to talk about what he had heard Zayd read with its learned rabbis and caretakers.

My father dropped into all of this as though out of the sky. He spoke eloquently of the connections between Muhammad and David, of how the Arabs were going to bring peace and prosperity to an Arabia torn to shreds by its feuds, of how they were destined to bring the City of the Temple into the fold of True Belief. Always he had answers, even to questions that had not yet been asked. And in no time at all had employed his prodigious powers to memorizing all the revelations that had descended upon the Prophet in the loneliness of Mecca's mountains, after which he took to clinching every argument with the words of God:

> *Say to the Bedouins who were left*
> *behind: 'You shall be called against*
> *a people possessed of great might*
> *to fight them, until they surrender.*
> *If you obey, God will give you a*
> *goodly wage; but if you turn your*
> *backs, as you turned your backs*
> *before, He will chastise you with a*
> *painful chastisement.*

～

In spite of the support of the Prophet's Companions, Ka'b's detractors found fresh arrows for their bows in the bitterness of my mother, who never took her husband's conversion seriously.

"You are an old man!" she would shout in the street so that everyone could hear. "Whoever heard of a man in his sixties changing his religion! Leave that for the boys, and stick to the ways of your ancestors."

I was born in a maelstrom of anger and resentment. To my mother's irritation, Umar was invited to our house on the day of my birth. "Surround your newborn with the blessings and protection of the prophets," the future Caliph advised, "for on Doomsday he will be called by his name and the name of his father." Then he rubbed the roof of my mouth with some dates that he had chewed, invoking God's blessing, and asked that I be named Ishaq in recognition of my father's abandonment of the name Jacob. Naturally, Ka'b agreed, whereupon Umar bent down and pronounced the call to prayer in my right ear. From that time onward this was the custom in the naming of Muslim newborns.

The final straw for my mother was Ka'b's resolve to remarry. I must have been about four years old at the time, because my only memory of my mother dates to the terrible fight that ensued between them.

"Did not all the great patriarchs and prophets have two, three, even four wives?" thundered Ka'b.

But my mother could only see a man who was daily becoming someone else before her eyes. Until now, his Jewish self had remained dimly discernible through the fog of new prophets, customs, forms of speech and dress, even a new name. Had Ka'b been younger, or in need of softer, whiter flesh between his sheets, it might have been a different story. She had been taught that God in His wisdom had put it in the constitution of men to love dalliance and the society of women. And she knew that the taking of several wives was common, as common among the Jews as it was among the Bedouins. Nor did it necessarily imply a diminution of the first wife's status and power over her husband—especially if the second wife was still young and malleable.

But the anxiety that choked at my mother's throat lay in her realization that Ka'b was too old for those to be his reasons for wanting a second wife. After all, the woman he had chosen was only ten years younger than herself. She was already spiced with her own flavor of maturity. My mother could see that her husband's desire to remarry was of a piece with his new role as seer of the Arabs, and with his dream of travelling to the land of milk and honey.

My stepmother was a widow of noble Bedouin stock with two sons from her former marriage. Her husband had been an early Believer who was martyred in the Battle of the Trench, the failed counteroffensive of the Meccans against Muhammad and his followers. Part of her fascination for me as a young boy was that halo of a fallen man's approval that she carried through her widowhood, and which she composed into a famous lament:

> A mote in your eye, dust blown on the wind?
> Or a place deserted, its people gone?
> To the pool that all men shun in awe
> You have gone, my husband, free of blame
> As the panther goes to his fight, his last,
> Bare fangs and claws his only defense.
> What have we done to you, death,
> That you treat us so?
> I would not complain if you were just,
> But you take the worthy,
> Leaving fools for us.

As a consequence of her husband's martyrdom and her eloquence, my stepmother was granted a handsome annuity from the spoils of holy war. But she felt hemmed in by the expectations of widowhood and yearned to move more freely in the new space that marriage opened up for her. In time, she grew very fond of Ka'b, and, I think, he of her.

Ka'b's motive was strategic. My mother was right about that. He had become a public figure by then, one to be reckoned with, especially if he was bonded through marriage to an important tribe of the Hijaz. My stepmother-to-be lived in the same quarter of Medina as Umar. Ka'b, never one to overlook his opportunities, had made his approach through his new friend. No one was going to refuse the Prophet's esteemed Companion, and no one was going to forget that Umar had been the intermediary in the making of the new alliance.

Umar handled all the arrangements; it was he who suggested that my care be entrusted to Ka'b's new wife. Thus was my father bound closer to Umar, even as he became irrevocably estranged from my mother. But the cruelest cut came when my father decided to take his new wife, her two sons, and me with him to Jerusalem, leaving my poor mother behind.

Ka'b was resolute. His first wife had become a burden. She reminded him of all that he wanted to leave behind; she seemed the very incarnation of Ezra's curse, forever deprived of repose and peace. He would not be dragged down with her, to wallow in guilt because of an ancient transgression. Ka'b was no longer lowly and impoverished like his kinfolk in the Yemen. He was on his way to the city of his dreams, the Holy House he had once thought resided only in Heaven. Through chance and circumstance, he had become a respected counselor to the Caliph. Nothing was going to stop him from walking with the son of Khattab "in the footsteps of the prophets," as he liked to put it.

As for my mother, when Ka'b returned to Arabia the following year leading a caravan load of Muslims on pilgrimage and looking for Jewish families to take back with him to resettle in Jerusalem, she was gone. "She joined a caravan headed for San'a," Ka'b was told. I was about six years old at the time. I never saw my mother again.

She left behind a letter for my father, dictated to a friend who had scrawled it on a scrap of leather. I have it still, kept in the same chest that Ka'b used to preserve the scrolls he had brought with him from the Yemen:

"As long as this wheel of fortune turns, nothing remains in its accustomed state, except for the one to whom God grants a respite.

May the Creator spare you and me the hostilities of time and its vicissitudes. May you never taste, or even witness, anything like that which I have gone through. May He accept what I have suffered as an atonement for your sins."

Coming to Jerusalem

Umar's age was come, and with him a faith unknown before that was sweeping empires off their feet.

Inside the great hall of the Persian King of Kings, where a golden crown studded with rubies and emeralds had once hung, a pulpit stood. Meanwhile, Heraclius, the Emperor of the Christians, was being tormented by a dream in which he saw his defeat at the hands of a circumcised man who called out to his men: "Ride, ye horsemen of God! Lo, the Garden lies yonder before you! Paradise rests in the shadow of your swords!" A multitude rode with him, their numbers stretching into the flatness of the desert, welding it to the sky. Stricken by the clarity of the dream, powerlessness seeped from the dreamer into his armies. By the banks of the Yarmuk, four hundred thousand Byzantines broke ignominiously under the blows of the men of Khalid—that brave son of Walid who would not stop until the going down of the sun. Fifty thousand of the emperor's men lost their lives to an army one-fifth their number. Awestruck, non-Believers took to whispering to one another in every town and village of Syria.

Fear of the Arabs had fallen upon the land.

Heraclius acknowleged defeat as he embarked for Constantinople, saying, "Farewell, Syria, and forever! Ah! that so fair a land should become my enemy's." To those left behind, he cried out, "O men of Byzantium, you are going to be slain on a dungheap because

you have desecrated the sanctity of the Holy City. It will be with
you just as it was with the Children of Israel, who were slain for
shedding the blood of John the Baptist."

In the City of the Prophets that the emperor had now deserted,
the commander in charge of defenses, a nasty Greek with a reputation for flogging deserters until they expired on the post, ran away
like his master. The lords and princes to whom he was beholden
abandoned their villas and rural retreats, all of which fell to our
zealous warriors without a casualty. Communication and supply
lines were in Muslim hands. The city was ripe for the taking on
almost any terms that Umar, Prince of True Believers, cared to name.
In the previous two years, an army of Believers had cut through the
hosts of Persia and Byzantium like a sickle through a sheaf of
wheat. The towns of Iraq and Syria, and those along the coastal
plains of Palestine, had one by one accepted Muslim sovereignty.

Ka'b's prophecy was being realized. And, indeed, everything
that Ka'b had prophesied four years earlier in the Prophet's mosque
in Medina would have come true exactly as he had foretold, had it
not been for the stubbornness of an old man.

Four days shy of his seventy-fifth birthday, Sophronius was elected
Patriarch of Jerusalem by local monks, against Heraclius's wishes.
He had only a few months to adjust to the burdens of the office he
as-sumed, in the autumn of the year that the Arabs swore allegiance to Umar, before the armies of Believers came knocking at
the city's gates.

With the flight of his cowardly commander, he was forced to
assume military duties on top of his religious ones. Hearing of the
favorable terms that had been granted to Christians in Damascus
and Homs, he held out the prospect of a peaceful transfer of power
to the commander of the Muslim forces, Abu Ubayda—a transfer
that would be least injurious to Christian interests in the Holy City
while offering the Arabs the kind of legitimacy that no army can
win at the point of a sword.

Abu Ubayda was tempted. The old Patriarch could be charming when he needed to be, and their meetings had gone quite well. Or so Abu Ubayda thought. At the very end, however, after everything had been agreed upon, Sophronius threw in one last condition: The dignity of his office required that he hand over the keys of the city to the person of the Caliph. No one else would do.

"That honey-tongued defender of the heresy that Christ is the Son of God and Mary!" Ka'b used to exclaim. "He pulled the wool over Abu Ubayda's eyes." The Patriarch was a sworn enemy of Muhammad. Satan himself nested in his head. It had been a grievous error, my father believed, for Abu Ubayda to accord him so much respect. Did not his public utterances exude hate of all things Muslim? And on Christmas Eve, after the town of Bethlehem had fallen to our zealous desert warriors, had not the old man delivered a sermon to his flock in which he said:

"For now the slime of the godless Saracens, like that of the gentiles at the time of David, has overrun Bethlehem and does not yield passage. They insult our cross. They feed human bodies to the birds of the sky. The abomination of desolation foretold by the prophets has descended upon us. What is to be done? For the love of Christ I call on you to stop committing acts that are hateful to Him. If we are beloved of God, we will live to laugh at the fall of our Saracen adversaries. We will witness their destruction. We will see their blood-loving blades enter their own hearts. Their end will furnish a new way for us, clear of hills and thorns. 'Glory to God the Highest, Peace and Good Will on Earth.' "

Unlike my father, Umar held Abu Ubayda in the highest regard. The Caliph often spoke of his courage during the Battle of Badr, of how he was one of the Ten Praised Ones who had been promised Paradise by the Prophet. He approved Abu Ubayda's instructions to his men not to kill a woman, or a nursing infant, or an old man in battle, nor to cut down trees, or strip palms, or destroy buildings, and to leave men found living alone in caves unharmed. Abu Ubayda lived, the Caliph said, by the code of a holy warrior. Thus it came to be that, on Abu Ubayda's advice, the normally fiery Caliph, so quick to explode with anger at the suggestion of a slight, disregarded the Patriarch's words and came to Jerusalem.

Sorted in small companies, with their bearers, womenfolk, and children in train, Umar and Ka'b were accompanied by a party of four thousand. They left Medina riding north, east of the Valley of the Villages. A mere six years separated the death of God's Messenger from that journey. I was five years old at the time and in the care of my stepmother and her sons. Our caravan strung itself along the crests of the hill chain that parallels the Red Sea. We looked down upon the coastal wilderness where, according to tradition, Solomon had exiled the demons who helped him build the Temple. Driven at a warrior's pace through the night until dawn, we slept during the heat of the day. Thus we rode until we reached the Desert of the Wanderings in southern Palestine—so named because it was there that Moses travelled to and fro with his children, looking for the Promised Land. A rock from which water once gushed and saved the Israelites served as our first camp, and my father remembered the words of scripture:

> *Behold I will stand before thee there,*
> *upon the rock in Horeb,*
> *and thou shalt smite the rock,*
> *and there shall come water out of it,*
> *that the people may drink.*

Lying between the Red Sea and the Syrian Sea, the desert extends for the distance of a seven days' march in every direction, and in this land of red sandstone hills and long sandy stretches are found deadly serpents a span long that spring up and hide in the litters of horses and camels, waiting for the right moment to lash out. Here and there the desolate wilderness is interrupted by salt marshes, or dry hollows where the dung of antelopes lies spattered like peppercorns, directing our trackers toward a cluster of palm trees nestled around a spring of fresh water.

Guided by the sons of Judham—Arabs who claimed descent from Jethro, the father-in-law of Moses—we approached the Holy City from the east on the twenty-sixth day of our departure from Medina. A glorious dawn was beginning to break, the light throwing the hills and ridges into sharp relief, bathing them with color. The only gap in the circle of hills surrounding Jerusalem faced Arabia, beckoning us on.

Like King David and Nebuchadnezzar before him, the Caliph took his first view of the Holy City from the Mount of Olives just outside the city. And there we set up camp, before a ravine filled with vineyards and caverns, cascading pieces of twisted rock, churches, the cells of anchorites and hermits, and many other remarkable things besides.

Across the ravine in the distance, a fortified town, vaguely square in shape, its spires and domes glistening in the sunlight, stretched westwards. The walls dictating the shape of the city contradicted the contours of the landscape, introducing another level of order, a higher order, which lorded over its surrounds. Inside the eastern wall sat the grand pile of what used to be the Temple—a mound of undecipherable stones baking in the sun.

Umar had come to the Holy City intent on seeing the place where David had sought forgiveness of his Lord, and where his son Solomon had later built the Temple. His inscrutable demeanor revealed not a sign of what he was about to do. My father, on the other hand, was overcome with sorrow; he pulled and tore at his clothes and had eyes only for the ruins of the Temple.

Umar and Abu Ubayda had to intervene forcibly. "You will perish of sorrow," they told him. "Restrain yourself!"

This is my earliest memory of the City of the Temple—my distraught father, an old man twisting and turning with grief like a reed in the wind against a backdrop of translucent blue.

An enormous assembly of the men and women who accompanied Umar on his thirty-day trek had started to form. Men discarded their weapons, laid them carefully aside, and lined up in rows; women took up the rear. A crowd of bare heads and undifferentiated limbs spread itself out slowly like the sea. Umar found himself at its head. Exhaustion and hunger were put aside as the Caliph led the daybreak prayers on the mountain summit.

And as he did, the crowd silently turned away from the Holy City before whose gates they had just arrived, turned away from the Rock, toward the titanic desolation of the desert across which they had just marched. They turned to face a different Holy City, at whose heart lay the Black Stone.

The Black Stone

When our angel ancestor was cast out of the Garden and landed upon the Rock, he was carrying the Stone toward which Umar and his people now prayed. Eve had fallen separately, in central Arabia. Adam traveled to find her, carrying the Stone with him. A month's camel-ride away, he caught up with her at the foot of Mount Abu Qubays, the tallest mountain in Arabia. After climbing the mountain, the first man set his precious load on its cone-shaped summit, and not wanting the Stone to remain exposed to the ravages of the weather and wild beasts, he decided to shelter it with cloth. Adam's tent was the first sanctuary to be established on Earth, and the predecessor of the most ancient house of the Ka'ba, whose origins lie in our father Adam's desire to protect the Stone from harm.

Two winters after Umar's conquest of Jerusalem, during the pilgrimage season, my father and I visited Adam's Stone.

Mecca sits flat and low, in a plain girdled by high and rugged mountains, destitute of all trees. Nothing of the city could be seen upon our approach, until suddenly we were on top of an area measuring two arrow-shots square, filled with houses jostled up against one another made of mud mixed with straw, a far cry from the dressed stone I had grown accustomed to in Jerusalem. God's most important words had been revealed to Muhammad here, Ka'b said, but all I could think of was the suffocating heat and the clouds of flies swarming around my head while the sun was still low in the sky.

Neither heat nor flies nor the throngs of unveiled women making the pilgrimage in the hope of finding someone to marry perturbed my father. He had eyes only for the Ka'ba, built by Abraham and his son, Ishmael, ancestor of the Arabs, over the Black Stone.

The Ka'ba is a cube whose walls are made of alternate layers of stone and wood draped in black cloth. Abraham, like Muhammad after him, had carefully placed the Stone in the southeastern corner of the cube, where pilgrims today begin their prescribed progressions around the building. When Muhammad was a young man, the old Ka'ba burned down when a woman was careless lighting incense. It is said to have been roofless with walls no higher than a man. The Ka'ba I saw was twice that height, its roof being made by a Christian carpenter from the planks of a Byzantine ship that had been cast ashore. Its door was placed high above the ground, so that you had to use a ladder to enter. Unwelcome visitors, Ka'b said, were pushed down from the high threshold. While it was being built, the people of Mecca quarrelled among themselves as to who should have the honor of putting the Black Stone in its place. Muhammad took off his cloak and convinced each head of a tribe to take one end. He then placed the Black Stone in the southeast corner because he liked to face that corner in prayer.

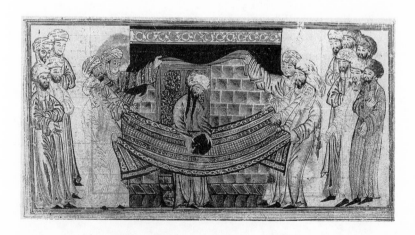

The Stone has been set chest-high above ground where the walls meet, two paces from the only door into the building. The Iraqi Corner, which faces northeast toward Iraq, is followed by the Syrian Corner, facing northwest, and the Yemeni Corner, facing southwest.

The Black Stone is actually reddish black in color, with embedded yellow and red particles. It is much smaller than its counterpart in Jerusalem, never having grown into a proper rock— the size of a large man's skull when I saw it. But that is, sadly, no longer the case. During the war between Mecca and Jerusalem that has only just ended, the Ka'ba was bombarded with stones from giant catapults placed on the encircling mountain slopes, and the Black Stone broke into three pieces. The pieces, I am reliably informed, have been bound together with a band of silver and mounted in a silver chasing shaped like a woman's vulva.

"The Black Stone is God's hand in the earth," Ka'b said as he bent down to touch and kiss the Stone; "he who touches it declares his allegiance to God." I reached up and followed suit.

We began our prescribed circling from this black corner. The seven circuits complete, we performed our early morning prayers facing the Stone, as the Prophet was wont to do. Only now would my father allow himself to sit down, spread his cloak, and relax.

From where we were sitting, Mount Abu Qubays could be seen in the distance, looming over Mecca. Its summit was as round as a dome and as high as an arrow shot from its foot; in capable hands that arrow might fall beside a stele said to have been erected by Abraham on the mountain's highest point. The Black Stone was found next to that stele during the Age of Ignorance that preceded the coming of God's Messenger. In fact, as I heard the story, two distinctive stones had been found on the summit of Mount Abu Qubays by members of the Quraysh, the Meccan tribe from whom the Prophet himself descends.

Unlike the large or oddly shaped rocks that the Arabs worshipped in the Age of Ignorance, these stones did not come from Mecca or her surrounds. They were brighter and more beautiful than anything anyone had seen before. Naturally, men concluded, they had fallen from the sky. Wanting everyone to admire their find, the tribesmen brought one of the two stones down to the valley.

"What happened to the other stone?" I asked Ka'b.

"It was stolen by followers of 'Amr, son of Luhayy."

"Who was he?"

"The first to introduce false worship among the sons of Ishmael," said Ka'b. 'Amr, he explained, had joined a caravan going to Syria for trade. Along the way he saw people worshipping stone idols.

"And why were they worshipping stones?" I exclaimed.

"Because, they said, when they prayed to them for rain, it rained. 'Amr asked if they could spare one or two for him to take back with him to Mecca. He was given a stone called Hubal, which he set up by a well near the Ka'ba. More and more Meccans began to serve Hubal and venerate him. Soon every household wanted an idol of its own to worship."

Idols, Ka'b said, were very much in demand in the time when the sister of the Black Stone was stolen.

"Until the Arabs stopped worshipping them," I said.

"Yes," he replied, "but old habits die hard as Muhammad, God's Grace Be Upon him and his Household, discovered. The sons of Mudar, for instance, persisted in thinking that a lofty rock in the desert near the shore of Jidda was God. One day one of them took the tribe's stock camels to the rock named Sa'd. He wanted his animals to stand close to Sa'd so that they would be blessed and give much milk.

"But when the camels, which were of the grazing type and had never been ridden before, saw the rock and smelt the dried blood shed on it over the years, they shied away and fled in all directions. This so angered the tribesman that he seized a stone and threw it at the idol, saying, 'God curse you! You have scared away my camels and that of all my kin. I came to you to improve the fortune of the sons of Mudar, but you have dissipated it. We will have nothing more to do with you, O Sa'd. You are nothing but a rock! You cannot make a right or correct a wrong.' Only then did the sons of Mudar abandon the worship of desert rocks."

"To change religion is not an easy thing," I ventured.

"Like herding camels on a rainy night," said Ka'b.

The last rays of the setting sun were lighting the summit of Mount Abu Qubays, which shone like a torch as darkness fell.

"Look at it carefully," Ka'b said, pointing to the Black Stone.

"Do you mean the Stone?"

"You call it a stone!"

"But of course I do. Is it not a stone?"

"In the beginning," said Ka'b, "it was a jewel that Adam brought down with him—just like the jewel that God plucked from underneath His throne and plunged into the abyss in order to fashion the ground upon which He stood while He went about creation. Later, the first man used it to cut a channel for his tears, which flowed for nine hundred years after the Fall."

"The same jewel that the tribesmen of Quraysh found on top of Mount Abu Qubays?" I asked, astounded.

"Yes."

"What kind of a jewel was it?"

"A sapphire," said Ka'b, "just like its sister on Mount Moriah."

"Then how did it turn black?"

"Menstruating women touched it in the Age of Ignorance."

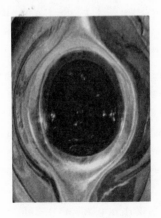

Mecca and Jerusalem, Ka'b went on to say, grew outward from their two Rocks in much the same way as a eucalyptus tree springs from a tiny seed. In fact, Ka'b claimed, the Rocks originally were not separate Rocks, but one Rock, parts of His throne. On both were found inscriptions—the ineffable name of God was chiseled in Hebrew letters on the Rock of Moriah; and on the Black Stone, words in a strange script that could be read only by a Jew. Or so a Meccan seer had told Ka'b.

The message on the Black Stone was this: "God is the Lord of Mecca."

Unlike the words written on Jerusalem's Rock by Ahithophel, King David's counselor, no one knows who wrote these words, or why. But for Ka'b, the messages of the Rocks confirmed the order behind all things.

None is like unto Him Who is the Hearer and the Seer.

"He intended the universe," Ka'b continued, "as a consonance of different parts, similar in ways and dissimilar in others," and then, in the clearest formulation of his great passion, he would add: "My work is to fit them back together again in the right way so that they return to harmony."

"But what is left that is harmonious between peoples who face different Rocks in prayer?" I asked. "What if dissonance, rather than consonance, is what we ought to learn to live with and work our way around?"

Ka'b would not entertain such a thought. God abhors the manifold forms of nature worship, he said. He wants us to search for His One transcendent essence.

But what if our feebleness is such that, in proportion to God's exaltation, to the fact that He is not a force of nature but Creator of all of nature's forces, He becomes cold and aloof, unapproachable to those who would worship him? Out of despair we turn first to this witless rock and then to that, knowing that the rock's soul is a mindless void. A mystery is its hatred, or its grace. Surely it is wiser not to care—to accept His variety without anger, and without love.

Such talk made Ka'b entirely lose control. "There *has* to be a connection," he thundered. "Never doubt it! It cannot be otherwise!"

In the end, I came to accept that, just as the idea of a flower is more enduring than the flower itself, the idea of the Rock was a more enduring reality for my father than the Rock itself. By endlessly contemplating it and instructing himself on its history, he was reaching to grasp that fleeting essence. Reality was not the Rock for Ka'b; it is through the Rock that He became real. Meanwhile, time was working, on him and the followers of Muhammad, a fatal substitution: Even as the Rock of my father's dreams was daily acquiring a life in the mind of Believers, was slowly but surely becoming real and strong for them, his knowledge of their passion for a different Rock was growing in clarity.

The Turmoil of Ka'b

hy do the Peoples of Moses and Muhammad face different Rocks in prayer? Men talked about the question
in the early days. Some said they knew why: God had
changed the sacred direction because the Jews did not accept
Muhammad as a Messenger. Woe unto them, they would say, who
have cried lies to the signs of God.

Why, thought others, should the perfidy of the Jews make God
change His sacred axis? Surely, no sin is big enough to change the
fundaments of creation, which He willed into existence before the
first man was fashioned out of the Rock's dust. The Rock stands as
an admonition to our inconstancy; either it carried the Truth yester-
day and still carries it today or it never carried it. Truth is profound;
it is foundational. That much reason Ka'b succeeded in instilling
in me.

I don't know why there are two sacred axes, not one. Can anyone know that which God's Messenger himself, Peace Be Upon
Him, never claimed to know?

To know belongs to God alone.

Certain things, on the other hand, it is given to us to know. I
know, for instance, that the prayer on the Mount of Olives terrified
Ka'b because it forced him to turn his back on the Rock. To be com-

pelled by force of circumstance to thus direct himself, and on the very threshold of the Holy City, was hard. And the effort magnified the task that lay before him, driving home the chances of failure—the price of which, he realized, would be borne by him alone.

The Arabs had done their part, as he had foretold. The armies of the uncircumcised had been routed. There remained only the conclusion of the vision that had made Ka'b so famous throughout Arabia—the return of all of Abraham's children, followers of Moses and Muhammad alike.

"No more shall they be kept from David's Sanctuary," Ka'b had said in Medina. And he would remind his listeners of God's words to Muhammad in the loneliness of his Exodus:

Surely He who gave thee the Book to be thy Law
will bring thee home again

At the time, that choice of words rang as clear and true as a bell. People woke up. But what did they sound like now that the Arabs were camped upon the place of Christ's ascent to Heaven, separated from the City of the Temple by a mere valley, all the while praying in the direction of the Black Stone with their backs to the Rock? How could a lowly southerner from the fallen star of the Yemen hope to convince these proud sons of the desert, upon whose good will he was dependent, to align themselves with a Rock different from the one they considered their own?

The initial flush of excitement at being so close to the City of the Prophets had long since passed, and Ka'b had recovered from the agitation he had felt when he first laid eyes on the ruins of the Temple. Then the waters had risen to the very seat of his breath. Now he was beginning to drown in a new kind of inner turmoil.

Would Umar allow the Jews back into liberated Jerusalem? For that matter, would they want to go back? Ka'b's kith and kin had rejected the appeal of the prophet Ezra to do so, finding the whole business of uprooting themselves and moving into the unknown too arduous. "Happiness is not all movement and change," my mother had said to Ka'b. "Even rushing water must settle down before it can be cleared of silt."

And who would pay for a new Temple? Not Umar. He forbade the accumulation of monies in the treasury for any purpose, preferring instead to assign the wealth of the Believers in the form of annuities to the Companions and family of the Prophet and to the fighters and families of those who had fallen in God's cause.

"I will not lead those who come after me into temptation," Umar had said, in response to urgings that he put aside revenues against times unforeseen. "Come what may, the only provision I will make against the time to come shall be obedience to God and His Apostle! That obedience is provision enough; it brought us here."

To such a man, a sumptuously decorated Temple was the Devil's own work.

On the other hand, my father must have thought to himself, might the man upon whose tongue God had struck the Truth think differently once he had come to grips with his responsibilities as the new master of the City of the Temple?

His own past was no longer a precedent for anything that Umar now found himself having to do.

Ka'b may have had a vision, but he had no plan. Calculation was not in his nature. He had taken things as they came, making adjustments according to circumstance. But the obstacles to the realization of his vision in Medina were now looming in his mind, like the stunning but unfriendly layers of rock spread out before his eyes.

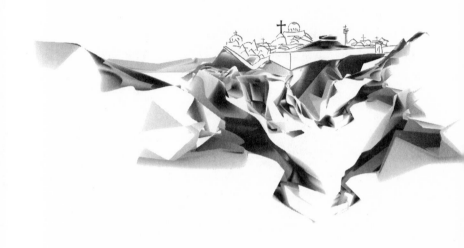

The Sins of David

tanding alone on the Mount of Olives, the Caliph and his counselor admired the walled hilltop city with its twenty-six towers, six gates, and towering stone walls that rose out of the narrow gorge known as the Valley of Hell.

"There are more stones on this mountain than there are people in Arabia," Umar mused, looking onto the sheer drop before him. He was standing next to a round church and the tomb of James, the brother of Jesus, which he shared with two Jewish prophets, Zacharias and Simeon. Across from him, on the other side of the valley, was the pinnacle of the southeastern boundary of what used to be the Temple. James had been tossed into the valley from on top of that meeting point of the southern and eastern walls, his body ripped to shreds on the stones below.

"The stones of Jerusalem impress themselves on all who wander among them," Ka'b replied.

Umar and Ka'b were looking for the pit into which the prophet Jeremiah had been dispatched. It could not be seen from where the two men were standing, the view being obstructed by a cascade of massive boulders down the slopes of the valley.

The stoniness of the landscape exceeded anything that even men accustomed to the desert had seen before—homes, roads, tombs, everything was either rock or made of rock. Heaps of stones were piled up here and there—in fact, wherever one looked. Many

walls and fences looked as though they had been thrown together
for no reason other than to get stones out of the way. Such disciplin-
ing of the landscape was always in vain, the removal of one stone
serving only to reveal others lying just below the surface.

"To each rock, large or small, rough or smooth, there corresponds a list of things we choose either to remember or to forget,"
Ka'b said. "Patterns made by boulders that have held up armies,
pebbles that have felled giants, tell stories that in other places are
told by tea leaves. Did you know, O Caliph, that blue-eyed David
was enamored of rocks?"

"How did his infatuation begin?" the Caliph inquired.

The seeds were planted early, Ka'b said, when God concealed
the stripling from Saul's jealousy inside the hollows of mountains,
amidst the swarming sea of stones that was Jerusalem's landscape.

"I take refuge in him, my rock, my shield, my stronghold, my
place of refuge," David, future king of Israel, had sung in gratitude.

Who is a rock but our God?
Blessed be my Lord, the Rock, who girds me with strength,
who gives me vengeance,
who makes my way free from blame,
who set me on a rock too high to reach,
who subjects whole peoples to me.

"Music is the Devil's own work, Ka'b!" cried Umar. "Beware,
lest it turn your head."

"Did not Muhammad choose men to recite to him from the
Holy Book because he liked the sounds of their voices?" Ka'b said.
"The Lord of the Worlds," he continued, looking toward the Temple
Mount, "gave David arts of sweetness to sing the primordial waters
under those ruins back to their right level. He blessed His servant,
wanting to transport him out of the grime of this world, and to have
his actions be guided by a higher purpose, one made accessible
through beautiful sounds."

"And yet in the end," replied Umar, "David, Peace be Upon Him, was denied the Temple, however much he ached to build it."

"He was denied it, O Umar," said Ka'b, "because of his sins, which were written on his hands until they rode roughshod over his art. When he was brought a goblet to drink, he could drink only half its contents because the action of raising a vessel to his lips exposed the wrongs held against him in the Heavenly Register. God's chosen wept, they say, until his joints were dislocated and the goblet had refilled with tears. On that occasion, he uttered these words:

> *My God, my God, why hast thou forsaken me?*
> *Why art thou so far from the words of my roaring?*
> *Our fathers trusted in Thee;*
> *and Thou didst deliver them.*
> *But I am a worm, and no man;*
> *a reproach of men,*
> *and despised of the people.*

Umar was now as visibly agitated as his counselor. He stood up abruptly and started pacing up and down alongside a boundary wall that overlooked the gravestones of seventy thousand prophets. "A worm? He spoke of himself as a worm! Tell us the story, Ka'b. Leave nothing out." And so Ka'b began.

David was anointed king in Hebron, where Abraham was buried, but he wanted to be king in Jerusalem because its stones had given him refuge and were a byword for impregnability and fortitude. The Jebusites were Jerusalem's rightful rulers, being the descendants of Heth, to whom Abraham had promised the Holy City in return for his burial place. Within earshot of David's army, the city's Jebusite defenders mocked the impudence of the fiery king: "David will never get in here," they said. "Our blind and our lame are enough to hold him off." Whereupon David placed a reward upon the head of every Jebusite. Then he took the city. As for the blind and the lame, David hated them for the rest of his life.

David called Jerusalem by his own name, and began to over-reach himself. Temptation sought him out in the shape of a woman. From his rooftop, he spied Bathsheba bathing. She was very beautiful to look upon. And the king was veiled from the Will of God by his desire for her. He lay with her, impregnated her, and then had her husband, Uriah, a holy warrior, sent to the forefront of the hottest battle to be killed. Bathsheba became his wife and bore him a son.

But what David had done displeased God.

Seventy thousand of David's men were cut down by the Angel of Pestilence. He was followed by the Angel of Death, who came to raze Jerusalem to its foundations. The king saw Death coming, colossal and irresistible, his drawn sword stretching over the city. As the angel reached the summit of Mount Zion, David and the elders of Israel, all dressed in sackcloth, fell to their knees. And David cried out: "God, O my God! I was the one who sinned. I was the one who acted wrongly. But these, the flock, what have they done? Let your hand lie heavy on me and on my family, but spare them!"

The prophet Muhammad, God's Blessings Be Upon Him, was fond of saying that David's remorse after that day was not like that of other men. Each one of his tears equaled a tear from all the other creatures that walked upon the earth.

But no amount of tears would deter the Angel of Death. As he was about to descend upon the city, he saw the ashes of Abraham's ram lying in a pile at the altar's base. They had lain there undisturbed for generations. It was at that very moment that a voice from up high thundered, "Enough now! Hold your hand!"

God stayed the hand of His wrath over the Rock as He had once before, over the same spot, stayed the hand of Abraham over his son.

Then He asked of David to go and raise an altar to Him on the threshing floor of Araunah the Jebusite. In those days Mount Zion lay outside the walls of the Jebusite city, dominating it from the north. A farmer owned the windswept summit, using the wind to winnow his wheat.

Dressed only in a loincloth, David obeyed, leading a procession of thirty thousand people up the mountain. They carried the Ark containing the broken stone tablets of God's words atop an oxcart refurbished for the occasion. The procession made music, and David danced for all he was worth the whole way up the mountain. At every step he sacrificed an animal to God. By the time he reached the top, the king was drunk with ecstasy, drenched in blood.

Araunah, who had been busy with his threshing, was horrified at the sight and prostrated himself at David's blood-soaked feet, saying, "Why has my king come to his servant?"

"To buy your threshing-floor," said David, "to build an altar to the God who has defeated your God."

"O King," said Araunah, "take my threshing-floor and make what offerings you see fit. Here are the oxen for the burnt offering, the threshing sleds, and the oxen's yokes for the wood. I am your loyal servant."

But David refused, saying, "I will not make an offering to God from a place that has cost me nothing."

So Araunah accepted the sum of fifty shekels for the Mountain's summit, and David placed the Ark of the Covenant on the Rock's surface. And there he built an altar as had Abraham before him, and fire came down from Heaven and consumed his offering, just as it had Abraham's.

"So David was forgiven," said Umar once Ka'b had finished. "Why then was the gift of the Temple denied him, to go to his son Solomon through Bathsheba, he whom the Lord kept safe from bloodshed and made king after his father?"

"David was never forgiven completely," exclaimed Ka'b. "His hands were too stained with blood. Nor did Almighty God want a Temple, O Umar. David set his heart on one because kingship had gone to his head. He wanted to be like the kings he had vanquished in battle, all of whom built Temples to their gods. And God disapproved:

> *Shalt thou build me an house for me to dwell in?*
> *Whereas I have not dwelt in any house,*
> *even to this day,*
> *but have walked*
> *in a tent and in a tabernacle.*
> *In all the places wherein I have walked,*
> *spake I a word with any of the*
> *tribes of Israel,*
> *saying, Why build ye not me an house of cedar?*

The hour was getting late. A cold west wind was blowing. Ka'b examined the Caliph's face; it was strangely expressionless and withdrawn. Umar looked tired, not like a conqueror who was about to take over Christendom's crown jewel, not like a hard-hearted man whose piety made him contemptuous of all frivolity. The flesh hung loosely from his sallow, sunken cheeks. It was not clear what, if anything, would be the consequences on the morrow of David's actions all those years ago. Umar, the Separator of Right from Wrong, as Muhammad had named him, whose shadow alone sent indolence and idleness scuttling like beetles in a campfire, looked unsure of himself.

And he said: "Would that Muhammad take me to that bountiful Garden where he must now be lying, underneath the spreading shade of a thornless lote-tree."

"That is surely your destination," said Ka'b.

"Not unless I die in God's cause."

"God forbid!"

"What have I to do with this world, O Father of Ishaq?" Umar said. "I am like a horseman who halts a little while in the shade and departs. A curse is upon his journey and all things along the way, save those signs that help him remember God. Perhaps the Lord mingled sin with the clay he used for the peopling of the Earth.

Think you that David sinned in his life more than we have done in ours?"

There was silence. And when Ka'b finally spoke, his voice was gentle. "David's sins were many and grave. But what do you, whom the Prophet always praised, have to be ashamed of?"

"One thing, old man, which still haunts my nights."

"Unburden yourself then, by this hallowed valley watered by the tears of the living and the dead. There is no better place."

And Umar unburdened himself. He told Ka'b of how he had made an offering of his six-year-old daughter to a stone in the days before Muhammad had come to light up the world, of how he had buried her alive under a pile of stones, of how the sounds of her fading screams turned into strangled grunts as the earth stopped her mouth, of how she had reached up tenderly to touch his face and brush earth from his beard even as he was digging her grave.

"This," said Ka'b, "is the music of Satan lamenting the loss of the world."

Whereupon Umar suddenly groaned, dropped his head, folded it in his arms, and began to weep uncontrollably. The Caliph wept so hard that day that his tears etched two lines on his face that remained until the day he died.

The Rock of Sacrifice

o console his Caliph and stiffen his resolve before the delegation from the Holy City arrived, Ka'b reminded Umar that, in the Age of Ignorance, the father of Muhammad himself had come within a hair's width of being sacrificed. The kind and generous Abd al-Muttalib, who would protect his grandson in later years from the wrath of those who would not believe in him, wanted ten sons at a time when he had none. He vowed to sacrifice one of them to the gods of the Ka'ba should he be granted his heart's desire. The wish was granted. It fell upon the future father of Muhammad to pay the old man's debt.

"By God! If you do a thing like this there will be no stopping men from sacrificing their sons," said a shaikh from the boy's tribe. Abd al-Mutallib was pressed into finding an expiatory sacrifice to save the boy.

The hand of God took the shape of an old Jewess from Khaybar. She told Abd al-Muttalib what he had to do. His son's life would be spared in exchange for one hundred camels slaughtered between Isaf and Naila, two lovers who had come to Mecca on a pilgrimage from Jurham in the land of the Yemen and could not control their passion for one another. After fornicating in the Ka'ba, they were discovered the next morning turned into upright rocks. These the Arabs of Quraysh relocated one hundred paces in front of the main door to their shrine, reserving the space between them for sacrifices like that which spared the life of the Prophet's father.

The story did not console Umar.

"Where is the hand of God in what I did to my daughter? Tell me that, Father of Ishaq."

"What else brought you here before the altar of the ancients," replied Ka'b, "if not His guiding hand? Is it a coincidence that He brought you in the first month of spring, the month of the creation of the world and the birth of the prophets? When the blood of a first-born is sacrificed on this threshold, the new year is purged of all the calamities of the old. Did not God say to the People of the Torah,"

> *Thou shalt not put off*
> *the skimming of the first yield of your vats.*
> *Thou shalt give Me the first-born among your sons.*
> *Thou shalt do the same with your cattle and your flocks:*
> *seven days it shall remain with its mother;*
> *on the eighth day thou shalt give it to Me.*

"The Lord placed such an onerous burden upon the Jews?"

"He did," said Ka'b. "Just as He commanded Abraham to sacrifice his son, Ishaq, in this very same month in which you stand before the gates of the Holy City. And you ask me about the whereabouts of His hand!"

Ka'b's eyes flashed their excitement.

"A son is the pearl of his father's eye," he went on, lowering his voice. "Abraham stood to lose everything by making a burnt-offering of the child of his old age. Not a daughter, mind you, but Sara's firstborn. Nor was God holding out the promise of a reward as he had at the beginning of Abraham's prophecy, or asking him to kill his son in order to keep his word. That would at least have turned Abraham into a hero like Abd al-Mutallib. No! That would have been too easy. At the time of the ordeal, not a soul was present; there was no one to witness, much less spread word of, Abraham's piety! Who would have believed Abraham's own account? Who could have believed that God would ask him to kill in silence, in utter isolation, out of the purest feelings of love, without hope of being understood by those nearest and dearest to him? Abraham was asked to kill, knowing that no one could possibly benefit from what he was about to do. Not even you, O Prince of True Believers, had to kill this way. Of all the different ways of killing, Abraham's was by far the hardest. All other sacrifices pale in comparison with what he did. And what are those sacrifices but constant reminders of the enormous merit of what Abraham did?"

Ka'b's outburst had the desired effect of calming Umar.

"What passed between Abraham and his son on that day, as you know the story?" asked Umar, his curiosity aroused.

"Instructed to enact the priest," said Ka'b, "Abraham set to work piling the faggots for the offering. These he gave to the boy, carrying in his own hands the fire and the knife. Father and son loaded their asses and traveled in the direction that God had indicated. For three days, they rode in silence, unhurried, at a leisurely pace. While the boy tended to the asses, Abraham cast his eyes to the horizon, looking for a sign. He did not know exactly where or when the offering was to take place. Then, on the morning of the fourth day, he saw a pillar of cloud rising from a mountain in the distance.

"There before you," Ka'b said, pointing to the ruins of the Temple across the valley, "somewhere in that mound of desecration, lies hidden the meeting place of Heaven and Earth upon which David so assiduously sought forgiveness, and where all the great sacrifices of the prophets have been offered."

"Am I to be tested like Abraham?" Umar asked.

"Since the time of Adam," Ka'b said, "the primary lure of the Rock has been as a testing ground for faith. Abraham set the standard for us all when he offered up the soul of him he loved the most. His ordeal was the ultimate proof of holiness, binding him to God by knots of love that outweigh all dignity. It was Abraham who rebuilt the altar of Adam, which had been demolished by the waters of the great flood. Noah tried and failed. Ever since, men and women of faith have been trying to measure belief by what the Father of Faith did. David tried by conquering Jerusalem. Solomon tried by consecrating his Temple through animal sacrifice. If the Jews still blow the ram's horn, it is to remember what Abraham did. If the followers of Muhammad cut the throat of a sheep during the forenoon of the first day of the Feast of Sacrifice, it is to remember that which Abraham did is what it means to have faith."

"Do the Books of the Ancients tell you anything, Ka'b, about what happened after the deed was done?" asked Umar. "Did he harbor any regrets?"

"Most certainly not," replied Ka'b, "but, worrying that his offering was not enough, he said these words in prayer: 'Master of the Universe, regard it as though I had sacrificed my son first and only afterwards sacrificed this ram.' "

Sophronius

The meeting of Sophronius and the Caliph was to take place on the day before Palm Sunday. It was a brilliant ploy on the part of Sophronius, unanticipated by Umar and his advisors, for it meant that the Arab takeover of Jerusalem would be lost in a show of Christian pomp and pageantry headed by the Patriarch himself. On that day, the Patriarch would gather with the faithful on the Mount of Olives to open the Great Week of festivities commemorating Jesus's entry into the Holy City.

With the crowing of the cock, Ka'b spotted a trickle of people leaving the city from its eastern gate toward the Mount of Olives. He began to have visions of being "lost in a sea of Christians unfurling their crosses like banners," as he put it to me years later. He hurried to Umar's tent to bring the situation to the Caliph's attention.

"You worry too much, Father of Ishaq." Umar was in too good a mood to bother with Ka'b's fears as he sat relishing the details of the city's surrender that had been worked out by his commander-in-chief, Abu Ubayda.

The Caliph had guaranteed the security of all Christian inhabitants of the Holy City—their families, property, churches, and crosses. That was his practice throughout the territories taken from the Byzantines. He had promised that no constraints would be put on individual Christians in matters of religion. He had promised that no site belonging to the Church or to an individual Christian would be expropriated, and no building demolished or forcibly converted into a mosque. That left the Christian character of the city dangerously entrenched, in Ka'b's opinion. Where would the Believers settle? Where would they build their mosques? But Umar was not looking into the future when he made all his promises.

In return for security, Umar demanded a ban on the building of new churches, cloisters, monasteries, and hermitages that were not expressly authorized by the Caliph. No Christian, were he or she so inclined, was to be dissuaded by his kin or by the Church from making submission to Muhammad, Messenger of the One and Only God. Church bells were to be tolled slowly at all times, and voices lowered during services. Voices were not to be raised during funeral processions, nor lights carried, especially not through streets inhabited by the Believers. Christian books should not be hawked for sale in any street frequented by Muhammad's people, nor in their bazaars.

In matters of attire and comportment, Christians should refrain from wearing caps or turbans similar to those worn by Muhammad's people; they had to keep to their existing style of dress, wearing belts about their waists at all times. Nor could they dress their hair in the fashion of the Arabs or assume Arabic names. They could not cut Arabic inscriptions upon their signet rings; swords were not to be worn in public or new weapons purchased. Above all, Christians should not seek to discover the private affairs of Muslims through their slaves. Spying upon Believers in any way would not be tolerated. To all of this, including a poll tax, Sophronius had already indicated his agreement.

"Our covenant with the Christians has been guided by your principle, O Ka'b," Umar said, "that of the separation of categories."

"Separateness in all things has been ordained by God," Ka'b replied. "It was present in the order of creation. Can a woman lie with a beast? Or a man eat flesh that is unclean? No. Because holiness is not abomination; it is separation. That is the reason,

O Caliph, why I am urging you not to enter the Holy City in the company of Christians carrying palm leaves and idols."

"What do we know about this Sophronius?" Umar asked, ignoring my father's desperate admonishment. The Caliph was more interested in his adversary's bold step of demanding Umar's presence as a condition of handing over Jerusalem without bloodshed. This was, after all, no common transfer of sovereignty. And Sophronius was the head of his Church, ruling from a city that had been the crown jewel of Christendom for three hundred years. It was the Christian who had asked to meet the Muslim face-to-face. The Caliph of God's Apostle had therefore been honored by the Patriarch. Such a thing had never happened before, not even to the Prophet. Umar, normally so unyielding to ceremony, was flattered.

But what kind of a man was his flatterer? Honorable or sly? Of genuine religious conviction, or a politician buying time while his emperor plotted in Constantinople to bail him out?

～

Ka'b's informant was an old trading partner of his uncle's, a Copt who had lived for many years in Alexandria. Sophronius, the Copt had said, had been born in Damascus a Greek-speaking Orthodox Christian. He had been brought up an emperor's man, contemptuous of the local Christians he had grown up with. His eyes on the glories of Christ's Empire, he felt hemmed in by the city of his birth. Alexandria, that staging post for all things Christian and Greek on the coast of Egypt, exerted a far greater attraction. The fame of the city had long before penetrated to Syria. His head swollen with thoughts of adventure, the young Sophronius had set out to discover its charms.

Sophronius used Alexandria as a base from which to explore the monasteries of Egypt, gathering material for a collection of sayings and stories of the saints. No sooner had he returned to Damascus than he had to flee his city, forced into exile by the wars of an illiterate centurion elevated into the highest office by disaffected units of the Roman army. He had settled in Alexandria, spending the years reading and studying in what remained of its great library after it had been burned by monks like himself who were trying to save Egypt from paganism. When the Persians invaded, Sophronius had fled Egypt like all Byzantines. Passing through Cyprus, he had sailed among the islands of the Aegean and visited Rome and Constantinople, but decided finally to spend the winter of his life in Jerusalem. He arrived in the Holy City for the first time on the eve of the Prophet's flight from his persecutors in Mecca.

"What made him become a monk?" Umar wanted to know.

"Alexandria," Ka'b replied. "The city attracts them and turns out new ones all the time. Its streets are bursting with black-robed monks, scuttling past colonnades, holding secret little conclaves, and conducting arcane debates."

"Travelers passing through Medina," said Umar, "tell fantastic tales about this city. They say that its streets shine so bright, awnings of green silk have to be hung over them to relieve the glare."

"Every wall and pavement is clad in white marble," Ka'b replied. "So white it is painful to the eyes."

"A white city," pondered Umar, "born of the whim of a soldier who was in a hurry to conquer the world, and peopled by Greek-speaking Jews and Christians who dress in black—a striking combination. I wonder if it is the glare of the marble that made the monks wear black?"

"The city is an unnatural mix of incompatible elements, each of which pulls in a different direction," said Ka'b. "Hence its susceptibility to licentiousness and abominations of the flesh. Caught between the sea and a desert that stretches into the heart of Africa, Alexandria chose to face seawards, toward Constantinople and all things Greek, turning its back upon its own people. In that orientation lie the seeds of the city's ruin."

"Such a fickle place, yet you say it has formed our man and shaped his thoughts, not Jerusalem," Umar said.

"Jerusalem faces the desert," Ka'b replied, "and just as Alexandria never really belonged to its desert interior, so does our man Sophronius not really belong to Jerusalem. His allegiances lie elsewhere."

"You are speaking in riddles, my friend."

"The arms of the cross span this man's life," explained Ka'b. "He has spent the better part of his life combating heresy in Egypt. There Christians have been at loggerheads with one another for as long as anyone can remember. He believed Egypt to be in dire threat of succumbing to the wrong kind of Christianity, and he stayed to heal the growing divide within Christendom. The danger was greatest in Alexandria. Sophronius believed he could change things. But he had no idea what he was getting himself into. Rivers of blood had been spilled over the Christian soul of Egypt—and nowhere as much as in Alexandria, a city of foreigners that hated all things foreign. And what was Sophronius if not a foreigner!"

"What is the argument between the Christians all about?" asked Umar.

Ka'b tried to explain that it all boiled down to the true nature of Christ. Did the Son of Mary have a single divine Nature, one that subsumed the human, as the local Copts believed? Or did He have two natures, divine and human, as the Orthodox, led by Sophronius, taught.

"How can any man have more than one nature?" an incredulous Umar wanted to know.

"Because all Christians uphold the heresy that Christ is both the Son of God and the Son of Mary," my father explained. "From this foolishness, many problems ensue. To extoll His divinity, as the Copts do, diminishes His humanity. As far as Sophronius is concerned, this belief renders meaningless the actual, physical sacrifice of Jesus on behalf of mankind, the pain that Sophronius says Jesus literally and truly experienced on the cross. The Copts, on the other hand, believe that placing undue emphasis on the humanity of Jesus is a heresy in the opposite direction that diminishes the transcendent nature of God."

"And the ordinary people of Alexandria," Umar asked, "do they concern themselves with such questions?"

"They are obsessed with them. If you ask a man on the street how much a certain thing costs, he is quite likely to reply with a discourse on the Immaculate Conception. And when you ask him the price of bread, he will reply that, before he can answer such a question, it must be put into the larger context of whether the Father is greater than the Son, or whether the two should be put on an equal level. If by now your head is spinning and you decide to ask your innkeeper to prepare a bath in which to relax, he is likely to demand that you agree with him in advance that the Son was made out of nothing, and not from his mother's womb."

"Where does the emperor of the Romans stand on all this?"

"All he wants is a united Church," replied Ka'b. "Doctrinal squabbles bore him. For this purpose, he had his cronies in Constantinople invent a third doctrine, a compromise between the two that proposed that Christ had two natures, as the Orthodox insisted, but only one will, as the Copts insisted. Everyone saw through this crass maneuver. Nonetheless, it was proclaimed the official doctrine and enforced at the point of the sword."

"I gather from all this that Sophronius's mission in Egypt failed."

"Miserably," Ka'b replied. "He made a fool of himself during the debate of the council of church officials in Alexandria. I am told that he fell on his knees at one point and begged his opponents to repent the error of their ways."

"And did they?" asked Umar.

"Of course not."

"What then did the old man do?"

"He promptly wrote a long treatise on the dual nature of Christ," Ka'b said, "which he dispatched to all the Patriarchates of the Byzantine empire. I am told that it is unreadable and greatly annoyed his emperor. However, no sooner had he sent it than our armies reached the gates of Jerusalem."

"A propitious omen," remarked Umar. "I still don't understand why such a man, so advanced in years, would choose to spend his twilight years in Jerusalem."

My father explained that Sophronius had spent his youth

in Alexandria writing passionate lyrics about the holy sites of Jerusalem. He spent his mature years fighting for the belief that the person of Jesus is on the same level as his divinity. Finally, when he was old and defeated, that same longing for the unattainable, which was the only constant of his turbulent life, brought him for the first time to the actual place where Jesus was born and died.

"My dear Ka'b," Umar said with a gleam in his eye, "I am told that such longing for a promised land is a state of mind perfected by the Jews. I want to know how a heathen city, infamous for its self-indulgence, can fashion a Christian monk who then pines after a different city than the one that made him! And when he finally reaches the object of all this yearning, he becomes so attached to the place that he refuses to leave it even after it is abandoned by its cowardly commanders. This Patriarch is a man of principle, undeterred by the odds. I respect that."

The last thing Ka'b wanted to do was to make Umar more interested in Sophronius. That crafty old fox had managed to stay in control without an army to speak of even as every city, town, and hamlet in Syria fell to our forces. His strength of purpose and personal style had proved persuasive enough to bring Umar to Jerusalem. Ka'b pinned his hopes of installing more caution in the Caliph regarding the kind of a Christian that he knew the old man to be.

"The problem, O Umar, is that, for Sophronius, the places of Jesus' life, and especially his death, hold deep meaning. He believes that, if he touches the rock upon which Christ died, or walks upon the cobblestones that he walked upon, he will receive more of Christ into himself. It is not in the nature of a man like this to be reasonable with us, whatever the show he may be about to put on today."

"Am I dealing with an idolater," asked Umar, "or a man of holy scripture who is doing the best he can to defend his city and his people?"

"That," replied Ka'b, "is what we are about to find out."

~

The tent in which Sophronius awaited Umar was not big enough to accommodate the large retinue the Patriarch had brought along with him. Most of the men were lingering outside when Umar, Abu Ubayda, and Ka'b arrived. Of the Christian delegates inside the tent, there was no doubting which was the Patriarch. He had come in full ecclesiastical dress, gold chains draped over his neck and shoulders, and long silk robes trailing behind in the dust.

Umar was dressed in the same worn-out, coarsely woven battle tunic that he had been using on the road. He was contemptuous of finery of any kind, especially when used to enhance the body of a man. There were times, even after he had become Caliph, when he would lead the Friday prayers in attire so ragged and worn you could see through the holes in his shirt. Worst of all, the Caliph was self-righteous about his attire, often to the point of embarrassing his daughters and those who kept his company. Arriving late for prayers one day, he said that he had been held up washing his shirt, the point being that one shirt was more than enough for a true Believer. "Nothing is allowed to Umar," I once heard him say to Ka'b, "beyond a garment for winter, one for summer, and enough for pilgrimage and the rites, along with food for his household but at the middling rate."

Such stories about the Caliph were commonplace in Medina, but they had not yet reached the ears of Sophronius. My father felt a wave of relief flood over him when he realized that the Patriarch did not know something known by every urchin in Arabia.

If Sophronius felt the incongruity of his attire, given the appearance of the man to whom he was about to surrender his city, it didn't show. Looking directly at Umar, he rose from his seat, bent slightly at the waist, and, through a weasel-faced translator on his right, extended his greetings:

"Your arrival from so great a distance does us honor, O Prince. We who are at your mercy greet you, as do the priests and the Church that I represent, the very same church that with deepest concern is entrusted to keep watch over the inhabitants of this fair city, all of whom call on the name of Our Lord."

"Your vigilance in the service of God is to be commended," replied Umar tactfully.

"If we were not vigilant," said Sophronius, "we could not excuse ourselves before Him who willed that we should be the sentinel."

Umar sat, and everyone followed suit. Up until then everything about the terms of the city's surrender had been done verbally. Imagine the surprise of the Muslims when the translator suddenly produced two scrolls from inside his robes and explained in stilted Arabic that he was holding the draft of a covenant based on the discussions held with Abu Ubayda. In the interests of lasting peace, said he, the Patriarch had committed these to writing. From the expression on Abu Ubayda's face, all this came as a surprise. Only now did Umar realize that his adversaries had something more than just his word in mind.

The Christian translator prepared to read out the Arabic version, while keeping the Greek one rolled up in his hands. Umar motioned for him to stop, and reached out for the scroll, which he began to read to himself.

"This is a document submitted to Umar, son of Khattab, King of the Arabs, by the Christians of the Holy City."

"Am I now a king?" Umar asked, turning to Abu Ubayda who was seated on his right.

"If you tax the land of the Believers too heavily and put the money to any use that the Law does not allow," Abu Ubayda replied, "then you are a king, and no Caliph of God's Apostle."

"By God!" Ka'b overheard Umar saying to himself, "I know not any longer whether I am a caliph or a king. And if I am about to become a king, it is a fearful thing."

"A turban is your crown!" exclaimed my father. "A plague on them and their kings!"

Umar returned to the text.

"No Jew will be authorized to live in Jerusalem."

Apart from this one sentence, the draft conformed with what had been agreed upon previously. Umar did not say anything; he just asked for a pen, and crossed out the offending sentence. He did it slowly and deliberately so that everyone inside that tent could see him doing it. I bring this up because so much doubt has been cast in recent years on whether or not the Caliph left the ban on a Jewish presence in Jerusalem in force or not.

The Christians are responsible for the confusion that later transpired. Long after Umar's departure, when their interests in Jerusalem looked as if they might be threatened because of new settlers, they took to flourishing a document they called the "Covenant of Umar." Muslims who wished to make a name for themselves, or who had developed business interests with Christians, took this forgery for the real thing. The scroll containing the prohibition crossed out by Umar is written in Greek. How could Umar have read, much less signed, such a document! The authoritative version was the Arabic translation, as amended by him. The fact is, no one in the Muslim delegation got to see the Greek version because it had been superseded by the Caliph's own amendments. No doubt it got buried in the Church's archives and resurrected when it suited the Christians, long after Umar's death.

Having gone over the terms carefully and consulted with Abu Ubayda, Umar added at the very top of the document, "In the Name of God, the Merciful, the Compassionate," and crossed out "Umar, son of Khattab, King of the Arabs." In its place, he wrote "God's servant, Umar, Commander of the Faithful." This was the first time that the title "Commander of the Faithful" was used by the people of Muhammad.

"Tell your master," Umar said to the translator, "that he has negotiated an honorable Covenant, which gives his people more than we have committed to elsewhere. This is in recognition of the respect with which we hold his office and his person."

Sophronius did not haggle over a word the Caliph had written. He agreed to all of Umar's amendments, knowing he could not afford to lose the Caliph's goodwill. His strategy was to avoid a war that the Christians would lose, and to gain a foothold instead inside the mind of his adversary.

And now, Sophronius looked to turn another of his city's splendid assets—its works of art and architecture—to his advantage. Looking Umar directly in the eye, he said: "As measure of our gratitude and goodwill, we ask of the King of the Arabs to join us on a tour of the Holy City. We would be honored to thus seal this Covenant between our two religions in a spirit of amity and respect."

"Splendid!" replied Umar. "We would be delighted to hear from you about the prophets whose footprints have blessed every rock and tree of this land. We are told that you are an authority. Above all, we wish to go to the Sanctuary of David. To the place where God tried David, and where he sought forgiveness, falling down on his face and bowing in repentance. It is our deepest desire to visit that particular place."

"A pious spirit breathes through your words, O King of the Arabs," said the Patriarch. "No priest of God clothed by Him in the sacred gown of His service can afford not to heed them. Jerusalem is the happy Church on which Our Lord, the son of David, poured forth all his teaching, together with his blood. On the merit of His blood, through us, his most unworthy heirs, this city lays claim to the holiest places in God's creation. We are honored to be your guide. I am at your disposal."

"As we are on the subject of how the Lord of Creation clothes His servants, I take it you think He demands extravagance," Umar remarked, pointing at Sophronius's golden chains.

"I am my office," replied the unflappable Sophronius. "Rules govern men like me. We do not stand over rules but subject ourselves to them. The function and appearance of my robes of office ensure that my person is always subordinate to those rules; I wear them not to adorn myself, but to hold in check the confusion and anarchy of the world. Thus does my dress make manifest the order that God has ordained in the world."

"But you were a monk," Umar pressed on, "and lived alone, dressed in black, doing God's business. Did you desire the life of this world and its adornment back then?"

"You are well informed," the Patriarch replied. "I remember

with sorrow what I once was, how I rose in contemplation above all changeable and decaying things and thought of nothing but the things of Heaven. Even as I speak to you now, I sigh as one who looks back and gazes at the happy shores he has left behind. Unfortunately, today, by reason of my office and pastoral care, I have to bear with the business of the world. In truth, after so fair a vision as I enjoyed as a monk, I now seem fouled with worldly dust. All the more reason not to let it show in my dress."

This was no ordinary priest, as even Ka'b now realized.

Tour of the City

Not a soul, circumcised and uncircumcised alike, was without foreboding on that Palm Sunday. The early morning mist clouding the horizon had already been dispelled by the touch of the rising sun, leaving the air cool and dry, as diaphanous as hidden intentions suddenly exposed.

Overnight, the Christian faithful had strewn the road from the Mount of Olives to the Holy City's Eastern Gate with palm fronds. Monks, priests, and bishops with ornate accoutrements, many of them carrying crosses, had assembled to head a huge procession. They mingled with those of the Prophet's Companions who had accompanied Umar, Conqueror and Redeemer, on his desert trek from Arabia. To forestall being swamped by Christians, it had been decided that all male Believers would enter the city.

Even Ka'b thought that would be enough. Still he left me behind at the camp with the servants and the women for that momentous entry. I was a mere slip of a boy at the time, old enough to want to be a man but not old enough to understand anything. "Too dangerous, too dangerous," he kept on muttering when I pestered him for permission to accompany him. "We could be walking into a trap. Who knows what these Christians have in store for us?" I bitterly resented being left behind.

Muhammad's followers, it transpired, were vastly outnumbered by those of Jesus who materialized as out of thin air, replete with whole families dressed in their finest and most festive garments.

Worshippers mingled with curiosity-seekers, men with women, children with fearless desert warriors who could ride for weeks on a diet of dried bread and dates.

Only the Arabs wore swords, and these had to be kept sheathed on Umar's instruction. Notables from both parties led the way. They were all on horseback—all, that is, except Umar. He surprised everyone by appearing wrapped in a cloak of camel hair like a simple Bedouin, and riding an ass instead of a horse.

His dramatic arrival upset those Arabs who had spent four years in Syria and had seen wealth and treasures unknown to their brethren in the Hijaz. These "princes," as they had taken to calling themselves, were frankly embarrassed by the sight of their supreme commander appearing in such a manner before those whom he had vanquished. And they told him so. The entry had to be delayed while the argument went on. Even Abu Ubayda abandoned his customary restraint and urged the Caliph to make a concession. It had to be a horse, not an ass, they argued, or at the very least a camel.

To make matters worse, Sophronius had sent fresh white linen garments as a gift to the Caliph. Did he do this to insult Umar, or because he did not know the person with whom he was dealing? I am inclined to believe that he still did not grasp that all excess in matters of appearance were as dung as far as Umar was concerned. Austerity and simplicity were his creed in all things.

True to form, Umar would have neither Sophronius's linen nor his commander's horse, saying to Ka'b, who alone among his advisors stood by him in his decision: "Nothing good can come out of making me into another person. I fear lest I grow too great in my own eyes."

In defense of Umar's decision to enter Jerusalem on an ass, my father said that it had long ago been prophesied,

> *Behold, thy king cometh unto thee,*
> *vindicated and victorious,*
> *meek and sitting upon an ass.*

Sophronius and his priests maintained a discreet silence as the Believers argued among themselves, seated cross-legged in a circle on the mountain summit.

The Patriarch's great liability in his endeavor to pull the wool over Umar's eyes was ignorance. As discerning a man as he obviously was, the information he had about the Arabs on his doorstep came from wild rumors that had been circulating in Jerusalem in recent years. The Arabs, he would have heard, were not interested in production, commerce, or religion, only in plundering and wars. Why, they did not even have sacred texts through which a learned man might know them! The Quran had, after all, not yet been collected into a book. Local gossip likened the Arabs to bloodthirsty wild animals. "They behave like beasts of prey, though they look like human beings," I heard a Syrian Christian say in the market only the other day.

Nonetheless, the measure of this Patriarch was that such talk did not deter him from acting as a guide to one who was insistent upon acting the fool, as he must have thought, an impostor making a show of piety designed to impress the common folk by entering Jerusalem the way Jesus had done.

After an excruciating delay, the Caliph had his way as he always did in such matters. With the sun already high in the sky, the party began its descent. Abu Ubayda's squadrons of thirty-five thousand soldiers stayed behind, keeping the city encircled; they were in full combat readiness, prepared to pounce like lions should any mischief befall their comrades.

At the foot of the Mount of Olives lies the garden of Gethsemane. Here, by a rock in the vineyard, Judas betrayed the son of Mary and Joseph, and was arrested. The Christian faithful are most diligent in offering prayer at this spot, holding that it is the place where Jesus first took upon his shoulders the evils of the world. Around the rock on which Jesus knelt to pray, the Church of the Agony has been built. Sophronius had to make a stop here. He invited Umar to join him in prayer. Wisely, Umar refused, not wanting to set a precedent in these circumstances and at this particular location.

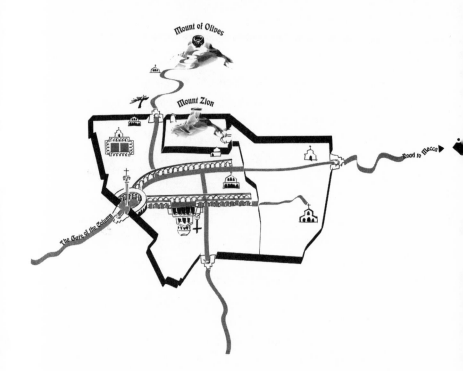

After Sophronius's prayers, the procession continued across the valley, winding its way down and then up again past the tomb of the mother of Jesus, toward the Gate of the Sheep's Pool on the eastern wall, which opens the Holy City onto the desert and the River Jordan. To the right of this gate, an olive grove was beginning to fill with people. Men and women were pouring down the mountain now that it was clear that there would be no hostilities. The Caliph and the Patriarch stopped beside the only fig tree in the olive grove. On this tree, said Sophronius, Judas hanged himself after betraying Jesus. It so happened, he said, that Jesus had cursed this very tree upon his triumphal entry into the city on Palm Sunday, because he was disappointed to find it fruitless. The tree stands there to this day, protected by a circle of stones, as barren as when Jesus first saw it.

In the olive grove around the fig tree, our warriors had meanwhile assembled, edging their way toward their Caliph while nervously fingering the hilts of their swords. Intermingled among them, and obstructing their passage, were an even larger crowd of unarmed Christian men, women, and children, carrying palm and olive branches and singing hymns. The very little ones, already overcome by boredom and fatigue, were carried on men's shoulders. A crowd of Bedouins and local peasants looked on from the rear and sides.

Clearly visible to the crowd, eighty paces southward along the city wall on the other side of the road, was the Gate of Repentance, last used by the emperor Heraclius during his triumphal entry into the city a mere six years before the arrival of Umar's army. He was returning to Jerusalem victorious from his defeat of the Persians, who had sacked the Holy City a few years earlier with the help of local Jews. The Persians had returned to Ctesiphon, their capital in Iraq, carrying what the Christians claimed was a piece of the cross upon which Jesus had been crucified. Heraclius seized this piece of wood after defeating their army and brought it back in triumph to the Holy City, passing through the Gate of Repentance. Men whose wisdom is not in doubt say that the threshold and entablature of this finely carved stone gate, which opens directly onto the Temple Mount, is all that is left of Solomon's Temple. But Umar and my father did not know that at the time; they found the gate mysteriously sealed, as it remains to this day.

At the foot of the flight of steps leading up to the Gate of the Sheep's Pool, Umar and Ka'b held a private conference, following which the Caliph strode up the steps alone in his camel-hair dress and in full view of the crowd of people. Without looking at them, he threw himself to the ground and lay prostrate in homage before the wide-open doors. Loudly he said the special greeting all pilgrims make when they visit the Holy City of Mecca: "Here am I, at your service, O God! I am here to serve, whatever be your will."

Then, on knees that had been hardened like a camel's from the frequency of prayer, Umar prayed until he had outdone Sophronius's demonstration of piety many times over. Watched over by hosts of incredulous and sullen Christians, the Believers threw caution to the winds and followed his example.

"Bear patiently what people say, and remember Our servant David, the man of might," Umar recited:

> *David was a penitent.*
> *With him We subjected the mountains to give glory*
> *at evening and sunrise,*
> *and the birds, duly mustered, every one*
> *to him reverting;*
> *We strengthened his kingdom and gave him wisdom*
> *and speech decisive.*
> *Has the tiding of the dispute come to thee?*
> *When they scaled the Sanctuary,*
> *and David thought that We had only*
> *tried him, therefore he sought forgiveness*
> *of his Lord, and he fell down, bowing,*
> *and he repented.*
> *Accordingly, We forgave him that.*

~

The hour was late. The crowd was getting fidgety because of the time it had taken to go down the mountain, and Sophronius had services to attend. He now took the lead. Hardly had he passed through the Gate of the Sheep's Pool than he took a sharp turn to the right toward the healing pools for which Jerusalem was famous. There he stopped to point out the Church of the Paralyzed Man, which overhangs a double pool with splendid porticoes on all four sides and another across the middle dividing it into two equal squares.

Here the sick and the melancholy come to sleep under the porticoes. Often they are awaiting a dream or the coming of an angel who will reveal himself to them by a sign, after which they wash themselves in the waters and are healed. Usually, people of every religious faith can be seen lying about at all times of the day and night. But not on this occasion. Apart from a handful of cripples, everyone had already joined the crowd following the Patriarch and the Caliph into Jerusalem.

Sophronius explained that, although the Church marked the place of Mary's birth, it was named after her son's miraculous healing of a man paralyzed from birth. "Arise, take up your bed, and walk," Jesus had said to him, and the paralytic had. His bed is kept in the Church. But Umar did not care to go and see it.

As a young man growing up in the Holy City, I often found myself visiting the pools, watching peasants who, after a hard day's work selling their produce, lingered by the cool waters to gape at the intricately carved marble inlay on the columns of the porticoes. There is much to delight in the passage from reflected light dancing on the water, to the cool shade of the portico, to the dark and enveloping enclosure of the old church. Perhaps it sparked memories in the old Patriarch. According to Ka'b, he did not move on right away in spite of Umar's impatience and the religious services that awaited him at our destination. Instead, in an inspired moment, and in a gently lilting voice, he began to recite a poem composed in his youth. Don't ask me how or why, but the poem written so long ago retraced the journey from the Mount of Olives to the Church of the Paralyzed Man:

Let me enter the church,
church of the all-pure Mother of God,
there in veneration to embrace
those walls, so dear to me.

Far be it from me, as I pass through the forum,
to neglect the place
where the Virgin Queen was born.
A most noble palace!

May I behold that floor
where the paralytic went
at the behest of the Healing Word
to lift his bed from the ground.

Spiritual bliss will fill me
when I hymn the glorious sanctuary
of Gethsemane, which has received the body,
the body of Mary,
who gave birth to God.
There they have built the tomb for the Mother of God.

How surpassing sweet thou art, O lofty Mountain,
from which Christ the Lord looked into heaven!

My father remembered this incident because he could see that, in spite of the blasphemous references to Jesus and his mother, and the clumsiness of the translation, Umar was moved. Sophronius may not have known it, but sweet words more than beautiful things moved the first generation of Believers. Umar, like my father, believed that the only reason for building anything was utility; he shrank from one who intentionally sought to add a gratifying effect to an object or a thing. Were one to give him a cheap building over a beautiful one, he would receive praise for being thrifty with the goods of the Lord. Building rudely was religiously justified, he said. How, asked his Companions? Because it meant elevating worship over place, Him over things, content over form, the next world over this one—and this surely was what the Lord intended.

> *Serve God, and associate naught with Him.*
> *God is not heedless of the things you do.*

∾

The stone-cobbled street down which Sophronius had chosen to travel headed due west from the healing pools, turned north, and led to a large open space inside the city walls opposite Saint Stephen's Gate. Since the conquest, Muslims and Jews had called this gate the Gate of the Column.

The name is derived from a great column that stands in the center of the semicircular forum around the gate. At one time, circuses and games were staged there. Some people say the column is a left-over from those pagan times. A cross sat on top of the column when Umar visited the city, reminding people, Sophronius explained, of how much the Roman empire had changed, and, more importantly, that this was where the Jews had tried to seize the body of Mary as it was being carried by the eleven Apostles for burial in Gethsemane. They didn't succeed. Later, Ka'b would agitate for the removal of that offensive cross. But no Caliph ever thought it politic to do so in such a Christian city, and it is still there to this day, lording it over the most important gateway into the city.

It was at the Gate of the Column, Sophronius was quick to point out to Umar, that Christianity had given up its first martyr to the faith.

"What happened?" Umar asked, genuinely interested.

"Filled with the Holy Spirit, and gazing intently up at Heaven, Saint Stephen saw the glory of God," said Sophronius, "and he cried out to the people, 'Look, there is a rift in the sky. Behold the Son of Man standing at God's right hand!' His words made the Jewish elders in the crowd grind their teeth in fury. They uttered a great cry and called upon the people around them to stop up their

ears. Then as one man they rushed upon the blessed Stephen, fling-
ing him out of the gate and down the steps, whereupon they set
about stoning him. As the stones rained upon him, Stephen fell to
his knees, and with his last breath, said, 'Lord Jesus, receive my
spirit. Do not hold this sin against them.' "

But Sophronius did hold it against them, as could be seen from
the way he told the story. He had already surmised that Umar's
advisor was a Jew. And he must have discerned Ka'b's mounting
anger and discomfort. But this was not the time or place for Ka'b to
intervene. His senses were still reeling from the Christian stamp
that had been affixed to every street and building of the City of
David and Solomon. He had never imagined there could be so
many crosses.

Grateful for my father's restraint, Umar turned to him and
whispered, "What drives these Christians! They are like women. No
sooner do they have a memory than they turn it into an ornament."

From the Gate of the Column, the party turned sharply south for
the final stretch of Sophronius's tour. They were now heading down
the most important commercial street in Jerusalem—the Cardo—
and into the wealthiest section of the city. The buildings were solidly
constructed and finely finished; the markets were the cleanest in
Syria and overflowed with cheeses, figs, olives of every variety, tanks
of pressed oil destined for export, celebrated raisins of diverse
kinds, apples, bananas, and pine nuts, whose equal was not to be
found. To each craft, there was a separate bazaar, where one could
purchase the finest quality leather and silver work, mirrors, lamps,
jars, and needles, cotton from Egypt spilling from brightly colored
baskets onto the large smooth paving stones of the street, all in such
abundance that it was enough to take a man's breath away.

But this is not what my father and Umar saw on that most
extraordinary of days. The stores were tightly shut, and the crosses
that one tended to lose sight of in the hustle and bustle of people
and goods stood starkly at attention.

～

Sophronius was silent. Everyone was now on foot, having handed over their horses, and Umar's ass, to attendants at the Gate of the Column. Umar broke the silence:

"How in God's name do you manage to keep your streets so clean?"

Sophronius needed to have the question repeated to make sure he had got it right. After a pause, the Patriarch replied, "Whenever too many camels, horses, asses, oxen, and their dung, clog the city streets, a truly wonderful event occurs to free us. An abundance of rain will pour during the night, washing away the dirt off the streets and freeing them of filth. God made the terrain of His city slope down from the mountain upon which His Church is built, toward the lower ground of the former Jewish Temple. In this way the heavy rain never collects in the streets, but rushes downhill. The flood of water from the Heavens flows out through the Eastern Gate by which we entered, taking with it all that disgusting dung and filth. The moment Jerusalem has been thus baptized, the downpour stops."

No sooner had he finished speaking than an enormous complex looming from afar suddenly came into full view through an opening in the colonnade. Arriving at that hour when a man can barely distinguish another in the light, a sequence of interconnected buildings marking the journey's terminus rose gradually in height as they stepped back from the street. The Church of the Resurrection, like the Jewish Temple that had inspired it, was situated on a longitudinal axis facing east, overlooking the desolate ruins of the Temple. Towering above it in the distance, Umar and Ka'b could see the great rotunda built over the tomb of Jesus. Not that the edifice had been constructed to look like a memorial. Far from it. The church was a celebration in stone to Triumph, to the Glory of Christ the Conqueror, he who had overcome death.

Capping the tall cylindrical tower of the rotunda was the largest dome in Jerusalem, the Dome of the Resurrection. A hole was cut out at the apex of the spherical surface, exposing the rock-cut tomb to the sky. The Dome bore a striking resemblance to the round, shaven top of Sophronius's head.

A flight of steps led up to an atrium surrounded by a portico held up by pillars bigger than any the Arabs had ever seen before. "Here, under one roof, over the mountain we call Calvary," Sophronius said, "are gathered all the places, which, together, have witnessed the providential history of salvation first set in motion by our father Abraham."

"All?" asked Umar. "But what of the Sanctuary of David, where the king of Israel begged the Lord for forgiveness? I want to go there."

"Forgiveness was granted to David by virtue of what Jesus did in this place," said Sophronius, waving his arm in the direction of the three massive doors that had mysteriously been thrown open for the party, revealing a long five-aisled Basilica of breathtaking sumptuousness. The walls were encrusted with colored marbles that shone like mirrorwork. The sculpted coffering of the ceiling presented itself as an endless wave. The ceiling coffers crested like a gently rising swell down the middle two-story nave, divided from the neighboring aisles by a forest of columns. A brilliant gold sheen followed in the wake of the coffering, growing denser and more brilliant still down the nave where the light came spilling through clerestory windows, causing the whole temple to sparkle with a thousand reflections.

"Please." Sophronius motioned to Umar. "You are my guest. I will explain inside."

"Do not go into that Sorceror's Temple, good Umar!" Ka'b suddenly whispered fiercely. "Do not approach those pillars by the entrance, for they are idols. The prayers of him who passes through them will be as if naught. A curse upon these Christians for not seeing the things to come!"

"Calm yourself, my friend. You are fencing with shadows. We have nothing to fear from this priest."

Sophronius observed them with an artificial smile and, looking down at Umar from his position on top of the steps, said, "You are having to contend with two Jerusalems. His crucified Christ," he said, pointing at Ka'b, "while ours worship Him in this blessed place. It is our greatest wish that you join me inside for prayer." And then he turned slowly, deliberately, to genuflect in front of the open doors.

The New Temple

My father's confrontation with Sophronius took place inside the great Basilica. The crowd having finally been shaken off, the Patriarch and the Caliph were looking at a natural outcrop of gray-speckled rock contiguous with the floor of the apse of the great church. The raw rock spread incongruously out of the ornately decorated floor, reaching a span's height above the floor at its highest point.

"What is this?" asked Umar.

"The summit of Calvary, upon which our Lord died," replied Sophronius.

"A slot has been cut into the tip," Umar remarked, pointing at a rounded protuberance like a skull cap which marked the rock's highest elevation.

"It was cut by the Romans in order to prop up the cross upon which our Savior offered Himself," replied Sophronius.

"You make it sound like a sacrifice, not an execution."

"Because it was," said Sophronius. "Jesus died during Passover, at the very hour of the Paschal offering. Like Isaac, who carried the wood for his own sacrifice to this rock, Christ carried his cross."

The leader of Christendom dropped to his ancient knees, genuflected, and kissed the sinuous protrusion neatly framed by marble moldings set into the floor. "Thus do we touch Jesus," Sophronius said, speaking so softly he could barely be heard, "at the moment at which he endured the agony that redeemed us." Then to Umar and Ka'b's evident discomfort, he began to intone words of mourning and praise as though they were not there.

Tears were in the old man's eyes by the time he had finished. Umar looked away. No one said anything—except Ka'b.

"Did you say that the son of Abraham was sacrificed on the rock of Jesus' crucifixion?" Ka'b asked, breaking the silence.

"I did," replied the Patriarch. "Unlike your forefather Ishaq, however, the Son of God died on the cross, slowly and terribly. At the moment of His greatest agony, he cried out, 'I have overcome the world.' By which the Son of God meant that He had offered Himself up for those sins that the blood of bulls, goats, and sheep cannot wash away. His death is the true Passover, fulfilling and terminating all the forms of sacrifice that used to take place in the old Temple."

"How can an offering meant to expiate the sins of the world," exclaimed Ka'b, "originate in one who called for the destruction of God's House? Did not Jesus say,

I will destroy this temple that is made with hands,
and in three days I will build another not made with hands.

"Three days! If he were truly God, then it would be over and done with in the blink of an eye. And if he were not God, his purpose would have been to delude men. If the blood of such a man was indeed spilled on this rock, then it is wasted blood."

"You are lying, Jew, confirming the curse that was laid upon your entire race!" Sophronius retorted, having regained his composure. "Your own most holy Isaiah recognized this curse when he declared how his own children, raised and exalted by their father, had sinned against him. He said:

An ox knows his owner, and an ass the manger of his master,
but my people did not know me. Israel did not recognize me."

"It was your prophets who first spoke about our Messiah. Yet you did not understand the words that foretold the coming of Him who wondrously shows His steadfast love and who is our rock of refuge. Jesus foretold the destruction of which you speak, but He never called for it. Your kind bore false witness against Him then, as they continue to bear false witness against Him now. *Not one stone will be left upon another,* were the actual words of Christ; *all will be thrown down.* And so it came to pass that the old Temple was destroyed, and a new one has arisen in its place."

"You mean this building," interjected Umar in an attempt to calm things down but keep his distance.

"I do," said Sophronius.

"And what is it founded on?"

"The body of Christ."

"I take it you mean his burial place."

"The Holy Sepulchre is empty," Sophronius patiently explained. "I mean His body, literally. When God came to dwell among us in the person of Jesus, the Word became flesh, the Father became the Son. The Apostles were witnesses to Him speaking of the temple of His body. True believers rallied around Jesus. They believed in Him, and by so doing became a community. Thus did His body become a Church, which is our Temple; the stone spurned by the old builders became a new cornerstone."

"However you want to put it," exclaimed Umar, "the point is you worship at the site of the death and burial of Jesus."

"And His resurrection, on the third day," Sophronius added. "You mustn't leave that out. For only at that moment did the New Temple come into existence—after the body had risen. We worship at an empty tomb, not a full one. God's people were judged, destroyed, and restored in the shape of the Risen Body of Christ. The New Temple may not be what the Jews expected at the time of Jesus, but it is the long-awaited Temple nonetheless. And it owes its existence to His agony and death, and, above all, to His resurrection."

"So that is what Jesus meant when he said he would build

another Temple not made with hands!" exclaimed Ka'b, thinking he had found Sophronius out. "He meant he would personally replace the Temple he wanted to see destroyed. Those whom you have so unjustly accused of bearing false witness said as much!"

"This is not the time for bickering," Umar said in an aside to Ka'b. He looked confused and irritable as he turned to address Sophronius. "In simple terms, exactly how was your church, or temple, or whatever you wish to call this building, built?"

"From the stones of the ruined Temple," replied Sophronius.

"The same stones!" exclaimed Umar.

"The very ones," said Sophronius. "We have traditions to that effect."

"So you wanted to keep a connection with the old Temple?" Umar asked.

"Not any longer," replied Sophronius.

"But I am told," Umar went on, gesturing in the direction of Ka'b, "that you celebrate the consecration of your Church on the same day that Solomon consecrated his Temple. Also, that in this very Church you have put on display the ring of Solomon and the horn that Jewish priests used to annoint the kings of Israel. Why?"

"The priests who tried and crucified our Lord Jesus on this spot forfeited their right to offer new sacrifices in the old Temple," said Sophronius. "Their hands were thus forever defiled. The holy artifacts that you mentioned, and many others besides that I could show you, had to be transferred to that place sanctified by His blood."

"But what about the Rock that was the first direction of prayer of true Believers?"

"That," replied Sophronius, "could not be moved. And besides, it no longer had a purpose after our Savior sacrificed Himself. From Calvary, where the head of the human race was held and death itself was destroyed, there began to stream the water that was the source of a new salvation. The Rock upon which the old altar rested used to mark the spot where the world's thirst was quenched. On the evening of the final day of the Feast of the Tabernacles, priests would so signify by pouring a golden flagon of holy water down the shaft at the side of the altar. But it is no longer that spot. Not after God revealed that *Out of His heart shall flow rivers of living water.* Henceforth the center and source of life was no longer a place, but the person of Jesus himself. His flesh became our Temple."

Adam's Tomb

ophronius told Umar that Calvary contained "the head of the human race," and by that he meant that our father Adam, the first man, was buried underneath the protrusion of exposed rock in the Basilica, in an underground crypt that the Christians call Adam's Chapel. The three men were standing there.

"As in Adam all die," said the old man, citing his Holy Book, "even so in Christ shall all be made alive."

"But I thought our angel ancestor was buried under a different Rock, the Rock of Foundation," Umar said, expressing his confusion.

Whereupon the Patriarch made the strange remark that it could not be otherwise, seeing as how "the origin of death was destroyed" in the place where Jesus had suffered. The sacrifice of Jesus, he was trying to say, had somehow overcome Adam's death, changing the essential nature of sin.

None of this made any sense to the Caliph. To illustrate his meaning, Sophronius turned to a mosaic that depicted Adam rising from his grave at the foot of the cross, holding a chalice to catch the precious blood of Jesus. The blood, having fallen upon Calvary and then run down its face to his grave, had recalled him to life. "The blood of Jesus, the new Adam," Sophronius explained, "is in this cross overcoming death even as it washes away the old Adam's sin." Then he sang these words:

We think that Paradise and Calvarie,
Christ's Cross and Adam's tree,
Stood in one place;
Look, Lord, and find both Adams met in me;
As the first Adam's sweat surrounds my face,
May the last Adam's blood my soul embrace.

Such smooth words! Even my father had to admit they were inspired. The old man, he said, was full of such words; was it any wonder men called him honey-tongued? But were they true? And if they were, what about what Ka'b had said to Umar in Medina, about Adam's fall and burial underneath the summit of Moriah?

During Umar's week in Jerusalem, Sophronius and Ka'b could find nothing on which to agree other than that the first man was originally buried on Moriah. This, remarkably, Sophronius took for granted. How then did the body get moved from Moriah to Calvary, some six hundred paces away?

Sophronius told Umar a story that began more or less where my father's story of the first man and his fall from the Garden had left off.

A tradition handed down to the Church Fathers, Sophronius said, told of Solomon finding Adam's skull in the cleft of a small rocky knoll that rose bare amidst a lush garden of palms, olive trees, and flowering plants. Solomon called the delightful place, including the bald protuberance of rock in its midst, Golgotha—the name by which the People of the Torah referred to Calvary.

Ka'b agreed that the word *Golgotha* meant "place of the skull." But, he immediately added, the skull was not that of Adam but rather had been found among the bleached heads of the condemned left lying about in what was, after all, a public place of execution.

Sophronius brushed this aside, insisting that the name referred to a single skull—the skull of the first man, our father Adam. Some monks, Sophronius went on to say, claimed that the rock itself had taken on the shape of the skull it entombed.

Adam was buried under Calvary, and the proof, according to Sophronius, lay in certain details that Ka'b had omitted from his version of the story of Adam and the Rock.

One day, said the Patriarch, Adam called his son Seth and said: "Go to the gates of the Garden and ask the guardian of the Tree of Life to give me the oil of mercy that God promised when he thrust me out of Paradise."

"Father, I am ready," said Seth, "but I know not the way."

"Go by that valley which lieth eastward. There you will find a green path blackened by footprints left by my feet and your mother's when we were turned away from the Garden. No grass has grown to cover them since."

Following his father's instructions, Seth reached the gates of the Garden, which he found guarded by an angel barring his entry. He was allowed but a glimpse of the Tree of Life. Its crown reached into Heaven, and its branches were covered with foliage and flowers and all kinds of fruit. Its trunk was gigantic and bare, with a terrible serpent wrapped around it, consuming everything within reach. The tree's roots descended into a precipitous chasm that reached into the very depths of Hell. There they became the tree that the People of Muhammad call Zaqqum. The only inhabitant of Hell was Seth's brother Cain, who was striving vainly to climb upwards. The roots of the Zaqqum were like live tentacles wrapped around him, pinning him down, their ends piercing his flesh.

Seth begged the angel for mercy. But the angel refused to give him the oil of mercy, saying that it could not be bestowed upon his father's race until many more years had passed. In token of future mercy, however, the angel gave Seth three seeds from the heavenly tree, and suggested that he bury them with Adam.

Adam died shortly after Seth's return, and Seth put the three seeds under his tongue before burying him under the Rock of Moriah, the site of the old Temple.

Adam's body, Sophronius said, did not lie undisturbed. On the authority of a blessed chain of transmission, it is known that Noah dug up Adam's body from under Mount Moriah's summit to protect it from the flood. He placed it in a teakwood coffin on his ark, and gave strict orders that it not be opened. When the raging waters of the flood had subsided, and the ark had reached its resting place, Noah ordered his son Shem to place the coffin on an oxcart pulled by a bull. Shem was to follow in the steps of the bull, and wherever the beast came to a stop, there he was to bury the coffin.

But Shem was greedy; he convinced himself that there were riches in the coffin. While awaiting the arrival of the cart, he opened the lid and there beheld Adam, beautifully preserved, all sixty cubits of him wrapped in a white shroud, whereupon he was consumed with regret at the terrible thing he had done.

When the bull arrived pulling the oxcart, as his father had said it would, Shem loaded the coffin and walked behind the cart. The bull stopped somewhere in Palestine, and there Shem reburied Adam. The three seeds from the Tree of Life germinated and produced three saplings. In time, these became one tree, with each component preserving its distinct nature. The tree was at once palm, cypress, and cedar, symbolizing, Sophronius said, Victory, Death, and Eternity.

Moses made his wondrous rod from this marvelous wood, the rod that drew forth sweet water from a rock in the Sinai. David replanted the tree in Jerusalem. Solomon attempted to cut columns out of its trunk for his Temple. But these kept growing even after they were cut and were therefore not suitable for construction.

Then the tree was stolen. A spring welled up to cover the place where it had been hidden, forming pools, the very same healing pools of the Church of the Paralyzed Man to which Umar had been taken by Sophronius. There the wood remained until the time of Jesus, when it miraculously floated up to the surface, and was unwittingly selected by the Romans to make the cross upon which Jesus died.

But where exactly in Palestine did the bull stop, Adam get reburied, and the three seeds from the Tree of Life begin to grow?

Now the story grew complicated. Sophronius maintained that the meaning of the name *Golgotha*, preserved in holy scripture, confirmed that the place had to be Calvary. Ka'b continued to disagree, saying that he knew Christians to disagree with one another over the matter. Some said the Tree of Life first grew in Mount Lebanon and was planted by Noah, not his son. Seeing as how Muslims and Jews deny that Jesus was crucified, Ka'b said he himself held no opinions on the Tree.

Umar said that Arab sages had told him that the torso of Adam was buried with his limbs in Hebron, while only his head was buried under the Rock in Jerusalem. Others, he said, were of the opposite opinion: Adam's head was buried in Hebron, beneath the sanctuary of Abraham, whereas his torso and feet were buried in the vicinity of the Rock. No one knows how the parts got separated from one another. Nonetheless, all agreed that they had.

Throughout this exchange, Sophronius remained adamant about the skull, insisting that it was buried in the place where Jesus was crucified, but open to suggestion regarding the other body parts.

Did Noah's bull really stop where Sophronius said it did, and was the head later transported to Calvary? I myself am of the opinion that our Father Adam's burial place is a subject fraught with confusion. Wise men had better drop the subject. God does not want us to know everything.

One thing, however, that He does want us to know, and that all Peoples of the Book agree upon: On the Day of Resurrection, on top of the old Rock, not the new one, God will restore the first man's head to his body. And He will set him upright, and say:

O Adam! Unto thee I assemble thy seed;
and all of them are assembled to do thee honor.

The Rock of the Cross

The raw rock of Calvary has been elaborately dressed up in masonry to the point of merging into the walls of the memorial intended to do it honor. Only the summit is venerated from the Basilica. And even it is not visible at first sight, being at floor level and dominated by a large new cross.

I see no reason to doubt that this was the site of the crucifixion. But it could not possibly have been the site of Abraham's sacrifice. For if you inspect the foundations of the apse and the base of the rock from the underground crypts of the church, namely, from Adam's Chapel, whose story I have just recounted, a reasonable man will realize that nowhere was Calvary flat enough to lay Ishaq across it. The old Patriarch saddled Calvary with too great a burden for common sense to carry.

I surmise that the rock upon which the Son of Mary, or another who looked like him, died (or was snatched away before he died, as some Meccan sages argue) was a tall, vertical block rising out of the corner of an ancient quarry.

By the time of Jesus, the quarry had been filled in. The earth accumulated around it, forming a mound out of which emerged the rock and the cleft tip that attracted Umar's attention. Perhaps it resembled a hillock ideally shaped to support and display the wooden instrument of torture beloved by the Romans. The Temple, further east, was the center of Jerusalem in the days of Jesus. Calvary would then have been just outside the city walls, in a visible place that the Romans would have used over and over again for public executions. At some point, the quarry must have become a garden cemetery, for it is written,

> *In the place where He was crucified,*
> *there was a garden,*
> *and in the garden a new sepulchre,*
> *wherein was never a man yet laid.*

The sepulchre was intended for Joseph of Arimathea. Considering its distance from Calvary, it had to have been hewn out of the opposing rock face of the quarry, a stone's throw away from Calvary. Here, according to the eyewitness of the two Marys, the body of Jesus was hurriedly placed and a large round stone was rolled across the entrance. But deep in the bowels of the earth, underneath the church and the dirt that had collected in the bowl of the quarry, the place of the execution and the burial of Jesus would have been conjoined into a single mass of rock.

Alas, none of this can be seen today. For the place is not even remotely as Jesus would have known it. The quarry has been turned into a beautiful open courtyard, paved with polished stone. Hundreds of lit candles cast dancing shadows on the ceiling and columns of the arcades that surround it.

On the far side of the Church of Resurrection lies the Rotunda, which is the building's beating heart. Day and night it is filled with chanting monks bearing candles that cast a distorting light upon their faces. Their prayers resonate within the tall cylinder and can be heard like a muffled drone from the courtyard outside.

The tomb of Jesus sits in the center of the Rotunda, just as the Ark sat in the center of the Temple of Solomon. In order to build the tower so that it dominates the city from all angles, the entire vertical face of the quarry had to be cut out. The tomb was thereby freed from the mass of rock of which it once formed an inextricable part until large crowds could walk comfortably around it. Masons must then have hollowed out the interior of the remaining stone block, forming a narrow chamber four arms and two thumbs long, barely tall enough to accommodate a person standing upright.

Inside this intricately carved chamber, a bench has been cut out of the rock. It is long enough for a body lying at full length. On this, the black-robed guardians of the tomb will tell you, the faithful Joseph laid the body of Jesus. When Umar entered the chamber, fifteen golden bowls stood in the place of that holy body. Filled with oil, they burn day and night, turning the normally light-colored limestone surround pitch black.

The mouth of the tomb faces east, toward Calvary. The stone that originally sealed this entrance, until it was mysteriously rolled aside, is situated at the western entrance. Bound with copper, it is anointed with holy balsam by the Patriarch once a year. During the week of Umar's visit, Ka'b told me, the veins at his temple bulging with anger, it served as a Holy Table. Indeed, Ka'b could see that the whole edifice had been conceived with the Jewish Temple in mind—from the great steps off the Cardo to the long walk down the five-aisled Basilica and the Rock of the Cross, from the arcaded court to the beautifully finished triumphal tower of the Risen Christ, which mocked the ruins of the Holy of Holies it had supplanted.

~

Since adolescence, I have admired the lines of the New Temple and wondered about those who must have labored so hard to put them in place. No ill that my father could think to say of it diminished my enthusiasm and curiosity. "Idolatry run amok," he would say of the place, forgetting his own passion for the Rock, which, to some people, also smacked of strange worship.

"The Church of the Dungheap," he would call it, changing a letter in the Arabic word for resurrection, *qiyama,* to *qumama.* Although my father's play on words caught on among some of Muhammad's People, I never use it. The real dungheap at the time was farther east. For one who did not live solely on memories like my father, there was nothing to admire about David's Sanctuary in those days. It was just a boring expanse of stone that took two decades to properly clean up. In contrast, the Christian areas of the city buzzed with life, variety, beautiful things.

One day, I don't remember how, the issue came up of who had commissioned the Church of the Resurrection.

"Christ raised her from dung to power," Ka'b blurted in anger. "She was a commoner, and yet the whole empire let her have her way and christianize the world."

"Who are you talking about?" I said.

"The strumpet who founded this Temple of Abomination with which you are so enamored," replied Ka'b. "She built it upon a relic that she came halfway across the world to find."

"You mean Calvary?"

"No! No! No!" exclaimed Ka'b. "I mean the cross. She stumbled upon Calvary by accident, pursuing a mad search for what Christians call the true cross, the two pieces of wood upon which they claim Jesus was crucified. Just imagine! A harlot who scalded her son's wife to death in a steam bath, and then decided to relocate the fulcrum of creation from Moriah to the place of her find, which she claimed was Calvary."

The woman my father was fulminating against was Flavia Helena Augusta, the mother of Constantine the Great, who had come to Jerusalem on pilgrimage three hundred years before the arrival of the sons of Ishmael. A long and tumultuous life had she, rising from lowly servitude in an inn to mother of the first Christian Roman emperor. She left Rome suspected of collaboration in the murder of her daughter-in-law, Fausta. Maybe finding the cross was her atonement. No one will ever know for sure. Certainly, the guardians of the Church of the Resurrection, who deemed her a saint, would vehemently deny my father's accusations.

But Ka'b was right about one thing. Helena had single-handedly reshaped the geography of the Holy City, and with it the fate of the world. She had cut right through to the heart of the matter with a devastatingly simple insight: The actual wood of the cross could bear witness to the story of Jesus in a way that no words could ever do.

No one had dared to think such a thought before. The empress just brushed aside the objections of her theologians, who thought it unseemly for Christians to revere a relic. They had simply read too many books.

I can see her driven by an all-consuming desire to see and touch the incontrovertible proof of the suffering of Jesus, and wanting to spread fragments of that proof, the wood of the true cross, until they filled all corners of her son's empire, touching the common folk with whom she so identified, giving them the opportunity for a magical union with Him, one in which the frail trappings of their miserable existence on earth—an existence her origins made her all too familiar with—could finally be transcended. The beaten and broken body of the Messiah, in Helena's eyes, was not just a story of suffering—it was one of community through the passion of Jesus. And the bonds of that community were going to be forged through the truth of the cross, a truth that Helena had extracted from the rubble and turned into the magnificent New Temple I grew up in awe of.

Finding the Cross

"How did she know where to look?" asked an incredulous Umar. The Caliph and the Patriarch had left Adam's Chapel and were standing beneath the basilica of the church in another underground crypt, this one bearing Helena's name. Here, Sophronius said, the true cross had been found.

Sophronius said that Helena had searched high and low for the cross for weeks, and as he recounted her many stratagems to unearth information, it was as though he himself had been there. The indefatigable empress, he said, had checked and cross-checked anecdotes from the locals, visited one holy site after another in the blistering heat of summer, and distributed bags of silver from wagonloads brought all the way from Rome. She followed every lead provided by priests, every clue volunteered by the army of soothsayers and would-be prophets who populate this city. She took to grilling carpenters on the types of wood from which crosses were made in the time of Jesus. She even questioned a blacksmith about the shape of the nails that might have been used by the Romans.

But it was all to no avail. Any clues that might have survived from the time of Jesus had been erased by the emperor Hadrian's workmen when they laid a new Jerusalem on top of the ruins of the one the emperor had razed to the ground.

"Why not build the church anywhere?" asked Umar. "Or use a

replica of the original thing? Why go to all this trouble to possess the actual cross?"

Human beings, Sophronius replied, treasure the mementos of the dead whom they have loved—the greater the love, the more intense the need. It was inconceivable for the Blessed Virgin and the Apostles to not seek the crown of thorns, the nails, the sponge soaked with the blood that had washed away their sins. There had probably been no need to bribe the centurions, who were, after all, ordinary Romans who had no stake in the murder. But what if they had been required to pay a little something? Surely, Joseph of Arimathea and Nicodemus, both men of wealth, would have paid the soldiers' price. No amount would have been too high when you think of what it meant to fondle such blessed things.

Nothing but the actual cross would satisfy Helena. She could not bear to continue living in the knowledge that the instruments of His Passion—the Pillar of the Scourging, the Crown of Thorns, the Holy Lance, the nails, and, above all, the cross—were lying buried in some obscure, forgotten place. Helena had come all the way from Rome to a pompous if provincial town of no great commercial or political importance to bring to light the instruments of His agony and the place of His Resurrection, so that all might be able to see and venerate them. God willed that she would not return without them.

"But she had reached an impasse," said Umar. "What did she do next?"

"She realized that the reason she could not find the cross was because it had been hidden so well."

"By whom?"

"By those who were of old the beloved of God, until they showed with their saliva contempt for Him who through His saliva opened the eyes of the blind."

"Who?"

"The Jews."

"But I thought they were no longer in the city!" exclaimed Umar. "You yourself said as much when you insisted that we maintain the ban on their presence."

"They come to weep," replied Sophronius. "We gave them permission to enter one day a year in exchange for payment. Just as they purchased the blood of the Messiah, we allow them to purchase their own tears. The day after Jerusalem was taken and destroyed by the Romans, one could see women dressed in rags, and the old bearing their tatters and their years, gather for a time of mourning, proving by their bodies and their dress the meaning of the wrath of the Lord. Every year, on the day of the destruction of the Temple, we let this rabble of the wretched gather on Mount Moriah, and while the wood of the crucifix of the Lord shines and glows and celebrates His Resurrection, and the symbol of the cross is topmost on the Mount of Olives, the children of this wretched nation bemoan the destruction of their former Temple. But they are not worthy of compassion, using as they do the occasion of our generosity to filter back into Jerusalem in ones and twos to live in hiding. It is impossible to police them. A number even now live and work in the city."

"Why would the Jews care what happened to the cross?" Umar asked.

"Because their forefathers had to conceal the proof of their terrible deed. Finding His cross would expose them, and bring down upon their heads the curse written in their own law."

"So what did Helena do?" asked Umar.

"Her soldiers rounded up several hundred infiltrators into the city. These were then forced to choose among themselves twenty with knowledge of the law. When the twenty were brought before her, she asked them to search out the one person most knowledgeable among them. They hesitated, wherupon she ordered all twenty to be burned at the stake. Only then did the oldest man in the group, a rabbi by the name of Judas, get pushed to the fore. It was claimed by his friends that the secret had been handed down to him by his father, who, in turn, had received it from his father. Judas tried at first not to confess. But Helena ordered him thrown into a well. On the seventh day, he relented."

"What did he say?" asked Umar, thoroughly absorbed in the story.

"He asked to be taken to the old Rock, the site of Solomon's Temple."

"Praise be to God!" exclaimed the Caliph.

The indomitable Helena, said Sophronius, seated herself on a makeshift platform on the Temple Mount. The empress's hair, which she wore knotted over the middle of her head, was drawn back severely. Her tight, thin-lipped face suggested a woman accustomed to being obeyed. From where she sat, amid the ruins of the Temple adorned with two desultory statues erected by Hadrian, she would have faced a colonnade of steps descending to the sacred pool in the southern half of the city. The emperor had built a square fountain surrounded by porticoes at this terminus. The steps leading down to the pool continued the cold, classical colonnade of the Cardo, effectively halving the pagan city that he had built.

"As Mary bore the Lord and gave Him to the world, so I shall uncover His cross and teach His Resurrection," said Helena. Your ancestors hid this wood, and I, a woman, have come to bring their tricks to naught. Now tell me why have you brought us to this pierced stone that your people come to anoint each year, and before which they rend their garments upon departing? Perhaps it is hidden here, in the cave that lies underneath? Why else would your kind visit here?"

"We come on the date of the destruction of our Temple," the old man said. "We come to mourn, the way you would mourn the death

of a loved one by visiting the site of his burial. In the year of Jesus'
crucifixion, our Temple was still standing here, centered on this
rock; it lay inside the Holy City, whereas your own scriptures say
that Jesus was led out of the city to be crucified—which is why the
cross cannot be here."

"Where is it, then?" said Helena. "The Holy Gospel says that
He was crucified at a place called Calvary. You Hebrews call it Golgotha. That is where I will find his sepulchre and the cross. Tell me
where Golgotha is. That is all I want from you."

"Golgotha," said Judas, "is known to us as the place of the
skull. But I don't know where it is."

"Are you choosing death with severe torments over a good and
gracious life?"

"Would a man in the desert, Your Highness, desire to eat
stones when he can eat bread?"

"Then get on with it!" demanded Helena.

Judas fell to his knees, prostrated himself upon Moriah's summit, and, according to my father, who heard it from Sophronius,
loudly made this appeal: "O God, who made the earth and meted
out its dust with the hollow of His hand. O God, who dwells in the
glorious light that no man can withstand. O God, who made the
countless Seraphim to continuously praise Him with their voices,
saying, 'Holy, Holy, Holy, Mighty Lord whose glory fills the earth.'
You, O God, are the Lord of the Universe. Everything is the work of
your hands. If it be your will that the Son of Mary reign, He whose
being is derived from you, I beg you, perform this miracle for me
and, just as you revealed the bones of Joseph to Moses, reveal to me
the treasured wood of your cross. If it is buried somewhere in this
Holy City, may the sweet smell of incense ascend from it. Then I too
shall believe in Christ who was crucified, He who will reign forever
and ever."

The sweet smell of incense did not ascend. No sooner had
Judas finished his speech than a luminous cross appeared in the
sky, extending from its foot over the Mount of Olives, to a place several hundred paces away from where Helena and Judas were stand-

ing. According to eyewitnesses, the brilliant light emanating from the cross surpassed the light of the sun and lasted for most of the day. Christian and heathen alike were inspired by a combination of fear and joy. They flocked to the churches to seek their salvation, now that the prophecy had been fulfilled:

> *And then will appear in Heaven*
> *the sign that heralds the Son of man.*

Helena and her entourage, with Judas in tow, hurried to the place indicated by God, and Judas was set to work. The Romans had spared no effort in filling the site with city waste and earth and rubble brought from elsewhere; all this Judas had to uncover. He found the cross at a great depth in a stone cave that had been concealed when the Romans raised the level of the ground and covered it with flagstones in preparation for the construction of a temple to the Goddess of Love. And yet the holy tomb that Judas revealed was remarkably well preserved. Right on top of the Rock of Golgotha, which Helena could finally see, and to which the cross had been fixed throughout the ordeal of Jesus, there stood a statue of Venus, naked, brazenly displaying her charms."

Only now was the empress convinced of Judas's good faith. She showered him with honors, had him baptized, and made him the first bishop of Jerusalem—but not before changing his name from Judas to Cyriacus.

∾

Sophronius concluded his tour by showing Umar a piece of the actual cross, mounted in a casket of pure gold and precious stones. I found out later that it was not the actual relic, which had been carried to Constantinople for safekeeping in the months preceding Umar's entry into the city. On Easter Friday, Sophronius said, the casket would be opened in a ceremony to which the Caliph was invited.

At this ceremony, which Umar did not attend but which many years later I observed, the Patriarch's chair is placed on the Rock of Calvary. He takes his seat. A table is placed before him with a cloth on it. The deacons stand round the table like sentinels. The casket containing the fake holy wood is then put before him. He opens it, and takes the piece of the cross out, placing it on the table. As long as the holy wood is on the table, the bishop sits with his hands resting on either end of it, holding it down. The deacons round him watch like hawks as now all the faithful, catechumens and communicants alike, come up to the table, one by one, with their hands behind their backs, to kiss the wood and move on. They keep their hands behind their backs, I was told by a monk, because on one occasion one of them bit off a piece of the holy wood and stole it away. That is why the deacons are anxious and wary as they stand guard, and why the worshippers stoop down and touch the holy wood with their foreheads, then with their eyes, and finally with their mouths, but no longer reach out their hands to touch it.

Finding the Rock

If the Patriarch's strategy was to feast the Caliph's eyes on the sumptuous buildings of the Holy City to gain a foothold inside the mind of his adversary, Sophronius realized the strategy had not worked after Umar refused to pray inside the Church of the Resurrection. Umar occupied another world, different even from that of his own followers. Had he been Abu Ubayda, the commander-in-chief, or that brave son of Walid who wreaked havoc on the Byzantine army and had a weakness for silk and red turbans with arrows stuck in them after the fashion of great warriors, it might have been a different story. "Heaven is as close to me as my sandal-straps, and so is Hell," I heard Umar say. The Caliph lived every hour of every day as though that were the literal truth.

Umar, impatient now, repeated the request that he had first made on the Mount of Olives, saying, "I would have you take us to the Sanctuary of David. Do you know where it is?"

"It must be somewhere amidst the ruins of the Temple," replied Sophronius. "But why do you want to go there? The place has been abandoned for years."

"I wish to pray there."

"There is so much more that I can show you," said Sophonius. "The New Church of the Virgin Mary, for instance, which is a truly splendid building, and the Church of Zion."

"I don't want to see any more buildings," Umar answered. "I want to be taken to the place where David sought God's forgiveness."

Gaining access to the site of the Temple was not as straightforward as Umar had imagined. Sophronius insisted that the hour was too late to go right away.

"If you must," said Sophronius, resigned, "I will take you there tomorrow, at the crowing of the cock."

Umar and Ka'b were given comfortable quarters for the night in an annex of the church. To decline the duty of hospitality might give offense, even to a Christian. Moreover, the Patriarch's invitation conferred upon the Caliph a measure of protection that the desert Arab immediately understood; and, conversely, Umar thought, the Christian was putting himself under an obligation to the Muslim that might come in handy later on.

The Patriarch was careful to show Umar his own quarters, which were part of a grouping of monastic cells organized around a courtyard north of the Rotunda. The room was tiny and bare, much less comfortable than those of his guests less than twenty paces away. Even my father was struck by its austere furnishings, which so contrasted with the Patriarch's silk and gold-tasselled attire.

Just before daybreak, when the only sounds on the streets are those of roosters and padlocks, sliding bars and rattling door boards, the party set out. Sophronius was in the lead. For some unknown reason, a dozen local peasants had been rounded up. There was a new spring to the Patriarch's step as he picked his way across cobbled streets less elegant than the ones they had taken the previous day. It was as though the old man, having slept on the dilemma that Umar represented for Christendom's holy places, had woken up with a new resolve.

The party worked their way south and east of the Church of the Resurrection arriving before a gate on the southern wall of the esplanade. Believers today call the entrance through which Umar first entered the noble sanctuary the Gate of the Prophet, because it looks as if it had been an important entrance to the Temple Mount in its time. But the entrance gate was blocked with piles of refuse. Now it became clear why Sophronius had brought the peasants along; they set to work clearing a path to the giant doors. As soon as these had been forced open, more rubbish came bursting out, raining down upon the heads of the workers and spilling onto the road that pointed in the holy direction of the Ka'ba.

The interior was a warehouse of filth, which had settled in huge piles on the floor. In some places it reached the ceiling. Umar and Ka'b found themselves standing outside what had once been an elegant sequence of paired square spaces—the pair closest to the wall being surmounted by two domes that gave the appearance of floating away from the walls, supported as they were by adjoining pairs of arched brackets.

Umar fell to the ground in horror, like a man suddenly paralyzed at the knees. Then he soberly and calmly prostrated himself before the rubbish-filled doorway, in a posture of deep and humbling submission, becoming as one with the earth. Slowly, he rose to his feet and stood upright. Raising his hands level with his ears, palms toward the cheeks, he said, "God is most Great!" Then he crossed his hands over his chest, the right palm over the left as prescribed by the Prophet, and inclined toward the Lord, his hands on his knees, said three times, "Glory to the Great One"; then he drew himself up slowly, saying, "God hears him who praises Him." Drawing himself upright for the second time, the Caliph said, "To You be the praise, our Lord," and then prostrated himself yet another time, resting his body on his forehead, knees, and the palms of his hands, his nose lightly brushing the earth.

Umar prayed and prayed. He prayed like a man washing himself over and over again in a running stream of clear water. Each time, he would repeat the same sequence of movements. He prayed not to an audience, as he had done at the Gate of the Sheep's Pool. He prayed as though his very soul were on fire and in need of quenching in the cool waters of God's praise. Solomon had done the same upon finding that the doors of the Temple were barred to him. The son of David had then repeated his father's prayers, imploring God to grant forgiveness. Solomon had prayed as much on his father's behalf as his own. Umar now prayed on behalf of all of them.

Rubbish was piled high on the steps leading up to the Temple Mount. So dense and packed was the dirt that not a single ray of the early morning sun could make its way through, not even after the doors had been opened. Once again, the peasants brought along by Sophronius were set to work. Only two men could work in the densely packed gateway at a time. After much delay, they managed to clear out the beginnings of a tunnel. Still, no light came through.

"It is impossible to proceed," Sophronius said, "except by crawling on one's hands and knees."

"So be it," Umar replied.

Whereupon the Patriarch, in spite of his age, went down on his hands and knees, oblivious of the consequences to his finely tailored garments. Before following Sophronius into the tunnel, Umar tightened his loosely wrapped outer mantle around his body, and tucked the extra material into his belt. My father took up the rear. Everyone else stayed behind on Umar's instructions until they had fully dug out the entrance and carted all the rubbish away.

What was it like, tunnelling through the refuse of centuries? Ka'b remembers bumping into massive pillars a man's length in diameter. Sophronius had dug out a space around them, pushing the rubbish to one corner so that Umar could see his way forward. The pillars rested on the bedrock of the mountain and had once held up a gigantic portico, which Ka'b said King Solomon had built; Sophronius gave the Romans all the credit. A part of that portico, on the southern boundary of the sanctuary, was still standing when the armies of Islam arrived.

Rare are the moments when the play and chatter of life in this world, the pageantry and the boasting, the competitive grasping after wealth and children, are all suspended—and suspended by

dint of sheer necessity, not because of thoughts of the grim doom
that awaits all God's creatures. Such was the bond between the
three men inside the tunnel that held the forces of competition,
prejudice, and hatred in abeyance for however short a while.

After considerable exertion, they worked their way up a flight
of steps, emerging into what looked like a gigantic court. They
looked around in all directions and pondered the scene for a long
time.

Ka'b was the first to break the silence: "By Him in whose
hands is my soul, this must be it! This is David's Sanctuary."

Then he removed his sandals, a custom of both the followers of
Muhammad and Moses, signifying that they make no claim to the
hallowed ground upon which they are about to walk. The ground
was thick with filth under Ka'b's feet; still, he felt a holiness seep
through the bare flesh of his soles. Umar did the same, but Sophronius would not follow their example. Instead, the old Patriarch
turned east and genuflected, as though to ward off some evil wind
that was turning his way.

Young Muslims cannot imagine what the noble sanctuary looked
like then—just as they cannot imagine a butterfly wrapped inside
the wrinkled carcass of its chrysalis.

Time, and the vindictiveness of men, had taken its toll. One-
fifth of the city was a warehouse of ruins—the very fifth that had
sustained its former splendor. The destruction of the Temple Mount
had begun in the time of Titus, the capital of whose kingdom lay in
the land of the Franks. When Titus came to the Holy House in the
first year of his reign, he fell upon the Jews, massacred thousands,
and enslaved the rest. He gave their city over to plunder. He put the
Temple and all its sacred scrolls to the torch.

His soldiers carried off the candelabra, trumpets, and holy
vessels of the Temple. They carried away the two pillars that had
adorned the entrance to Solomon's Temple, and which carried

God's name. Every year, on the day of the destruction, eyewitnesses say, these pillars pine away in their place of exile until tears stream down their rounded sides.

Titus banished the Jews from their city and forbade them from ever re-entering it. The few who had survived his siege emerged from their hiding places to salvage bits and pieces of their lost treasures, but they would never again govern themselves in the same way, much less resurrect on the torn and shredded landscape the monument of their former days of glory.

The powerlessness of the People of Moses brought out the worst in the Romans. Helena, mother of Constantine the Victorious, had the pillars and capitals that remained intact on the Temple Mount carted away to adorn her New Temple on Calvary. Then she ordered that the site be turned into the city dump. And so the newly Christian city began daily to empty its bowels on what was left of the Jewish one. Excrement and refuse had been gathering for three hundred years when Umar, Ka'b, and Sophronius found themselves picking their way through it.

Piles of garbage sat alongside heaps of building rubble, broken pots amidst broken columns, pediments, and architraves. Ka'b did not know one part of a monument from the other. He did not have the faintest idea how these parts might once have fitted together. Blades of grass that had been fertilized with human excrement were

growing in a strange receptacle. Was it once a kitchen pot, or a broken urn, or even a piece of the great altar of sacrifice itself?

The Temple that lived in his imagination, and through him, Umar's as well, was built of words—and was all the sweeter for it. An unbearably wonderful thing was firmly lodged in his mind's eye in spite of being unseen, but its physical expression was not only gone, it had been destroyed over and over again until it had been ground back into the dust of the mountain.

The words, however, he knew by heart; they lived on—in a way that broken artifacts could not. And the words said that, corresponding to His House on Earth, was an absolutely perfect counterpart in Heaven. When Moses ascended to Heaven without having walked the streets of the Holy City, the Lord made it up to him by cleaving the seven firmaments to show him its heavenly equivalent. The two cities faced one other. The same services were performed in both, so that, when the high priest was sacrificing and burning incense on Earth, the Archangel Michael was doing the same in Heaven. What was the Archangel doing now? What had he been doing for the last three hundred years?

Ka'b stumbled about in a daze; he was looking and not looking at the same time. Thoughts cascaded through his head, yet he did not know what to think about any one in particular. My father was in a strange state for the next several days: utterly distracted, unable to attend to me or any practical matter, seeking every opportunity to go back to the desecrated sanctuary, desirous only of wandering aimlessly among the refuse and the filth. I think the desire to knit together the scattered remembrances of his life around the Rock turned into an obsession on that day.

How did my father know where he was on the sanctuary? And how did he go on to find the precise spot where David and Ahithophel had long ago found the Rock?

The desire to offend has a smell to it. Ka'b followed his nose.

Helena had singled out the Rock. She had ordered that the smelliest scourings be dumped there, including the manure of the city's stables. Ka'b found the Rock because the dung reeked most foul and was piled highest over the precise spot where the Holy of Holies had once stood in David and Solomon's Temple. He was assured that he was standing in the right place when he spied the menstrual cloths of Christian women collected there.

Umar asked Ka'b and Sophronius to step aside, and set to work alone, throwing the dung with his bare hands into his mantle, which he had placed flat on the ground. Taking the four corners of the cloak into his hands, he carried it on his back, doubled over with the weight, to the wall of the noble sanctuary. There he threw his load over the wall into the Valley of Hell, where the kings of Israel had buried the ashes of the idols that had desecrated their Temple in olden times. Before following his example, my father prophesied the fall of Constantinople, and said: "Be joyous, O City of the Temple! For to you has come the Redeemer, who will cleanse you of your contamination." Sophronius stood aside and watched while all this was going on; he was joined by the rest of the party, who had in the meantime cleared the entrance gate. Umar and Ka'b labored at the pile until enough of it had been cleared to ascertain that they had indeed found the Rock.

To every prophecy in an unsettled age there comes a time of ful-fillment, a time when one begins to see in the present and toward the shape of things to come. Such a time was now settling upon my father. The Rock, he realized, stood in for a greater reality than was suggested by its appearance. Such a time had also come upon Sophronius, who, having failed to leave an impression on his uncouth visitors, clung to the hope that he could redirect their prodigious energies away from Calvary. And it had come upon Umar, he whom all the Peoples of the Book were now calling the Redeemer.

"Where should I build my mosque?" Umar asked, speaking to no one in particular.

"Has not your heart found that which it was looking for, O King of the Arabs?" Sophronius replied. "Honor that which sent it forth on its long and difficult journey. I say you should build on top of this hard, flat piece of rock that your hands have uncovered; it will elevate your house of worship so that it overlooks the desert from whence you came, and provide a solid foundation for the things that you wish to do."

"What do you think of the suggestion, my good friend?" asked the Caliph, turning to my father.

Ka'b did not pause to think. The Commander of the Faithful and liberator of Jerusalem could not be beholden to a Christian monk for the site of his mosque.

"The Rock is without any redeeming value in this priest's eyes," he said. "Quite the opposite. He wants to see it desecrated, so that the so-called prophecies of Jesus will look as though they have come true. Knowing that his religion has lost the power of des-ecration, he would have you bury the Rock on his behalf, hide it under a building that draws attention to itself like his dungheap of a church. I say, therefore, O Umar, beware his forked tongue. Remem-ber that the Rock uncovered is his Church unmasked. Leave His Sign clean and exposed, for all to admire and see. Build north of the Rock, not on it. In that way God will doubly favor you for giving Him back His foundation stone and for being the one who brought back into alignment the two holiest directions of Moses and Muhammad."

"I see you still lean toward the Jews, O Father of Ishaq," Umar replied with a twinkle in his eye. "I have made up my mind. Our mosque will be south of the Rock."

"But then we shall be praying with our backs to the Rock!" exclaimed Ka'b, horrified.

"So be it," the Caliph replied.

Facing Whose Rock?

Umar's mosque was cobbled together hastily. Aside from his decision to build south rather than north of the Rock, no consideration was given to the sanctity of its location. There was neither art of proportion nor technique of construction in the place of prayer that the Prince of the Righteous constructed. Men would have to put their foreheads to the ground inside a square shed assembled from thrown-away boards and beams collected from a Christian dump. The Caliph was in a hurry to return to Medina. His stay in the Holy City lasted only a week.

The son of Khattab identified the religion of Muhammad with proximity to the Prophet, which he measured by distance from his grave in Medina. In Umar's eyes, the Prophet's Companions were the only rightful rulers, and their roots were sunk deeply in the soil of the holy cities of Arabia. Jerusalem was just too far away.

A multitude of poor Bedouin Arab tribesmen, the first converts to Islam, made the rule of the first four Rightly Guided Ones possible. These were the great fighting men of the desert who had taken Iraq and Syria in the blink of an eye. By heading northward with their families, they became holy warriors like those who had accompanied the Prophet David, Peace Be Upon Him. Umar recorded their names, genealogies, battles, and the year of their conversion to True Belief, in registers. He made them live in closed camp-cities, separated from the non-Arabs of the conquered territories; he held them to stricter standards than anyone else; he tried, not always successfully, to prevent them from holding and cultivating land outside Arabia. Then he compensated them with handsome annuities out of revenues collected by taxing everyone else.

Umar's bias against non-Arabs did not affect his fondness for Ka'b. He took pride in the conversion of his friend. When the Caliph expelled the People of the Book from the Hijaz, my father was already his counselor. In fact Ka'b had a role in the resettlement of Jews in Palestine. Forty-two of these, scholars and experts on scripture to a man, he turned to Islam.

"Two religions cannot subsist together," Umar said by way of explaining his decision not to let any captive over the age of puberty reside in the two holy cities of the Hijaz.

In due time the Caliph had to soften the harshness of his new orders, allowing Jews, Christians, and Magians to visit Mecca and Medina on business so long as they stayed no longer than three days. But always he longed for a pure and untainted Arab state, one that continued to expand from its center in Medina.

For all his bluntness, Umar was not unaware of Ka'b's distress at his decision to build south of the Rock.

"Did He not send down His Word as an Arabic Book?" he urged upon Ka'b in Mecca, on the day of rest that follows the slaughtering of the camels during the first pilgrimage season that followed his departure from Jerusalem.

"He did," replied Ka'b.

"And did the Lord of all Being not reveal Himself to an Arab heart so that He might warn them in a clear, Arabic tongue?"

"I suppose so," said Ka'b, not wanting to contradict the Commander of the Faithful.

"And did He not do so in order that His Messenger could warn those who dwell in the Mother of Cities, Mecca, home to God's most ancient house?"

"Yes, but . . ." Ka'b said, before being interrupted by his increasingly excited friend.

"What did God say about facing Him? Tell me, what did He say?"

"The good Lord said many things. He said, for instance,

> *Every man has his direction*
> *to which he must turn in prayer.*"

"He specified one particular direction, as the Father of Ishaq well knows,"

> *From whatsoever place thou issuest, turn*
> *thy face toward the Holy Mosque; it is*
> *the truth from thy Lord. God is not heedless of*
> *the things you do.*

"But which Holy Mosque do the words refer to?" replied Ka'b. Whereupon Umar became angry, detecting impropriety in the question.

"Other verses were revealed in Medina, in the seventeenth month following the Apostle's flight from Mecca," he said in a colder, more clipped tone of voice. "Was I not in the room when Gabriel spoke in Muhammad's ear to tell him that God had changed our most sacred axis of prayer? Can a man forget what happens in such an hour? The Prophet, God's Grace Be Upon Him and His Household, was leading the afternoon prayers. He had just finished two prostrations facing Jerusalem, when suddenly he broke his rhythm and, with the uncomprehending eyes of the whole assembly boring into him, he slowly turned a half circle until he faced the Holy City whose guardians are the Prophet's own House of Hashim. He faced Mecca. His back, mark you, Ka'b, was now to Jerusalem! I was paralyzed with fear, transfixed with horror! We, his closest companions, had been given no warning. Not that Muhammad could have warned us, because the Spirit of the Lord was descending upon him at that very moment, in our presence. I tell you, Ka'b, I could see the Spirit in his face. Like a man in a trance,

he began to utter beautiful new words that no one had heard put
together in that way before."

> *We have seen thee turning thy face about*
> *in the heaven; now We will surely turn thee*
> *to a direction that shall satisfy thee.*
> *Turn thy face toward the Holy Mosque of Mecca;*
> *wherever you are, turn your faces toward it.*
> *Those who have been given the Book know it is*
> *the truth from their Lord; God is not heedless of*
> *the things that they do.*

Muhammad had inaugurated an earthquake on that day in
Medina when he changed the Sacred Axis. His community was
deeply troubled. "O Messenger of God," they asked of him, "what
is the condition of our brothers who died before this change?" But
the Prophet would say nothing, which troubled them even more.

If Umar had been frightened by this turn away from the Rock of
Moses, what about his counselor? Ka'b had prayed in the mosque
where the change had taken place. Standing inside its walls he had
foretold the conquest of the City of the Temple. In the course of the
great oration that had brought Ka'b such fame throughout Arabia,
his eyes must have lingered on the old niche in the middle of the
northern wall facing Jerusalem. Two stones used to sit on either
side of it. After the new verses were revealed, the stones were relocated to a new niche in the southern wall. The old niche was
blocked up, but its impression remained. So men took to calling the
place the Mosque of the Two Sacred Directions. After his speech,
Ka'b would have had to turn to the new niche, his back to the Rock.
How else to pray in a city that sits between Mecca and Jerusalem?

Ka'b's distress had led the normally taciturn Umar to make one
of his longest speeches. The Caliph of the Arabs found his tongue
whenever he needed to suppress doubt.

"His word was sent down as an Arabic judgment," thundered
Umar. "Face the facts, old man—the torch has passed over the
heads of those who were favored of old; it has been passed to the

sons of Ishmael, not Ishaq. The Black Stone has replaced the Rock, just as Arabic has replaced Hebrew. Abraham's descendants by Hagar, not Sara, are the newly chosen ones. You will find peace only after you accept God's will."

Ka'b could not accept it. Not because he was a descendant of Abraham through Sara. Nor because he was from the land of the Yemen, and a southerner with an inferior line of descent, according to his northern cousins. And certainly not because he was inclined toward the Jews, as Umar had implied (an implication that handed to Ka'b's detractors the barbs and insults that would henceforth be used against him).

Perhaps Ka'b had lived a fantasy—call it the final delusion of an old man—that Medina had been a detour, and that Umar's coming to the resting place of the pure would be a new dawn visible to anyone with eyes. Only now the Arab Redeemer, as he had dubbed him, had turned out to have feet of clay. Ka'b found that hard to accept in a man he thought of as his friend.

My father couldn't accept Umar's decision because he never understood it.

"Those who can see lift their eyes to the Heavens and contemplate its manna. Those who cannot see look at the onions in the ground," he said to me by way of expressing his disappointment.

Umar's piety was homespun and unrefined, his tolerance limited. Ka'b's knowledge, his expertise in the Torah, had elevated him above other Believers at a critical juncture in the life of Muhammad's fledgling community. Every Companion of the Prophet had his scripture expert, and circumstances brought Umar together with one of the best. Ka'b defended his sponsor's coarseness, provided biblical justifications for his harsh treatment of his wives, and when Umar had his eldest son lashed to within a hair's breadth of his life for having tasted wine, Ka'b stood against the approbation that descended like a sandstorm and vanished as quickly.

Umar was not an imaginer of genius like Muhammad. He could

not cut through time and circumstance like a knife through cheese. He was a follower, a deputy of the Messenger of God, as he called himself. The Believers in Medina needed to believe in someone if they were to hold together as a community after the death of their Prophet. Abu Bakr had passed away after only two years. So they followed Umar, who turned following into a state enterprise; he incarnated the principle of following. Umar knew how to turn people into followers, how to rank and reward them in accordance with how good they were at it. Ka'b understood that this was not easy; his friend and protector had a gift. How else to capture half the world and its crown jewel in six short years after the Prophet's death! It took a genius for following and for being followed.

The one thing that my father forgot, however, is that a follower is not, and can never be, the Messiah.

In the winter of the year in which he presided over the surrender of Jerusalem to those whom he deemed barbarians, Sophronius died. From his deathbed, the old Patriarch had struggled to defend Christian sites in the Holy City. This leader of men, whose life had been an affair of places not of the heart, died unhappy and broken, still in anguish over the concessions he had been forced to make. Even my father had come around to a grudging admiration of the stubborn priest into whose company he had been thrust by chance and circumstance.

The quarrel between Umar and Ka'b was also an affair of place.

So long as the Holy City remained in Christian hands and the problem was how to wrest it from them, the quarrel lay dormant, like a sleeping giant whom no one even suspected was there. When Umar said, "We are the People of the Sacred Direction," Ka'b would agree. As soon as Umar chose to build south not north of the Rock, however, the giant woke up.

Shortly after Ka'b had been pressured into turning his back on the Rock, first on the Mount of Olives and then on Mount Moriah, I asked him a question, the kind only a boy can dare to ask.

"Why does God, who is the One, have two holy Rocks? And why did He change the sacred axis of prayer from one to the other, so that Jews face one Rock while we Muslims face the other?"

He replied by citing these lines of scripture:

To God belong the East and the West;
He guides whomsoever He will to a straight path.

Ka'b was talking around my question. He went on to say that, since there were three holy cities, not one, men were prone to make mistakes in ordering them by merit. What kind of mistake? He would not elaborate. Then he went on to say that the Messenger of God, unlike his Companions, was lenient in matters of direction. By way of illustration, he told me the story of Bara' the son of Ma'rur, a Meccan with whom he used to be on good terms. Bara' was a Believer long before the Exodus to Medina. He liked everything Muhammad had to say about God—with one exception. Bara' was unable to pray with his back to the Ka'ba because all the idols of his ancestors were housed there.

"I decided," he told Ka'b, "that I was going to be a follower of Muhammad in all things except this. I had to pray as my ancestors had done, facing the Stone that I was most comfortable with."

Muhammad's Companions, especially Umar, were outraged. Those were the days when everyone prayed facing the Rock of Moses, which they had never seen. Being God's Messenger, Muhammad was asked to rule against Bara'. But he would not do so. All he would say was: "You would have had a Sacred Direction if you had kept to it."

Every man interpreted these words in his own way. The lesson that Bara' drew from the Prophet's reply was to position himself south of the Ka'ba during prayer. In this way, he told Ka'b, his face would be aligned with the Black Stone and the Rock of Jerusalem at the same time. That is where my father got the idea that he put to Umar in the City of the Temple.

God had something in mind when he changed the direction of prayer, Ka'b kept on saying. But he could not give a satisfactory account of how the two Rocks came into being, or of the relation between them. Nor did he like talking about the subject. For upon the choice of which Rock to align one's toes with during prayer, the most important friendship of my father's life had foundered.

Ka'b never answered my question. Instead, he followed the example of Bara', which meant avoiding at all cost praying inside the mosque that Umar had built. He located himself out in the open at prayer time, on the sanctuary esplanade, north of David's Rock. Like Bara', Ka'b had both holy Rocks in alignment with one another. He felt at peace, not because he knew he was doing the right thing but because he did not have to think about choosing between the two Rocks.

Growing Up in Jerusalem

My childhood ended six years after the conquest of Jerusalem, with the murder of the son of Khattab at the hands of a disgruntled Christian slave who blamed Umar for the amount of tax he had to pay. When Abu Lu'lu'a's double-bladed dagger pierced the Prince of True Believers in the twenty-first year after the Exodus, its ugly tip found its way into my father's heart. Suddenly he aged. "Your father has gone into his dotage," my stepmother said as she fussed and rearranged and took over his daily routines in a way she had never done before.

An age of chivalry and noble religious purpose had come to an end. Along with Sophronius, dead of a broken heart, Abu Ubayda of the plague, and, most importantly, Umar, murdered by means so foul, died the kind of wisdom that had allowed so peaceful a transfer of sovereignty in the City of Peace. People began to turn their oaths into screens for their misdeeds. Recrimination filled rooms like foul-smelling smoke. Politics was stripped of its noble purpose to become the pure distillation of rumor.

"The luck of Islam was shrouded in Umar's winding-sheet," Ka'b took to saying.

My father had been too close to power to avoid getting entangled in the veils that were now being cast over men's hearts. His warning to Umar, for instance, about the dangers facing him in the conquered territories, was taken for a prophecy of the Caliph's assassination. The conversation that gave rise to this interpretation took place three days before Abu Lu'lu'a did his terrible deed in the presence of Abu Dharr, my father's bitterest foe and a Companion of the Prophet from the earliest days. No sooner was Umar killed than word spread like wildfire that my father had foretold the precise manner and timing of his benefactor's demise!

Ka'b knew the power of wagging tongues. Had he not been lifted by them from the status of a bedraggled and vanquished Jew to that of an Arabian seer within a short time of his arrival in Medina? He was visibly shaken at having acquired the dubious reputation of being the first person to have predicted the assassination of a Muslim Caliph. With my stepmother's encouragement, he cut himself loose from public affairs, refusing all public engagements, including an invitation from Mu'awiya to become his counselor. All he wanted now was to be allowed to live out the rest of his years peacefully in Jerusalem.

I was apprenticed to a local bookbinder who had learned his craft in the Yemen. The craft was new to Muhammad's People and in great demand. At first, my duties were to glue sheets of papyrus to the inside of two wooden boards that held the book together. As soon as I proved adept at this, I was upgraded to the outer covering—leather pasted onto the board and embellished in accordance with the book's importance. I took to this task like a sparrow to flight. In no time I was sewing ornamental leather strips onto the outer leather cover and rubbing or scratching patterns into the surface. By the end of my formal apprenticeship, to Ka'b's great pleasure, I was tooling leather and doing inlay work that was as good as that of any Greek or Christian craftsman in Jerusalem.

Umar's successor, Uthman, was the first son of the House of Umayya to govern Muhammad's People. Eight years had now passed since the conquest. Uthman was loyal to the Prophet. But the House to which he belonged had been of recognized nobility in the days of ignorance and had led the struggle against Muhammad from Mecca until its defeat in the year that my father and mother arrived in the Hijaz. The House of Hashim, from which the Prophet descended and which brought Mecca into the Muslim fold, had come into its ascendency at the expense of the princes, merchants, and noblemen of Umayya, who had to swallow their pride and mark time.

In the power struggle that now raged between the House of Hashim and the House of Umayya in Arabia, my father chose to ally himself with the latter. He supported the victor, Uthman, against Ali, the cousin and son-in-law of the Prophet.

Under the rule of Uthman, the very Islam that had been such a thorn in the Umayyads' side turned into their greatest opportunity. The time had come, they judged, to restore their House to glory. They were on their way to becoming a power to be reckoned with in Syria, especially after Uthman undid all of Umar's strict edicts against Arab accumulation of wealth and ownership of land outside Arabia. An appetite for reckless spending and lavish display was unleashed upon Syria and the Holy Land.

The problem worsened when Uthman confirmed Mu'awiya as governor—he whose accursed father had fought pitched battles against the Prophet, and whose mother was called Hind the Liver-Eater, because she had eaten the liver of the Prophet's uncle in front of all the knights of Arabia after the Believers had killed her father in battle. Such was the stuff of which Umayya's sons were made, among whom I must not forget to include Abd al-Malik, the Caliph I now serve.

Uthman lavished the goods of the Believers on his own kin during the twelve years that he ruled. He gave his great-nephew Marwan, the father of Abd al-Malik, a fifth of Africa's revenue. Those riches paved his family's road to power. The Caliph was generous with himself as well; he died a wealthy man with estates valued at over one hundred thousand gold pieces, and large herds of horses and camels. By the end of his reign, he had earned the reproach of good men. To justify his nepotism, Uthman used to say, "Does not the Quran enjoin us to show kindness unto our near kindred?"

Uthman continued Umar's practice of ruling from Medina.
Apart from setting aside the gardens of Silwan for the city's poor,
he did not intervene in the affairs of Palestine. His new governor
in Syria, however, more than compensated for this neglect. He
encouraged Arabs from Medina claiming descent from the Yemen
to settle in the City of the Temple. He also urged his kinsmen to
buy land from Christians, especially in the areas adjacent to the
sacred precinct. Mu'awiya had the esplanade cleared of what
remained of the rubble. He rebuilt some of the walls and repaved
the northern part of the platform. There was even talk of ambi-
tious new building plans for the area. Nothing came of them during Mu'awiya's years, first as governor and then as Caliph. Ka'b
eagerly followed these plans, but he was counting on self-interest
to drive the House of Umayya to do what was right by the Rock—
seeing as how the House of Hashim was too firmly entrenched in
Mecca and Medina, and too preoccupied with prophecy and matters of the next world. Ka'b, you could say, adopted a pragmatic
stance toward Uthman's reign, never having experienced himself
its pecuniary and grasping nature, which my generation found so
odious.

Before my peers and friends, many of whom had been born to followers of Jesus, my father's hatred of all things Christian was
embarrassing. Their illustrated manuscripts, which often came my
way in the course of my work, were the models of our vocation. It
was from such books that I learned to enclose the chapter headings
of God's Book in a gold frame surrounded by tracery, twisting lines,
and geometrical patterns. On one occasion, I returned from work
flushed with excitement because I had seen my first picture in a
Coptic work, which I was rebinding. It was of a tree with branches
curling upward into the sky and different, exquisitely painted birds
sitting on each branch.

Ka'b went livid with rage, saying that the copying of living
things is strictly forbidden; it is one of the great sins that will be

severely punished on the Day of Judgment. "Even if it is a tree without spirit, or a bird that is not made in His image?" I protested.

"Yes," he thundered, "because it is an imitation of the Creator's activity! On the Day of Judgment, the makers of such images will be eternally condemned to try to breathe life into their pictures, and fail. They are like dogs, classed among the worst of creatures. Angels will not enter their houses." Ka'b was angrier than I had ever seen him. He rued the day that he had put me in harm's way by apprenticing me to one who dealt in such "Satanic filth," as he called the book.

We took to arguing. I would needle him with my escapades into the cavernous interiors of the great Church, whose builders, I imagined, must have burned with overpowering love for their work, the kind of love that only the young of heart understand. If the monks would not let me in through the main doors off the Cardo, I crept in through the back to find a spot all to myself, near a pillar or in the shade of an arcade.

I began to explore every nook and cranny of the Christian city around me. The dazzling monuments and churches worked a kind of magic on us children of the first generation of Muhammad's followers to settle in the Holy City. When I sneaked into the Church of the Resurrection with my friends during High Mass, for instance, the music and liturgies in praise of God made my knees buckle under with emotion.

The Church of the Ascension, crowning the summit of the Mount of Olives and open to the sky to commemorate the place of Jesus's passage into Heaven, was another favorite haunt. At the center of the tall tower lies a set of Jesus' footprints, marking the precise point of his ascent. Besides these, carved out of the rock, stands an altar around which Christians gather for their rituals, under the blue dome of the sky. Against the round walls of this remarkable church rise columns; two in particular remind visitors of the men who said "Ye men of Galilee, why gaze ye into the sky?" The monks tell people that, if a man can squeeze between the wall and the column, he will be freed from his sins. There is not a pilgrim who will not attempt this feat after a fast lasting three days.

A bright light emitted from lamps placed behind windows set below the tower's parapet shines fiercely at night, lifting the steps leading into the valley and to the city out of the shadows. Their brilliance would lift my soul along with the shadows, bringing a sense of reverence that was both attractive and alarming. Headstrong as I was, I sought out priests and monks to talk to about these things.

Walking back home after long and stimulating discussion with my Christian peers, I could not help but see the Rock, which I passed on my way, as plain—no different from hundreds of other rocks in a city that was in any case endowed with more than its fair share of them. Its stories, which I all too often had heard regaled, appeared flat and featureless. My father's zeal for it, I began to think in the waning years of my adolescence, was worthless, the most worthless human activity imaginable.

Ka'b and I had our most bitter exchange after one such ramble through the city. Amid the chickens that my stepmother reared, we were sitting on the roof of our house overlooking the esplanade. The evening sun had intensified the color and size of the surrounding mountains, giving them the appearance of heaving up toward the Holy City, presenting to her the threshold of the Arabian desert immediately above the hills of her own wilderness. The platform in the foreground had been cleared of all of its debris; it lay rolled out flat as a carpet before our eyes, empty and ghostlike, its paving broken by the looming presence of the Rock.

"Father," I began, "I have been considering what you once said about how the color of the Rock and the Black Stone changed."

"Oh," he said. ". . . Are you referring to their defilement?"

"Well, yes," I replied. "Defilement or veneration, I don't suppose it makes much difference."

"I don't follow you," he said, letting his voice and head drop as though preparing himself for the worst.

"An old man I was talking to in the city said that, if the Black Stone lost its brightness during the Age of Ignorance, it was not because menstruating women touched it, but because the people of Quraysh were in the habit of smearing the Stone with the intestines, excretory organs, and genitals of the animals they sacrificed. Inside these organs, they believed, reside the emotions most closely bound up with religion—remorse, grief, compassion, sex."

"You make too much of old wives' tales," he replied, looking directly at me even as I tried to avoid his gaze. "And what of it?"

"These organs exude large quantities of blood when cut out of a carcass. It was this blood, rather than impure bodily fluids or dirt, that stained the Stone and turned it black. Think of how much blood our own Rock must have seen. Every day I see Jews wringing the neck off chickens and sprinkling the blood all over its surface. But long before we came here, before even the time of David, strange gods were worshipped on the Rock. Baal, god of all that was renewable about nature, was ritually killed and resurrected on its surface. The prophet Jeremiah confirmed that this was done through a surrogate, the most precious imaginable—a firstborn child. Have you ever considered that all that spilled blood is behind the change in the color of the Stone?"

"I don't see why you are bringing yourself to a boil about this," my father said.

"I want you to consider the possibility that the stones were always dark gray and mottled black."

"Nonsense," exclaimed Ka'b. "Those are not God's colors. Somehow, sometime, the color changed. That is what is important."

"This old man said something else," I said, determined to press my point to the bitter end.

"I see you are going to tell me whether I want to hear it or not."

"He said that slitting the throat of a sheep and smearing its blood to make a sacrifice is as primitive and barbarous as the practices of a Baal worshipper."

"He did, did he . . ."

"Yes," I said, "and he made much of the fact that neither the head nor the heart of an animal features in the sacrifices of Muslims and Jews."

"Being the seat of reason and love, they have nothing to do with God," said my father.

"His point," I continued, "was that idolatry, which was not allowed in the front door of Jewish and Muslim worship, crept in the back. Stories such as those you have vigorously pressed upon me exude the same odor as those of the worshippers of Baal and the long-gone stone idols of Arabia. They invoke false worship and strange gods, he said—not the God of Moses, Jesus, and Muhammad."

"I never equate either the Rock or the Black Stone with God," Ka'b said defensively. "I simply teach that, like the angels, they have a divine origin. And they stand alone, absolutely uniquely in the world, with no rivals and no equals. They are complete unto themselves, signs from Him for those who would see."

"In other words," I ventured, "they share in His attributes."

"God preserve us from such a thought!" my father exclaimed.

"You said it, not I," I replied, and pressed on, unable to stop myself. "In a certain class of human minds, the principle of idolatry is never truly eradicated. It is, after all, a principle that has given form to the faith of many different kinds of people throughout the ages. This principle requires that, for the exercise of faith, some tangible object should be available to the bodily senses—whether in the form of a relic, a holy spot with which an act may be associated, or an image that will represent what their minds are too lazy to conceive; it matters little whether this thing be the true one or not, so long as it answers their purpose. You have chosen to spend your life first searching, and then living beside, that Rock that you are convinced is the navel of creation. But who is it that speaks: Ka'b the Jew, or Ka'b the Muslim? Because the People of Muhammad are still unsure of themselves. I have met some who will tell you that the Black Stone, not that Rock, is the center of the world. Both can't be right. It seems that neither the Jew that you were born, nor the Muslim that you became, have eradicated a principle from your soul that you know to be false."

"A monk has got his claws in you!" Ka'b exclaimed in hurt and anger. "Is this why they walk upon the pathways that Jesus walked, embrace the Rock upon which he died, gaze starry-eyed at the lance that pierced his body, and stand on the Mount of Olives, where they say he ascended!"

"I despise that kind of monk!" I retorted.

"What kind do you find attractive, then?"

"The kind who believes that God's Temple is holy, that it is not a specific place but rather in the heart of every true believer. The kind that holds that, when the Lord invites the blessed to their inheritance in Heaven, He does not include amongst their good deeds a pilgrimage to a rock—be it in Jerusalem or Mecca. Change of place brings a man no nearer to God, who comes to us only if the chambers of our soul are so filled with thoughts of Him that He can dwell and walk in them."

"How can a Believer fill his heart with thoughts of Him," Ka'b replied indignantly, "if you would deny him the evidence of God's work? It says in the Book of Wisdom that God created the world according to number, weight, and measure. And it says that God saw all that He had made, and found it very good. There is a meaning, then, in the things with which He furnished the heavens and the earth. Abraham, David, and Solomon understood this meaning, and set out to provide us with proof of it from His works. That is the point of all my stories."

"True religion is not storytelling," I replied.

"What is it, then?"

"Love," I said, "about which I have composed these verses":

A church, a temple, or a Ka'ba Stone,
Quran or Bible or a martyr's bone—
All these and more my heart no longer tolerates
Since my religion now is Love alone.

Those lines hit Ka'b like a bowl of cold water in the face. The old man reeled back, as though physically hit. He could not get up from the floor and pushed me away when I rushed to help. He tottered up. For a moment, I thought he was about to be overcome with emotion. My heart was in my mouth. Somehow he managed to get to the stairs. He left without speaking a word. As my stepmother took over, I was flooded with guilt. God had given the Rock to Ka'b in the way that a cradle and a mother are given to a child; he couldn't rightly turn toward a different cradle and mother. But there was nothing I could do. For weeks he would not look at me. Others had made the charge of idolatry to his face; my barbs were more subtle. Worst of all, they came from *me*.

Mine was a hollow victory that day. Can one love that which one cannot see, touch, or provide an account of? I had scored on rhetoric, not on substance. Perhaps I will be forgiven on account of my youth. Youth is vanity.

Shortly after our terrible exchange the Angel of Death, Izrail, began to stalk Ka'b. In imperceptible steps, his walk turned into a shuffle; his handwriting became less legible. He lost most of his teeth and lived on yogurt, rice, and mashed dates. Death was visibly eating little chunks out of his body. My father was already prone to attacks of dizziness and fainting, and, after my shameful performance, they came with greater and greater frequency. His memory appeared and disappeared, as though it were playing games with him.

The Rock, whose numinous presence and endless stories had once filled our evenings with lightness and mystery that bound father to son, was now a millstone around my neck. It was with such evenings in mind that my father had bought our house in the year of the conquest. He not only sought to live as close as possible to the center of the world but to make sure that no one in his family ever forgot that was where they lived. Who could have imagined that it would be at the price of such discord between my city and his?

The Death of Ka'b

W ho are you?" were the last words I heard my father speak as Izrail hovered over him.

"I am he who separates loved ones!" the angel replied. "I am he who subdues the power of the sons of Adam. I will inhabit the grave with you until the coming of the Day. Not a creature lives that does not taste me."

When God created Death and named him Izrail, He forced the other angels to watch. Izrail is so big he can hold the entire Earth in the palm of his hand. His wings stretch from the farthest point in the east to the farthest point in the west. So terrible was the sight of him that the other angels fell into a swoon for a thousand years.

Izrail brings us to Him one by one to await the Hour of our second life. The first began inside our mother's womb. The second, which goes on eternally, will begin on the Day of Resurrection. In between lies the wait in the grave. The angel appears to each son and daughter of Adam differently—as he or she merits. For Believers, the angel spreads his wings wide; for sinners, he shuts them closed like pincers. It is not given to us to know how Izrail appears to anyone other than ourselves; each death, like each life, is different, if only in small ways.

The power to decide when our first life will end is not accorded to Izrail, however. That has been recorded from the beginning of

Creation in the heavenly register, and is unalterably fixed. The Angel of Death is simply informed by a sign. When the time has come to take a soul, forty days before, a leaf on which is written the person's name falls from a tree located between God's throne and the holy Rock. As soon as the angel sees the leaf, it knows that a soul's first life is about to terminate.

Ka'b's leaf fell on the first day of spring in the thirty-fifth year of the Prophet's Exodus from Mecca. It fell seventeen years after Umar, Sophronius, and he had been thrown together by chance and circumstance to talk about the places that God had chosen for them to inhabit. It fell in the year that the men of Iraq turned to the House of Hashim, saying to Umar's successor, Uthman, "We'll have no more to do with you!"

It fell at the right time. For it would have broken Ka'b's heart to witness the great rift that was about to open up among the Believers. If he died at odds with his headstrong twenty-two-year-old son on matters religious and political, at least he was at peace with himself.

> *Praise be to God,*
> *the All-merciful, the All-compassionate,*
> *Master of the Day of Doom.*

Ka'b's leaf did not fall in the City of the Temple, as he had wished; it fell in the Syrian city of Homs. The shaikh who helped me bury him in the cemetery outside the city walls said that a speck of soil from the place that a man is destined to die in is planted in his mother's womb. Ka'b's demise in Homs had been written with the celestial reed in the Mother of all Holy Registers during Creation. And yet I would have moved mountains to have had his body interred in the Holy City. Tradition overruled me; it is against the custom of the followers of Moses and Muhammad to prolong a burial. A man has to be buried in the place where he has died. The speckled crow of fate, which so filled my father's heart with love of a place, played a most unhappy trick by making him die among strangers.

We had gone to Homs at Mu'awiya's insistence to provide information to the local governor about Abu Dharr, a Companion of the Prophet who had it in for my father. Mu'awiya was considering sending Abu Dharr back to Medina in disgrace for fomenting discord against his House. Abu Dharr had dared to imply in the local mosque of Homs that the House of Umayya was implicated in Umar's assassination. My stepmother worried that Abu Dharr would exploit the nine-year-old rumor that Ka'b had predicted the assassination of Umar in order to implicate him in an Umayyad plot against Umar.

"Son of a Jew, are you trying to teach us our religion!" Abu Dharr spat at Ka'b in front of a large group of men. His enmity dated back to a public slight made by Ka'b out of zeal for Uthman. Everyone outside the circle of the House of Umayya thought Ali, not the weakling Uthman, ought to have become Caliph. Abu Dharr was a partisan of Ali, as was I at the time of my father's death, as were all men of principle who had not entrusted the reins of their restless hearts to strange and corrupted passions. "But of what use is the sword in distinguishing Right from Wrong," Ka'b would retort, "when it destroys the spirit together with the body?" The civil wars that tore Muhammad's people apart over Uthman's successor made me lose my zeal for politics. Would the bloodletting and sedition inside the Community have been averted had Ali ruled before matters soured as they did? I am no longer sure it would have made that much difference. From ignorance to wisdom to senility, time turns like a waterwheel in whose cycles we are held to ransom. Even the best of times are only a respite granted to us by God.

And yet it was foolish of my father to make an enemy of such a man. Because of his reputation, Abu Dharr was unassailable; men compared his piety and humility to those of Jesus. The harsh exchange between them left bitter memories that haunted Ka'b in his last years. Now it had brought him to Homs in Mu'awiya's service. The governor of Syria needed to do damage to Abu Dharr's name before exiling him to Medina. I wanted nothing to do with the whole business but had to go along because, at that stage, my father needed someone to tend to his needs.

The five-day journey up the Syrian coast exhausted Ka'b. The weather was unusually humid that summer. Upon arrival in Homs, he looked ashen and complained of dizziness and fatigue. I prepared a straw pallet at the inn and laid him down to rest. That is when I began to notice that his nose was more pointed than normal, and that the sockets of his eyes were slightly caved in. The tips of his ears were cold and flaccid to the touch. The most striking change was apparent in his complexion; it went dark and pallid. I thought little of these signs at the time. Now I realize that he was about to yield up the leasehold of his days.

I fretted, wiping his face and trying to arrange for help. Ka'b would have none of it. He wrapped his fingers feebly around my wrist to calm me down.

"When destiny digs in its claws, amulets of any kind are useless," he said, grimacing with each breath. "To every man and purpose under Heaven there is a time—a time to be born, and a time to die. For some years now, I have seen Izrail lurking in the sagging of my flesh. Today, my stomach and entrails burn and throb; he has his hands clasped tight like a band around my heart. I can hardly breathe. My rope is about to be cut."

"Father! What would you have me do?"

"Anoint my head with oil. Put kohl around my eyes."

I made his sunken cheeks and bald dome shine, while the tip of his nose was turning a light shade of blue and his nostrils flared up with each breath.

"Prop me up," he rasped. "I want people to say that Ka'b met his Maker the healthiest of men." With the innkeeper's help, I pulled him up, pressing cushions into the small of his back and all around his sides, until he sat upright.

No sooner had we finished than his breathing got louder and

more erratic. A rattling noise was emanating from somewhere deep inside his throat. He tried to speak. His face was pointed toward me as he spoke his last words, but his eyes were looking through me as though into a void. How long we remained in that state, I no longer remember. All I remember is the unspeakable ugliness of this last stage of our lives, even in the absence of violence or disease.

Ka'b did not die well. Perhaps he had escaped life's woes for too long, like a man marked not by fate but by God's grace. It is harder to give ground after twice as many seasons as is afforded other men. Ka'b left unwillingly to his allotted place in the beyond, letting out a bellowing roar as his head jerked backwards into the pillows. He gasped as though he were choking and being strangled to death, and then he threw his hands up to clutch at his throat. The calm and repose with which he had prepared for this moment were gone. His eyes bulged out of his head and looked terrifying. Somehow the kohl had smudged and spread around the sockets in big smears. Panic-stricken, he tried to call out, but the only sound to emerge from his lips was a hoarse rattling. As death's flood brimmed up in his heart, his last breath was a long, gurgling exhalation.

A good soul slips out of a body easily, like water jetting out of a water skin. Four angel helpers of Izrail, on the other hand, descend on bad and profligate spirits, pulling the soul out through the toes and fingers of all four limbs after tying up the dying man's tongue. That kind of death is hard and painful; the soul squeals and squeaks out of the body like a skewer drawn through metal mesh. My father had his failings, but he was a good man. He should not have died like that.

I took his face in my hands, shut his eyelids, and kissed the different parts of his face again and again. I cleaned up the smudges of kohl, relined his eyebrows, and applied more oil to his forehead, cheeks and neck. Only then did I turn his face sideways to face the Holy City in which he had always wanted to be buried.

When the Angel of Death paid his visit in Homs, it seemed as if

I were Ka'b's only legacy on this earth. His death went unnoticed in the world that had so celebrated him two decades earlier in Medina. Storytellers like him shaped the first generation of Muhammad's followers. They borrowed their authority from death, which was the sanction of everything they had to say. Ka'b's own death, however, did not carry the sanction it deserved.

My father died on the edge of bad times. His withdrawal after the assassination of Umar coincided with a decline in the importance of Jerusalem in the affairs of the Community. Is this why the Companions of the Prophet, whom Ka'b had taught, did not come to pay homage? Is this why the Caliphs and their sons and advisors, who had so often sought his advice, also did not come? No one came to honor the man who had done so much for the religion of Muhammad. Mu'awiya ordered a small tomb to be built in Homs. But no one goes there, because the rewriters and inventors of traditions want Believers to forget my father. Whispering tongues took to attacking him after civil wars had taken their toll; they feared the Jew that he was more than the idolaters they used to be. Meanwhile, Ka'b lies in his grave, forgotten, a flagstone at the feet of Time.

The solitude of the grave is hard enough on those who mourn. But it passes. The silence of a whole generation does not; it lies like a blot on the future. It was not only Ka'b who was being forgotten; the story of our beginnings was being rewritten.

Truly the world is as soft to the touch as the adder is sudden in its venomousness.

After I turned Ka'b's face toward the Holy City, it looked rested, as though finally he had found comfort and was without a worry in the world. The loneliness of his declining years, exacerbated by my youthful indiscretions, rubbed out the lines of his face. His choices and decisions now lay in the past; only their consequences remained, and these lay in other hands. At the time, I was aware only of how much this dead face meant to me. Lying there, stretched out on the ground, his hands folded on his chest, facing the sacred Rock that he had venerated more than any other man, he seemed to me an angel of the Lord.

Verily, to God do we belong, and to Him shall we return.

The Wait in the Grave

H e is like a bridegroom sleeping off the ardors of his wedding night," my stepmother said of Ka'b in his grave just before she herself expired of fever. She looked upon his death as though it were a painted sleep, the purest kind of release from the mire and dung of this world. Left without the man who, in exile, had brought the world to her feet, she spent the intervening years between his death and her own picking and choosing among his memories as though in a flower garden. She passed away imagining his coming resurrection on the Day as a joyous reunion of spirit and body, like that experienced awakening from a night under the dome of Heaven, gloriously bathed in the rising light of God's candle.

"They are the most frail and vulnerable of God's creatures," she said of her husband's critics and slanderers. "At the same time, they are the most arrogant. They see themselves as exiled to the lowest part of the universe, farthest from the vault of Heaven, but put them in a position of ascendency over defenseless men, and they will turn themselves around and forget everything, planting themselves above the circle of the moon and dragging the very sky down beneath their feet."

What could I say to such sweetness? She had not been there in Homs. The awakening she wished for Ka'b is reserved for a mere handful of prophets and martyrs. For the rest of us, the grim shape

of things to come is a noose in which we have already been ensnared, long before we reach the height of our powers. My father
died before Muhammad's People wore themselves out with strife,
and before his son had come to terms with him. Perhaps that is why
he died such a terrible death.

"Your father was a man of worth," my stepmother said by way
of showing her disapproval of my disrespect toward Ka'b in the
declining years of his life. "And in a man of worth, the claims of
fatherhood cannot be denied."

~

The night after I washed my father's body, wrapped him in his
winding-sheet, and lowered him into his grave on the outskirts of
Homs, his spirit paid mine a visit.

I was tossing and turning in bed. In the throes of a terrible
dream, I saw myself getting out of bed and walking aimlessly, without realizing what I was doing. At some point I must have become
aware that the light of the sun had disappeared. I was in a deep,
dark shadow. Looking up, I saw the gargantuan mass of the Rock
hovering above my head, suspended between the earth and the sky.
I woke up in a cold sweat, terrified.

Standing over me, watching, was the spirit of my father, which
had dressed itself in the shape of his body but looked as thin and
white as the muslin cloth in which I had wrapped him. How small
and shrunken he looked, compared to the pulsing, lean strength of
the man who had been the lodestone of my childhood! It is the
spirit that breathes length and breadth into a man's torso and
limbs. Dead as he was, I nevertheless had the feeling that he had
seen me preparing him for burial earlier in the day. Or was it his
spirit that was doing the seeing? It takes time, men say, before the
spirit can irrevocably break with the body that has housed it for so
long; it clings like a faithful animal to the old flesh and bones, lingering and inhabiting the same grave when there is room, or sitting
nearby stricken with grief if there is none.

Ka'b's spirit said that it had heard my footsteps departing from his grave. It tried to stop me from leaving. Only I did not hear it calling; I heard the earth mocking Ka'b instead:

"You used to enjoy yourself on my surface. But from today you, who are all wound up in shrouds and packed in by earth poured all around, are going to grieve in my interior as you have never grieved before. You used to eat all kinds of delicacies and move freely on my surface. From today the worms will eat you while you are held tightly on all sides, unable to move a muscle."

Two blue-eyed questioners of the dead arrived. One had a beautiful face, lovely clothing, and a sweet fragrance. He ordered my shriveled-up old father to sit up. Somehow he could. He then told him that his body would not stir from its prison in the earth, and be resurrected, until he accounted for his youth—how he had worn it away—then his life—how he passed it—and finally his wealth—how he had none. Ka'b crossed these hurdles easily. But then the other angel, who emitted a noxious odor and whose face was black, spoke. In a piercing tone that rang in my skull like a whistle in a hollow chamber, he asked: "Who is your Lord?"

"God."

"What is your religion?"

"Islam."

"Who is your prophet?"

"Muhammad."

"What is the direction of your prayer?"

"Toward the Rock."

"Which Rock?"

"Both Rocks."

"And what if you are situated between the two holy Rocks?"

"Then it depends."

"On what?"

"On circumstance."

"What circumstance?"

"Whether I am with other people or by myself."

"And if you are among company?"

"Then I pray toward the Black Stone."

"And if you are alone?"

"Surely the direction in which one prays matters less than how one prays."

"It matters. Answer the question!"

"If I am alone, I pray facing Jerusalem's Rock."

"You know what that means!"

"I am not sure."

"It means you are a wolf in sheep's clothing, a Jew and a hypocrite!"

Ka'b had lived his life teetering on a rope that stretched between two holy cities. Keeping the balance for which he had become famous depended on choosing to walk purposely toward one city or the other. That task had become more difficult once both holy cities were under one dominion. Now everywhere the followers of Muhammad were asking: If both Rocks are holy, surely one is holier than the other. One of them had to be preferred by God. Which one? And why? How were the two related in their holiness? Why does Ka'b not speak about these questions, he who claims to hear the silence of God by pressing his ear to the surface of the Rock?

In truth, Ka'b did not know what to say. The wildness in him had long since brimmed over. After becoming a follower of Muhammad, he had tried not to look as if he were choosing between the Rocks. As a result, he appeared foolish. "He is a man weighed down by the Torah," Abu Dharr said mockingly, "the way an ass is weighed down by the books it is carrying on its back."

Ka'b was saved from his ignorance by his belief that religion and worldly things were able to join hands. For most men, it was easier to carry two watermelons under one armpit than it was to maintain the thought of such a union. I, for one, failed the test; he never did. Back and forth, like a juggler on a plank, Ka'b was most adroit at balancing the two watermelons of worldliness and the life to come.

How did he do it? Perhaps, it began to dawn on me, the secret was in what Ka'b said when he talked about the span of a man's life being but a speck in the larger scheme of things.

"Keep the Day, not your own death, daily before your eyes," he would say, "the Day that follows the work of the maggots and the bleaching of your bones. Never doubt it is coming. If piety means anything, it means to believe that the Day of the Raising of the Dead is drawing near, and on that day every soul shall be afforded its due. And no amount of remorse will avail the unbelievers."

> *What, does man reckon*
> *We shall not gather his bones?*
> *Yes, indeed: We are able to shape again*
> *even the little bones of his fingers.*
> *Was he not a sperm-drop spilled?*
> *Then a blood-clot,*
> *created and formed.*
> *What, is He who made this*
> *not able to quicken the dead?*

I used to scoff at Ka'b for living his life transfixed on Judgment Day, as I scoffed at him for his obsession with the Rock.

Today, however, I too keep an eye out for the Signs that will precede the coming of the Day. I reflect upon the moment of Resurrection, when all the men and women who have ever lived will rise bodily from the grave, complete in soul and thought. Then I measure my few atoms' worth of good and evil against one another, as I will do for the final time on Judgment Day, and consider what I should do on the morrow.

Before the final Reckoning, however, lies the wait in the grave. In this first station of our afterlives, my father waits. What is it like for such a man to be tucked away under the earth, knowing that his eternal fate has been prefigured even as the worms are fastening on him?

Are there any among us who have not forgotten their prayers at least once, or who have not prayed without performing their ablu-

tions? Is there anyone who can swear that he has never passed a
child or a blind woman in need of help without stopping to do what
he can? I can't. Nor could my poor father, who has been waiting in
that terrible place for forty years. The wait in the grave is for people
like us. Upon the truest of Believers the surrounding earth presses
more gently, "like the compassionate mother stroking the head of a
son who is complaining of headache," said the Prophet, trying to
console his young wife Aisha, distraught after a Jewish woman had
thanked her for some kindness by saying, "May the Lord give thee
refuge from the torment of the tomb."

The punishment of the grave is real. The external peace and
quiet of the cemetery is deceiving. No contrast is more striking, no
affliction more terrible, than what goes on inside each little house
of worms. Martyrs and prophets excepted, each one of us, Believer
and un-Believer alike, will undergo some torment, heavy or light,
depending on the quality of his faith and works. If we escape the
worst, because of how we have lived our lives, then the punishment
that will go on eternally, and that comes after the Hour, is light. And
yet none of us, between the moment of our deaths and His Judgment on the Hour, can escape the torments of the tomb.

"What are our years on the earth," Ka'b used to say, "compared to being squeezed like an egg under a boulder for many times
their number? And what is being squeezed like an egg under a
boulder for a number of years compared to roasting in Hell for all
eternity?" Someone should have asked that of Muslims after the
murder of Umar. But when Ka'b died, the last person who worried
about such questions also died.

Like Umar, Uthman and Ali, the third and fourth Rightly Guided
Caliphs, were also murdered. With them died the practice of nomi-
nating a council of wise men to decide matters of succession. A
pattern was being undone. By putting family before Community,
Umar's successor, Uthman, undid all that his predecessors had
achieved. His death was brought about when he would not deliver

to justice his cousin and chief advisor, that son of a blue-eyed woman, Marwan, after he had conspired to have the governor of Egypt killed. Family and feeling were all that it was taking to kindle a sense of intolerable wrong; trivial matters were eliminating things of weight throughout the land.

But did Uthman's wrong justify the terrible way in which he was killed and the uses men made of his death?

A party of those whom Marwan had plotted against laid siege to Uthman's house in Medina, demanding that he give up the conspirator. Marwan was inside hiding with his son, Abd al-Malik, then a lad of ten. Father and son, destined to be the eighth and ninth Caliphs of Islam, witnessed the murder that was to bring grief and sedition in its train; it also brought their House of Umayya to the pinnacle of earthly power.

When Uthman refused to give up his cousin, three men climbed into the Caliph's courtyard unseen by the guards on the roof. They found Uthman reading the Quran with his wife. Grabbing him by the beard, they cut his throat in front of her. Marwan and Abd al-Malik got away; their servant took Uthman's shirt, gory as it was, and rode off with it to Damascus.

While the holy cities of Arabia were giving their oath of allegiance to Ali of the House of Hashim, Mu'awiya, still governor in Syria and a cousin of Uthman, was pinning up the bloodied shirt of his kinsman in the court of the mosque of Damascus. Barely had Uthman's grave been filled when fresh ones were being dug all over the empire. A fever for revenge such as the Arabs had not known since the Age of Ignorance devoured the land.

A new age began with Mu'awiya's cry of vengeance over Uthman's shirt; it ended with the community tearing itself apart. Deeds that should have been hidden were not. Men were held in thrall to the idea that only through more killing, and more dying, would there be a recovery from it. Everyone wanted the Caliphate for himself. Ali of the House of Hashim, the Prophet's cousin, was the most deserving. But even he could not lance the boil of desire mixed with loathing that now fixed men's hearts on hateful things. His short reign was eaten up by the first great wars of sedition. Four years after succeeding Uthman, Ali's forehead was hewn with a sword as he prayed.

Hasan, the son of Ali and the Prophet's own grandson, conceded leadership to the House of Umayya in that year of ill omen, the forty-first year after the Exodus. He was Caliph for a matter of months. Hasan had not wanted his followers to be butchered for a kingdom's sake. Arabia grumbled at the deeds of Hasan, he who of the Prophet's family most resembled the Messenger of God. Idle tattlers called him a weakling, even after he was poisoned in Medina. But no one can upset the hour when words fall silent and destiny springs its trap. Wrong had triumphed over Right. God clearly had no intention of uniting Prophethood and the Caliphate in the same House—not in the House of Hashim.

In the gathering gloom of Muslim affairs that followed my father's death, I turned to business, opening a stall on the Cardo. I conducted a general trade in books. Buying, selling, transcribing, all now fell within my purview. I even dabbled in calligraphy. But my real vocation remained bookmaking and its associated arts: cover and border design, leather tooling, floral and geometrical inlay in which I pioneered various new combinations of ivory, bone, multicolored wood, and gilding.

But the visitation of those fearsome angels kept on recurring in my dreams. Little by little, their skulking presence made headway during sleep, when my senses and defenses were at rest. In that state, echoes from times past and shadows of things to come are able to crowd upon the troubled mind unimpeded. Slowed down by the inaction of the senses, the mind is unable to sort out the meaning of what it sees. Memory is confused, and foreknowledge, though also confused by the veils of memory, is imaged in shadows from our waking moments and pursuits. The mind smolders like a fire heaped over with chaff.

The Footprint

u'awiya was interested in all things related to the Holy City. His authority rested upon Syria, a province still overwhelmingly Christian. He had learned to navigate his way through all the factions and sects of the city during his inauguration as Caliph, which had taken place in Jerusalem. As the Christians like to put it, Mu'awiya was "crowned" in their midst.

Mu'awiya had arranged a most elaborate ceremony immediately following the news of the murder of Ali, his archenemy and the leader of the House of Hashim. The charged atmosphere of the moment was dissipated into pomp and circumstance! The strategy worked. All the tribes that had come from Arabia and settled in Syria trooped in to the Holy City, competing with one another to be the first to attach their banners to his pole. Within months of his inauguration, Hasan, son of Ali, had conceded the Caliphate to him. No other Caliph since Umar had so singled out Palestine, and made of it a substitute for the Hijaz, a fact that was held against the House of Umayya throughout Arabia. But in Syria and Jerusalem, it worked in his favor.

I was in attendance when he toured the holy sites on the day of his inauguration and I heard him assume a title previously bestowed by God on Adam and David alone. In the outer courtyard of the Church of the Resurrection, Mu'awiya declared: "The earth belongs to God and I am His Deputy."

All of Muhammad's Rightly Guided successors had spurned this title. God had given the Prophet Companions for whom humility was a watchword; they loved his person more than their own. Such men did not seek the world, however much it sought them. When a fawning petitioner tried to curry favor with Umar by calling him God's Deputy, he was pushed to the ground and rebuked sternly. Reminded of this incident, Mu'awiya smiled and said:

"What's approved today was reproved once. Things now abominated will someday be embraced."

He was right. The title stuck. Every Caliph since Mu'awiya, including his protégé and admirer, our own Abd al-Malik, has adopted the same heresy of a direct line of communication between himself and God—a heresy whose legitimacy his own Arab constituency interpreted as being confirmed by God after Mu'awiya was approached by both Peoples of the Book to arbitrate their dispute over a footprint.

~

In the waning years of Mu'awiya's rule, a Jewish leather worker, Joseph by name, observed an impression on the surface of the Rock that no one had observed before—a footprint. Greatly oversized, but a footprint nonetheless. Everyone was convinced of the authenticity of his finding. But to whom did it belong?

Joseph, renowned for his piety and trustworthiness among both circumcised and uncircumcised alike, said it belonged to the prophet Jacob during his communication with God while asleep on the Rock. A footprint was left behind as a sign that God's Holy House would one day be erected here. The Jews of the city were inclined to agree with Joseph. A pigeon's neck was wrung as an offering over the impression, and its blood sprinkled over the rest of the Rock's surface.

The monks of the Church of the Resurrection disagreed. The matter was taken up by their leadership council, which, since the death of Sophronius, had been in charge of Christian affairs in the city. The council had been unable to agree upon a Patriarch to replace Sophronius. Now it found something to agree upon. Amidst great publicity, the council announced that the footstep belonged to Jesus, and that it was made when he used to teach in the old Temple before the coming of the abominations which he foretold would destroy it.

The decree caused an uproar. It looked like the Christians were trying to claim ownership of the very place that they had treated with such contempt. A group of rabbis, newly settled from Arabia, issued a counter-declaration. Couched in abrasive language, it caused spirits to grow even more heated. The argument spread throughout the towns and villages of Palestine. Everywhere, men feuded over the identity of the footprint. Words spilled over into blows. Christians and Jews died. The Holy City was turned into a tinderbox. To avert total disaster, both parties appealed to the Caliph to adjudicate. He agreed and called upon me to help him resolve the dispute.

"Son of Ka'b, know that I do not use my sword when my whip will do. Nor my whip when my tongue will do. Nor my tongue when another man's tongue will do. Let a single hair bind me to my people, and I'll not let it snap; when they slack, I pull; but when they pull, I slack. Know these things, and tell me what your father had to say about this footprint."

Ka'b never mentioned a footprint. Had he suspected there was such an impression, I would have known about it. I was naive enough to tell this to the Caliph.

Mu'awiya would have none of it. Ideas on the footprint were cropping up daily. An alliance of Muslim and Jewish scholars had started to claim that the footprint was left behind by Abraham, as he was preparing to strike his son with the knife. When challenged as to how a mere mortal could leave an impression on stone, they replied that in the days of Abraham the Rock was soft, like clay, as evidenced by the shells and sea animals impressed on similar types of rock in the vicinity. Why then was there only one footprint? retorted the incredulous. Why did the son's feet not leave an impression next to his father's? The scholars replied that after the Rock had hardened, God erased all the other footprints. No one was convinced.

Mu'awiya's real problem was not this alliance but Yasar, a former slave turned tailor from Medina, who was making a name for himself because as a young boy he had heard the Prophet preach.

Yasar was going around Damascus claiming that the Rock was the spot from which the Messenger of God had ascended to Heaven. The footprint bore witness, Yasar said, to a miraculous journey he had heard Muhammad describe, from Mecca to Jerusalem and back again in one night, during which, he alleged, the ascent occurred.

Yasar was busy showing crowds of people gathered around one corner of the Rock what it felt like to touch the precise imprint of the Prophet's heel who, he said, was not wearing sandals at the time.

Lifted up on his father's shoulders, the young Yasar had supposedly heard the Prophet tell throngs of people:

"While I was sleeping near the Black Stone of the Ka'ba one day, the Angel Gabriel came and stirred me with his foot. I sat up but saw nothing and lay down again. He came a second time and stirred me with his foot. I sat up but saw nothing and lay down again. He came to me the third time and stirred me with his foot. I sat up and he took hold of my arm and I stood beside him and he brought me out to the door of the mosque and there was a white animal, half mule, half donkey, with wings on its sides with which it could propel its feet very fast."

When the Prophet tried to mount this extraordinary creature, it shied away from him. This made Gabriel upset. He grabbed the creature's mane, and shouted,

"Are you not ashamed to behave in this way? By God, none more honorable before God than Muhammad has ever ridden you before."

The creature was so ashamed that it broke out into a sweat and stood still until Muhammad mounted. With the help of this steed, Muhammad and Gabriel were able to cover the distance between Mecca and Jerusalem in the blink of an eye, stopping at Mount Sinai on the way.

Upon arriving at David's Sanctuary, the Prophet found himself welcomed by an assembly made up of all the prophets from the past.

"I have never seen a man more like myself than Abraham," Yasar reports Muhammad as saying of this encounter. "Moses was a ruddy-faced man, tall, thinly fleshed, curly-haired with a hooked nose. Jesus, Son of Mary, was a reddish man of medium height with many freckles on his face and lank hair as though he had just stepped out of a bath. One would suppose that his head was dripping with water, though there was no water on it."

The assembled prophets asked Muhammad to lead them in prayer. Gabriel told Muhammad that this meant he had been guided to the most primordial of all the religions of the Book. Following the prayer, the Prophet was led by Gabriel to climb onto the Rock's hard, flat surface. As he reached its summit, the Heavens began to open up in preparation for his ascent. The Rock even tried to rise with him, which it might very well have done were it not for the quick-thinking Gabriel. He grabbed hold of the massive platform from two of its sides, and pulled down on it with all of his strength, crying out:

"Your place, O Stone, is on earth. You have no further part in what the Prophet must do."

The long ridges along the edges of the Rock of Ascension, as Yasar had taken to calling it, are the traces of Gabriel's fingers as he clutched at the formidable hardness, terminating its rise, and eventually fixing it back in place on top of Mount Moriah. Muhammad's ascent, it turned out, was to be by means of a ladder of light, just like Jacob's. The ladder came down from the Heavens and rested on the Rock. Muhammad described the ladder as "that to which the dying man looks as death approaches." The footprint was left behind as Muhammad pressed down hard to spring up with the other foot.

The two companions travelled through the Heavens, meeting and conversing with various angels and prophets. Gabriel informed the Guardian of each heavenly gate that his companion had been sent for. The Guardian was always helpful. Eventually the pair reached the highest Heaven and were in the presence of God. The encounter turned out to be something of an anticlimax the way Yasar spun out the story, because its only outcome was the imposition of an obligation of fifty prayers a day upon the followers of Muhammad.

At this point in Yasar's telling of the tale, someone in his rapt audience wanted to know how the fifty had been reduced to the customary five. Whereupon Yasar claimed to remember word by word Muhammad's reply:

"On my return from the highest Heaven I passed by Moses. He asked me how many prayers had been laid upon me. When I told him fifty, he said, 'Prayer is a weighty matter and your people are weak. Go back to your Lord and ask him to reduce the obligation on your community.' I did as he recommended and God reduced the number by ten. Again, I passed by Moses who still thought the number was too high; so I went back, and God reduced the number by another ten prayers a day. So it went on until only five prayers for the whole day were left. Again, Moses gave me the same advice. But this time I told him that I was ashamed to go back to my Lord and ask him to reduce the number again."

Nothing good would come of Yasar's story, Mu'awiya said; the man was inspired by the Devil. Lines of anxiety creased his face when he spoke of him. No one could predict the alliances that might unfold amid such allegations. Yasar had no learning. But,

Mu'awiya realized, he had animal cunning and a sense of timing which more than compensated for it.

By turning a Messenger from God—a mere warning that the beginning of the end was nigh—who himself rejected every superstition regarding his person, into a miracle-worker, Yasar was challenging both the Jews and the Christians in their city, and laying down a new, purely Muslim, claim to the Holy Rock. The uproar that had already claimed lives could get worse. Nothing a Christian could say about Christ's ascension into the Heavens from a different spot on the Mount of Olives could compete with a Muslim's description of Muhammad's visit to Paradise and Hell, and his return in body and spirit to tell everyone about it.

Yasar had the tailor's gift of weaving entirely separate pieces of cloth into a whole so seamless that the customer did not even notice that his beautiful new tunic was made of rags. And he was hard to suppress, given that he claimed no prophetic powers.

But what was the Caliph to do? Seal off the Rock from the throngs that were daily gathering around it to see and hear the famous tailor of Damascus—even as he deployed the rest of his soldiers to keep Jews and Christians from scratching each other's eyes out? That would only add to Yasar's credibility. The Caliph would be seen as afraid of him.

A story is as good as its chain of transmission, I suggested to Mu'awiya. Not all transmitters can be trusted. There was nothing wrong with hearsay, when passed on by a transmitter of good character and reputation. My father, I said, had never mentioned anything about a night-journey and ascension in spite of spending the last years of his life seeking out the great storytellers of his generation. Perhaps Yasar was simply a fraud trying to further his own interests. Mu'awiya should investigate his background and motives, and then expose him.

The Caliph was not convinced.

"We have fattened a dog, and now he comes to eat us. What else is there to know about the man? He lived in Medina as he claims. There he almost certainly heard the Prophet preach before large groups. Everyone did in the old days. Perhaps he actually heard the Prophet describe a vision like Jacob's that came over him during sleep. Am I to be seen haggling with a former slave over whether the ascension was a dream or an actual event while the Holy City goes up in flames all around me? Yasar has nothing to lose from attaching the Rock to the person of the Prophet. It is a clever move bound to gain him supporters. I am surprised no one thought of it before. The man does not seek to win an argument but rather to acquire a reputation. No, we will have to outwit him on his own territory: the footprint. Return to the footprint, son of Ka'b. Think! Search for an explanation of its origin, one worthy of your father."

That night, for the first time in years, I tried to recall all of my father's stories. I put them in chronological order from Creation to the destruction of the Temple. I listed every prophet who had had anything to do with the Rock, and then painstakingly eliminated them, one by one from the roster of possible owners of the foot behind the print. Jesus, David, Solomon, Jacob, and all the lesser prophets were either not old enough, or had not had an appropriate opportunity to leave an imprint that would go unnoticed all these years. Adam was too frivolous. Ishmael lived in Jerusalem only as a young boy; the impression was too big to be his. How about my namesake, Ishaq? Unlikely. It would be his father's before his. I struggled particularly hard over Abraham. Even Yasar stressed the physical resemblance between Abraham and Muhammad. How, then, could he distinguish between their footprints? For that matter how could an imprint have been left on solid rock by a mere man?

Suddenly, while considering this argument, the slate of my uncertainties was wiped clean, and from my father's stories, the truth dawned like one of those universal forms of the Divine that owed no allegiance to time or place but had to be a sign of our salvation. The name of the Truth was God.

In the twelfth hour of the sixth day of Creation, on Friday the sixth of Nisan, after the First Man had been cast out of the Garden, stripped of his Garment of Light and admonished for his transgression, God put His foot on the Rock to ascend back to Heaven. Ka'b had said so. Therefore, the footprint had to be God's own impression, left behind just before He took himself outside His own creation, angry at the degraded thing that Adam had made of himself. He became forever transcendent because of the First Man's transgression and had left His mark behind as a reminder of all that we had lost.

Mu'awiya was delighted. The very next day, citing the authority of Ka'b and a number of other luminaries he had lined up for the occasion, he announced that the impression on the Rock belonged to the Lord of All the Worlds. No mention of Yasar or the story of the Prophet's ascension was made.

The monks felt vindicated because in their eyes God was Jesus Christ. The Jews were happy because it was their story of Creation that Mu'awiya had just ratified. The Rock of Foundation, not Calvary, was the navel of the universe. And Yasar had been checked because the stakes had been raised. He now had to deny the Caliph's assertion that it was God's footprint on the Rock, and this looked like blasphemy. Like a piece of limestone dropped in acid, the dispute dissolved.

War of the Holy Cities

The peace of the sword did not leave the sword in peace for long, as Yazid, Mu'awiya's son, quickly found out.

The nomination of an heir did not sit well with supporters of the House of Ali in Iraq; it smacked of kingship. Nor did it sit well in Mecca and Medina. No one outside Mu'awiya's clan wanted the Caliphate to be a plaything of his progeny; by right, it belonged to the family of the Prophet. Many Meccans, become rich overnight because of Umar's conquests, watched as their wealth slipped away along with their power into the hands of newly converted tribes, settlers, and even Christians from the rich northern provinces. "These upstarts do not grasp Muhammad's message," they said to themselves. Yazid derived support from them. Worse, he encouraged games of chance and riotous feasting, and was the first to employ eunuchs in the women's quarters of his palace. All that people talked about in his court was women and food. "Look! How they veil their beards and sell their arrows for spindles," men said of the Caliph and his court.

It came as no surprise, therefore, that as the Arabs of Damascus played musical instruments and drank openly in the streets, the holy cities of Arabia refused to give Yazid their allegiance.

Yazid's murder of Husayn, the son of Ali, the Prophet's favorite grandson, had been the final straw. Husayn had inherited the mantle of leadership from his brother Hasan, who had conceded it to

Mu'awiya. "So long as Mu'awiya is alive," Husayn had said at the time of his brother's poisoning, "let every man stay in his own house and draw his cloak over his head." But Yazid did not carry his father's weight. And Husayn would not keep his head cloaked for a drunkard with an appetite for revelry shared by all those he set in power.

The son of Ali came to Kufa in Iraq, where the people were swearing allegiance to him and cursing the House of Umayya. But Yazid's army intercepted his small party of followers and friends, and denied them water on the parched fringes of the Iraqi desert. With his tongue stuck to the roof of his mouth, Husayn drank the bitter draught of death instead of the sweet water of the Euphrates. Two sons, four brothers, five nephews, and five cousins died with him on the plain of Kerbala. Only after they had fallen did Husayn take to horse against his foes. He smote until he fell, having been struck seventy-two times. Only two of his sons were left alive—a babe in arms, and a lad sick in bed.

"Short work!" Yazid's men told their commander. "Time enough to butcher and dress a camel, or to take a little sleep." When the severed head, still in the flower of youth, was put into Yazid's hands, he turned it round and round. With an air of indomitable insolence, he struck it on the mouth.

"Enough!" cried out a man in his court, unable to control himself at the horror of the deed. "I have seen God's Apostle kiss those lips."

The manner of Husayn's death sparked the bloodiest unrest yet among the Arabs. The bitterness spilled into a war lasting eleven years. We escaped unscathed in Jerusalem. Still, it felt like the end of the world. The sunlight glared saffron yellow on the walls of the city the day a messenger arrived with the why and wherefore of the massacre of the scions of the House of Hashim on the banks of the Euphrates outside Kerbala. Men went out into the streets, lashing out with their swords like frenzied camels in heat making directionless tracks in the sand. Not a stone was turned in the Holy City on the day that Husayn rose to his Maker but that fresh blood was found underneath. The very earth trembled at the slaying.

Truly, we are an aggregate of elements that emanate from the deep well of our beginnings. Yazid, that accursed son of an accursed father, whose father God's Prophet himself did curse, had spilled innocent blood as if it were water. Mu'awiya had spilled it for a reason; his son didn't need reasons, thinking himself freed by power to shape the lives of Muhammad's followers in ignorance of who he was and where he came from. In that act of forgetting, the license to wild impulses and the illusion of freedom was born, dragging vanity and vaulting ambition in their train.

On their hearts is the stain of the ill which they do.

Exploiting men's horror of Yazid's deed, Abdallah, the son of Zubayr, proclaimed himself Caliph in Mecca. His father had been the fifth Believer in Muhammad. Abdallah himself was thought blessed for being the first child born into Muhammad's religion after the Exodus. His mother was the daughter of Abu Bakr, and sister to the Prophet's favorite wife. No man in Medina was better tied to the House of Hashim on all sides. His father, Zubayr, had become a very wealthy man, accumulating valuables worth fifty thousand gold pieces, along with vast numbers of horses, slaves of both sexes, and estates. With this wealth, Zubayr's sons built themselves town mansions in Medina made of plaster-work, brick, and teakwood imported from India. But the flow of revenues from the conquered provinces that had made all this possible had recently dried up. The new seat of the Caliphate in Damascus was drawing everything to itself. If Husayn's death was not the only reason for war between the holy cities of Syria and Arabia, it was, nevertheless, the excuse used by men intent on fighting to the finish.

Abdallah denounced the practice of ruling from Syria instigated by Mu'awiya. Muhammad's People, he said, must be ruled from the cradle of prophecy, the land of the Hijaz. The Prophet was a son of Mecca, not Jerusalem. And Yazid was descended from the House that had led the struggle against him in the Age of Ignorance. Abdallah chose Mecca, not Medina, as his seat of government, because it housed God's most ancient Temple built around the Black Stone.

Thus did a rift between the Believers turn into a festering wound. While Abdallah consolidated his hold over Mecca and the Hijaz, garnering support from his guardianship of the Holy Places and playing Yazid's tyranny to his advantage, dissension and strife escalated. Had not the governor of Basra executed eight thousand in promulgation of Yazid's new rules of punishment? men asked as they, in turn, entrusted the reins of their restlessness to passion and desire. Revulsion at the House of Umayya grew to the point that Yazid had difficulty raising an army willing to attack his foe in Mecca. When he finally did, it was swallowed up in the desert and disappeared from the face of the earth. Yazid then took to paying poets and scribblers to hurl taunts rather than spears on his behalf:

"If Abdallah were a Caliph, as he says, he would show himself. He would fight like a man. Instead he plants his tail in the shadow of the Black Stone like a female locust laying its eggs."

Yazid died waiting for Abdallah to budge from his desert fortress. He had ruled for three years and left no successor. The father of Abd al-Malik, Marwan, of the same House, wrested the Caliphate from rivals but ruled in name for less than one year; he died as ingloriously as he had lived after enraging one of his wives for refusing to name her son his successor. She was a corpulent lady, who, shortly after copulation, took her revenge by spreading the cheeks of her buttocks and squatting on her husband's face until he suffocated. Or so at least men say.

Verily, only to the Omniscient One belongs knowledge of such abominations.

While such goings-on ruled the men and women of Damascus, Abdallah rested secure in Mecca. He was as hard as he was inflexible. He had his own brother executed and stuck on a gibbet outside

Mecca for having disagreed with him. In this obdurate nature were sown the seeds of his demise.

$$\sim$$

Abdallah found his match in Marwan's son, Abd al-Malik, he who had witnessed the murder of Uthman as a boy of ten. Abd al-Malik had been driven out of Medina a second time by Abdallah at the start of his revolt, becoming governor of Jerusalem at the time of his father's death. He had been groomed for leadership by Mu'awiya, who recognized the young man's prodigious talent from when he tended to his father's affairs. "This man will one day rule the Arabs," Mu'awiya said, by which he meant unite them. Abd al-Malik happened to be seated with the Holy Book in his lap when he heard of his father's ignominious demise and was pressed, for his House's sake, into accepting the mantle of leadership. He closed the Book and said, "This is our last time together." He was thirty-nine.

In the son of Marwan, the Arabs found an embodiment of the saying, "He who takes revenge after forty years is in a hurry." Abd al-Malik was as flexible and patient as Zubayr's son was intractable and stubborn. He understood that the success of Muhammad—the fact that his followers now ruled half the world—meant that they could no longer be ruled from Arabia. Believers had to be at the center of things; the locus of authority had to change. But it would take time for Mecca to give way to Jerusalem. And so Abd al-Malik first secured Egypt and its revenues. Then he amassed his forces to attack Abdallah's allies in nearby Iraq, leaving his nemesis to grit his teeth in the desert.

The only man in Syria who had no qualms about laying siege to the Holy City was Hajjaj. Lean as a gray wolf who breakfasts poorly, he was put in command of an army of Syrians and dispatched to Mecca. Hajjaj did what no man had done before; he set up giant catapults on the slopes of Mount Qubays and shot stones and flaming torches into the sacred sanctuary where Abdallah and his men had taken refuge.

The Meccans had never thought to build a wall around their city. The depth of the desert was more secure than the highest wall. When the city became overcrowded, however, Umar had walled in the sacred enclosure of the Ka'ba for the first time. The ends of the alleyways, which used to open onto a large open central space, were turned into gates. From inside this wall, the son of Zubayr waged his defense.

Abdallah repulsed the Umayyads at first, but not before severe damage had been inflicted on the building of the Ka'ba. A passing traveler, eyewitness to the destruction, described the scene to us in Jerusalem:

"I saw a dog hurled by a catapult, its corpse toppling a pot in which Abdallah's men were cooking bulgar. Half-starved by the siege, they ate the dog instead of the bulgar. I saw stones as big as boulders rain on the Ka'ba until its clothes of black brocade became rent like the cleavage of a woman's blouse."

Abd al-Malik was distressed when news reached him of the damage. He was, after all, a son of the Hijaz, born there eight years after the conquest of Jerusalem. No one could have held its holy cities in greater esteem. So he wrote to Hajjaj:

"Do not bombard the Black Stone or tear asunder the veils of the Ka'ba, or even startle its birds. Rather, corner that scorpion in Mecca's ravines and tunnels. And wait until he dies there of hunger."

But the knife had cut through to the bone, and Hajjaj would have none of it. This was no ordinary city on whose conquest he had staked his honor. His family's name was at stake. "Permit me to do battle with this man as I see fit," he dared to write back. "For if you do not, his numbers will grow, and he will become impossible to dislodge."

Abd al-Malik rescinded his order and let Hajjaj have his way. Whereupon he arranged a deception, ordering his men to prepare to make the pilgrimage to the sacred precinct. As keeper of the House, Abdallah was unable to refuse this request. The siege was lifted so that both sides might perform the sacred obligation. Hajjaj led the pilgrimage, wearing his helmet and a coat of chain mail, while his reinforcements secretly infiltrated the city. When the fighting resumed, the stones of the catapults on Mount Qubays rained down on the Ka'ba even heavier than before.

Eyewitnesses say the Ka'ba was hit so often that it became fragile. At some point a thunderstorm appeared, and a bolt of lightning hit one of the catapults, burning it and killing twelve operators. That terrified Hajjaj's men. They stopped fighting until he said:

"Generations before you made offerings, and always a fire was sent down to consume them. This happened to the prophet David when he took Jerusalem; it happened to Abraham when he offered his son and God took a ram in his place. God has given you a sign that your offering has been accepted. So finish what He has ordained."

Tucking the skirt of his tunic into his belt, Hajjaj then rolled up another catapult with his own hands. He loaded it with stone. "Shoot!" he commanded. The bombardment continued more ferociously than before. When the Syrians finally rushed down from the mountains, they trapped the son of Zubayr inside the hollow of Mecca's valley where the holy sanctuary lay. He fought like a lion, even after he was abandoned by two of his sons.

Those who finally got to shake their swords in Abdallah's ribcage swear that he met his fate laughing; they say they saw his back teeth as they pulled out their swords. Hajjaj hung Abdallah's headless body from the same gibbet that Abdallah had hung his brother's. Tariq, the son of Amr, who had led the final assault into the sanctuary, was outraged. "Women have borne none manlier than he," he said.

"Will you praise one who disobeyed the Commander of the Faithful?" Hajjaj retorted angrily.

"Yes," replied Tariq. "He freed us from blame. Were it not for this man's valor, we would have no excuse for what we have done to God's House. He had no trench, knee-high walls, no stronghold. Yet he held his own against us for seven months."

Abd al-Malik declared Tariq right. Still, he allowed Hajjaj to treat the people of the holy cities harshly. Companions of the Messenger of God who had supported the claims of the House of Hashim against Umayya had to wear lead seals around their necks. Those who had not stood by Uthman during the siege of his house in Medina thirty-five years earlier were executed. Criers went through the streets of Mecca singing songs of praise to Abd al-Malik, rubbing his victory in the faces of all of the city's residents.

> The red-white camels, snorting through their nose-rings,
> Brought you a noble man from Umayya, impeccable,
> Like a great white hawk,
> His countenance gleaming like a polished sword.

Abd al-Malik ordered the demolition of what remained of the Ka'ba. He flattened God's most ancient house, and then he rebuilt it. But he did not rebuild the Ka'ba as it was when Abdallah was lord and master of Mecca. The Temple was rebuilt "according to the dimensions of Muhammad's day," the crafty Caliph ordered.

The construction took but two weeks. The Ka'ba was, after all, a simple building, four straight sides of a square. In Muhammad's day, the walls had been built of loose stones and were low enough for nimble goats to jump over. There was no roof. Abd al-Malik used mortared stone for the walls and put on a timber roof. The Ka'ba was in accordance with its original dimensions in name only. In the southeastern corner, the one farthest from Jerusalem, he had the broken pieces of the Black Stone framed and fitted into the wall chest-high above ground, as first Abraham, and then Muhammad, had done before him.

The war of the holy cities had at last ended. The Black Stone was in Syrian hands. The son of Zubayr was dead. But it was the new Ka'ba that marked the real end of Abd al-Malik's struggle against Abdallah. Old memories had been erased by the new construction, and like a grave that men have abandoned and ceased to cherish, Abdallah's spirit was lost in the rubble.

Meeting Abd al-Malik

A bd al-Malik had been Caliph for less than a month when his soldiers, a group of fierce-looking Syrian Bedouins in full battle gear, appeared before my house amidst a gawking crowd of onlookers to escort me to Damascus. I was given a day to get my things together and settle my affairs.

Abd al-Malik and I had met once before, briefly, while he was serving as deputy to his father in Palestine. For a while, he was based in Jerusalem, and when I went to pay my respects, he spoke highly of Ka'b.

Iraq was in open rebellion over the excesses of Mu'awiya's son, Yazid. The emperor in Constantinople was retaking Syrian towns from which he had been evicted four decades earlier. Christians and Jews were at loggerheads in Jerusalem yet again. Abdallah's fortunes were at their peak; he was gaining adherents in Syria and crowing over his victory in the Hijaz. On the streets, men were saying that the desert had swallowed up Yazid's army because of God's displeasure with a House that dared to denigrate His holy cities. The talk of Damascus was of how Marwan had died at the hands of his wife. The stench of defeat lay like a heavy blanket over the House of Umayya.

"Our cousin Mu'awiya, God Rest His Soul, said you identified the footprint on the Foundation Stone of Solomon's Temple." These were the first words Abd al-Malik spoke to me.

"I did, O Commander of the Faithful."

"And what do you say about that footprint today?"

"That it was left by the King of Absolute Sovereignty, who is the light of Heaven and Earth, and not by any of His Messengers."

"How do you know He has a footprint, or for that matter any kind of a shape? The Holy Book says: *Naught is as His Likeness.*"

"The source of all shape must Himself have a shape. The verse you have cited assumes it, even if that shape is like no other. Formlessness as an attribute of God is the refuge of lazy minds. He is the thing that He is named. What do we know about this thing? The Good Book says He has a throne, which encompasses the heavens and earth. God sits, in other words. And He moves. Did He not rise to Heaven after Creation? Does He not have two Houses, one in Mecca, the other in Jerusalem? Did He not travel to Mount Sinai and reveal Himself by voice to Moses? The Holy Book specifies that the Heavens shall be rolled up on the Day of Resurrection with His right hand. If He has a right hand, then why not a left? If He has a hand, then why not a foot?"

"Do you know what He looks like?"

"No, my Caliph. My examples are merely aspects of what God must look like just as His ninety-nine names are merely attributes of His nature."

"Do these aspects and attributes encompass Him?"

"Nothing can do that. It is not given to us to know what He looks like. But it is given to us to aspire to know. In fact, it is demanded. Were we ever to cease striving to know Him, our faith would be of an ill-fated and lowly sort."

"Yet you claimed to know that the mark on the Rock is God's own footprint."

"I made no such claim, O Caliph. I merely deduced the likelihood that it was His by way of argument from the lore of my father and the prophets."

"You do your father credit, son of Ka'b," Abd al-Malik replied. "I see that I have not wasted my time inviting you to Damascus."

~

Abd al-Malik used to give five audiences every morning after the Dawn Prayer. These began with the Reporter bringing him news from all over the empire, after which he would read a thirtieth part of the Holy Book in private before entering the audience hall. First to be admitted were his personal officers, with whom he would chat for a while, and then his ministers, who would talk over matters that had arisen during the course of the previous day. At this audience, a breakfast would be served made up of the remains of the previous evening's supper—cold lamb, chicken, or some such dish.

"Page, set out the chair!" he would call out once he had finished. Then, he would proceed to the mosque, where, after ablution, he would take his seat on the chair that had been set for him, lean his back against the screen, and allow suitors to approach him as they would. I have met beggars on such occasions, wandering Arabs from the desert, women and children, destitute folk upon whose heads some calamity had fallen. After the customary "How is the Prince of True Believers this morning?" or "God prolong your days!" to which Abd al-Malik would always respond, "By the Grace of God," they would unload upon him their tales of woe and misfortune.

Abd al-Malik had the talent of listening. This was a man with no intimates, and yet he was capable of paying attention to trivia and drivel for hours on the grounds that it would one day be useful to him. Occasionally, he would act upon a particular injustice— ordering redress, or sending guardsmen to put a stop to some encroachment, or, when no immediate course of action appeared feasible, initiating an inquiry.

When no more suitors remained, he would return to his palace paved in green marble and sit an hour by the great fountain in the court, which flows at all hours, watering a garden of flowers, trees, and birds. Occasionally I would be taken into this garden. But more often than not, we would meet in the audience hall, and I would speak before scores of nobles, secretaries, officers, and petitioners.

"Talk," he said to me early on when he was setting down the rules of our relationship, "so long as I want to listen, but do not, whatever else you say, give me flatteries or exhort me to righteousness."

Talk about what? Of what use could I be to a new Caliph beset with enemies and problems on every side? Abd al-Malik was in dire need of soldiers and strategists who had knowledge of tribal genealogies and rivalries and feuds that stretched back for generations. Perhaps they could suggest alliances that could help prop up the empire that was collapsing all around him. I knew nothing of such matters.

Abd al-Malik wanted to talk about Ka'b. He wanted to be armed with his wisdom, he said. The truth is that Abd al-Malik had not brought me to Damascus for myself; it was my father's lore he wanted.

What really happened between Ka'b and Umar in Jerusalem half a century ago? Abd al-Malik asked. He wanted to know the direction of Ka'b's prayers, and God's reasons for not allowing David to build a House for Him over the Rock. Was it because God did not want to be housed in a Temple made of cedar, however magnificent? Or was it because of David's sins? What exactly were those sins? Should a kingdom be bequeathed to one's sons if there were the danger that it might not remain intact due to the father's sins?

Rubbing knees with so attentive a listener as Abd al-Malik for long stretches at a time was not easy. To be sure, he was a tall and handsome man to look upon, with an aquiline nose that added stateliness to a comeliness that not even an attack of smallpox in childhood had succeeded in marring. What could be wrong with being favored by such a powerful and handsome man?

Foul breath. Unfortunately, God had endowed his regal countenance with breath so bad that his wives could not fall asleep in his presence and grew sick from lack of sleep. Whispering tongues say that Sukayna, the daughter of Husayn, the son of Ali, would not

marry Abd al-Malik because of the foulness of the air whenever he
was in her presence. But the marriage was a strategic one from the
outset, designed to improve the standing of Abd al-Malik's father
among the Hashemites; it would have become untenable after Abd
al-Malik fled Medina at the start of Abdallah's revolt.

The Caliph's breath earned him the nickname Father of Flies.
The hateful creatures forever hovered around his face, attracted by
the smell and traces of blood that leaked from his mouth. A courtier
accused of using the epithet was once hauled before him in my
presence. "My arse contemplates those who talk behind my back,"
Abd al-Malik said before ordering the fellow beheaded. Flies were
certainly in evidence around that hapless head when it was brought
on a platter before the Caliph.

Some people said that the Caliph was afflicted with a disease
that gnawed away at his gums, requiring him to have gold bands
aligning his teeth. Others said that his bad breath was the price of
the curse that the Prophet had laid upon Mu'awiya's father and his
House. More likely than not, Abd al-Malik never picked his teeth
with sticks from the tamarisk tree and had too great a fondness for
the sugared curd-tarts and pilgrim-cheer pastries which were forever being passed around in his court.

Abd al-Malik talked about his breath to no one. On all matters,
he kept his thoughts sealed tight as a clam. Perhaps his economy
with words came from his affliction. It is, of course, the height of
folly to initiate a conversation with anyone about anything remotely
connected with the faculty of smell. Naturally, therefore, I suffered
Abd al-Malik's breath in silence, for as long as it took him to
squeeze from me all the stories of Ka'b, stories which I had once
spurned.

Abd al-Malik's interest in the City of the Temple exceeded that
of all the Caliphs who had preceded him. But storytelling was not
all he had in mind. I was being measured and sized up for another
purpose. Or was what I was saying being turned around and laid
out for inspection in the back rooms of the Caliph's mind? Looking
into his fathomless eyes gleaming above flashes of gold, I felt as

uneasy as a moth drawn to a lit candle. What did Abd al-Malik
have in store for me? Either he was not yet ready to say or did not
know himself.

"How do you think your father would answer those who claim to
see Jewish leanings in his claim that Adam fell in Jerusalem?" he
asked toward the end of his first year in office, just before the call to
the Sunset Prayer had sounded.

Before I could reply, he waved his hand dismissively in the
direction of a group of older, bearded men. "These pious souls say
he fell in India, on a mountain called Wasim in a valley called
Bahil between Dahnaj and Mandal, carrying with him seeds from
the Garden. These Adam spread around. From them came all good
fruit, many varieties of which are still found only in India. Eve fell
separately, they say, in the environs of Mecca. There, the first man
traveled to meet up with her. Neither fell in Jerusalem. What would
Ka'b have said to that?"

"If Ka'b is a Jew for thinking that Adam fell in Jerusalem, O
Abd al-Malik, then he is in the company of the most notable members of your House. Why, Mu'awiya said as much the day he was
proclaimed Caliph in Jerusalem. And what if there is a difference
of opinion between the followers of Muhammad on such questions?
On no other point concerning Creation do these critics disagree

with my father. Whether Adam landed in India or on the Rock in the Holy City, everyone is in agreement that he carried the Black Stone and landed on a mountain, one that happens to be the closest to Heaven of all the mountains of the Earth."

"Too close," interjected a tall, elegantly dressed man often seen by Abd al-Malik's side, "for I am told that his head poked into Paradise and frightened the angels. Some Rock this is that causes such consternation in the heavens!"

The speaker was a Christian poet from the tribe of Taghlib in Mesopotamia—a court favorite ready to praise or revile anyone to have his mouth filled with gold. Famous for his loquaciousness and flabby ears, either one of which could have earned him the name Akhtal, he knew how to please a paymaster even as he steered perilously close to offending him.

I saw him appear in court one day, drunk and flaunting a huge gold cross on a chain on his chest. Irritated, Abd al-Malik demanded that Akhtal embrace Islam. He offered ten thousand gold pieces in return for an instant public conversion. "If I accept," Akhtal replied with extraordinary effrontery, "will you allow me to continue drinking wine?" He had a reputation for needing drink to compose.

"What is the use of your wine," Abd al-Malik replied. "Its beginning is bitter, its end intoxication."

Whereupon Akhtal smacked his lips and said, "That may be so, but all in between is such that, compared with one properly mellowed draught, deepened to amber with time, your whole empire counts as a drop of water from the Euphrates licked off the fingertip." Abd al-Malik burst into laughter, and the same man who could carry on a discourse on the likeness of God gave Akhtal the money without making him convert.

I was new to court and kept quiet at Akhtal's taunt. He was not a man to trifle with. One scathing line of verse could make my life hell. Men's ears tingled with anticipation of them from Arabia to Egypt. Abd al-Malik, however, was in good humor and egged on the conversation himself.

"I expect of our poets to show more reverence for the point of creation of the universe and the place where our angel ancestor fell."

"I don't dispute that Adam fell there, O Caliph. Perhaps he even lived on the Rock. But like myself, he did not have in him the ascetic temperament," Akhtal said, stroking his sumptuous silk attire with the palms of his hands in a clownish gesture.

"By the way," he added as though he had just had an afterthought, "have you seen the Rock?"

"Of course, many times during my governorship."

"Well, then, you know what a bare and unwelcoming thing it is. How would you like to have Ka'b's Rock staring at you day in and day out like the cold, gray eye of an embittered old man? No wonder Adam became so irritable and bitter. Perhaps its unforgiving, diabolical shape suggested to the Jews their ghastly theology. Better, I say, for the Caliph of Muhammad's People to have nothing to do with it."

There is no more intoxicating draught than anger swallowed down for God's sake. My insides were seething. But I kept silent. Who, I thought, does this Akhtal think he is? At heart he is a descendant of those pagan bards so beloved by the Arabs. From time to time, he divorces his wife, returns to the desert, remarries, and throws himself into a tribal feud. Having replenished his virility, he comes back to court, where the princes of Umayya swaddle him in luxury, loving the way he vents his wild Bedouin nature in poetry. Personal piety had imposed restraints on the first generation of Muhammad's followers, who were now all gone. Syria's cities today turn out singers, not fighters, Arab men—and women, God forbid!—who set passages of Bedouin lore to music for dancing girls. Every luxury and new experience is eagerly sought, to be experienced vicariously through court jesters like Abd al-Malik's poet.

What does Akhtal know of religion to insult Ka'b? A Christian, he may think he is. Sophronius would certainly not have thought him one. He grovels before a priest one day, and makes fun of another the next. Once, I am told, a priest passed by his house. Akhtal instructed his pregnant wife to run after him and touch his robe. He thought to bring the poor woman luck. But she could not run fast enough and only succeeded in touching the tail of his donkey. "Don't worry," Akhtal said to her, shedding his piety as quickly as he had adopted it. "There is not a great deal of difference between him and his donkey's tail."

Can a man seek revenge through his work? Was I going to let myself be driven into the arms of an Umayyad Caliph by Akhtal and everything such so-called poets represent—I, who had carried a deep distrust of the House of Umayya since my youth?

Abd al-Malik, however, was not the kind of man that Akhtal took him to be—and that Abd al-Malik wanted him to think he was. Nor was he like the other members of his House. He belonged to the first generation brought up from birth in the religion of Muhammad, not in the desert by Bedouin women with reckless instincts. He grew up in the first God-fearing city, Medina, where every person was a deeply devout and committed follower of the Prophet. Until he assumed the Caliphate, he was considered one of the four most trustworthy scholars of law and religion of his day.

This was a man who was being serious when he bantered with his court jester to people's amusement. He had the ability to do both things well at the same time. So why did he bring a book illustrator to Damascus from Jerusalem? What was the connection between Ka'b's stories and his plotting to turn the troubles of a kingdom around? Since no one around the Caliph could see a connection, they assumed he was as flighty and irresponsible as they were. I, too, was attracted and repelled, intrigued and confused— not knowing in which direction to turn or what it was the Caliph was seeking from me. However intimate my knowledge of him eventually became in the course of time, I never made the mistake of thinking that I understood this Caliph's mind.

When his soldiers first appeared, making such a commotion outside my house, no one outside Damascus would acknowledge Abd al-Malik as their Caliph. By the end of seven years, however,

Believers from Africa to Khurasan were falling over one another to do so. They cheered him on in the very year that he flattened the Ka'ba, toward which every one of his acclaimers prayed five times a day. Why did so few mourn the fate of Abdallah and God's most ancient House? What arresting stroke of genius on a man's part can so quickly change the hearts and minds of people toward him?

His advisors say that he used up all the wealth hoarded by Mu'awiya and decades of successful campaigning in foreign lands to defeat Abdallah and turn people around. In order to devote himself to his internal problems, they say, Abd al-Malik signed a truce with the Byzantine emperor that required him to pay 365,000 gold pieces, one thousand slaves, and one thousand horses annually. The deal untied his hands. Still, how could he afford such an onerous sum and have enough left over to defeat Abdallah hunkered down in Arabia? If Mu'awiya's frugality and Abd al-Malik's truce explain his military victory, they do not explain why Abdallah was forgotten in the year that the Ka'ba was destroyed. Habits of the heart are not purchased with gold or changed by the sword.

Abd al-Malik had intuited that military means alone were not enough. But to which direction would he turn with this intuition? The Caliph was holding back, perhaps even from himself. Suddenly, however, a year after I had been going backward and forward between Jerusalem and Damascus, I saw the Caliph's purpose flushed out. Three seminal conversations wiped clean the slate of his uncertainties. They flared up on the day following my encounter with that worthless windbag Akhtal.

Mecca and Jerusalem

The first conversation took place in private, during Abd al-Malik's noon meal. There were no secretaries or petitioners. I was called in and invited to help myself to some chicken roasted with garlic. No sooner had I taken a mouthful than Abd al-Malik said:

"The son of Ka'b should not have let himself be needled by our poet."

Mercifully, I had foreseen this rebuke and answered, "I was held back, O Commander of the Faithful, not by Akhtal's rudeness, but because his words sparked a moment of illumination on to which I needed to cling for a while."

Looking into Abd al-Malik's eyes, I continued: "Our forefather, Abraham, was driven from the City of the Temple to the City of the Black Stone. But what drove him away? Ka'b gave this question much thought. Perhaps it was the Rock's cold and forbidding nature, to which Akhtal alluded."

"What are you talking about, Ishaq?"

"After his trial on Moriah, Abraham did not want to be buried under the Rock—unlike Adam, who yearned to return to the Garden and sought the place on Earth closest to it as his final resting place. The Knight of Faith had a nightmare in which he imagined that he was the Rock upon which the terrible ordeal had been enacted. He did not know that he had ever been anything but the

Rock. Suddenly, he awakened and realized to his astonishment that he was Abraham. But it was hard to be sure whether he was really Abraham and had only dreamt that he was the Rock, or was really the Rock and was only dreaming that he was Abraham. For a split second, the father of the Arabs and the Jews was confused."

"What is there to be confused about a rock?"

"The Rock was no longer just a rock, sitting there at the summit of the mountain, silent and unyielding, indifferent to all that was unfolding around it; it had metamorphosed into the lodestone of Abraham's worst nightmares, the meeting point of his most hidden desires and fears. Abraham was relearning the meaning of fear. The memory of what he had been about to do weighed upon him. He ached to put distance between himself and the mountains of the Holy City looming over him like giant parched bones. He had to die somewhere else. Not that he knew what would bring him peace; all he knew was that it could not be a thing that took its form from his own deepest fears, from suddenly resurrected memories of bridled impulses and expiated joys. He who had called his own father wretched had spent a lifetime running away from wretchedness. But, like furies, the memories stayed in hot pursuit, catching up with the old man during his nightmare. Furies began to inhabit the frail frame of the man who so willingly would have given up his own son on the Rock, and wherever he turned, he found himself chased by them until they coalesced into the unforgettable shape of an enormous hulk of limestone."

"Men are saying he is buried in Hebron."

"In a valley treed with sycamores and carobs, filled with orchards of grape, fruit, olives, and figs. He found peace in a land that is as soft and green as the Rock is hard and gray. No more harsh shadows and dramatic vistas. No more infinite horizons and star-filled skies. But it is not his resting place that came to my mind while Akhtal was speaking."

"What, then?"

"His flight to Mecca."

"To build the Ka'ba . . ."

"And achieve atonement. He took to the road in search of his firstborn, the long-lost Ishmael, dispatched upon Sara's whim into the desert after the birth of Isaac."

God hears the voice of the boy, wherever he may be.

"Who said those words?"

"The Almighty said them to Moses long after Abraham's time, as he had said them to Abraham before, which is what sent him to the desert where Ishmael and Hagar now lived."

"Separation breeds strange habits of the heart."

"Attraction grows with distance, like a distant bridegroom pining for his faraway bride. Abraham was drawn to Ishmael just as the Black Stone will be drawn to the Rock from which it was long ago separated; he was fated to atone for what he had done on the Rock by repairing that which his abandonment of Ishmael had torn asunder."

"It is fitting, I suppose, that the father of the Hebrews and the Arabs should be destined to return to his firstborn. But why were the two rocks separated in the first place?"

"Why was Ishmael cast out in the desert and the hands of men

turned against him? God intended it that way. Perhaps He wanted
to test His children, as Jews friendly to Muhammad say. Or perhaps
He intended a curse on both peoples' heads, like the mark that
branded Cain for killing his brother. Knowing in such matters
belongs to God alone."

Abd al-Malik went quiet. The Caliph was lost in a private
world. Breaking out of his reverie, he said: "What are you suggesting with all this, Ishaq?"

"To the origins of the two holy cities, O Abd al-Malik, to Mecca
and Jerusalem, to what separated them in the first place, and to that
which must one day bring them back together."

"But was there a Mecca at the time of which you are speaking?
All was desolation and destruction, relics of the Deluge."

"There was the Black Stone."

"Abraham fled one Rock to run up against another . . ."

"He took the same route as Adam when he met up with Eve.
And surely enough, a month's camel-ride away from Mount Zion,
he found Ishmael and the prize that the First Man had brought with
him from the Garden."

"The Black Stone."

"The very same. Tarnished by time, but recognizable. Abraham
found the Stone in the valley at the foot of Mount Abu Qubays,
where the winds and wild beasts had pushed it. The father who had
nearly lost a son on one Rock now set to work building a Temple
with the other. The Stone had to be protected. The house that Adam
built around it had long since gone. Only its memory survived. The
prophets, including Muhammad, knew of it, the Jewish sages of
Arabia knew of it, and Ka'b knew of it."

"What did Adam's house look like?"

"It was made of black cloth and wooden pegs, Ka'b taught,
which is why weaving is the first craft and lies at the origin of the
art of shelter. All the rules of geometry were suggested by the
straight lines, from which a square piece of cloth is still made.
Bookbinders make their papyrus sheets the way Adam made his
cloth. Adam's tent, called a tabernacle by the Jews, opened onto an

enclosure marked out as a sanctuary. The doorway faced the gateway into the outer enclosure of the sanctuary, which, in turn, faced the direction from which Adam had come—Moriah's summit. Thus was created the first direction toward which the prophets turned in prayer, and the prototype of the tent used by the Children of Israel during their wanderings."

"The Mother of All Books teaches that Abraham and Ishmael built the Ka'ba, carefully setting the Stone into its southeast corner because there it would be protected from flooding. But they used stone, not cloth."

"They draped the walls in black cloth, annually renewed by men ever since to remind them of the house that Adam had built. The Stone, whose color was on its way to blackness when Abraham found it, had been exposed to the ravages of flash floods, sandstorms, and the blazing heat of the sun. Abraham had to improve upon what Adam had done. Thus did the first shelter made of cloth become the first building made of stone clad in cloth. Around this primordial square grew Mecca, a city that received both its form and its meaning from the Stone."

"Abraham the priest had become Abraham the builder."

"The two roles later combined in Solomon, as they were to combine for the last time in Muhammad when he rebuilt the Ka'ba. Solomon built a Temple around the Rock that had so unsettled Abraham. As Mecca grew around Abraham's Ka'ba, so did Jerusalem grow around Solomon's Temple. Guarded by fearsome cherubim, Solomon placed the Ark on top of the Rock, inside a room known as the Holy of Holies. That room, the heart and soul of Solomon's grand design, was built of stone in the same shape as Abraham's Ka'ba."

"A cube!"

"Precisely, O Caliph. Duplication is here a sign of God's majesty; it is the affirmation of the as yet unwritten covenant between the two holiest cities in creation. Memory was hard at work."

"Solomon's Temple, I am told, far exceeded the Ka'ba in beauty and magnificence."

"It certainly did. Yet the Ka'ba is the most ancient house, in God's words, the first sanctuary to be established on earth. Age is to the Ka'ba what beauty was to the Temple."

"What did Solomon do after the completion of his Temple?"

"He prayed and offered sacrifice to God in Jerusalem, just as our father Abraham had done before him in Mecca. His words, Ka'b always said, were Abraham's own. Solomon finished his work on the tenth day of the first month of the year, Yom Kippur, the very day that the Ka'ba annually receives its new clothing of black."

"Praise be to God!"

"Like nature's cycles, such temporal recurrences are proofs of His Design."

"I inherit a deeply divided kingdom. What happened to break the covenant between Mecca and Jerusalem?"

"Time passed. Memories dimmed. Desires multiplied. Cities grew larger in concentric circles around the two Rocks. Distance from the center forged new memories and desires inside new forms. Men disagreed over what had happened in the past, and why. Desires and memories washed over both holy cities until the descendants of Abraham could not tell the one apart from the other. All that they remembered was what they wanted to remember. The present prevailed as the frailties of the First Man were passed on to his heirs. The inhabitants of Mecca and Jerusalem even forgot one another's existence. Sons of the same father began to conspire against their own souls, forgetting God, not even knowing that that was what they were doing. He, however, did not forget them. He sent Messengers to bring men back to his bosom. Muhammad was the last among these. He came after the Temple of Jerusalem had been destroyed, its Rock desecrated with statues and Christian dung."

"So Ishmael's descendants in Mecca were singled out by the coming of Muhammad, Peace Be Upon Him."

"Because there was nowhere else for His Messenger to go. The hand of fate carried him there. To every nation He raises a witness against itself. His coming meant that the time of those who were born to die for His Name by the sword had arrived: the Sons of Hagar would no longer stay in the desert. They had to join with the Sons of Sara and come to Jerusalem. We must not forget both sacred Rocks were jewels in the beginning. Adam landed on one and carried the other. Both featured in Creation. Both have a divine origin. They were even defiled in the same way. Did not Ka'b and Umar find menstrual cloths and filth on the first day of the Muslim conquest . . . ?"

"The day on which Jerusalem and Mecca were reunited."

"Long-lost lovers brought back into an uneasy embrace. But an embrace nonetheless."

"The signs of that shared destiny are not in evidence today. One last question remains, Ishaq. In His wisdom, the Holy One chose to complicate our lives by changing the axis of prayer in the second year of the Exodus from one Rock to the other. What did your father have to say about that?"

"He said that everything has its origin as its destination. God does not command an abomination. The strife that the religion of Abraham forbids is not part of His design. The Rocks, on the other hand, are. Their story is. Through them, for better or for worse, the destiny of the peoples of Moses and Muhammad are inextricably intertwined."

"And what if the story has a bad ending?"

"It is still one story."

The second conversation followed late in the afternoon of the same day, after Abd al-Malik had recited his mid-afternoon prayers. Normally, he retired then, receiving no one. On this occasion, however, I was brought to his private quarters overlooking the courtyard in the palace.

"Our Syrian Rock is bigger than Abdallah's Black Stone. What did your father have to say about the importance of size?"

"Adam had to land on one and carry the other. Size in itself does not bestow greater or lesser sanctity."

"I was not suggesting otherwise, son of Ka'b. Surely, however, size has some implication for the Temples housing the two stones."

"As does the future reunion of that which the First Man estranged through his travels."

"Would that be a physical act that you are talking about?"

"It would."

"Truly, this would be a wondrous sign! What said Ka'b about it?"

"It was he who foretold that it would happen. He said that it will be one of the signs of the Hour; that the Stones will not be annihilated like the rest of Creation on Judgment Day but will conjoin like a man does with a woman."

"How will my heart rejoice over that which my eye will never see?"

"God's signs are there for those who know how to draw consolation from them."

"No man can be consoled from the annihilation of all things."

"No. But he can from the knowledge that the Rock and the Stone are the last things to be annihilated. Their nature is to consume Time, rather than be consumed by it."

"What exactly did Ka'b say will happen to the two Stones on the Day?"

"The Black Stone will say to the Rock: Are you ready to receive me? You who are the first creation of the Holy One, Blessed Be He, and I who am His envoy? And the Rock will reply, Yes, come to me. The Black Stone will then rise in the air, uprooting the Ka'ba from its foundations, and carrying with it all those who have over the generations made the pilgrimage to Mecca. It will come to Jerusalem to be received by the Rock. The Rock will open like a woman opens herself to receive a man. The Stones will mate in a final cataclysmic embrace, an implosion of passion and desire such as has not been witnessed during Creation, the wildest rutting season of all. So powerful will be the urge, it will fuse back together again that which He once separated."

The third conversation took place in the Caliph's audience hall. It was the morning of the following day. Officers, ministers, and secretaries were present. But instead of addressing them as was his wont, he turned to me, saying, "Do you like your profession?"

"Bookbinding is the source of great solace. I would not exchange it for another under any circumstances."

"Describe what you do."

"I turn wisdom into an artifact that men engage with and attend to."

"How do you begin?"

"The wisdom has to be there, like the plan according to which God laid out Heaven and Earth and all that lies in between."

"Wisdom precedes, in other words, what you do."

"Precisely. As the idea of a circle precedes its drawing."

"If I recall, those were your father's words."

"You have a prodigious memory, O Abd al-Malik. They are his very words used to describe the place of the Rock in Creation."

"Go on. Describe how you make something out of this wisdom."

"I take pieces of papyrus cut directly from the plant. These are dried, woven in layers at right angles to one another, then wetted, hammered together, pressed, and smoothed in the workshop. Upon such sheets, using reed and ink, words are passed on to posterity. I deal in all that has to do with making it possible to fix and house such words between two covers."

"Even when the Words are God's own?"

"Especially if they are His. For then I know that the Book I am about to make is Divine, as will become the method, manner, and even the materials of its making."

"I want to build such an artifact as you describe to house that place in the City of the Temple that sits on the very threshold of Heaven. There the prophet David sought refuge. I want to cover God's Rock as his son Solomon did, and as you would His words. Only I want my Book to be in the shape of a Dome, a Dome built directly over the Rock, a Dome larger, and more beautiful, and more richly adorned than any other."

A Moment of Decision

The Rock was all that was left of God's work on the first day. It was the height of hubris to imagine that I could connect that visible trace with His invisible Presence, the always absent Purpose of everything. My entire upbringing weighed against the idea of trying to do so.

Had not Solomon himself entertained regret after building his Temple? "The Heaven and Heaven of Heavens cannot contain thee," he cried out upon seeing his magnificent monument. "How much less this house that I have built!"

Ka'b taught that the soul is most beautiful when it is naked. Building, through the extent of its artifice, its freezing into place the melting flux of nature, bodes ill for the Rock in its natural setting. Under the cool half-light of the moon, the spectacle of bare Rock against the starlit canvas of the sky draws the breath right out of a person. Time comes to a stop; the only sound is silence, a silence that takes the mind out of itself to meditate on other worlds. Truly, this is the first rung on Heaven's ladder, I used to think to myself. To be transported, all one needs is to be there at night and look—look at God's Rock set against His upturned bowl of a sky.

Imprisoning His Rock in a gilded cage, dressing it up in ceramics, marble, precious stones, gold lettering—"a whore's glitter," Ka'b would have said—was anathema. Had the ghost of Sophronius reached out from the grave and bewitched Abd al-

Malik? Was he about to do to my father's Rock what the Patriarch's queen had done to Calvary? Strip out the sheltering tent of the sky, and what are you left with? A relic like Golgotha. A cross laid out in a coffin made of silver and gold.

Can memory and conscience take shape against these as a backdrop?

The craft of bookbinding teaches that it can.

What is a book if not an artifact unfixed in time and space? A mobile receptacle for memories that would otherwise be lost? Ka'b adored the few scrolls and leaved books he had brought with him from the Yemen. The little wooden chest in which they sat partook of a kind of holiness. I was brought up to treat it like a reliquary, as inviolable as the holy Ark itself. No one was allowed to sit, or put anything, on top of it. No one was allowed to drink or eat when it was being opened. My first lesson in the value of books began with the chest that housed them.

Perhaps Abd al-Malik intuited this, and used it to turn me around to his way of seeing things—just as his Dome was going to turn the whole Community of Muhammad against his rival, Abdallah, holed up in Mecca.

Perhaps I was being seduced in the way a moth is seduced by the flame that will consume it? Even if I could bring myself to disturb the Rock in its natural setting, to forgo my former pleasure in the hope of wresting out an even greater one, could I trust this Caliph? I disliked and mistrusted his House, however much I had come to respect the discernment of the Caliph himself. Intelligence, after all, can be put in servitude to a man's organs as easily as it can to the glory of He who made those organs in order to serve Him.

The Caliph needed me to justify forms selected on the basis of stories that he wanted to be like the mortar that bonds materials together, invisible to the eye but indispensable to the larger structure of things. The prospect both thrilled and terrified me.

The success of Muhammad, the very speed with which his followers had become rulers of half the world, demanded an answer to the question of where they ought to be ruled from. Arabia was too remote. Mu'awiya, and even Ali, understood this. But only Abd al-Malik was able to translate the understanding into realities on the ground. Only Jerusalem, he had intuited, could put Muhammad's People at the center of things, where they belonged.

Was not the City of the Temple the Holy Land to which all the prophets had emigrated? It had, therefore, greater merit than Mecca. Was that not the truth that my father taught and which I myself had passed on to Abd al-Malik? This Caliph was no innovator; he was simply restoring a balance that had been confirmed by God during the week in which He fashioned the world. Muhammad, God's Grace Be Upon Him and His Household, was the seal of the prophets. God willed that his followers should crown the epic encounter between Him and all His creations—an encounter that reached its apogee on the day that the first Believer and his son underwent their great ordeal at the place that Abd al-Malik now wished to pay homage.

Thus did I reason myself into the whirlpool of my father's obsession and Abd al-Malik's desires. I was appointed advisor on matters of the Dome's form and appearance. My task was to find a Syrian master-builder and justify a shape that would support and enhance Abd al-Malik's Dome—a Dome that had to be bigger than the biggest Christian Dome in the city, that of the Church of Resurrection.

The Father and the Son

In Medina, on the day of my birth, long before he knew he would come to Jerusalem, Umar placed upon me a terrible burden—my name. Truly, the coming of the Redeemer to this land, and Abd al-Malik's decision to build over the Holy Rock, was foreshadowed in that choice.

My father left out the merit of the son in the story of the great sacrifice that he told Umar on the Mount of Olives. Nor did Umar raise the question with him, perhaps because that is not what a man beside himself with grief at the sacrifice of his own daughter needed to hear at the time. For him, as for Umar, that was not where the true meaning of what happened on the Rock resided. But Ka'b was wrong to leave out the merit of he whose name is on the dying breath of every martyr in God's cause.

The monks of the Holy City contend that the People of Muhammad follow too blindly in the footsteps of the Jews. What happened to Abraham and Ishaq they say, was but a preamble, a dress rehearsal, for the supreme sacrificial act of all time carried out by Jesus in the place where they have erected their Church. Because of what Jesus did, the whole tradition of bloodletting practiced in the old Temple was rendered null and void. Abraham did not offer himself. And Ishaq was just a boy who was offered by someone else; he too did not offer himself. Worst of all, he did not die; he was not even hurt. Not one drop of Ishaq's blood was shed, they argue most persuasively to the young Arab scholars who search them out. How could either Abraham or Ishaq, venerable prophets that they were, be compared with the Son who was Himself God, and who died so nobly on behalf of all of us?

The true meaning of what happened on the Rock during the great trial, therefore, needs to be re-examined. Mine is a moderate view, rooted in the teachings of the Holy Book; it starts, not by denying what Ka'b said to Umar on the Mount of Olives, but by adding to the story all those things that my father did not say. Is there equal if not greater merit in him who was to be sacrificed than in him who did the sacrificing?

After Moriah had been pointed out by God, Abraham and his son left their asses at its foot and climbed the mountain. On the summit, Abraham sharpened his knife. He built the altar, and he trimmed and arranged the wood in the right order for a burnt offering. Then he embraced the boy, who only now, even as he was being bound hand and foot, began to realize that something was amiss.

Like a soft-spoken dove, Ishaq whispered:

"Father!"

"I am here, my son."

"I behold the fire and the wood. But where is the lamb for a burnt-offering?"

"The Lord will look to His lamb, and draw it to His bosom."

Between the question and the answer, Abraham would have had to look into his son's eyes. He would have had to look into his eyes yet again as he raised the knife to dispatch him. Tradition demands that, in the case of an unblemished offering, the killing must be done in a single stroke. If, in the act of slaughtering, there occurs a pause long enough for a whole other stroke to take place, the sacrifice must be disqualified.

But according to the Jewish sages whom I have consulted, that is when the exchange of words took place. There would not have

been enough time for the sacrifice to be done correctly. Abraham's
ordeal would have been for naught.

Suppose, however, the exchange of words took place before the
binding. Or suppose there was enough time to make the cut precisely as it should be made. How could *this* be a true sacrifice if
the offering's own blood was not shed? All the wise men that I
have consulted teach that sin can be expiated only with blood. Tradition demands it, and only the blood of the victim himself counts
for true atonement. The blood of a substitute will sometimes be
accepted, as Muhammad's father, Abd al-Muttalib, found out to his
relief, but it is never as good. We know why God accepted a substitute on that particular occasion. Because He wanted His Messenger to be born. But how could He accept a substitute in the case of
the supreme sacrifice, Abraham's sacrifice of his son on the Rock?
The Christians have an unimpeachable point here that needs to be
accounted for.

Perhaps the Patriarch inflicted some kind of wound that released blood that washed over the Rock but left the boy alive.
Would that consummate Abraham's offering?

No, say the sages of blessed memory. It would not be enough.
Where are the ashes? Tradition demands ashes. To be properly sacrificed, an offering must release blood and leave behind ashes.
What happened to the ashes of him who was the perpetual offering?
If they were not there, then Ishaq was not killed. What precisely
happened on the Rock to confer merit on both Abraham and his
son?

The first time I heard the story was the day that we settled into
our new house situated eighty-six paces away from the story's setting. No sooner had our baggage been set down than Ka'b took my
hand and hurried to the esplanade, which was still covered in filth.
Beside the Rock that he and Umar had uncovered, he told me the
story of the origins of my name. I wanted to know whether or not the
boy had been afraid. Ka'b said,

"Perhaps, but the fear went away after his father spoke."

"Why did he submit to being tied up?"

"He trusted his father."

"Did he struggle to release himself?"

"No."

"But then his faith was being tested as much as his father's."

"It was."

"What would be the point of binding him, depriving him of the possibility of failing God's test?"

Ka'b was silent. He did not know what to say. That silence led me to search in new directions. And this is what I have concluded.

Of course Abraham's sacrifice was a true offering, and as such, the boy had to have died. Otherwise, how can the sacrifice of a would-be victim, taken down from the altar sound of limb, be greater than that of an actual victim, like Umar's daughter, whose body became food for worms? The Christians have a point: He who does not act out a plan, whatever his intentions, is not like one who carries it out. How, then, did the boy die *and* go on to spread his seed until his descendants were as numerous as the sands on the seashore?

Abraham would have pinned Ishaq down with his knees. Had the arm clenching the knife in its fist faltered, as it might, Abraham would have steeled himself and made it strong. That was his nature. With steadied hands, according to the rite, he slaughtered the boy. But did he kill him? The boy may have died of fright before the blade struck, as some people say. Still Abraham had to slit Ishaq's throat because a full quarter of the boy's blood had to spill on the Rock. Whether it was the blade that did the deed, or Ishaq's own terror, there is no escaping the conclusion that Abraham's son was the first true lamb of God.

No sooner had the deed been done, and the body consumed by fire, than a resurrecting dew fell upon those ashes of righteousness. The boy revived. God, who commands the wind, showers the rain, and nourishes the living, also quickens the dead. In the blink of an eye, salvation sprouts, bringing life where before there was only death. There and then on the Rock, the son of Abraham was resurrected as proof of his great virtue. Thus it had to be with him whose binding was intended to be more than just a test of Abraham's submission, and whose blood has watered the gardens of the pure ever since.

What did the father do now? No doubt he seized the newly arisen boy by the shoulders to slaughter him again, as God had commanded. Only just before the ministering angels intervened with Him on high to save the son by substituting the ram in his place, the boy himself asked to be bound. He feared for his father's sake; his offering would be found wanting if, in a moment of weakness, he cringed and the knife were deflected from its purpose.

"O my father," Ishaq said, "if you desire my sacrifice, nothing is imposed on you by me. Your punishment for shedding my blood is by this diminished. Only make my bonds fast, for if the death is hard I do not believe I will be able to endure it when I feel death's touch. Hone your knife so that you can finish me off quickly and release me from my agony. When you lay me down for sacrifice, lay me down on my face, not on my side. For I fear that, if you look at my face, you will soften and abandon God's command. If you wish, return my shirt to my mother; it might be a consolation to her. Now, proceed. Do it!"

The Importance of Eight

For weeks I walked like a man in a daze up and down the cobbled streets of Jerusalem, visiting my old haunts. I sat for hours in the convoluted halls of the Church of the Resurrection, looking at how Calvary's rock had been fitted to its church. The building meandered from the great steps of the Cardo, to the Basilica, to the central court, to the Rotunda, with Adam and Helena's tomb tucked away underneath. The giant envelope of a form fitted these different places connected with the death and burial of Jesus arbitrarily. Calvary was all but lost in the confusion. One stumbled upon it by accident. It was not in the center, because the Church of the Resurrection had so many of those. A center has to be there all at once, all the time, and from every direction; it has to be suggested by the large and the small in the whole edifice. Every surface and detail has to strive toward it.

I climbed the Mount of Olives, approaching the Church of the Ascension on its summit from different angles, considering afresh the question of its rotund shape, so unlike that of any other edifice that I have ever seen. This unroofed building that was all wall and columns never failed to lift my spirits. The sky was its canopy—its only decoration, constellations of stars blended into the firmament like smoke from a sacrifice. What arresting stroke of genius had conceived of that for the place that Jesus had been called upon to return to Him on High? Like the Muslims that I grew up with—and unlike my father—I never excluded the possibility that Jesus the Prophet, not the Son of God, God forbid! might have ascended from here into Heaven, as the church's caretakers tirelessly tell their visitors. Perhaps those *were* his footprints embedded in the sandstone in the center of the church.

But the Churches of Jerusalem had not been founded on the Prophet's truth. The willingness to suspend disbelief, which is what I do when I walk up the Mount of Olives or go into a beautiful church, is not True Belief—not, at any rate, as we followers of Muhammad understand it. True Belief is the certainty that God returned to His heavenly place of abode from the plain, gray, ordinary-looking piece of Rock that nestles in the sanctuary beside my house. My task, therefore, was to celebrate the wordless equivalent of that certainty, to sate the hunger of all men to believe from a place of deep humility.

I consulted Nicholas, a Greek master-builder responsible for many of the finest churches in Syria. Knowing that the secrets of his trade were handed down from father to son and could be imparted only under the strictest of vóws and never to a man of alien faith, he refused to talk to me about his craft at first, fearing both the admonition of his Church and the ire of his family. By appealing to our years of friendship—we had enjoyed an interlude of companionship as young men—and the pride he took in his considerable skills, I eventually won Nicholas over, and enticed him into a conversation on the setting out of domes.

"Give me a point, and a square," he said after crossing himself repeatedly to ward off the possibility that he might be commiting a grave sin, "and I can erect any dome you want."

The point sat at the center of the square, where its two diagonals intersected. From the same intersection, another square could be drawn at right angles to the first. Thus were created eight equidistant points.

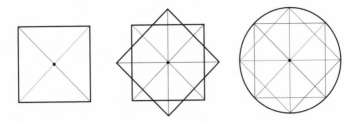

"Now think of these as describing the circumference of a circle. That is the drum of your Dome, and that is how I would mark it out with pegs on the ground."

I took to playing with this geometry, using a stick in the sand— as I often did when deciding upon a frame for chapters of the Holy Book, which I would then execute in gold on parchment and surround with twisting tracery superimposed on patterns of straight lines.

In so tracing lines on a prepared patch of fine sand, I stumbled upon a remarkable consequence of Nicholas's rules. By taking the original superimposed set of squares and extending all eight of their sides, a new set of intersections was harmoniously generated. I had made a new octagon, bigger than the first, but as perfectly derived from its archetype as the ripples made by a stone thrown into the stillness of a pond.

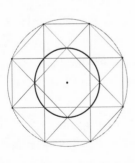 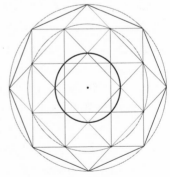

Extending the sides of the octagon in the sand generated yet another pair of superimposed squares, larger than their predecessors. One could go on and on, I realized. The pattern emerging was

like a living crystal, infinitely extendable around a point of origin
and always with perfect symmetry in every direction. Connecting
the outer eight points gave me an outer enclosure, the boundary
wall enveloping two interior ambulatories, which, in turn, enclosed
a circle out of which was going to rise the highest and most splendid Dome imaginable. There before my eyes in the sand was what I
had been looking for—a graded passage from this world to the next
by way of the Rock.

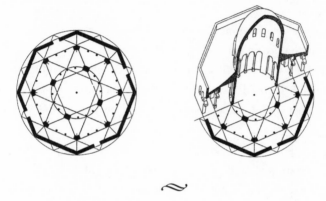

Eight is the number of Paradise just as surely as Arabic is its language. God provided His creatures with eight paradises and only
seven hells, Ka'b used to say.

"Why the difference?" I asked.

"Because His mercy is greater than His wrath. Is not the
covenant between a newborn and his Maker made on the eighth
day, the day his foreskin is cut? And did not the Prophet say that
the Garden of Refuge for the Companions of the Right, virtue's ultimate reward, is the eighth level of Paradise?"

Four rivers—of water unstaling, of milk uncurdling, of honey
purified, and of wine delightful—irrigate this highest level. The
Garden is near the Lote-Tree of the Boundary under the Throne of
God, itself carried by eight angels, all hovering in the Heavens
directly above the Rock. Fountains gush everywhere. Shade trees,
date palms, pomegranate trees, and other fruit trees abound. The
air is redolent of musk, camphor, and ginger. In such a place the

God-fearing shall dwell in the presence of their King Omnipotent, and find out that all their Lord had promised them was true.

Believers know these things because they are written. But not all of them know about the importance of eight. A bare handful realize that all the Peoples of the Book are folded under that number's divine wings.

Christians say that Jesus rose to Heaven on the eighth day of the Passion. The pool in which they circumcise the hearts of their children is shaped like an octagon. Baptism, as they call it, makes the newborn a companion of Jesus on the Day of Resurrection. My Dome was in the shape of this number of the afterlife. The thought of it brought tears to my eyes.

In the course of a lifetime, a man is lucky to be granted two, three at most, insights into what is unmistakably right. Normally, the mind contents itself with shuffling around the dead facts of experience, trying this and then that, invariably settling on a compromise of sorts. But in the rare event of such an insight, the veils are stripped off life's clutter to reveal the bright forehead of exactitude. The soul has grasped a living truth! The Beautiful, a deeply overpowering sensation that fills the soul with the warmth of Rightness, is revealed.

What is Rightness if not also Truth and Justice? My commission was one of immortalizing in stone the Truth and the Justice of my father's Rock. Nothing about it was contingent. Like a harmonious chord, the building had materialized in my mind as an emanation of cosmic laws. The architecture was rhythmical and sequenced as it should be; it rejected the confusion of the superficial. Even the circumference of the Dome fell into place by itself, as it were, according to a definite proportion and in perfect harmony with every other dimension—as did the locations of the piers and columns that fell naturally on the points of intersection of my lines. I did not choose those points; they made themselves known to me. Nor did they conceal one another in the plan, but rather permitted, from any point in the interior, a view all the way across to the other side.

Transparency, as all men know, is the rule in Paradise.

Can rotating a square around a point accomplish all this? Can it determine the appropriate correlation between His ineffable nature and built form? To find shapes properly grounded in scripture and the stories of the prophets from so few rules is more reminiscent of Him than months, even years, of knowing Him through words alone. And all of it happened while I was playing like a child in the sand. When His Design was traced out with my stick, I was blessed with a glimpse into the dawn of what was to come. I knew then that, finally, I had awakened from the dream of this life to the reality of the next.

Two problems had to be resolved—the location of the Rock's center, the building's starting point, and the dimensions of the square that Nicholas had talked about.

The Rock sprawled irregularly over a much larger area than is apparent to the eye today. Who dared to vouch on his or her own authority where the all-important center was? Scrambling over the surface, I drove a small wooden stake into the crevice that Ka'b had always said marked the Rock's center. That stake became the marker from which the whole edifice was laid out.

The second problem was more complicated. Nicholas had said—and it was borne out by my drawing—that everything depended on the dimensions of the square: the diameter of the Dome, the outer perimeter of the octagon, the width of the two ambulatories, to say nothing of the area of the Rock left visible. All of these would fall into place only after the length of the square's diagonal had been determined. I needed a criterion by which to determine this critical dimension.

The solution came to me like a bolt from on High. The template that I needed for Abd al-Malik's Dome in Jerusalem must derive from Abraham's Ka'ba in Mecca. The cube that housed the Black Stone was, after all, destined to return to the Rock on the Day when all things would be annihilated. That is what Ka'b had said. The Black Stone would uproot the Ka'ba from its foundations and travel with it to Jerusalem. The two holy Rocks would then conjoin in a cataclysmic embrace. Abd al-Malik's Dome had to accommodate its counterpart in Mecca. All three dimensions of the Ka'ba had to fit inside the new Temple that Abd al-Malik was building over the ruins of its predecessors in Jerusalem. The diameter of the Dome had therefore to be equal to the height of its drum from the ground, whose dimensions were, in turn, derived from the diagonal of the Ka'ba, whose four corners are the four piers in the plan of the Dome of the Rock.

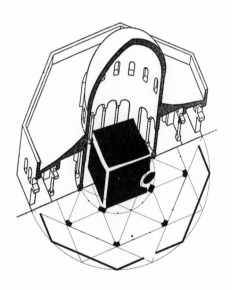

Stone into Light

"Y̱ou will no doubt have to prepare the surface of the Rock, cut it into shape, smooth it over, and dress the surface," Abd al-Malik said after the plan that Nicholas and I had carefully drawn on animal skins had been explained to him.

"Absolutely not!" I blurted out, horrified. "The Rock must not be touched, no matter what else we do."

"How can it remain in such a crude and ugly state when it occupies pride of place inside a great monument?" asked the incredulous Caliph.

"The Rock is beyond our canons," I replied. "It may terrify, be wondrous, awesome even, but it is not and can never be merely beautiful. It is, after all, His first creation and the cornerstone of the entire cosmos."

"Where is the Beautiful, then, in what you are proposing?"

"It is in Abd al-Malik's Dome in the first place, followed by all the other surfaces that hold it up. Imagine a delicate and intricately embroidered canopy suspended over the Rock. The Dome is to the Rock what the sky is to the earth, what the night stars are to the celestial pole. It is the mirror to the Rock's opacity, the beacon of its Truth."

"Do you not aspire to any kind of likeness between the Dome and the Rock?"

"None whatsoever. To Him alone belongs sublime similitude.

The Rock and its Dome harmonize through contrast and opposition. Similitude and continuity between them would be the Devil's embrace. When you cannot compete with something or even simulate its meaning, it is wiser to do something else entirely. Then the Dome, and that which it celebrates, are together enhanced."

"How should the Dome look?"

"A landmark, visible by virtue of height and color from every approach to the city and every point within it. From within, looking up into the cupola, its inverted roundness must present a spectacle of small, smooth, delicate, subtly colored parts that lead the eye of the beholder on a wanton kind of chase to sights worthy of Heaven. The mind delights in variety that is intricate, elusive, and intertwined, as long as it is also ordered and contained, held within an overarching uniformity. The Dome is unity, like the tent from which it derives. Contained within it is a primal force, the rugged craggy summit from which He fashioned everything. I would have the raw Rock rising like an eruption from a sea of polished marble, an island in glassy-smooth coral waters."

"How can what you describe be achieved?"

"With the use of precious, glittering materials, perfectly cut and set to an invisible order mimicking that of the plan before your eyes. By human artifice, we will adorn your Dome with that which really belongs only to Him, and with which He has decorated Paradise."

"Is this how Solomon decorated his Temple?"

"It is. But we have gone a step further than Solomon. He cloaked the Holy of Holies in darkness, whereas we shall flood the Dome with light."

"Why were there no windows in the Holy of Holies?"

"Because Solomon's advisors said God resided there, and, thus, they believed His light physically radiated from that place. And because Solomon copied the pagan temples he saw around him, all of which had dark, inaccessible centers. In place of their idols, he put the Ark of the Covenant in the Holy of Holies. When the Ark was lost, the chamber was left a dark and empty cube, like the Ka'ba, qualities the Israelites associated with the brooding presence of the Lord. The Romans, who were used to brightly decorated temples reeking of incense and filled with the golden effigies of their idols, thought them mad."

"How could you possibly know what the Holy of Holies looked like?" interjected Raja', son of Heyweh, a theologian and collector of traditions about the Prophet, whose advice was highly regarded in Abd al-Malik's court. "There is no description of it in God's Book, and the Prophet said nothing about it."

"I know it from the Book of Moses, which my father was taught in the land of the Yemen."

"A Book thick with praise, but thin on the matters of shape and form that you are talking about." Raja' considered himself an expert on the City of the Temple and its holy places.

"I think the son of Ka'b has arrived at a commendable plan, O Commander of the Faithful," Raja' said, turning away from me to address the Caliph. "But I am troubled by the distance that his building takes from God's Words. These represent Revelation's most palpable miracle; wrought by Him, they were made manifest in our Arabic tongue. Christians choose to ignore and falsify their scripture with pictures. But we are a People of the Book, the final link in the chain of those who have been admitted to the secrets of the Celestial Register, the Mother of all Books. Was not the very first word of God to His chosen Messenger, 'Recite'? And did God not say that men will suffer no injustice on Judgment Day because He had given us words that set forth the Truth? If our own Book, that which paved our way to the Holy Land, is not somehow in the Dome that will carry your name, men will say that Abd al-Malik has built just another Christian monument."

"Well spoken, Raja'. What say you, Ishaq? You are, after all, a bookbinder. Your vocation is to value His words. What were you proposing to make out of jewels of different colors and precious stones?"

"Follow the words of scripture, which say, *He is the Light of the Heavens and the Earth.* I was proposing to illuminate. Was not light

His first creation? And did the first ray not shine outward from this
interior to illuminate the world? Physical brightness illuminates
spiritually. It points to a journey from the material to the immate-
rial. Cast the bright light of day on His footprint, and the eyes of
visitors to the Rock will be directed toward His Light up above,
which is what they will confront on the Day of Doom. If His image
is absent during our sojourn in this life, it is because light is the
mark of His presence. He is Omniscience and Omnipresence," I
said to the Caliph in one great outburst, "and that is Light, the
Light of the Heavens and the Earth, the likeness of which

is as a niche
wherein is a lamp
(the lamp in a glass,
the glass as it were a glittering star)
kindled from a Blessed Tree,
an olive that is neither of the East nor of the West,
whose oil well-nigh would shine, even if no fire touched it;
Light upon Light;
God guides to His Light whom He will.

God, who knows all things, had set these verses as a parable for
men, I told Abd al-Malik. The Dome is the niche, within which sits
a lamp. The lamp is the glass through which His light passes. The
Rock is the Truth without which the niche is nothing. Thus does
His Truth come to all Believers through the agency of light, which
we can see, and be uplifted by, and love.

❧

"Parables will not sell my Dome to ordinary people," Abd al-Malik
said to me. The son of Haywa had elicited in the Caliph a desire for
more directness. I had to come up with a simpler solution.

Since there was so much light—the design allowed for fifty-six
windows piercing the walls and drum of the Dome—did it not make

sense to give men something to read? I decided to decorate the walls in the exemplary miracle of His Arabic script.

The knowledge of a True Believer exists in his heart, or it does not exist at all. The sinuous lines of brightly colored calligraphy linking different surfaces together are not intended to teach the good Book, but to corroborate and reinforce what everyone already knows; they represent memories without falling into the trap of making likenesses of them. When Believers enter a mosque, they begin to recite aloud, swaying their bodies from side to side with eyes half closed, their voices like the roaring ocean. In the Dome, my calligraphy enacts those bodily movements before they have been set in motion; it envelops Believers in His praise before they have had a chance to begin praising Him.

Building on the Rock

Abd al-Malik loved the idea of applying calligraphy to the surfaces of the Dome. But he never gave me full credit for it. He saw my contribution as a mere fleshing out of his original concept of a Dome and what the son of Haywa had said. In recognition of the latter's contribution—and out of consideration of the respect he enjoyed as a man of religion even in the holy cities of Arabia—Raja' was appointed supervisor of the project, directly responsible to the Caliph for matters pertaining to the Dome. He chose the verses from the Holy Book to adorn the surfaces of the Dome, even though it was I who would execute the fundamental correlation between Architecture and His ineffable nature. Raja' was as blind as a bat in matters of form and color. Thankfully, he was intelligent enough to leave these realms to me in the knowledge that the glory was going to him. He was the kind of man who enjoyed exercising control through the strings of a purse. All expenditures, changes, and major decisions had to be authorized by him. My days of easy access to the Caliph had come to an end.

Shortly after the appointment of Raja', son of Haywa, I convinced Nicholas to serve as master-builder for Abd al-Malik's Dome. The Church held the threat of excommunication over his head even though it had no new buildings upon which he could deploy his talents. But his reasons for accepting were not entirely pecuniary, seeing as how friendship and respect had flourished between us in the course of our collaboration over the plan of the Dome.

Work on the Dome began in earnest in the sixty-ninth year after the Exodus, while Abd al-Malik was still preoccupied with the rebellion of Abdallah's brother in Iraq. We had raised the square platform around the Rock by this time. Four sets of steps led up to the platform, to the four doors of the Dome facing the four cardinal points of the cosmos.

The height of the platform's retaining wall was determined by the amount of rubble we had to dispose of. Much of that rubble had been shovelled northwards in the days of Umar and Mu'awiya, clearing the southern two-thirds of the esplanade and turning the northern third into an even bigger blot on the city. But the esplanade had to be big—a massive expanse if possible. So we had the whole area cleared, using some of the rubble as fill inside the new retaining walls that Nicholas had built. Large pieces of stone—cut and uncut—along with usable bits of columns, were kept aside. Everything else—Roman, Jewish, Christian, or pagan—went underneath the raised platform upon which the Dome was going to sit. The greater the amount of rubble at our disposal—the greater, in other words, had been Roman and Christian desecration of the site of Solomon's Temple—the higher would our platform rise, and the more triumphantly would Abd al-Malik's Dome tower above the city skyline. Was this God's way of punishing those who had so abused His Rock? Thus did I wonder at Destiny's Design while watching the Rock I had known as a young boy get buried until only its tip was left exposed.

All that is left of the Rock today when one walks into the Dome is a dark, primitive, and yet gently tilted mass, inclining toward its counterpart in Mecca, the Black Stone. I measured out sixteen-by-twenty paces of it to be our building's inner sanctum, and the new floor was cut around the irregular shape and simply recessed at the edge where the raw limestone slides under polished marble. The exposed surface in the middle looks weatherbeaten, ravaged by time, colored in grim grays and gray-blues flecked with spots of brown and black. Identifiably human markings gouged into its worn-out countenance have become even more pronounced, holes and lines that must have been cut into the stone for the drainage of water or blood—sacrificial blood, animal and human. In spite of these markings, the surface feels parchment-like, with a texture and polish that comes from years of touching and kissing and stroking, so smooth it suggests the aged but well-preserved skin of a beached whale. Thus have we accentuated the disjunction of the Rock from its mountain carcass; to visitors, it seems to float like some unnatural distant apparition.

Nicholas marked out the building with plaster in time for the Caliph's visit. In spite of troubles brewing in Iraq where Abdallah's brother was governor, Abd al-Malik decided to come to inspect the works. Upon learning that we had used plaster to set out the lines, he ordered it swept away and replaced with flour, "the emblem of fertility," as he put it to me. Nicholas returned the next day and wordlessly began to mark off the piers, columns, and outer walls, which revolved around the Rock like the spokes of a wheel.

Following Nicholas's lines, peasant laborers dug the foundations, into which a graduated mixture of broken stone and mortar would be poured. They dug until they hit the Rock that they had just covered up. The ring of Rock we had covered with new flagstones was flat until the point at which the outer face of our octagon-shaped walls ended. At this edge, the supporting rock slopes sharply downward. Had our building been any bigger, or smaller, it would not have fitted its mountain as perfectly. I had not foreseen or adjusted for the contours of the Rock when drawing the plan. God willed everything to fall in place. The first great work of architecture to be commissioned by Muhammad's followers in the name of their faith had been tailored by Him on High to crown Mount Zion perfectly.

I took this as a sign and stopped all work for the day. Each man, after the fashion of his religion, was called upon to give thanks to the Lord.

It took Nicholas six months to put up the piers and external walls. He used rough blocks of stone, crudely hewn, with very thick joints, knowing that they were never going to be seen without their finished coat of glazed tiles. Each of the eight outer walls was subdivided into seven tall panels ending at the top in a semicircular recessed arch. Nicholas wanted to make them all blind; he said that it was not fitting for a house of worship to have so many windows. But I insisted on the light.

The compromise we finally worked out was to leave the lower half blind, while putting windows in the upper half of five of the seven panels. As a consequence, there are forty windows in the external walls of the octagon, which, along with the sixteen windows of the drum, make a total of fifty-six.

I selected the columns for the interior from what we had salvaged from the esplanade. The careful observer will notice that no two columns are alike in the Dome. The striated marble shafts vary slightly in diameter as well as in coloring. The capitals in particular diverge from one another. A handful do not even belong to the shafts to which they are currently attached. One had a cross chiselled into it. How it got there, I don't know. But cross or no cross, the quality of the carving was excellent, and I was loath to discard it. Raja' was away in Damascus, and I decided to let it pass. Perhaps he wouldn't notice; by the time he came back, it would be too late to make a fuss.

The different heights of the columns caused many problems. Adjustments had to be made through trial and error. If a column was too short, we used thick layers of lead at the base to raise it. This material forms a good bedding because of how it allows the weight to distribute itself evenly over the junction with the shaft. The messy result was then concealed under paneled boxes of white marble. In spite of Nicholas's best efforts, further fine-tuning was often required at the top. To make these with the greatest flexibility, he added a plain block of slightly recessed stone above the capital, upon which rested the wooden tie-beams running through each arcade. Adjustments in the thickness of the stone would compensate for any differences in level from one column to the next.

As the neck is carried on the torso, the drum of our dome is carried by the four piers and eight columns of the circular arcade. A long neck is a mark of graciousness in a person; I aspired to a very high drum. Nicholas built it of squared blocks of stone following the lines of the arches below. In order to support the enormous weight, he strengthened the four piers so that they acted as buttresses rising through the roof. The height from the ground to the spring of the Dome—the drum's top edge—was equal to the diameter of the Dome. In other words, we had generated a cubical interior around the Rock, perfectly squared to accommodate the Ka'ba on the Last Day.

Attached to the drum in a fanlike fashion are a series of wooden trusses sloping down to the walls of the outer octagon. These carry the roof over the two ambulatories. Rafters rest on the trusses parallel to the sides of the octagon. Upon them, we laid an exterior finish of sheets of lead.

The crown of any such edifice is its dome. Domes test the true art and mettle of a builder like no other element. Ours began going up a year or so after Abd al-Malik's visit to the site.

Nicholas insisted on constructing it out of two shells, independently fitted to one another like inverted cups. The curved ribs of each dome were bent, not cut, and held in place with crossbraced wooden struts as in a ship's hull. It was stronger that way, Nicholas said. More importantly, the height I aspired to on the outside would not be marred by a tunnelled effect on the inside. Praise be to God who put proportion in that good man's mind where all true works of architecture are carried, enabling him to see the consequences of geometry and arithmetic before they materialize on the ground.

The effect, while walking around inside the structure, before the roof was laid down, was one of striped light shimmering and dazzling the eyes as one passed under the symmetrically aligned trusses. The beauty of expressed structure tells its own story, and I needed no other argument to leave the beams and struts exposed rather than hiding them under coffered ceilings hanging off roof trusses, as had been done in the Basilica of the Church of the Resurrection.

Thirty-two ribs spring upward from a wall-plate fixed to the top of the drum. These converge at the apex, where all tensions are resolved. I insisted on thirty-two so as to maintain a symmetry based on a factor of four, the number of sides of the Ka'ba: four doors, eight sides, sixteen drum windows, and thirty-two ribs. On the inside of the Dome we had the wall-plate cantilever beyond the wall to support a stucco cornice girdling the drum, which I thought provided a handsome transition from the starkly vertical to the gently sweeping curve of the dome. Similarly, on the outside, a cornice separated the Dome from its drum, which, again, is only fitting, seeing as how a change of material occurs there.

I wanted the decoration to be as lavish and rich as Nicholas's

structure was spare. Had not Solomon's Temple been filled with golden trees and sumptuous fruit? That which God has blessed has to have its riches come bursting out of all its surfaces.

Working from pattern-books that my mosaicists presented to me, I chose according to what my father had taught me of the shapes and colors of the mansions and trees of Paradise. Vine-scrolls, five-pointed leaves, pinecones, bunches of grapes looping out of trees or vases, and chains of half-palmettes were carved or painted on plates of wood and attached to the exposed roof beams. I wanted them to be overwhelming in quantity and variety. The tie-beams, being closer to the ground, were clad in metal, upon which craftsmen applied finely painted gilt, sometimes working the metal surface directly in a variety of ways. Likewise, the piers were decorated with vinelike plants rising from acanthus leaves, their stems laden with expensive ornaments and jewelry.

Golden trees, and treelike forms with multicolored trunks, luxuriant blossoms, and clusters of fruit, spill from the surfaces of the arcade. Sometimes I had sinuously curving vegetal forms growing out of jewelled vases. These I would have necklaced in collars of gold studded with chips of mother-of-pearl. The golden trees bore real fruit, just as Ka'b had told me they had in the lush gardens and courtyards of Solomon's Temple. On the soffits of the arches, in cubes of mosaic, my craftsmen depicted grapes, dates, figs, pears, apples, prunes, quince, olives, cherries, lemons, and pomegranates.

While building his skeletal structure, Nicholas scrambled about on the scaffolding as though he were putting together Noah's Ark. He picked only the finest pieces of oak and cedar for the Dome's ribs, even though the difference could hardly be seen from the ground. These species of wood are not subject to the attacks of worms, he said, when Raja' tried to get him to obtain cheaper alternatives.

It was while he was working on the final stages of the inner dome, nailing boarding that had palm-tree fiber glued on to hold the plaster, that he slipped and fell onto the craggy surface of the Rock below. Nicholas's back was broken. We carried him to his house on a stretcher, but he was beyond the art of the doctors and died the following day.

I was distraught. We lost much of our Christian workforce that week, because word spread that Nicholas's misfortune had been caused by his disobedience to the Church. A priest's instruction should be heeded, one of the marble-setters said to me, for it is not his words that bind, but those of Jesus:

> *What you bind on earth,*
> *will be bound in the heavens,*
> *and what you unbind on earth*
> *will be unbound in the heavens.*

I appealed to Raja' to dispense one hundred gold pieces to Nicholas's family in recognition of his service on the Caliph's behalf. But Nicholas had died uncircumcised, reminding everyone that, in spite of half a century of Muslim governance, Jerusalem was still Christian. In that was considerable loss of face for the followers of Muhammad. Raja' refused to pay more than Nicholas was due on the day that he died. I decided to appeal directly to Abd al-Malik.

It took the Caliph weeks to see me. This was our first meeting since his visit to the site just under two years before.

"Nicholas, the master-builder, served his Caliph well," I argued with all the passion at my disposal. "He did excellent work and met his death in the service of God."

"Not for the sake of God did your friend meet his end but for the sake of money," Abd al-Malik replied.

Generosity comes to this Caliph like sweat to a stone, I thought to myself as I rode back to Jerusalem.

All Is Vanity

When Nicholas fell from the Dome, no one was converting
to Islam in Syria. The Church of the Resurrection was
dazzling Muslims with its size, its magnificent mosaics, marbles, and gilded metalwork, not to mention the music
that could be heard coming from inside. The great bells ascending
and descending, the hypnotic chants of the monks, the high-pitched
tones of the child choir, the ecstatic responses of worshippers to
their priests—all this acted as a kind of bewitchment that worked to
blur the word-filled edges of religious differences between men.
Beardless men much further down the road to defection were asking
what kind of victors we were who could not make pleasing things
and sounds as well as those whom we have vanquished?

Abd al-Malik was completely dependent on Christian craftsmen like Nicholas for his building projects. And when criticism
mounted that too many Christians were working on the Dome, Abd
al-Malik snapped his fingers and said:

"Solomon turned to Hiram of Tyre for his architects, craftsmen,
and materials. I am doing no more than he!"

The Caliph was enamored with the person of Solomon. Building had gone to his head. Before an assembly of courtiers and advisors, he said one day:

"David came out of the desert and waged a holy war of conquest for the land, an achievement which his son consecrated by

building the Temple and making Jerusalem the capital of the sons of Ishaq and of the world. The sons of Ishmael can do no less."

Ka'b had taught that Solomon's House was endowed with columns that propped up a mass of gold so bright the eyes flinched. So, Abd al-Malik instructed that his Dome shine like a lamp on a moonless night. But whose jewels and gold would encrust the walls? Believers had none of their own. All had been acquired as spoils of war.

"Precisely!" Raja' said. "Include those. Did not the noble Umar hang crescent-shaped Persian insignia in the Ka'ba as a sign of the submission of the King of Kings?"

Thus did pictures of crowns, bracelets, diadems encrusted with precious stones, breastplates, necklaces, and other ornaments and insignia make their way into the inner face of the drum and the arcades. They hung from golden branches bursting with fruit redolent of Paradise. Facing the Rock, the crowns of the kings whom the followers of Muhammad had trampled into dust circled and paid homage to it.

I selected the trees from the pattern books of my artisans. Then, on pieces of wood that were to act as templates for my mosaicists, Raja' ordered me to ink:

O ye People of the Book,
overstep not bounds in your religion;
and of God speak only truth.

In clear, unornamented letters which were to fit above the arches of the arcade, I wrote,

Believe in God and His Messengers,
and say not Three.
Refrain; it will be better for you.
God is One.
Far be it from His glory that He should have a son.
The Messiah does not disdain being a Servant of God.
The true religion with Him is Islam;
and they to whom the scriptures had been given
differed through jealousy.

Simple words. Orthodox words. God's own words lettered in gold mosaic against a background of bright green. Every Muslim knew them by heart. And now they girdled the Rock. The craftsmen, who thus spelled out the errors of their own faith in glittering mosaic made to sparkle with mother-of-pearl, came from Antioch and Saloniki. A handful of the best were from that kitchen of thieves, Constantinople. The emperor's artisans did not read Arabic. They made mistakes, which I did not uncover until after the tiles were glazed. Words were left out from one verse, which no one has so far noticed.

What is the point of addressing Christians inside a building they made with their own hands but are unlikely ever to throng? Abd al-Malik, it seems, had in mind his own defecting Muslims, not the followers of Jesus. This Caliph's mind worked in convoluted ways. Why else would I be ordered to both wage polemics against the religion of Jesus and draw attention to the high regard in which he was held by Muhammad's People?

"The Son of Mary is only a Messenger," Raja' said, acting as his master's voice. "Is a Messenger any less a prophet for being His servant?" And so it came to be that, in the best-lit spot in the entire building, was written the commandment:

> *Pray for your Messenger and your servant,*
> *Jesus Son of Mary!*

∼

If Abd al-Malik had hoped his Dome would supersede the Church of the Resurrection in beauty and excellence, he positively relished the fact that it would do so over the spot that Christians had desecrated. He wanted to rub the noses of the monks in the smell of his authority. Three hundred Guardians of the Noble Sanctuary—as the Temple Mount was being called—were appointed, including descendants of the seventy Jewish families that the caliph Umar had transferred from Tiberias to Jerusalem with my father's help.

These Guardians maintained its cleanliness and were charged with carrying out rituals that Raja' said had been practiced in the days of Solomon. Among the Jews were glassmakers, descendants of the men who ran the great workshops in Sidon producing mold-blown glass vessels for the Temple and the Jewish Feast of the Tabernacles. Abd al-Malik wanted them to make lamps for the Noble Sanctuary, which is most generously lit, as well as spittoons and storage jars. I personally oversaw the installation of five thousand lamps with their chains—four hundred and sixty-four of which were in the Dome of the Rock.

The salaries of the Noble Sanctuary's extravagant number of Guardians are paid directly by the Treasury in Damascus, from the fifth share of the spoils to which the Caliph is entitled. Whenever one of these Guardians dies, the rule is that his first son take his place, followed, in turn, by his son, and so on for as long as the family continues to bring forth offspring.

At each of the Dome of the Rock's four gates, from among the three hundred Servants, Abd al-Malik placed ten Jewish gatekeepers. Their duties included kindling the interior lights daily, using oil made from the seeds of the ben tree, a species of moringa. The ben oil is mixed with the purest olive oil to make the one hundred candles consumed on average every night. On the days that the Dome is closed to visitors, only its special Guardians may enter.

Such rituals were more lavish than anything I had imagined when I first agreed to work for a man in whom the grasp of religion seemed so firm—unlike the other princes of his House, whose religiosity dissipated as quickly as the enormous wealth they suddenly acquired from the conquered territories of Iraq and Syria. The inquiring, self-effacing man who had employed me to tell him Ka'b's stories was gone. In less than seven years, he had changed into a king afflicted with the disease of caring only about how he appeared before others. On the day of the opening of the Dome, I heard him chuckle, "Solomon, I have outdone you."

The monks were furious with Abd al-Malik's Jewish appointments, the announcement of which coincided with the first appearance of copper coins issued in the Holy City showing a branched candlestick resembling a Jewish menorah.

The air of the city crackled with anxiety. Stories began to circulate of Jewish glassblowers who threw their sons into the furnace for consorting with Christian youths. An all-out conflagration was narrowly averted when a former monk and his followers dressed in hair shirts were caught preparing to clear an old abandoned tunnel under the esplanade. The party had been intent on secretly storm-

ing the Noble Sanctuary on the eighth day following the opening
ceremony for the Dome, the day on which their Savior had been
resurrected. The men, fully expecting to die, intended to hold
the Sanctuary long enough to destroy the Dome, thus fulfilling the
prophecy of the destruction of the Temple before the coming of the
Messiah.

The men had thirsted for death so much that it had made them
slipshod in their preparations. They were spotted by a watchful
Jewish Guardian of the Sanctuary. Just before his beheading, the
monk who had led the group described a vision of the End of Days
which had come upon him. He had seen a white horse walk through
the portals of Heaven, which were opening in front of his eyes.

"He that sat upon the horse," he said, "came in righteousness
to wage war. The armies of Heaven followed Him, clothed in pure
white linen. Out of the Rider's mouth I saw a sharp sword big
enough to smite nations. I saw the Beast and his false prophet surrounded by the kings of the earth, all gathered to make war against
Him who sat upon the white horse. But the Beast was taken and
cast alive into a lake of fire and brimstone. The rest were slain.
Then I saw the souls of them that had remained steadfast. They
came down from Heaven to reign in a New Jerusalem. The Holy
City was filled, like a bride adorned for her husband, with the glory
of God, her light clear as crystal and brighter than a jasper. In that
New City, I was told, I would reign with Jesus for a thousand years,
until the Hour when all the dead would be awakened."

If I had wept for joy at resolving the cube of the blessed Ka'ba
into the Dome of His Rock, it was because the number of the afterlife had materialized out of my lines in the sand, but after hearing
that half-crazed speech, I had to ask myself if the resolution had
been a blessing or an omen. Had grim destiny marshalled the strife
needed to bring dead stones back to life as a harbinger of darker
times to come? And was destiny's herald happy or angry with the
stones I had helped Abd al-Malik bring back to life?

Ka'b held that a beautiful building is like a beautiful woman
bedecked with ornaments. Men play with her until they become

besotted. If she gives no thought to her end, allowing herself to be played with, then she will be ravaged, her body defiled, her most intimate places exposed and violated. So it was with the rape of the Temple of the Hebrews, whose stones we had now turned into a Muslim Dome. Twice, this jewelled daughter of the sons of Ishaq had been despoiled, her ruin willed to be as vast as the sea.

"Why was her ruin so great?" I asked Ka'b.

"Because she drew eyes to herself, away from God," he replied. "God wanted to show the People of the Torah that vanity is of no comfort in this life, much less the next. So he lit a fire under their feet until His Rock was laid bare to the world's gaze. Jackals roamed over the place that David had promised would be his cornerstone and the followers of Jesus had spurned. No curse could compare with the one that descended over this holiest of places."

I had paid no attention when Ka'b spoke of that curse in earlier days. But now that Abd al-Malik had exceeded himself, I remembered it. Were glitter and human artifice, however marvelous, about to replace the invisible order of justice and peace among tribes that Islam was intended to bring back into the world? Were we, the People of Muhammad, in danger of visiting upon ourselves the grim fate of which my father spoke, and which none but he had foreseen? What was in the Temple of Abd al-Malik to stop it from succumbing to the fate of its predecessor?

Building the Dome carried graver consequences than simply arousing the ire of local monks. After news of the huge sums being expended on the City of the Temple reached Arabia, Abdallah's poets and scribblers accused the Caliph of "reviving the ways of an ignoble people, the Jews." They pointed to prophecies that foretold of Jewish salvation at the hands of an Ishmaelite king. Unscrupulous wags dreamed up a whole stable of new sayings that they attributed to the Prophet. According to these, Muhammad himself had denigrated Jerusalem out of anger with the Jews.

"A prayer in the mosque of Mecca," the Prophet was reported to have said, "is better than a thousand prayers in any other mosque except that of my mosque in Medina."

Abd al-Malik's propagandists countered with lies of their own: "You shall only fasten the saddles of your riding beasts for three mosques," they had the Prophet saying, "the sacred mosque in Mecca, my mosque in Medina, and the farthest mosque in Jerusalem."

Apocryphal tales sprang up like spring grass throughout the conquered territories. One young laborer, newly converted to Islam, told me that his father had approached the Prophet on the day of Mecca's conquest, saying, "O Messenger of God, I vowed to pray in Jerusalem on this day. Should I go right away?"

To which the Prophet is supposed to have said, "Just one prayer in that place will absolve you of sin until you become as you were on the day your mother bore you."

The war of words got nastier. Fanatics accused Abd al-Malik of changing one of the pillars of True Belief—the pilgrimage. Abd al-Malik, they said, intended to divert the pilgrimage to the new Temple he was building in Jerusalem, which would one day replace the Ka'ba.

Believers could see their Caliph in Damascus praying toward the Black Stone five times a day. But Abdallah was appealing to their feelings, not to their reason. They became confused. The learned among them worried that there would be no legitimacy left in a Christian province were their Caliph to repudiate the font of his authority and power in Arabia.

There was a grain of truth to Abdallah's accusation. Abd al-Malik employed every trick at his disposal, short of force, to reduce the number of Syrians going to Mecca. He wanted Syrians to go on believing that his House was the sole surviving continuation of the Prophet's own. His rule depended upon it. But it was hard to do that if people kept travelling backward and forward between Syria and the seat of rebel activities in Mecca. People might begin to think that the House of Hashim, from which the Prophet and his murdered grandson Husayn descended, lived on in the person of

Abdallah who, although not a Hashemite, was bonded in kinship to the family of the Prophet on both sides. Abd al-Malik needed to distract his subjects, turn them away from thoughts of Mecca. What better than a massive public works program that outdid the uncircumcised in their own city!

~

Can a Temple refashion the clay of a man's heart? The monks of Jerusalem thought so. Abdallah thought so. Above all, Abd al-Malik thought so. In fact, he counted on it.

"You see that old man?" Abd al-Malik said, pointing to an Arab praying in the Dome on the day of its opening. Tears streamed down his cheeks as he mumbled verses from the Holy Book to himself. "We were like him once, but our hearts have grown harder since."

"His tears watch over us," I replied, noting to myself that the old man was performing his prostrations so as to face the Rock and the Black Stone at the same time. "On the day they stop, we should worry."

The Dome changed people's hearts in many ways. If some of Abd al-Malik's subjects were crying, the eyes of others were popping out of their heads in astonishment. You could see visitors silenced, with dropped jaws, standing beside others incanting incessantly, like the hoopoe bird, "What is this that our Caliph has built?"

You heard pious folk to whom the Dome had become a kind of salvation saying to one another, "This is not a building! It is a sweet-smelling vision descended from another world. Thanks be to God who has seen fit to bless the stricken followers of Muhammad."

In truth, no Believer had laid eyes on so marvelous an artifact before—and built to cover the Lord's own footprint, in a place that had witnessed a father and his son's supreme test of faith. The same marks on the face of the Rock once used to drain the blood of my namesake were now used to drain water, the buckets and buckets of it needed to wash the Rock on the Monday and Thursday of every week. And not any kind of water—only the sweetest-smelling, further perfumed by a secret concoction of crushed roses, mistaqi, and saffron.

All kinds of new smells were enveloping and soothing suffering souls. On the morning of the same Monday and Thursday on which the Rock was washed, the Jewish Guardians would prepare a mixture of ambergris, rose water, and saffron, and from these would make a special kind of incense intended only for the Dome. The rose water was pressed from the best red roses of Persia, left to mature and put in censers of gold and silver inside which lay an odoriferous Indian wood rubbed over with musk and myrrh extracted from Arabian trees considered divine. Then the Guardians would lower curtains made of variegated and decorated silk until they hung down among the pillars. Now the incense would encircle the Rock entirely, condensing and clinging to all its surfaces. When the curtains were raised, the subtle odor, bearing a hint of the fragrance of cloves and sweet as a zephyr's breath, wafted out to fill the city.

"Come one, come all!" the public herald would call out. "Abd al-Malik's star-studded Dome, intimating in its perfection the world to come, is open. Come and perform your visit."

And the people would hasten to pray in the Dome as if pious and serene thoughts, not smells, had begun to exude out of every joint and pore of stone; they would depart saying that they had been reminded of Paradise, whose fragrance is of musk, camphor, and ginger. On whomever the odor of the incense was found, it was said of this person that he was "in the Rock."

Myself, I tried not to enter the Dome after it was opened. It was too full of visitors, streams of people coming from the four corners of the empire, who wanted nothing more than to be able to say that they had the air of Paradise on their clothes. I would see them going to and fro from the rooftop of my old house, hear them telling one another, with rapt faces, how on the same two mornings of every week, the Guardians of the Sanctuary would enter the bathhouse to wash and purify themselves. They would go to a room in which there was stored the special perfume intended for washing down the Rock. There, they would take off their clothes and put on garments of silk brocade adorned with figures made for the occasion. A girdle embellished with gold would be fastened tightly around their waists. After dressing themselves, they would rub down the rock-face in front of all the visitors. When these visitors returned where they had come from, expressions of awe travelled back with them, rippling over the anxieties and fears of the age like a smooth, sweet-smelling balm.

Travellers from far-flung provinces described half-shut eyes, wearied by decades of sedition and civil strife, opening like full moons upon hearing the heavenly vision described to them. Drowning men and women clutched in desperation at news of the wonder, as though the Dome were a plank bobbing in the ocean of their sorrows and fears. Terrible memories were erased overnight because of what Abd al-Malik had accomplished. Not in their wildest dreams would Muhammad's People have imagined that such beauty and ceremony could belong to them without having been confiscated from Christians. Perhaps now they had something to live for, not just be against. Is it any wonder that Muhammad's People forgot Abdallah and flocked to pay allegiance to the man who had brought about such a transformation?

Warfare is the art of biding one's time while reading the future from the habits of men's hearts. Only after Abd al-Malik had reaped the grand harvest of the Dome's reception by the Believers did he turn his attention to Abdallah, stewing away in his desert fortress. Such was the virtue of patience in Abd al-Malik that, by the time that fighting actually broke out in Arabia, the Dome was all that anyone was talking about throughout the length and breadth of Syria.

Wars and military victories were no longer enough for the fol-

lowers of Muhammad. Victory had to be converted into a currency
other than territory or gold. Abd al-Malik had converted it into
stone. His achievement had the appearance of a spontaneous eruption, coming out of nowhere, like the Israelites bursting out of the
desert and substituting a Temple for a tent. Phoenicians, not Jews,
were supposed to be Temple builders. Christians, not Muslims,
liked to paint and decorate their holy places. But if David could
make Jerusalem his capital, and if his son Solomon could conse-
crate that achievement with a Temple destined to be remembered
until the end of time, so could Abd al-Malik.

The seventy-second year after the Exodus is the Year of the
Dome. Abd al-Malik had his name and the year inscribed as a
mosaic frieze inside the monument, thus ensuring that he would
stand out in the annals of Islam because of his Dome, and not
because of Abdallah's corpse stuck on a gibbet outside Mecca.

Preparations and planning had gone on for four years; construction took an additional three. The crowning glory of Abd al-
Malik's reign was not slapped together in two weeks like the Ka'ba
it supplanted, or like that embarrassing shack of a mosque that
Umar had built south of the Rock, which the Caliph ordered torn
down. As the pomegranate tree takes years of cultivation to swell
up with red spring flowers and fruit worthy of a king's banquet, so
too a Temple that is able to so uplift the soul of its community.

As a rule, men live to be admired by others of their own station. I,
for instance, a bookbinder, live to have my work admired by other
bookbinders. Warriors live to be admired by other warriors. And
rulers live to be admired by fellow rulers. A handful of rulers, however, are unique. They occupy a different space from the rest of us.
These are the builders of dreams—ordinary men's dreams, builders
who are in some ineffable way able to account for every human
impulse imaginable, seekers after the universals that cater not just
to one but to every religious taste. Such rulers can be the hardest of

taskmasters, the most unpleasant of men. Nothing is too small in their eyes, too small to be taken care of by someone else. Every detail has its place in a scheme that, by its very nature and not through the inclination of their own hearts, is grander than their own persons.

Abd al-Malik traveled a road paved in blood to become such a king. He bribed infidel emperors, cut off heads, and humiliated those Companions of the Messenger of God who had supported the claims of the House of Hashim. And yet he made the future live in the shadow of his Dome.

How will this Caliph be judged on the Day? Will he be judged by the merits of his building, or by his vain desire to be remembered for having built it? And what are we to make of the fact that, as it was being opened, Abd al-Malik's army was gathering to besiege and attack the Ka'ba? Are these two acts of construction and destruction bound together by grim fate? Who decreed that the Stones Umar had so sweetly brought together should so horribly be ripped apart by factious war, and then just as horribly yoked back together again by the harsh terms of Abd al-Malik's victory over Abdallah? Perhaps the Ka'ba that Abd al-Malik ended up destroying will never be redeemed by the Dome that he built. The passage of time does not change the nature of a sin. But that is a judgment for the next world, not this one. Is it by dint of our feebleness that we admire Abd al-Malik for what he did, forgetting how he did it, we who know only how to laugh or weep, or is it in accordance with the design of Him whose deeds are without blemish and all of whose ways are justice, He who made laughter and tears?

The eyes attain Him not, but He attains the eyes;
He is the All-Subtle, the All-Aware.

The Rock of Judgment

When the Egyptians took a stand in relation to their world, they faced south. The word for "south" was the same as the word for "face." "North" was the same as "back of the head." A whole world in which east was left and west was right was described in accordance with the idea that the Nile, flowing from the south and cutting a green gash teeming with life through the desert, was God.

The Christians converted the Egyptians to praying east because, their sages said, east was the direction of the earthly Paradise from whence Adam had come.

Ka'b read all the sins of the monks and the pharaohs into this. In the search for God, he said to Umar shortly after their acclaimed find on the site of the old Temple, one must disregard the four cardinal directions given by the sun and the stars and the rivers and the mountains. God was not in this or that creation; He was pure orientation.

"Which is why," Ka'b concluded, "when the Peoples of Moses and Muhammad take a stand in relation to their world, they face rocks."

"But a rock is good for nothing, unlike a great and fertile river like the Nile," objected Umar. "Had I not seen the Prophet himself kiss the Black Stone, I would never have done it."

"In its uselessness lies its strength, its eternal correctness, its irreproachability," my father would reply. "The greater a rock's uselessness, the less likely it is to be confused with Him who is the only life-giving force. A rock is dumb, mute, and dense; it knows only how to sit, not to move; it is a marker forever singling out one point on the surface of the earth. At such a point, and nowhere else, did the Holy One manifest Himself during the act of Creation—and He will do so again on the Day of Annihilation. However brief His manifestation or however far back in the mists of time, and for whatever reason it took place, the fact that it happened is all that is important. Nothing else about the Rock is of the slightest interest."

"The father of Ishaq is singling out a thing over its meaning!"

"His meanings are unfathomable. All that is given us to know is that at the moment of His first appearance, the undifferentiated material of the universe began to break out of its formlessness. The things that we can see and touch and smell began to happen, suddenly, out of nothing, as though by magic. Beauty erupted into the world. Not prettiness, mind you, whose nature is trite, but beauty, which sinks to the depths. David stumbled upon it when he unwittingly unleashed the chaos of the Waters. The Rock, the beginning of all Creation, checked the impending catastrophe lying just under the surface of the world. It stood as a reproof to the inconstancy of even the greatest of kings. How much greater an admonition does the Rock offer to our own frailties! Rocks are explosions of form in unformed space. They are authority and strength. Anyone who has seen them looming like parched bones in the desert will understand what I am saying. How else to order and discipline the treacherousness of sand? When the first Rock told the First Man where he was located in Palestine, the world, stretching from the farthest ocean to the Indus valley, was born."

God's chosen instrument both in the time of Moses and in the time of Mohammed was a People of the Sacred Direction. For in the beginning there was only one Rock and one Direction. This common orientation created deep ties of knowledge and experience between the peoples of Moses and Muhammad—from astronomy to pilgrimage, from the separateness of the categories of creation to proper rules of sacrifice, from ideas of cleanliness and defilement to architecture and the geography of Heaven and Hell.

True Believers prayed facing the Rock that David and Ahithophel had uncovered. The heads of animals about to be slaughtered were turned toward it. And while the first Muslims were undergoing persecution in Mecca, they took the greatest of care never to spit or to relieve themselves in this holiest of directions—the first sacred axis of Islam, which Umar himself had returned to True Belief.

Ka'b lived through an age of prophecy and unsettled customs, an age in which wisdom did not lie in teaching what had been revealed; it lay in revealing what ought to be taught. He wrestled with his soul as hard as Jacob with the angel before accepting Muhammad. But accept him in the end he did. He attached himself to Muhammad's mission while his own people were lost in lamentations over their subjugation and the destruction of their Temple. My father did not speak of the Rock, until his visit to the Holy City. Perhaps he thought the Arabs would not know what to make of it. Perhaps he did not know what to say.

Umar was the first to know. But his knowledge remained unpolished. At the moment of his greatest triumph, the great Redeemer allowed religion to become subordinated to politics. He worried about what people might think if the sons of Hagar looked too much like the sons of Sara. And so he chose to define the People of Muhammad by expunging from them what was rightfully owed to the People of Moses.

If Ka'b considered this unworthy, it was not because he thought Umar ought to abide by what the Jews believed. It was because the great Caliph was denigrating the actual place of God's ascent and Abraham's sacrifice. He was denigrating all those prophets who predicted the destruction of the world and yet foresaw redemption coming only out of this mountain upon which I am now writing.

"I am laying in Zion a foundation stone, a tested stone, a precious cornerstone," Isaiah had said. The Rock of Foundation:

Foundation, not only as a story about origins, but as an ongoing holding together of the world. For around this Rock, Isaiah prophesied, all nations would end their warring and gather for a final reconciliation. Such a lodestone could have provided a clarity that was both welcome and necessary in the confused and confusing state of affairs in which Believers found themselves immediately after the conquest.

But Umar turned his back on the Rock. And later generations, for whom Umar's bones were warmer than their own flesh, continued to build their mosques in the direction the Conqueror of Cities had built his. The Rock was ignored, turning into a thing toward which one gradually became indifferent. The unerring spirit of an age that had begun with such promise, that had conquered half the world in a handful of years, foundered; it was entombed within a stone that lay like a troubled conscience upon the land.

Muhammad would not have recognized the Believers as his followers. They grew idle and soft. The City of the Rock was being turned into a mine for profit in this world, not the next.

The moment Umar made his fateful decision, Ka'b knew that he had failed. Other men might have bent like reeds in the wind. But Ka'b harbored one of those abiding passions that ripens and deepens in adversity. The Rock was his probe; having worn out his sandals searching for it, only to be misunderstood, he gave himself up to the Rock.

A thing belongs to the one who remembers it most obsessively. Only through such remembering can we defend the mystery against the sorcery, worship the incomprehensible while rejecting the absurd, dispel the superstitions that complacency brings swirling around Him, and separate out of the inexplicable what is necessary and true.

~

"Remember what happened to the king who strove to build the tallest tower! He sought to scale the heavens above the clouds, imitating Him who is Most High. Instead he was ensnared and scattered by a whirlwind, flung aside to lie on a mattress of maggots, swaddled in a blanket of worms. Turn this world into a bridge over which you cross, my son, but on which you must never build. The living are but passersby on their way to Judgment."

Like a blind man proud of his blindness, Ka'b never saw the point of a beautiful building. A permanent one, built of stone, was the gravest sin:

"What! Would you alter the structure of the universe!"

The Rock, which had honed and tested my father's mettle, left him saddled with a vision that so encompassed the world that he lost touch with everything else around him. Perfection of the life is better than that of the work, taught the man whose own life's work had dissipated like sand between his fingers.

For years I took for granted that, by not leaving behind anything new, or any kind of imitation of Him, the scroll of my good deeds would outweigh the bad. I lived quietly, honoring through my bookbinding only that which was given to men by God. I tended to my business, just waiting to be ensnared by the Decree from which there is no refuge—until a son of Umayya came along, wanting to be regaled with my father's stories.

I do not share in Abd al-Malik's conceit that due consideration of His first Work would admit me into the Almighty's good graces on the Day. A man does not enter Paradise just because he has painted his own picture of it. But, perhaps by returning to childhood's stories of Paradise one can enhance his sense of its mystery. Whenever I start to worry about whether or not I did the right thing in serving a Caliph whose intentions were not mine, I recall what David and Solomon built around Abraham's deed on the ordinary-looking mountain summit above which I placed my Dome. It was not easy translating that story into permanence. I had to work the earth of my heart, in the place where the struggle against weeds is first felt as a pain in the knees and back.

The Father of Faith was asked to kill his favorite on a rugged and distant mountaintop in complete isolation. He was asked to kill with no hope of being understood by those nearest and dearest to him, knowing that no one could possibly benefit from what he was about to do. He did not protest God's justice as he had done in the case of the destruction of Sodom and Gomorrah. Throughout his ordeal, he was silent, resolved, completely resigned. Of all the different places to undergo such an ordeal, Moriah's Rock was the unlikeliest. And of all the different ways of doing God's will, Ishaq's was the hardest.

The blood of the ram would have mingled with that of my namesake; it would have run down the gently tilting face of the Rock, inside the lines and down the perforations of its craggy surface. As it spread, the blood changed that which it was washing over. The blood of my namesake, the first martyr to true Belief, is not about the loss of life; like the Dome I was resolved to build, it is about the birth of new meaning: bright red blood coagulating to dark black, delineating the boundaries of a new holiness.

But what is left of that new beginning, of that original act of foundation? The wood upon which Abraham was to sacrifice Ishaq was consumed in the fire along with the ram; the rope with which Ishaq was tied up has rotted, the knife long since been lost.

That leaves only the Rock.

Only the Rock to remind us of a fragile string of feelings and traditions. The Rock: last surviving trace of horror's resolution into ecstasy. The Rock: sole surviving witness to the passions that have driven men to become little Abrahams on this mountaintop over and over again.

What happens to an otherwise benign piece of the landscape when it is converted into an executioner's bench, and then into an instrument for the working of that great force of change, memory? Its ordinariness is unmade before our eyes, all its prior meanings annihilated.

Can the children of Abraham, the one taken by God for His Friend, afford to forget such an annihilation, or continue to pray with their backs to the greatest Enigma, an act for which they will surely have to account one day? And if a man does not pray with his back to the Rock, is it enough for him to eat figs in its shade, entrusting himself to God's will?

My patrimony came burdened with the problem of direction, the inheritance of a whole generation, all of whom were born to converts in an age of conversions.

Building taught me that Ka'b was wrong: True Faith is not a precondition for coming to God. Good works are. If there is a difference between other men and women of the Book who advocate commendable attitudes and do good deeds and we who have the True Faith, it is that we are in duty bound to show greater gentleness, forgiveness, and tolerance. Otherwise, in His eyes, we are all the same.

Say you: We believe in God, and
in that which has been sent down on us
and sent down on Abraham, Ishmael,
Isaac and Jacob, and the Tribes,
and that which was given to Moses and Jesus
and the prophets, of their Lord;
We make no division between any of them, and
To Him we surrender.

I, Ishaq son of Ka'b, born Jacob of Judah, believe that we have a duty to remember and honor both the submission of the Father and the submission of the Son on this Rock. Time is irredeemable. The Lord of Creation sees our end in our beginning. Abraham's deadly seriousness stood a witless world on its head. Fused with my namesake's merit, it forged mankind's most sublime act of submission. And submission is at the core of what Muhammad preached.

I have ensured that the true legacy of the man who happened to be my father will no longer be forgotten. Not that the old curmudgeon will ever thank me for it. The Lord of Creation will do that before he ever will. But it was his unworldliness in the end that brought the Dome of the Rock into the world. It is his lore that allowed me to shape a stone so beautifully it will stand until the

End of Time as a reproof to men's penchant for forgetfulness and smallmindedness.

The Dome of the Rock was a kind of solution. Through the hands and the eyes, connections often become visible to the heart where, before, words had reaped only confusion and division.

The decision to build may begin out of anger, spite, vanity, or even sweetness. But to succeed at it requires reaching beyond such motives to a moment of tranquillity when, by the grace of God, one is able to see the forms in which His words can once again be heard.

Intention sits at the heart of Judgment. Abraham will be judged, not for what he did, but for what he intended to do. I, on the other hand, served a Caliph whose wars and vanities were not mine. Do the merits of what I built outweigh Abd al-Malik's intentions?

God knows everything that was in my heart. He culled a building out of me that outweighs those intentions to call upon Time's two extremes—creation and annihilation. The Rock does not belong to the followers of Moses any more than it belongs to the followers of Muhammad. First and foremost, it is His Rock, to which He will return on the Day when all motives will have dissolved into nothingness and a new reality will have unfolded in which will be exposed the whole slew of intentions that have shaped our destiny from the moment Adam ate of the forbidden fruit.

In the Name of God the Merciful
the Compassionate

The gentle Muhammad was sent to fold his wings in tenderness over the Believers and warn them that the beginning of the end will come as a terrible breakdown in the proper order and comportment of people and animals. Sedition, defilement, and fornication within genders and across species will be the rule. For seven years there will have been no leader in prayer worthy of a following, and not a soul will have visited the Dome.

On the morning of the last day of the seventh year, men and women shall rise to discover that the Ka'ba has disappeared without a trace. They will turn to their Holy Books only to discover that the text has evaporated from the page, leaving glistening white parchment. Not a letter will have been left behind. The memory of God's Book will have been blotted out of all hearts. Not a word shall be remembered. For their amusement, men will have returned to the songs and tales of the Age of Ignorance.

If they see a sign they turn away and say,
"A continuous sorcery!"

Like seeds buried in the earth, all the teachings of the Holy Book have to rot in order to bear fruit once again.

When people are so far gone that they eat like cows, when piety has given way to pride and truth to lies, when usury, adultery, and fornication on the street are customary, when people's hearts have become wolflike, then will a Divinely Guided One come to herald the end of the world.

"How soon will He come?" the people of Jerusalem ask.

"Three things catch men unawares," I reply. "A found article, a scorpion, and the coming of the Divinely Guided One."

"How will we know whose staff to follow?"

"His nose will have an aquiline shape. His head will be bald. He will be from the family of the Prophet with a pedigree in the Yemen on His maternal side."

"Where will He come?"

"To the Rock. You will find Him preaching in the Dome."

Redemption will follow His coming like a dawn breaking on the horizon. At first, it will barely be visible; then it will shine forth more brightly. Afterwards, it will break forth in all its glory.

As the Divinely Guided One gains dominion among Believers, He will rule among the People of the Torah according to their uncorrupted Torah, and among the People of the Gospel according to their uncorrupted Gospel, and among the People of the Quran according to His Last Words spoken in Arabic. He will restore the world to the way it was before the onset of sedition, civil war, and corruption. The earth will bring forth its fruit for everyone. No man will have to hoard or steal. Whenever a man will get up and say, "O Divinely Guided One, give me," He will answer, "Help yourself!" Then he will die, a sign that

The Hour has drawn nigh: the moon is split.

The Hour will be announced by the Master of the Horn.

"Who is the Master of the Horn?" people want to know.

"A winged angel carrying a trumpet."

"Where will he stand?"

"On that corner of the Rock," I reply, pointing to an elevated *spot due north of the stone mass, facing which today on the northern arcade is a sumptuously decorated entrance into the Dome called the "Gate of the Master of the Horn."*

The sound of the horn will be louder and more terrible than thunder; it will pierce the mind and transfix the soul. Upon hearing the horn, every living creature shall taste death's bitterness. The angel will blow the trumpet on God's command, announcing the Hour of Annihilation when all things perish except His face,

When the sun shall be darkened
when the stars shall be thrown down,
when the mountains shall be set moving,
when the pregnant camels shall be neglected,
when the savage beasts shall be mustered,
when the seas shall be set boiling,
when the scrolls shall be unrolled,
when Heaven shall be stripped off,
when Hell shall be set blazing,
when Paradise shall be brought nigh,
when the souls shall be coupled,
and the buried infant shall be asked for what sin she was slain.

~

A second time the trumpet will blow, and God will bring forth the living from the dead as He brings death to the living. Flesh, which in this life decays and rots inside the earth, will turn as fresh as that of a newborn's still dripping from its mother's fluids.

Thrown out of their tombs, throngs of corpses as numerous as particles of sand will swarm hither and thither like flies, all quickened in the blink of an eye. Conjoined with their souls, released from their place of confinement inside the mountain, they will race pell-mell toward the place of their gathering, where the most remarkable sight shall unfold:

Two enormous crowds will gather separately—one destined for

Paradise, the other for Hell. Both will have to pass through the Gate of Paradise in the Dome of the Rock on their way to the next life. Opposite this Gate, God will have created a bridge narrower than a hair and sharper than a sword. It will stretch over the roaring flames of Hell. The faces of those destined for Paradise will be smiling, joyful, and brimming with hope; they will cross the bridge in the twinkle of an eye. The faces of the Wicked will be veiled in darkness and covered in dust; they will fall into fire everlasting.

Two crowds assembled in the knowledge that each can no longer grow, not by one person, not even at the other's expense as they have been doing since the time of Cain and Abel. Everyone—Jews, Christians, Muslims, prophets, martyrs, saviors, unbelievers—even the angels—will be in one or the other crowd, which, together, will contain the sum of all generations who have been, or ever will be, born.

∾

*F*ollowing *the motion and commotion of the gathering comes the unbearable silence of the Standing.*

Each person stands for the very first and the very last time in the same seamless white shroud of death. For just as one may not look upon the Black Stone unless dressed in such clothes, so after death one may not look at the Rock unless one's dress stamps upon its bearer the character of a particle of sand.

"Where will we be standing?"

"In circles around the stillness upon which He stood during Creation. The Rock graced by its Dome will be all that is left of a turning world. For the first to be created is the last to be destroyed. The Day of Annihilation will unfold in reverse of Creation. Only the Rock will hold for the duration of the Reckoning. Afterwards, even it will be annihilated."

"How long will we stand?"

"Time past and time future have already collapsed into time present. The Standing lasts an eternity."

"Will He come?"

"Veiled like the overcast sky."

"Upon which hallowed spot will He alight?"

"His foot will descend upon the spot from which it last ascended in anger and disappointment."

"What will we be thinking?"

"Of Him who made and destroyed you. Of the imminence of the danger that looms. You will stand with faces cast down, your souls suspended in astonishment, transfixed by apprehension, not in community or any kind of sympathy with one another, but one by one, alone—utterly and completely alone."

*N*ever has there been, or will there ever be again, such loneliness, such single-minded preoccupation with the possibility of eternal pain. Never has there been such a breakdown of every confining partition of the mind so as to keep everyone who has ever been born wholly transfixed on the consequences of his own selfishness.

From Creation to Judgment turns the wheel of all Believers. From time past to time future, it spins around the still axis of the universe. It turns in the direction of what will happen at the moment that He, among whose ninety-nine names are the Avenger, the Dominator, the Abaser, the Exalter, and the Merciful, will alight upon the Rock.

The face-to-face encounter with the Judge of all Judges will be like tumbling down into a bottomless chasm. It will be like being lost in the vast expanse of a starlit desert, listening to the howling of hungry wolves. Looking to the Rock, every person who has ever been born shall be struck by Terror as though by a thunderbolt from the sky, a terror that is the ruling principle of the Sublime.

And what shall teach thee
what is the Day of Judgment?
A day when no soul shall possess the slightest power to help
another;
a day when all Power is God's alone.

A Historical Note on Ka'b and the Rock

The most holy spot on earth is Syria; the most
holy spot in Syria is Palestine; the most holy spot
in Palestine is Jerusalem; the most holy spot in
Jerusalem is the Mountain; the most holy spot on
the Mountain is the place of worship, and the most
holy spot on the place of worship is the Dome.[1]

T he author of this passage, Abu Khalid Thawr ibn Yazid al-Kala'i,
lived in Homs, Syria, in the eighth century. The Dome to which he refers
was built over a rock on the *Haram al-Sharif,* the Noble Sanctuary,
known to Jews as the Temple Mount, in the year 692. Written in mosaic
on the Dome's interior surfaces, in some of the finest craftsmanship of
the period, are the oldest verses of the Quran in existence. In fact, with
the exception of some foundations and some coins, little else remains
that is indubitably Muslim and of the seventh century to hint at the great
encounter that took place between Muslims, Christians, and Jews in
Jerusalem. To be sure, there were manuscripts and artifacts produced
during that remarkable century of turmoil and change. But they are
lost or destroyed and survive only through recollections in later documents—works of history, geography, and biography written at least a
century after the Arab conquest of Jerusalem, which took place sometime after 634 and before 638.

As it so happens there were three holy rocks in the seventh century,
not one. And to each rock corresponded a Temple: The Rock of Calvary
had its Church of the Holy Sepulcher; the Black Stone had its Ka'ba in

---

[1] Cited by Ibn Asakir in his *Ta'rikh Madinat Dimashq,* and al-Wasiti in his *Fada'il al-
Bayt al-Muqaddas.* I have used the citation by Joseph van Ess in his invaluable article
"Abd al-Malik and the Dome of the Rock," in *Bayt al-Maqdis: Abd al-Malik's Jerusalem,*
edited by Julian Raby and Jeremy Johns (Oxford: Oxford University Press, 1992).

Mecca; and then there is our own story's Dome of the Rock, whose builders may have thought they were rebuilding Solomon's Temple, the first Temple of the Hebrews destroyed by the Babylonian king Nebuchadnezzar in 597 B.C.E.

Three is a curious number in human relations. Jews and Muslims have an aversion to it. And yet Islam, the third great monotheism, saw its mission as one of healing the damage caused by the previous division into two. During the time frame of our story, 630–692, the fortunes of these three Rocks waxed and waned at one another's expense. At the heart of this competition were the big questions of life, death, and the shape of the afterlife. The story has attracted many great scholars over the centuries. But, unfortunately, no amount of scholarship will be able to do it justice. We know too little. So much has been irretrievably lost.

In the preceding pages, fiction has stepped into the breach—a fiction of assembly. A variety of stories culled from the literature of three religious traditions have been put together like a mosaic. With few exceptions, I have not allowed myself the liberty of changing the original sources from which the pieces were taken (the exceptions have to do with language, continuity, and the modification of a detail in order to eliminate repetition and confusion). Still, the outcome is unmistakably fiction, mimicking the assembly of a building to a new plan using the detritus of greatly esteemed predecessors as its raw material—predecessors that were designed to celebrate the same much-revered site.

This way of making stories corresponds to that of the chief protagonist of this book, a seventh-century learned man and former Jew (perhaps even an ex-rabbi), Ka'b al-Ahbar, who accompanied the Muslim caliph Umar ibn al-Khattab during his conquest of Jerusalem. Muslim tradition has preserved accounts of the events that occurred during the week or so that Umar spent in Jerusalem, many of which have been integrated into the text and can be found in the sources. Perhaps they are not enough to prove that the historical Ka'b was as taken with the Rock on Mount Moriah as I have made him out to be. But then I make no claim that this is how things actually were—just that they are in accordance with the sources as I have chosen to thread my way through them.

Jewish and Christian sources tell us nothing about Ka'b. The little that we know comes from Islamic literature in which Ka'b occupies a rather shadowy place (highly respected growing to deeply compromised in later sources). As far as anyone can judge, Ka'b is the oldest authority among Muslims on Jewish scripture. Mu'awiya, the founder of the Umayyad Caliphate and a contemporary of Ka'b, is cited by the highly respected compiler of traditions Bukhari as saying that Ka'b "possessed knowledge like fruit, but we were remiss in relating it from him." Mu'awiya also said that Ka'b was "the most reliable of those transmitters [of traditions] who relate on the authority of the People of the Book, but in spite of this we used to test him for falsehood."[2]

Notice the circumspection in the second half of the sentence. Was this a later addition to what Mu'awiya said? Or was it present in how Ka'b was viewed by his contemporaries? The highly respected compiler of historical anecdotes, al-Tabari, reports that Ka'b refused to become Mu'awiya's counselor in Damascus.[3] Perhaps there was a personal grievance between the two men. The sources do not allow for certainty in such matters. The task I set myself was to make allowances for both possibilities while sticking to the "fact" that Mu'awiya, and after him his protégé Abd al-Malik, clearly held Ka'b in very high regard.

Ka'b is said to have died in Syria, at the extremely unlikely age of one hundred and four, during the reign of the third Muslim Caliph, Uthman ibn Affan (644–656).[4] On the basis of traditions transmitted orally for at least a century before being recorded, Ka'b was an Arabic-speaking Yemenite who arrived in Medina around the time of the Prophet's death. According to one version of events, he is said to have accepted the prophecy of Muhammad during the Caliphate of Abu Bakr (632–634). Allegiance to Muhammad as God's Messenger was all that conversion to Islam entailed during those years.[5]

But what kind of a Muslim did that make Ka'b? After all, all Muslims were converts of one sort or another in those early days. Was Ka'b a Believer in Allah and in His Messenger with all that later generations of Muslims read into that statement? Or was he a dissembler, a fraud, and an opportunist, as has been claimed by Western scholars and modern

---

[2] Cited in G. H. A. Juynboll, *The Authenticity of the Tradition Literature: Discussions in Modern Egypt* (Leiden: E. J. Brill, 1969), p. 123.

[3] See Muhammad ibn Jarir al-Tabari's *Ta'rikh al-Rusul wa'l-Muluk* (History of the Prophets and Kings), vol. 3, *The Children of Israel* (New York: State University of New York Press, 1991), pp. 2474–5.

[4] On Ka'b's age, see EI2 and Moshe Perlmann, "Another Ka'b al-Ahbar Story," in *The Jewish Quarterly Review* 45–46 (1954–1956), pp. 48–58.

[5] See W. Montgomery Watt, "Conversion in Islam at the Time of the Prophet," in *Early Islam: Collected Articles* (Edinburgh: Edinburgh University Press, 1990). The elastic nature of Jewish–Muslim allegiances during this period can also be adduced from early Jewish apocalyptic writings, an example of which I attribute to Ka'b in "The Conquest Foretold."

Islamists alike?[6] The difference between such characterizations is not in the sources; it is in the eye of the beholder. I have tried to straddle both views to some extent, leaving it to readers to make up their minds as they interpret the facts laid out by the narrator of this book—Ishaq, Ka'b's son, a practicing Muslim and true Believer by anyone's standard (and about whom nothing exists in the sources other than a reference to Ka'b as "Abu Ishaq," the father of Isaac).

The license to invent or to imaginatively fill in gaps is in part justi-fied by the impossibility of separating the historical figure of Ka'b from the legends that have been woven around him. Nonetheless, he does seem to have inspired confidence in those who met him and greatly esteemed Muslim writers of later centuries. Al-Jahiz, for instance, in his *Kitab al-Hayawan*, considered him trustworthy and rose to his defense on the question of interpreting the Pentateuch. Al-Kisa'i, as well, in his *Qisas Al-Anbiya'*, attributes many legends to Ka'b, including those sur-rounding the prophet Joseph, among the most colorful and erotic in Muslim tradition.[7]

What exactly did Ka'b do? It is probably safe to conclude that he was a *qassas*, or popular storyteller and preacher, a forerunner in the genre of storytelling that later produced such great works as *One Thou-sand and One Nights*. Ka'b's vocation, its fortune and reputation, fluctu-ated over the centuries, combining as it did exegesis of sacred writings, soaring flights of imagination, and outright charlatanism. There is every reason to think that Ka'b took his storytelling as seriously as his listen-ers, for whom it was a way of dealing with the great metaphysical ques-tions of existence. Ka'b, after all, had the reputation of being a very wise man. But so have many scoundrels in the past.

Ka'b dealt in a genre of stories known as *Isra'iliyat* (Judaica), which eventually fell into disrepute and were frowned upon by Muslim schol-ars. Even though Ka'b had been dead for at least a century by the time such distrust became widespread, traces of it probably existed during his lifetime. Indeed, it would be surprising if this were not the case.

---

[6] Guy Le Strange is among the pioneering scholars of Islam who, without explanation, writes that Ka'b was "a great liar" who "considerably gulled the simple-minded Arabs of the first century." See *Palestine Under the Moslems: A Description of Syria and the Holy Land from 650 to 1500* (Original edition is 1890. Reprinted by Khayats, Beirut, 1965), p. 142.

[7] Muhammad ibn Abdallah al-Kisa'i, in his *Qisas al-Anbiya'* (Tales of the Prophets), probably written around the end of the eleventh century; see the translation by Wheeler M. Thackston (Chicago, Ill.: Great Books of the Islamic World, 1997).

Ka'b's storytelling methods have to be gleaned from partial references in a wide variety of Muslim sources. I imagine our hero cobbling together the Bible, the Quran, rabbinical literature, Southern Arabian oral and folk lore, his personal likes and dislikes, and, above all, what he felt his audience wanted to hear. I think of the historical Ka'b as an entertaining rogue, a man with an agenda but also one who liked playing to the gallery. His modus operandi, not his truthfulness, is what makes his contribution to the raucous and imaginatively wide-open world of early Islam so invaluable. In its early years, Islam needed men like him to flesh out its appeal, because such men knew how to ground the Prophet's message in a larger cultural framework than that of Mecca and Bedouin Arabia. This contribution of marginals like Ka'b, Wahb ibn Munabbih, and others, has largely gone unappreciated by modern Muslims in part out of a fear that such acknowledgment might undermine the authenticity of their faith. Acting on that same misplaced impulse, a senior Palestinian negotiator asked his Israeli counterpart in the summer of 2000 how he knew that his Temple had been located on the Haram. Not only are such fears belied by the whole premodern corpus of Muslim tradition, they make total nonsense of it.

The unambiguous evidence is that early Muslims were ardent seekers of Jewish lore and scriptural interpretations. Long before the advent of Islam, Christian writers were commenting on the affinity between the beliefs of the Arabs and the Jews. We know from Bukhari that, in Muhammad's time, Jews used to read the Torah in Hebrew and interpret it to the Prophet's followers in Arabic.[8] However, starting in the eighth century, the doctrine that the Old and New Testaments had been corrupted by Jews and Christians, respectively, was developed. Muslims were discouraged from reading them. This later Muslim doctrine crops up in different versions of the story of Ka'b's conversion, confirming their implausibility. Over time it developed into the idea that the "People of the Book" should not even be taught the Quran (for fear, presumably, that they would corrupt God's words in the way that they had corrupted their own Holy Books).

The apogee of this school of thought is the modern idea that some converts, like Ka'b, were subverters of Islam from within. In 1946 an

---

[8] Cited in the "Introduction" to Gordon D. Newby, *The Making of the Last Prophet: A Reconstruction of the Earliest Biography of Muhammad* (Columbia, S.C.: University of South Carolina Press, 1989), p. 12.

article was published entitled "Ka'b al-Ahbar, the First Zionist." The author, Abu Rayya, a disciple of the Islamo-Arabist leader Rashid Rida (1865–1935), set out to prove that Ka'b had been involved in a conspiracy to murder the caliph Umar.[9] The article was heavily criticized by fellow Egyptians and is by no means representative of all Muslim theologians and scholars. But it is suggestive of the new wounded and defensive mindset that was to surface with the creation of the State of Israel and the escalation of the Arab–Israeli conflict.[10]

The most delightful thing about Ka'b, from my point of view, is that, in telling stories about the summit of Mount Moriah in Jerusalem, he did not favor one source or religious tradition over another. Like Ka'b, I ardently hope that my readers have a difficult time discerning whether a given tale in this book, or a particular detail of one, is Jewish, Muslim, or Christian in origin. Nor would Ka'b have dreamt of telling the story of Jerusalem's most famous rock by adherence only to what was undoubtedly authentic about it. Authenticity, as far as he and this book are concerned, has nothing to do with historical fact, or quarrelling about "who came first"; it is a quality established by age and by a certain deference to age. In any case, fact-finding scholarship already exists, scattered in hundreds of excellent books. Ka'b, as I have portrayed him, was engaged in a different kind of enterprise.

He was seeking to interpret the human significance acquired over time by a piece of the natural world. Perhaps, from our modern point of view, the mysteries of the godhead are an odd angle from which to pursue such a search. At least he was doing so in search of a foundation, a common ground, upon which to stand and engage the whole world, and not just one little parochial part of it.

But why would he do so on a rock, and what could he have known about a seemingly innocuous piece of the Jerusalem landscape, living as he did in the Yemen, an arduous month's journey away?

[9] For a full discussion of Abu Rayya's argument, see G. H. A. Juynboll, *The Authenticity of the Tradition Literature: Discussions in Modern Egypt* (Leiden: E. J. Brill, 1969), pp. 129–133.

[10] A modern Muslim work of scholarship on Jerusalem that illustrates this wounded mindset is *Bayt Al-Maqdis wa Al-Masjid Al-Aqsa*, by Muhammad Muhammad Hasan Shurab (Damascus, 1994).

It is plausible to think that Ka'b knew and perhaps even taught a passage like the following from the Midrash Tanhuma, written in the third century:

> Just as the navel is found at the center of a human being, so the land of Israel is found at the center of the world. Jerusalem is at the center of the land of Israel, and the Temple is at the center of Jerusalem, the Holy of Holies is at the center of the Temple, the Ark is at the center of the Holy of Holies, and the Foundation Stone is in front of the Ark, which is the point of Foundation of the world.[11]

At any rate, somebody like him, perhaps even one of his students, had to have passed it on to Abu Khalid, whom I cited at the outset of this essay, and who died in Jerusalem in the third quarter of the eighth century.

The name "Rock (or Stone) of Foundation" also appears in the form of this early midrashic recollection of the duties of the high priest inside the Holy of Holies during the days of the Herodian Temple:

> When he [the high priest of the Temple] reached the Ark he put the fire-pan between the two bars. He heaped up the incense on the coals and the whole place became filled up with smoke. He came out the way he went in, and in the outer space he prayed a short prayer. He did not prolong his prayer lest he put Israel in terror. After the Ark was taken away a stone remained there from the time of the early prophets and it was called *Shetiyah* (Foundation). On this he used to put [the fire-pan].[12]

The rock appears to have grown in importance from the simple, physical description of the Midrash Yoma to the thunderous cosmic implications of the Midrash Tanhuma. If so, why?

The question is even more interesting when one considers that there is no unambiguous linkage between the *Even Shetiyah* of Jewish

---

[11] Cited in John M. Lundquist, *The Temple: Meeting Place of Heaven and Earth* (London: Thames and Hudson, 1993), p. 7. With adjustments, and with no particular source to base myself upon, this passage has been put into the mouth of Ka'b al-Ahbar at the conclusion of "The Rock of Foundation."

[12] Yoma 5:2 in the Mishna, as cited in F. E. Peters' anthology, *Jerusalem: The Holy City in the Eyes of Chroniclers, Visitors, Pilgrims, and Prophets from the Days of Abraham to Modern Times* (Princeton, N.J.: Princeton University Press, 1985), pp. 29–30.

tradition—soon to become the *Sakhra* of Muslim tradition—and the Bible. Ka'b could not have relied on the Bible alone to arrive at his conviction that the rock that Umar and he had uncovered on the Temple Mount was the place of Adam's fall and burial, the site of Abraham's sacrifice, the threshing floor of Ornan the Jebusite, and the place where David prayed to avert God's wrath, as well as being a part of Solomon's Temple.[13] He needed to know the work of the rabbis in the first centuries of the Common Era, for they are the ones who first established the link between the rock and these stories. Because of them, the rock was elevated to prominence, and only then was its role rationalized backward into the whole corpus of stories with which Ka'b regales his son and Umar ibn al-Khattab. And how could that not be the case? After all, why should anyone want to magnify the significance of a piece of rock when a perfectly magnificent temple was sitting right on top of it (until it was destroyed in the year 135, it hid the rock from view)?

Describing the outcome of that final act of destruction in 135, the third-century Greek historian Dio Cassius wrote:

> Very few Jews survived; Julius Severus took fifty of their most notable forts, 985 of their villages were laid in ruins, and 580,000 men were slain in skirmishes and battles, while the number of those who perished by starvation, plague, or fire cannot be reckoned. Thus almost the whole of Judea was laid to waste, even as had been foretold to its people before the war. For Solomon's tomb, which they regard as one of their holy places, fell to pieces and was scattered abroad of its own accord, and many wolves and hyenas came howling into their cities. Many of the Romans also perished in this war. . . . [14]

How were the rabbis, who, along with the Temple, were in danger of losing their reason for existence, to deal with such a catastrophe? They were living in an age in which the channel of prophecy, as Alan Mintz puts it, was closed. "The only possible response was reading."[15]

---

[13] The relevant biblical citations are: Genesis 22; I Chronicles 3:1; I Chronicles 21:14–17; and I Kings 5–7. Oleg Grabar makes this point in his important essay "The Umayyad Dome of the Rock in Jerusalem," *Ars Orientalis* 3 (1959), p. 38.

[14] From F. E. Peters in his *Jerusalem: The Holy City in the Eyes of Chroniclers, Visitors, Pilgrims, and Prophets from the Days of Abraham to Modern Times* (Princeton, N.J.: Princeton University Press, 1985), p. 127.

[15] See "Midrash and the Destruction" in Alan Mintz, *Hurban: Responses to Catastrophe in Hebrew Literature* (Syracuse, N.Y.: Syracuse University Press, 1996), p. 50.

A curious example of how biblical texts were read and reread in that period is found in a midrashic story pertaining to the site of the Temple after its destruction (which does not mention the rock directly):

> Long ago as Rabban Gamliel, R. Eleazar b. 'Azariah, R. Joshua and R. Akiba were . . . coming up to Jerusalem together, and just as they came to Mount Scopus they saw a fox emerging from the Holy of Holies. They fell a-weeping [; only] R. Akiba seemed merry. "Wherefore," said they to him, "are you merry?" Said he: "Wherefore are you weeping?" Said they to him: "A place of which it was once said, And the common man that draweth nigh shall be put to death, is now become the haunt of foxes, and should we not weep?" Said he to them: "Therefore am I merry; for . . . so long as Uriah's prophecy [of doom] had not had its fulfillment, I had misgivings lest Zechariah's prophecy [of happiness] might not be fulfilled; now that Uriah's prophecy has been fulfilled [by the destruction of the Temple], it is quite certain that Zechariah's prophecy also is to find its fulfillment." Said they to him: "Akiba, you have comforted us! Akiba you have comforted us!"[16]

Akiba's laughter would not have comforted for long, and certainly not to less learned men and women,[17] who needed a less abstract and more tangible response to the loss of their most precious symbol.

I conjecture that the edification and glorification of the rock in traditions passed on to the Arabs by men like Ka'b began as such a response to total catastrophe. There it was, after all, the last remnant of what the rabbis believed had been the Temple, poking out of the ruins as a kind of proof that at least one indomitable thing remained of Israel's former glory. Perhaps the rock actually dominated the platform once the walls of the Temple had been torn down, being the highest point of Mount Moriah and rising above the ground floor of the highest level in the Temple, the Holy of Holies, according to the evidence of Yoma.

But this is speculation. One cannot be sure. We do not even know if the rock had actually ever been part of the Temple structure. But some-

---

[16] Makkoth 24a. I am indebted to my student Jonathan Stern for finding this story.

[17] The same Rabbi Akiba was a spiritual leader of the Bar Kochba revolt (132–135). He was brutally executed by the Romans a few years after the events. He was, therefore, in the story I have just cited, justifying his own people's defeat in a fashion common to revolutionaries of all ideological persuasions.

thing happened to elevate the importance of this particular bit of Jerusalem's stony landscape. Of that there can be no doubt, because in the year 333 primitive little rituals had grown around the rock, as observed by an anonymous visitor known only as "the Pilgrim of Bordeaux":

> In the sanctuary itself, where the Temple stood which Solomon built, there is marble in front of the altar which has on it the blood of Zacharias—you would think it had only been shed today. All around you can see the marks of the hobnails of the soldiers who killed him, as plainly as if they had been pressed into wax. Two statues of Hadrian stand there, and, not far from them, a pierced stone which the Jews come and anoint each year. They mourn and rend their garments, and then depart.[18]

Hadrian had banned any kind of Jewish presence in Jerusalem. The ban was renewed by Constantine. Jerome, the biblical scholar who lived in Palestine and wrote toward the end of the fourth century, noted that an exception was made for one day of the year:

> Silently they come and silently they go, weeping they come and weeping they go, in the dark night they come and in the dark night they go. . . . Not even weeping is free to them. You see on the day of the destruction of Jerusalem a sad people coming, decrepit little women and old men encumbered with rags and years, exhibiting both in their bodies and their dress the wrath of the Lord. A crowd of pitiable creatures assembles and under the gleaming gibbet of the Lord and his sparkling resurrection, and before a brilliant banner with a cross waving from the Mount of Olives, they weep over the ruins of the Temple; and yet they are not worthy of pity. Thus they lament on their knees with livid arms and disheveled hair, while the guards demand their reward for permitting them to shed some more tears.[19]

---

[18] From John Wilkinson's translation in *Egeria's Travels to the Holy Land* (Jerusalem: Ariel Publishing House, 1981), pp. 156–157.

[19] From Jerome's commentary on Zephaniah 1:15, which has been put into Sophronius's words in "Finding the Cross." Here, I have cited the translation used in Thomas I. Idinopulos, *Jerusalem Blessed, Jerusalem Cursed* (Chicago: Ivan R. Dee, 1991), pp. 100–101.

This is how things remained at the site of the former Temple until the arrival of about four thousand Bedouins headed by the caliph Umar ibn al-Khattab, accompanied by his learned councilor and expert on the holy sites of Jerusalem, Ka'b al-Ahbar, formerly a Jew from the Yemen named Jacob or perhaps Akiba, son of Mati.[20]

---

[20] On the names of Ka'b, see Israel Wolfensohn's dissertation *Ka'b al-Ahbar und seine Stellung im Hadit und der Islamischen Legendenliteratur* (Frankfurt, Germany: J. W. Goethe University, 1933). I am indebted to Chris Berdik for providing me with translations from parts of this work.

Sources

I once read somewhere that sources in a book are like dead ghosts inhabiting an empty house; their presence is what gives meaning to every stick and stone in the edifice. It matters hardly a jot whether or not you believe in ghosts. All that matters is that someone at some point in time did. As the majority of my sources are at least a century—more often than not, several centuries—removed from the events they describe, the use of a particular fragment, or record of a deed, can hardly be justified by its correspondence to historical fact alone (at least not by me). All that is required of a source from this book's point of view is that it be plausible, even as an invention that might have been in circulation in the seventh century, and that it have found resonance with me. Where I have erred or indulged in anachronism—and I am sure that I have, for my purposes are not history—I have broken the rules that I set for myself for constructing this story.

It is not always easy for readers to discern from the narrative whether a given story, or a particular detail within a story, or even a passage of scripture is Jewish, Muslim, or Christian in origin. This was the way things were in Ka'b's time and place, if not in ours. Such ambiguities are hopefully resolved in the essay on sources below. Sources are identified in full at their first occurrence; thereafter, the author's name is used, alone or with an abbreviated title for those authors with more than one work cited. If a source is used for the same purpose in more than one location in the book (for example, the various descriptions of seventh-century Jerusalem), then it is not repeated. Scripture is italicized, as are some passages of a prophetic or apocalyptic nature (for example, in the opening and closing pages). For citations from the Quran, I have used the numbering of A. J. Arberry in *The Koran Interpreted* (New York, 1996), with occasional modifications of the translation. For many of the events of this story, it should be noted, the Quran was not yet codified and compiled into its final form.

In the Name of God . . .

The opening italicized passages are adapted from the Quran (13:15, 16:4, 30:21) and the tenth-century historian and exegete Muhammad ibn Jarir al-Tabari's introduction to his multivolume commentary on the Quran, *Jami' al-Bayan 'an Ta'wil ay al-Qur'an* (Bulaq, 1905).

The Creation story draws from Tabari's multivolume *Ta'rikh al-Rusul wa'l-Muluk, History of the Prophets and Kings*, the English translation of which put out by the State University of New York Press I shall henceforth refer to as Tabari's *History*. See *General Introduction and From Creation to the Flood*. vol. I, (1989). The tradition that light and darkness were the first creations is attributed to Ibn Ishaq, the eighth-century biographer of the Prophet.

The story of Adam is based on the Muslim version, which incorporates many nonbiblical elements drawn from Jewish and Christian tradition. See *"Khalq," Encyclopaedia of Islam* (Leiden: E. J. Brill), henceforth *EI2*. Jewish tradition tells of the clay used to shape Adam's body in the *Targum Yerushalmi* to Genesis 2:7 and the *Sanhedrin* 38a. The beauty and length of the body are mentioned in the Quran 95:4, as well as in Jewish sources (*Sanhedrin* 38b; *Bereshit Rabba* 8:1, 12:6). Tabari's recounting of the story of Adam can be found in his *History*, vol. I. The bowing of the angels before Adam, except Iblis (Satan), is from the Quran (15:26–38); Iblis's reply to Adam later on in the chapter is an interpretation attributed to the Sufi mystics Junayd and Hallaj. The importance in Muslim tradition of the first Arabic letter, *alif*, is discussed in Edward Lane's *Arabic–English Lexicon* (Cambridge: The Islamic Texts Society, 1984). The reference to a fiery garment of light and the significance of Adam's fall can be found in *The Zohar*; Gershom Scholem discusses *The Zohar*'s emphasis on the fall of Adam in his *Major Trends in Jewish Mysticism* (Schocken Publishing House, 1941). The story of Eve's creation from Adam's shortest and most crooked left rib is from the ninth-century collector of "sound" tradition, Muhammad al-Bukhari. See his *Sahih al-Bukhari* (Cairo, 1969). That God ascended from the rock to Heaven after the Creation is in Abu Bakr al-Wasiti's eleventh-century *Fada'il al-Bayt al-Muqaddas*, as cited by Nasser Rabbat, "The Meaning of the Umayyad Dome of the Rock," vol. 6, *Muqarnas*, 1989. The post-Fall status of Adam and his complaint to God are in Tabari's *History*. The conversation between the Fish and the Eagle, and the angels' burial of Adam, are from material attributed to Ibn Ishaq, as edited and translated by Gordon Darnell Newby in *The Making of the Last Prophet: A Reconstruction of the Earliest Biography of Muhammad*

(University of South Carolina Press, 1989). A later version of the story of the Fish and the Eagle is attributed to Ka'b al-Ahbar by Muhammad ibn Abdallah al-Kisa'i, in his *Qisas al-Anbiya', Tales of the Prophets;* see the translation by Wheeler M. Thackston (Great Books of the Islamic World, 1997). On the Jewish and Muslim tradition that has God rubbing Adam's back and Adam ceding fifty of the thousand years alloted to him to the prophet David, see *EI2* under *"Adam."*

Prologue

The earliest Arabic name for Jerusalem is *Madinat Bayt al-Maqdis* (or *al-Muqaddas*), which I have translated as "the City of the Temple." But it could just as well be "the City of the Holy House." *Bayt al-Maqdis* derives from the Hebrew for the Temple, *Bet ha-miqdash.* Today's Arabic name for Jerusalem, *al-Quds,* is a later derivation from *Bayt al-Maqdis.* Not until the end of the seventh century was the Temple area singled out from the rest of Jerusalem by the phrase *al-Haram al-Sharif,* the Noble Sanctuary. The narrator's reference to the Temple Mount as the place of David's repentance is based upon the Quran 38:15–24, which records that David sought the forgiveness of God by bowing and throwing himself to the ground on this site.

The best general account of Ka'b is in EI2. See also Israel Wolfensohn's dissertation *Ka'b al-Ahbar und seine Stellung im Hadit und der Islamischen Legendenliteratur* (J. W. Goethe University, 1933). The traditions of the origins of the Jews of the Yemen cited by my narrator, Ishaq, are in Reuben Ahroni's *Yemenite Jewry: Origins, Culture, and Literature* (Indiana University Press, 1968). Jeremiah's prophecy of doom that prompted the departure of the Jews is found in Jeremiah 38:2: "He who remains in this city shall die by the sword, by the famine, and by pestilence; but he who goes forth to the Chaldeans shall live." Baladhuri's view of the origin of the Jews of Arabia, in his ninth-century *Kitab Futuh al-Buldan* (Leiden, 1968), is that they settled there after the destruction of Bayt al-Maqdis by Nebuchadnezzar. The expression "the most Jewish and the most Arab of all Jews" was coined by S. D. Goitein, the scholar of medieval Jewry, as quoted in *A Mediterranean Society,* vol. 5, *The Individual* (University of California Press, 1988).

The description of the city of Jerusalem given in this and later chapters relies on Oleg Grabar's *The Shape of the Holy; Early Islamic Jerusalem* (Princeton University Press, 1996) and John Wilkinson's work based on pilgrim accounts, *Jerusalem Pilgrims Before the Crusades* (Warminster, Wilts.: Aris & Phillips, 1977). It also conforms with the most important source for the early-seventh-century city, the mosaic Madaba map in Jordan (excluding the Temple Mount area, which is hardly in evidence on the map). Throughout his narration, Ishaq uses "Mount Zion" interchangeably with "Mount Moriah" because that was Jewish tradition. See Jon Levenson's *Sinai and Zion: An Entry into the Jewish Bible* (HarperCollins, 1985). Today's Mount Zion is a different mountain altogether, to the west of Moriah.

We know nothing about what the rock looked like at the time of the Muslim conquest. The Muslim sources belong to a much later period and will be cited in relation to what Umar and Ka'b found on the site when they first arrived. Clearly, a much larger part of the rock was visible than can be seen today inside the Dome, as can be surmised from what B. Bagatti saw when the pavement surrounding the rock was removed for repair work in 1959. In different parts of the text, I have borrowed from B. Bagatti's description in his *Récherché sur le site du Temple de Jerusalem, I–VII siècle* (Jerusalem: Franciscan Printing Press, 1979).

Stories about the cave beneath the rock are found in local Jewish and Muslim folklore. Zev Vilnay's collection, *Legends of Jerusalem* (Philadelphia: Jewish Publication Society, 1973), contains many of them. A Muslim tale not found in Vilnay concerns the question of why the rock, which used to hover above its mountain, no longer does so. "One day," goes the tale, "a pregnant woman walked underneath the Rock. As soon as she reached the center of the Rock suspended above her head, she became afraid and dropped her child. So there grew around her this construction until she was safely concealed from the eyes of people." From *Al-'Uns al-Jaleel bi Ta'rikh al-Quds wa al-Khalil*, as collected in A. S. Marmarji's compilation of Arabic texts on Jerusalem, *Buldaniyah Filastin al-'Arabiyah* (Beirut, 1948). Rabbi Binyamin Lilienthal, who visited the Holy Land in 1847, had a different explanation of the origin of the walls supporting the floating Foundation Stone of Jewish tradition. He thinks Jerusalem's Turkish rulers built the walls that reach up to the Foundation Stone, which is not fastened but "is suspended above the floor." The Turks did this because "when the stone falls, it will be the sign that the Messiah comes. Therefore they have built a base and a support . . . to prevent the advent of the Messiah of Israel" (Vilnay, *Legends*).

The treasures of Solomon's Temple are thought to have been hidden inside an underground cave located beneath the cave. Local Palestinians call it *bir al-arwah*, "the well of souls." In 1911, during archaeological excavations in the City of David, at the edge of Mount Moriah, a rumor spread that English excavators had penetrated the sealed cave at night, through hidden labyrinths, and made off with the treasures. The rumor caused days of apprehension and disturbances in Jerusalem. No treasure was found.

The image of mountains as signs of God is adapted from a passage by the eleventh-century Muslim scholar al-Ghazzali, which I have since lost. The verse "We shall show them Our signs in the horizons and in themselves" is from the Quran 41:53.

The Rock of Foundation

The tradition of a midwife naming a child as she cuts the umbilical cord is an old Turkish custom recorded by Yahya ibn Sharaf al-Nawawi in *Kitab al-adhkar* (Cairo, 1894). For Ishaq's general discourse on the importance of names I have borrowed from Annemarie Schimmel's *Islamic Names* (Edinburgh University Press, 1989). Reference to the rock as a stumbling stone can be found in Isaiah 8:14. The phrase "Rock of Ages" is used in the hymn "Jesus: His Cross and His Passion," composed in 1776 by A. M. Toplady. The idea of a name as proof of excellence is based on the Arabic proverb, "A multitude of names proves the excellence of their bearer." The Quran addresses the importance of names in 49:12, "An evil name is ungodliness after belief." Names are either enveloped by a taboo or carry *baraka*, the power of blessing. The argument concerning the relationship between the name of a thing and its essence is adapted from al-Ghazzali's treatise on the ninety-nine names of God, *Fi Sharh Asma' Allah al-Husna*, translated into English by D. Burrell and N. Daher as *The Ninety-Nine Beautiful Names of God* (Cambridge: The Islamic Texts Society, 1995).

"There was no heaven, no earth, no height, no depth, no name" is the opening line of "The Babylonian Poem of Creation." See N. K. Sanders, *Poems of Heaven and Hell from Ancient Mesopotamia* (Penguin Classics, 1971). In this Creation story, which dates to the second millennium B.C.E., Babylon, Jerusalem's nemesis, is the fulcrum of the cosmos. The city is named "The House of Foundation Between Heaven and Earth," an idea later associated with Jerusalem and implied in the story of David and Ahithophel told in "The Fundaments of the Universe." The position of God on His throne upon the water during Creation is mentioned in the Quran 11:7. Tabari cites traditions he attributes to Ibn 'Abbas (who may have been Ka'b's student), which contend that God was seated on His throne above the heavenly waters before Creation and that the first thing He created was the pen. The idea of the Rock as originating as a jewel underneath God's throne is in *The Zohar;* see Vilnay, *Legends.* The words Ka'b attributes to wisdom and the idea that it was by wisdom that God founded the earth are from Proverbs 8:22–27 and 3:19. James L. Kugel, in *The Bible as It Was* (Cambridge, Mass.: Belknap Press, 1997), argues that Ka'b's reasoning was commonplace among interpreters of the Bible from the beginning of the Common Era. The idea of a site or sacred structure as the navel of the universe and the focal point of Creation was prevalent in the ancient Middle East; its application to Jerusalem can be found in many midrashic texts, like the third-century Midrash Tanhuma with which Ka'b concludes the "Rock of Foundation." See Mircea Eliade's *The Sacred and the Profane: The Nature of Religion* (Harcourt Brace, 1987). Luis Stadelmann discusses the Hebrew notion of the center of the world in *The Hebrew Conception of the World: A Philological and Literary Study* (Rome: Pontifical Biblical Institute, 1970).

Locusts and Christians

The description of the rock in Solomon's Temple is based on those descriptions given in the Talmud and repeated by rabbinic commentators from the second century onward. See Thomas Chaplin, "The Stone of Foundation and the Site of the Temple," in *Palestine Exploration Fund, Quarterly Statement* (London, 1876). Ancient Yemenite Jewish marriage practices are discussed by Ahroni, who notes that these continued well into modern times. The descriptions of life in the Yemen, in particular the scourge of locusts, are adapted from those recorded by Ahroni following interviews he made with Yemeni Jews arriving in Israel in the late 1960s. The reasons for Ka'b's departure from the Yemen at a very advanced age (by one accounting he would have been eighty-two years old upon arriving in Medina) are not known.

The verses cited in the recounting of the Dhu Nuwas story are from the Quran 85:4–9. The description of the Dhu Nuwas massacre is from one of the earliest Arabic sources, Ibn Ishaq's *Sirat Rasul Allah*, an eighth-century biography of the Prophet, edited by Ibn Hisham and translated by A. Guillaume under the title *The Life of Muhammad* (Oxford University Press, 1955). I shall henceforth refer to this book as Ibn Ishaq's *Life*. The massacre is confirmed in Christian sources, although there are no Jewish accounts. Dhu Nuwas's death is recorded in Tabari, vol. 5, *The Sasanids, the Byzantines, the Lakhmids, and Yemen*. The saying "If you fatten your dog, he will eat you" is attributed to the Meccan Abdallah ibn Ubayy, who was insulting the Prophet shortly after the *hijra*, the Prophet's forced emigration from Mecca to Medina in September 622. It is cited in Nabia Abbott, *Aishah: The Beloved of Mohammed* (London: Saqi, 1985). Early Muslim adoption of Jewish practices, such as praying toward Jerusalem and keeping the Day of Atonement, are discussed by W. Montgomery Watt in his *Muhammad: Prophet and Statesman* (Oxford University Press, 1974). The Christian Church historian Sozomen, writing in the fourth century, was already well aware of how closely Arab religious practices resembled those of the Jews; see F. E. Peters, *Mecca: A Literary History of the Holy Land* (Princeton, N.J.: Princeton University Press, 1994).

Ka'b's tale of the false messiah leading followers over a cliff is based on an incident that occurred in Crete at the end of the fifth century, as presented by Jacob Marcus in *The Jew in the Medieval World, A Source Book: 315–1791* (Meridian Books, 1960). Ezra's curse on Yemeni Jews was recorded by the Yemenite Rabbi Schelomo 'Adani in his sixteenth-century work, *Maelecket Schelomo*. The passage concerning Jabbar and Antar is adapted from Steven M. Wasserstrom's *Between Muslim and Jew: The Problem of Symbiosis under Early Islam* (Princeton University Press, 1993). The envoy sent by Muhammad to the Yemen was Ali ibn Abi Talib. The ninth-century chronicler al-Waqidi records an encounter between him and Ka'b that led to the latter's conversion; see *Kitab al-Maghazi* (Oxford University Press, 1966).

Abraham's distrust of the Arabs, the sons of Ishmael, are in part based on a Geniza letter written about the arrival of Bedouins in Jerusalem; see Goitein, *A Mediterranean Society*, vol. 5. More fundamentally, however, Ishmael's outcast nature is based on Genesis 16, which has an angel of God saying to Hagar of her son: "A wild donkey of a man he will be, his hand against every hand, and every man's hand against him, living his life in defiance of all his kinsmen." At the same time, the angel predicts that the descendants of Ishmael will be "too numerous to be counted." Isaiah 21:7 tells of the prophet's vision of deliverance. The passage from Isaiah was interpreted as Ka'b has interpreted it in a Jewish apocalyptic work of the mid-eighth century, the "Secrets of Rabbi Simon ben Yohay," which preserves a messianic interpretation of the Arab conquest. Bernard Lewis discusses this work in "An Apocalyptic Vision of Islamic History," *Bulletin of the School of Oriental and African Studies* 13:2 (1950), pp. 308–338. Under "Elijah," the *Jewish Encyclopedia* notes the prophet's habit of dressing as an Arab and offers a midrashic tale by way of illustration. I am indebted to Patricia Crone and Michael Cook's thought-provoking discussion of the phenomenon of Jews accepting the credentials of an Arabian prophet in *Hagarism: The Making of the Islamic World* (Cambridge University Press, 1977); the figure of Abraham was suggested by an early-seventh-century Greek tract cited at the outset of their book in which a certain Abraham asks an old man: " 'What is your view, master and teacher, of the prophet who has appeared among the Saracens?' He replied, groaning mightily: 'He is an impostor. Do the prophets come with sword and chariot?' " The verses on the stone in Zion come from Isaiah 28:16; the allusion is to the Messiah, argues Kemper Fullerton in "The Stone of Foundation," in *The American Journal of Semitic Languages and Literatures* 37:1 (October, 1920), pp. 1–50. Abraham's reaction to Ka'b, it seems to me, would have been typical of the majority of Arab Jews in southern and central Arabia. Muhammad, however, was shocked to be received this way, and his bitter disappointment with the Jews of Medina in the second year of the *hijra* is suggested in the Quran; see verse 2:95, cited in the following chapter.

Medina

The phrases "on a night that like sea swarming had dropped its curtain" and "as bare as an ass's belly" come from the *Mu'allaqa* of the sixth-century pre-Islamic Arab poet Imru' al-Qays. See the translation in Robert Irwin's *Night and Horses and the Desert: An Anthology of Classical Arabic Literature* (Penguin Press, 1999). That some Jews acknowledged Muhammad as a prophet and still retained their Judaism is discussed by Norman Stillman in *The Jews of Arab Lands: A History and Source Book* (Philadelphia: Jewish Publication Society of America, 1979) and by Wasserstrom. Ka'b's romanticization of the Bedouin way of life was to become a pronounced feature of life under the Umayyads, as observed by Ishaq in his later dealings with Abd al-Malik. Maysun, the wife of Mu'awiya and mother of Yazid, for instance, hated her courtly life in Damascus. Of her husband, the caliph Mu'awiya, she composed these lines: "The crust I eat beside my tent is more than any fine bread to me; And more than any lubbard tub of fat, I love a lean Bedouin cavalier." Translated by R. A. Nicholson, *A Literary History of the Arabs* (Cambridge University Press, 1953).

Ka'b's reply to his wife's complaint is taken from Jeremiah 29:7. There are numerous accounts of Muhammad's death, differing in matters of detail; I have drawn upon Tabari's *History*, vol. 9, *The Last Years of the Prophet*. The description of depression as a "noonday demon" was used by desert monks, according to Kathleen Norris, *The Cloister Walk*

(Riverhead Books, 1996). Abu Bakr's repudiation of the renegades is cited by Eric Schroeder in *Muhammad's People: A Tale by Anthology, A Mosaic Translation* (Portland, Me.: Bond Wheelwright Co., 1955). I am grateful to Roy Mottahedeh for pointing out this marvelous book to me, from whose rendition of Arabic phrases and wonderful selection of material I have benefited greatly. Schroeder's sources, however, leave a lot to be desired; in this particular instance, I was unable to track down the original Arabic. The saying "Better than holy war is war against self" is traditionally attributed to the Prophet. Wasserstrom, in *Between Muslim and Jew*, attributes to the Prophet the phrase "Believe in the Torah, in the Psalms and the Gospel, even though the Quran should suffice you." Ka'b's assertion that the coming of Muhammad had been foretold in scripture is based on Isaiah 42:1–5. In al-Waqidi's *Kitab al-Maghazi*, Ka'b asks the Prophet's envoy to the Yemen to describe Muhammad. After Ali ibn Abi Talib does so, Ka'b (who is supposedly still a Jew) says, "He is in our books as you describe!" H.A.R. Gibb recounts the tale of Muhammad's gentle shaming of his closest companion, Abu Bakr, for overreacting during a pilgrimage, in *Mohammedanism* (Oxford University Press, 1970). The northern Arabs of the Hijaz and the southern Arabs of the Yemen evolved different and competing genealogies. I have avoided the complicating factor of the politics of these genealogies in my story, which is not to say that they were not very important. The seminal book in this regard is by Jawad Ali, *Al-Mufassal fi Tarikh al-'Arab Qabla al'Islam* (Beirut, 1976).

The information on Ibn Abbas, considered a pioneer of Quranic exegesis, is in Muhammad ibn Sa'd's ninth-century *Al-Tabaqat al-Kubra* (Beirut, 1957–68) and Baladhuri's *Futuh*. See *EI2* under "Abdallah ibn Abbas." Ibn Abbas's question to Ka'b about whether or not the angels got bored praising God is in Wolfensohn's *Ka'b al-Ahbar*. I am grateful to Nasser Rabbat for pointing out to me that Ka'b was called a *mawla* of his former student Ibn Abbas. *Mawla* is a legal term in Arab–Muslim history, with a long history of meanings. It derives from the verb *waliya*, which means "to be close to" or "connected with" something or someone. It has also the meaning of "client" or "protégé." Ka'b, as a Yemeni Jew who aspired to membership in Arab society, would have had to derive protection from someone in the early Islamic period. I think Ibn Abbas would have been too young at the time of Ka'b's stay in Medina. My story assumes that Ka'b's sponsor was Umar ibn al-Khattab, with whom he is closely tied in all the sources; Umar is therefore a plausible choice, even though Ka'b is nowhere called his *mawla* in the sources.

Umar invariably appears in Muslim sources as the epitome of the stern, uncompromising, and incorruptible ruler—a kind of Khomeini of his times. His disdain for levity, his unpopularity with women, his austere temperament, and the story of his conversion to Islam as told by Ishaq have become the stuff of legend. They even make an appearance in general surveys of Arab–Muslim civilization. See, for instance, Marshall Hodgson's *The Venture of Islam*, vol. I, *The Classical Age of Islam* (University of Chicago Press, 1974). Ka'b has been recorded in Muslim tradition as being the first Jewish convert to Islam, though there were probably earlier Jewish converts; see Sarah Stroumsa, "On Jewish Intellectuals Who Converted in the Early Middle Ages," in *The Jews of Medieval Islam*, edited by Daniel Frank (Leiden: E. J. Brill, 1992). Ka'b personified the Jewish influence on the earliest Muslim community, and the fact that he is most consistently connected with Umar in the sources speaks to the importance of the Jewish–Muslim nexus in the first half of the seventh century. I adapted Ka'b's argument for salvation through Adam from a passage in Ibn Rumi that I can no longer locate.

The Fundaments of the Universe

On the Temple as a "Palace of Peace," see I Chronicles 28:2–3 and I Kings 1:50–53, 2:28–31. The story of David moving a piece of the rock exists in many versions, notably in the Babylonian Talmud; Raphael Patai discusses these in his book, *Man and Temple in Ancient Jewish Myth and Ritual* (London: Thomas Nelson & Sons Ltd, 1947). Patai points out that tales about the rebellion of the primeval waters underneath the foundation stone, *Even Shetiyah*, are found in rabbinic literature as late as the fifth century. Yet they contain ancient Near Eastern motifs going back to traditions two millennia earlier. Among Muslim traditions of the same family cited by Tabari is one linking the Rock of the Temple with the source of the sweetest water in the world. The story of the sealing of the surging waters of the abyss with God's name is in the Jerusalem Talmud. See Daniel Sperber in "On Sealing the Abysses," *Journal of Semitic Studies* II (1966).

Jesus was the subject of a curious legend concerning the name on the stone: "Jesus of Nazareth went secretly to Jerusalem and entered into the Temple where he learned the holy letters of the divine Name. He wrote them on parchment, and, uttering the Name to prevent pain, he cut his flesh and hid the parchment therein. Then, again pronouncing the Name, he caused the flesh to grow together. As he left the door, the lions [guarding the gate as in Sumerian Temples] roared and the Name was erased from his mind. When he went outside the city, he cut his flesh again and drew out the parchment, and when he had studied its letters, he learned the Name again" (see Vilnay, *Legends*).

The association of Moriah with the House of the Lord is found in 2 Chronicles 3:1; Charles Warren expands on this association in "The Comparative Holiness of Mounts Zion and Moriah" in *Palestine Exploration Fund, Quarterly Statement* (1869–70). David's use of music and liturgy to bring the waters of the deep back up to the appropriate level turned into an annual ritual performed in the Hebrew Temple, discussed at length by Patai in his chapter, "The Ritual of Water-Libation," in *Man and the Temple*. Louis Ginzberg's *Legends of the Jews*, vol. 4, (Philadelphia: Jewish Publication Society, 1947), also describes this ritual. Finally, Patai observed in the 1940s that "the inhabitants of *Kafr Silwan* (Siloam), the Arab village next to Jerusalem, go down in procession in times of drought to the same well of Siloam out of which the water was drawn for the libation of the second Temple."

The Conquest Foretold

This version of Abu Bakr's death is from Abu al-Faraj al-Isfahani's tenth-century *Kitab al-Aghani*, and the story of the three-tiered pulpit is from Tabari; see extracts in Schroeder. Ka'b's poem is an adaptation of the text of an actual seventh-century Jewish apocalyptic poem on the Arab conquests, as published by Bernard Lewis in "On That Day," in *Mélanges D'Islamologie*, ed. Pierre Salmon (Leiden: E. J. Brill, 1974). The original, first published by Louis Ginzberg, is from the Geniza documents held in the Schechter collection at the Jewish Theological Seminary of America; it is preserved as a fragment on a single sheet, 11 by 8 cm. Ginzberg dated the poem back to the Crusades, but Lewis showed that the poem had to have been written "during a period of messianic expectation generated by the apocalyptic events of the Arab conquest. . . . It must be assumed that the poem was composed during or immediately after the Arab victory. Since the fall of neither Jerusalem nor Caesaria is mentioned, it may well be that the poem antedates the surrender of these two cities."

In Muslim tradition, Umar is closely associated with the title *al-faruq*, one meaning of which, according to al-Biruni's twelfth-century *al-'Athar al-Baqiya*, translates as "the great redeemer." While many sources, including Tabari, contend that the Prophet bestowed this title on Umar, Ibn Sa'd in his *Tabaqat* writes that "the People of the Book were the first to call Umar *al-faruq*." Crone and Cook argue for this view in *Hagarism*; they suggest that the origins of the title lie in a Jewish messianic idea attached to Umar by Jews early in the seventh century. Suliman Bashear offers a linguistic argument in support of this thesis in "The Title 'Faruq' and Its Association with Umar I," in *Studia Islamica* 72 (1990). The Patriarch of Jerusalem, Sophronius, attributed the same title to Jesus Christ in an undated rendering into Arabic of a manuscript attributed to him found in the Monastery of Saint Catherine on Mount Sinai. The need of the Prophet and early Muslims to seek out Jewish and Christian traditions is discussed by Newby in *The Making of the Last Prophet*. The Quranic verses used by Ka'b to clinch his arguments are 47:24–28 (Arberry).

The reference to God endowing mankind with a love of dalliance comes from the ninth-century *Kitab al-Shi'r wa-l-Shu'ara* of Ibn Qutayba, as translated by R. A. Nicholson. Ka'b's dream image of the Holy Land is adapted from Psalm 98. The poem that I attribute to Ishaq's stepmother was composed by al-Khansa' (575–645) for her two brothers lost in tribal warfare; see Irwin. The final letter of Ishaq's mother is adapted from the text of a letter found among the Judeo–Arabic documents of the Cairo Geniza, dating between the tenth and twelfth centuries; see *A Mediterranean Society*, vol. 5. These discarded writings, which could not be thrown away because they might contain the name of God, were edited by S. D. Goitein and have proved invaluable for my purposes regarding matters of phraseology and forms of address and language.

Coming to Jerusalem

The description of the golden jewel-encrusted crown of the Persian King of Kings is taken from the eleventh-century *Book of Kings* by Firdawsi. The dream of defeat at the hands of a circumcised man is cited in M. Ling's biography of the Prophet, *Muhammad: His Life Based on the Earliest Sources* (London: George Allen & Unwin, 1983). F. D. Donner presents an account of the Byzantine battle losses in his *The Early Islamic Conquests* (Princeton University Press, 1981). The phrase "Fear of the Arabs had fallen upon the land" is borrowed from a Muslim source in Schroeder's anthology.

Heraclius's farewell to Syria is recorded in Baladhuri's *Futuh* and in Tabari's *History*, vol. 12, *The Battle of al-Qadisiyyah and the Conquest of Syria and Palestine*. The warning of Heraclius to the men of Byzantium is drawn from the ninth-century historian Theophanes and the fourteenth-century work *Muthir al-Ghiram*, or *The Book of Inciting Desire to Visit the Holy City and Syria*, written by Jerusalem native Jamal al-Din Ahmad; extracts are translated in Guy Le Strange's *Pales-*

tine under the Moslems: A Description of Syria and the Holy Land from 650 to 1500 (Palestine Exploration Fund, 1890, reprinted by Khayats, Beirut, 1965). Le Strange offers a collection of extracts from medieval Arab geographers. The anti-Muslim sermon delivered by Sophronius is adapted from two of his actual sermons, on Christmas Eve of 634 and Epiphany of 635. The term *Saracen*, the Anglicization of *Sarakenoi*, or "empty of Sara," carried also the pejorative meaning of being an outcast and illegitimate descendant of Abraham's union with the slave Hagar. Sophronius's speech, as reported by John of Damascus, is one of the earliest on record conveying the negative connotation of "Saracen," a word which became common during the Crusades.

Heribert Busse recounts Umar's esteem for Abu Ubayda in "The Sanctity of Jerusalem in Islam," *Judaism* 17:4 (1968). The military code of conduct described in the narrative is attributed to the Prophet by al-Waqidi in his *Kitab al-Maghazi*. Other Muslim accounts, including Ibn Asakir's twelfth-century *Tarikh Madinat Dimashq*, as well as the Christian historian Eutychius, attribute it to Abu Bakr. The verses on the water of Horeb come from Exodus 7:6. The description of the desert is adapted from the *Mu'allaqa* of Imru' al-Qays. Ibn Sa'd writes that the great-grandfather of the Prophet, Hashim, sojourned with the sons of Judham while on his way to Gaza for business. The time frame for the journey from Medina to Jerusalem is in Peters, *Mecca*. The valley separating the Mount of Olives from the Holy City is known to Muslims as *Wadi Jahannam*, the Valley of Hell. They took this name from the Hebrew *Ge-Ben-Hinnon*, which referred to the deep gorge to the west and southwest of Jerusalem. The valley to the east was in Jewish lore the scene of the last gathering on Judgment Day, and so it remained in Muslim tradition. It is described by the tenth-century geographer al-Muqaddasi as follows: "Now, the Wadi Jahannam runs from the south-east angle of the Haram area to the furthest (northern) point, and along the east side. In this valley there are gardens and vineyards, churches, caverns and cells of anchorites, tombs, and other remarkable spots. . . . In its midst stands the church which covers the Sepulchre of Mary, and above, overlooking the valley, are many tombs, among which are those of [the Companions of the Prophet] Shaddad ibn Aus ibn Thabit and Ubadah ibn as Samit."

The Black Stone

Many of the early traditions about the Black Stone and Mecca used here and in "Mecca and Jerusalem," come from Uri Rubin, "The Ka'ba: Aspects of Its Ritual Functions and Position in Pre-Islamic and Early

Islamic Times," *Jerusalem Studies in Arabic and Islam* 8 (1986), and Ibn al-Kalbi (737–819), *Kitab al-Asnam* (The Book of Idols), edited by Ahmad Zaki (Cairo, 1965). In a different Islamic tradition regarding the origins of the Black Stone, Abraham the first believer (Quran 3:60), not Adam, receives it from God in a state of immaculate whiteness. Abraham then sets it into a wall of the Ka'ba which, according to the Quran (2:122–126), he built. Around this stone, the *hajj* is instituted. The ritual of circumambulation of the Ka'ba, or circling, has biblical parallels; see Psalm 26. The idea of women making the *hajj* in order to marry was noted by the poet Umar ibn Abi Rabi (644–721). On the breaking of the Black Stone into three pieces during the war between the Umayyads and Abdallah ibn al-Zubayr, see *EI2* under "Ka'ba." The sources say the three pieces were held together with a silver band, but I have no information on the shape of the frame that was used by either Ibn al-Zubayr, during his reconstruction, or the Umayyads. The photograph depicts the frame in use today. Reference to the Black Stone as God's hand in the earth comes from Alaa al-Din Ali al-Muttaqi bin Husam al Hindi, *Kanz al-Ummal*. The story of the two stones found on Abu Qubays is from Abu Abdallah al-Fakihi's ninth-century *Tarikh Makka*. The stories of Amr ibn Luhayy, and of the rock called Sa'd near Jedda, are from Ibn Ishaq's *Sira* and Ibn al-Kalbi's *Kitab al-Asnam*. The description of Abu Qubays is adapted from Nasir Khusraw's eleventh-century description of Mecca in his *Safar-Nameh*, translated by Le Strange as *Diary of a Journey Through Syria and the Holy Land* (New York: AMS Press, 1971). Finally, Ishaq's reflections upon human frailty and the attractiveness of rocks are an adaptation of lines from Firdawsi's *Book of Kings*, as cited in Schroeder.

The Turmoil of Ka'b

The idea of knowledge being only with God is a theme in the Quran 46:23. Umar's refusal to put aside revenues or make monetary provisions for the future is in Tabari's *History*, vol. 12. Umar is known as "the man upon whose tongue God had struck the Truth," as used by Ibn Manzur and others. Ibn Sa'd records a tradition that has the Prophet saying, "God put the truth on the tongue and heart of Umar and he is the *faruq* by whom God made the distinction between truth and falsity"; see Bashear, "The Title 'Faruq.' "

The Sins of David

The valley before which Ka'b and Umar were standing is *Wadi Jahannam*, the Valley of Hell, coming from which the eleventh-century traveller Nasir Khusraw reported: "you may hear the cries of those in Hell"; see Le Strange. The story of James's death is adapted from the account of the sixth-century pilgrim Theodosius. Ka'b and Umar's reflections on the stoniness of Jerusalem borrow from Herman Melville's obsession with the same. See the account in his *Journal up the Straits: October 11, 1856–May 5, 1857*. David's songs are from Psalm 18 and 22, respectively. See also Psalm 61.

The tradition of Muhammad having men recite to him from the Quran is found in Hujwiri's eleventh-century *Kashf al-Mahjub li Arbab al-Qulub* (The Unveiling of That Which Is Hidden for People of Hearts). The conclusions regarding David's sins and the building of the Temple are made by Tabari in his *History*, vol. 3, *The Children of Israel*.

The story of David that Ka'b tells is from 2 Samuel. The account of the blind and the lame defending Jerusalem from the conquering army of David is from 2 Samuel 5. The wrath of God on Jerusalem is found in 2 Samuel 24 and 1 Chronicles 21: 14–17. Isaac Kalimi discusses the Angels of Pestilence and Death, and the presence of ashes from Abraham's ram, in "The Land of Moriah, Mount Moriah, and the Site of Solomon's Temple in Biblical Historiography," *Harvard Theological Review* 83:14 (1990). The procession up the mountain and dealings with Araunah can be found in 2 Samuel 24: 10–25. The passage of years have not lessened the importance of the transaction between David and Araunah. In August 1967 Zerach Warhaftig, the ultra-Orthodox Israeli minister for religious affairs, said that, seeing as how David had paid the full price to Araunah all those years ago, the Israeli government legally owned the Temple Mount and all the Muslim structures on it. "The minister went on to say that while there was no doubt that Jewish rights on the Temple Mount overrode those of the Moslems, and while Jews even had a right to raze the mosques there, they had no intention at the moment of actually doing so." Amos Elon, *Jerusalem: City of Mirrors* (Little, Brown and Company, 1989).

Umar's words to Ka'b on Solomon's being kept safe from bloodshed in order to build the Temple are adapted from Tabari's *History*, vol. 3. Ka'b's response, that God never wanted a Temple to be built for Him in the first place, are based on Nathan's prophecy to David warning him against building the Temple, in 2 Samuel 7 (a prophecy which suggests that building a Temple was as controversial among the Israelites in the time of David as the Dome of the Rock was controversial among Muslims in the time of Abd al-Malik). Tabari attributes to the Prophet the analogy with a horseman who lingers in the shade and departs. See Schroeder, *Muhammad's People.* The Quran offers many images of Paradise as a garden; see, for instance, 56:28–33.

The story of Umar sacrificing his daughter is of obscure Shi'ite origin. I grew up with it, as have Lebanese and Iranian Shi'ites. It is rejected by Sunni Muslims, but it is in the tradition and so is fair game from this book's point of view. Reference to the tale and discussion of the practice can be found in Mahmud al-Qimmni's *Al-'Ustoora wa al-Turath* (Cairo, 1993); he argues that the practice of female infanticide was not economic in origin as has been claimed. Ibn al-Kalbi's *Kitab al-Asnam* supports this. The description of Umar's tears can be found in Abu Nu'aim al-Isfahani's *Hilyat al-Awliya* as cited in Heribert Busse, "Omar b. al-Hattab in Jerusalem," *Jerusalem Studies in Arabic and Islam* 5 (1984). I am indebted to Chris Berdik for translating this article for me from the German. Umar's language of mourning is taken from the Quran (53:2) and from the Sufi mystic al-Hallaj (857–922), who was tortured to death for his heretical views, and who is said to have described the mournful strains of a flute in the night as "Satan weeping for the loss of the world."

The Rock of Sacrifice

The story of Abd al-Muttalib's sacrifice is recorded in Ibn Ishaq's *Life,* in words that suggest it was a religious offering. The would-be sacrifice is recorded as having taken place near the two idols Isaf and Na'ila until the Quraysh came out of their assemblies and stopped it. The Arabs gave the large or oddly shaped rocks that they worshipped until the advent of Islam names. The story of two such rocks, Isaf and Na'ila, is found in both Ibn Kalbi's *Kitab al-Asnam* and Ibn Ishaq's *Life.* The Prophet's favorite wife Aisha seems to have been particularly taken with the tale. Ibn Ishaq reports her as saying: "Isaf and Na'ila were a man and a woman of Jurham who copulated in the Ka'ba. That is why God transformed them into two stones."

Ka'b recites Exodus, 22: 28–29 regarding the sacrifice of firstborn sons. Abraham's attempted sacrifice of Isaac is from Genesis 22. I have benefited from, and followed in broad outline, Jon Levenson's masterly treatment of the subject in *The Death and Resurrection of the Beloved Son: The Transformation of Child Sacrifice in Judaism and Christianity* (Yale University Press, 1993). From this book, I have also cited at the end of the chapter a poignant midrashic conversation between Rabbis Phinehas and Benaiah, in which Phinehas says that Abraham prayed asking God to regard his sacrifice of the ram, "as though I had sacrificed my son first and only afterwards sacrificed this ram."

Sacrifices on the rock of Mount Moriah, perhaps even the early tradition of child sacrifice, have been connected to the worship of Melchisedek, a legendary Canaanite priest-king of Jerusalem who is thought to have anticipated monotheism. Hebrew scripture depicts Melchisedek standing on the sacred stone of Jerusalem, consecrating an altar to El-Elyon, the "god most high," whom the Israelites would name Elohim, "Lord;" Thomas Idinopulos discusses this in *Jerusalem Blessed, Jerusalem Cursed: Jews, Christians, and Muslims in the Holy City from David's Time to Our Own* (Ivan R. Dee, 1991).

The Quranic account of Abraham's sacrifice, found in Sura 37: 102–107, does not mention the name of the son, and his identity was debated by Muslim scholars in the early centuries of Islam. Among the earliest Muslims, however, the *dhabih*, or sacrificed one, was more often than not portrayed as Isaac (Ishaq), not Ishmael (Isma'il or Ishmael). The scholar Qutb al-Din explicitly states that this was the view of Umar ibn al-Khattab and Ali ibn Abi Talib. Ibn Qutayba and Tabari shared the view that Isaac was the son almost sacrificed by Abraham. Later Muslim opinion, however, converged on Isma'il (Ishmael), the son of Hagar and the ancestor of the Arabs, as having been the son in question. Al-Kisa'i, in his *Qisas al-Anbiya'*, cites Ka'b al-Ahbar as his source for Isaac, the son of Sara, as the son in question. Kisa'i alludes to the debate that was still alive in the eleventh century; he attributes to Ibn Abbas the view that it was Isma'il (Ishmael), and to Ibn Umar ibn al-Khattab, Hasan ibn Ali ibn Abi Talib, and Husayn ibn Ali ibn Abi Talib his own view that it was Isaac.

Sophronius

Al-Waqidi, in his ninth-century *Futuh al-Sham*, writes that the formal opening of Jerusalem to the army of Umar ibn al-Khattab took place on Palm Sunday and began on the Mount of Olives, where Umar and his army had made camp and where the Christian community gathered with their Patriarch to carry out their procession into the city on the following day; on this issue, see Busse, "Omar b. Al-Hattab in Jerusalem" (1984). The observance of rituals following the order of events of Christ's passion during the Great Week of festivities described by my narrator, Ishaq, first evolved in Jerusalem in the fourth century. See the account by Egeria, a nun probably from a western province of the Roman Empire on the Atlantic coast, who visited Jerusalem between 381 and 384; Wilkinson translates her diaries in his *Egeria's Travels* (Ariel Publishing House, 1971). See also Wilkinson's *Jerusalem Pilgrims* (1977). Incidentally, there is no evidence that Ka'b ever met Sophronius. But it is plausible that he did.

The guarantee of security and property to Christians is part of the so-called Covenant of Umar, a treaty of capitulation between the Muslims and Christians concerning Jerusalem. The text of this agreement appears in one of its fullest forms in Tabari's *History*, vol. 12. One clause of the document—that continuing the Roman and Byzantine policy of excluding Jews from Jerusalem—is contradicted by all other evidence, and modern scholars have generally tended to discount it as a later forgery; F. E. Peters addresses this issue in *Jerusalem* (Princeton University Press, 1985). The terms of surrender for Jerusalem as set out in Tabari emphasize the poll tax; they do not include the details concerning comportment, dress, weaponry, and spying that I have added. Such restrictions are found in other deeds of surrender from the same period, reported in Baladhuri and Ibn 'Asakir. These were negotiated with the locals of Damascus and other Syrian cities. See Schroeder and Moshe Gil, *A History of Palestine 634–1099* (Cambridge University Press, 1992).

The discussion of separation as ordained by God and defining what is holy draws upon Mary Douglas's argument in *Purity and Danger: An Analysis of the Concepts of Pollution and Taboo* (Routledge & Kegan Paul, 1966). The collection of sayings and stories of the saints compiled by Sophronius is entitled *Spiritual Meadows;* it was jointly authored with John Moschus, Sophronius's mentor and companion on his travels through Egypt. Moshe Gil contends that Sophronius arrived in Palestine in 619, while the country was still in Persian hands, and became Patriarch in the autumn of 633. The description of seventh-century Alexandria, as discussed by Umar and Ka'b, is based on a variety of Muslim descriptions of the city. The term "Greek" is used in the story for the benefit of the modern Western reader. Practically the only Arabic term used in Muslim sources to describe the people of the Byzantine Empire is *al-Rum*, the Romans. The description of the ordinary people of Alexandria and their obsession with theological debate is adapted from the words of the late-fourth-century church father Gregory of Nyssa, who described the population of Constantinople in the words that Sophronius uses; see Speros Vryonis, *Byzantium and Europe* (Harcourt, Brace & World, 1967), and Idinopulos.

The description of Umar's clothing when meeting Sophronius is recorded in many sources. The details vary, but the gist is as Ishaq has it in his account. See Idinopulos (1991), Schroeder (1955), and Busse (1968). Tabari tells a nice tale, not included in Ishaq's narrative, of how Umar began to stone his commanders in Syria upon arriving from Medina and finding them dressed in brocade and silk. Grabar, in *The Shape of the Holy*, argues that a man like Sophronius would have been able to speak the local Arabic or Aramaic dialect of Jerusalem. However, in the beginning of such a formal occasion as the meeting of the Patriarch and Umar, Sophronius would probably have spoken through a translator. Sophronius's formal greeting to Umar is adapted from the text of a letter sent in the third century by Rome to the Churches of Africa, as recorded in *The See of Peter*, ed. J. T. Shotwell and L. R. Loomis (Columbia University Press, 1927). Umar's expression of concern over whether he is a caliph or a king occurs in a conversation with Salman al-Farisi, not Abu Ubayda. See Schroeder.

The politics of dress in the encounter between Umar and Sophronius is apparent in the *Chronographia* of the eighth-century Greek historian Theophanes, whose version of events is historically the closest to the actual Muslim takeover of Jerusalem. As translated by Le Strange (1890), Theophanes writes that "Umar entered the Holy City clothed in camel-hair garments all soiled and torn, and making a show of piety as a cloak for his diabolical hypocrisy, demanded to be taken to what in former times had been the Temple built by Solomon. This he straightaway converted into an oratory for blasphemy and impiety. When Sophronius saw this, he exclaimed: 'Verily, this is the abomination of desolation spoken by of Daniel the Prophet, and it now stands in the Holy Place'; And the Patriarch shed many tears."

In the *Formation of Islamic Art* (Yale University Press, 1987), Oleg Grabar makes the observation that Eastern Christianity "had always liked to use the emotional impact of music and the visual arts to convert 'barbarians.' That such attempts may have been effective with the Arabs is shown in the very interesting, although little studied, group of accounts dealing with the more or less legendary trips of Arabs to the Byzantine court in early Islamic times, or sometimes even before Islam. In most cases the 'highlight' of the 'guided tours' to which they submitted was a visit either to a church . . . or to a court reception." I have lent this important insight to Sophronius, who, after all, invited Umar to come to Jerusalem, according to the sources.

That Umar deeply desired to visit the place of David's repentance (Quran 38:15–24) is well attested to; see Peters's account, based on the authority of al-Walid ibn Muslim. On the many parallels between Umar and David in the sources, see Busse (1984). Sophronius's response to Umar's request, describing Jerusalem as "the happy Church on which Our Lord, the Son of David, poured forth all his teaching," includes language adapted from the African theologian Tertullian, as cited in Eamon Duffy, *Saints and Sinners: A History of the Popes* (Yale University Press, 1997). Sophronius's reflections on his monastic past are based on the words of Pope Gregory (540–604), as included by Duffy.

Tour of the City

Jamal al-Din Ahmad, in his fourteenth-century *Muthir al-Gharam*, puts a very different spin on the events of Umar's entry into Jerusalem than does Theophanes. Tracking down a long chain of transmission, the author arrives at what purports to be an eyewitness description of the Caliph's entry: "Umar, as soon as he was at leisure from the writing of the Treaty of Capitulation . . . said to the Patriarch of Jerusalem: 'Conduct us to the Mosque of David.' And the Patriarch agreed thereto. Then Umar went forth girt with his sword, and with him four thousand of the Companions who had come to Jerusalem with him, all begirt likewise with their swords, and a crowd of us Arabs who had come up to the Holy City followed them, none of us bearing any weapons except our swords. And the Patriarch walked before Umar among the Companions, and we all came behind the Caliph. Thus we entered the Holy City. And the Patriarch took us to the Church which goes by the name of the *Qumama* [Dungheap, a play on the Arabic word *Qiyama*, Resurrection], and said he: 'This is David's Mosque.' And Umar looked around and pondered, then he answered the Patriarch: 'Thou liest, for the Apostle described to me the Mosque of David, and by his description this is not it.' Then the Patriarch went on with us to the Church of *Sihyun* (Zion), and again he said: 'This is the Mosque of David.' But the Caliph replied to him: 'Thou liest.' So the Patriarch went on with him till he came to the noble Sanctuary of the Holy City, and reached the gate thereof, called [afterwards] the Gate of Muhammad" (Le Strange, 1890).

The prophecy that Ka'b recites regarding Umar's decision to enter Jerusalem on an ass comes from Zechariah 9:9. R. J. McKelvey in *The New Temple: The Church in the New Testament* (Oxford University Press, 1969) argues that the use of an ass is a sign of messiahship, an acting out of the parable of the coming of the kingdom of God. Umar's entry into Jerusalem recalls that of Jesus in more ways than one. Mark 11:11 records that Jesus, upon entering into Jerusalem, had proceeded to the

Temple as Umar did; and Umar's throwing himself on the ground in prayer before the Gate of the Sheep's Pool is reminiscent of Jesus' passionate prayer in Gethsemane. In Arabic the pilgrimage prayer spoken by Umar is: *"labyka, allahumma, labayka bi ma huwa ahabbu ilayka."* Its use in the context is discussed by Busse (1984). Typically, it is recited during the *hajj* at the early stages of *ihram* and then repeatedly during the rest of the pilgrimage. The Arabic traditions that cite this prayer by Umar at the gates of Jerusalem are obviously those that tend to equate the religious status of Jerusalem with that of Mecca, not those that elevate Mecca over Jerusalem (which, much later, come to the fore and dominate the tradition). Busse also compares Umar's prayer before the gates of the Holy City with that of Solomon upon his completion of the Temple. Solomon had the keys but could not open the doors of the new Temple until he had uttered David's prayer asking God to forgive him. The text of the Muslim prayer featuring David asking for God's forgiveness that appears later in the chapter is from the Quran 38:15–24.

The negative opinions and rumors circulating in Jerusalem regarding the Arabs are based on those of several ancient Christian sources. Moshe Gil writes that Nilus described Arabs as uninterested in anything but plundering and war, and I have cited the words of Antonius of Chozeba, who called Arabs "beasts of prey" that happen to "look like human beings."

Several pilgrims described Gethsemane as Ishaq does. See Eusebius, fourth century, and Hesychius of Jerusalem, fifth century, in Wilkinson's *Pilgrims* (1977). Also see John Wilkinson's *Jerusalem as Jesus Knew It: Archaeology as Evidence* (London: Thames and Hudson, 1978). The fig tree cursed by Jesus, which subsequently withered to its roots, is discussed by McKelvey. The unprofitable fig tree was turned into a Christian symbol of Israel's unfaithfulness and wretchedness before God. The Gate of the Sheep's Pool went by other names in the seventh century: the Gate of Benjamin, perhaps even the Gate of the Paralyzed Man (Wilkinson, 1977). Descriptions of the Christian crowds present during Umar and Sophronius's entry into the city are from an account by the pilgrim Silvia, as cited in George Jeffery's *A Brief Description of the Holy Sepulchre* (Cambridge: Cambridge University Press, 1919).

The Gate of Repentance, *Bab al-Tawba,* is more commonly known as the Golden Gate or the Gate Beautiful. The earliest Arabic sources refer to it as *Bab al-Rahma,* the Gate of Mercy, and the Gate of Repentance. Myriam Rosen-Ayalon, *The Early Islamic Monuments of Al-*

Haram al-Sharif: An Iconographic Study (Jerusalem: The Hebrew University of Jerusalem, 1989) suggests that both names were used as a way of distinguishing between the two doorways. Rosen-Ayalon also notes that these names may relate to the elaborate traditions concerning the Day of Judgment and the Mount of Olives, which is opposite the Gate of Repentance. Muslim sources note that the gate was sealed when Umar arrived (as it is to this day), to be reopened only on Judgment Day. The description of the Gate of Repentance is taken from the pilgrim of Piacenza who visited Jerusalem around 570 (Wilkinson, 1977). Muslims of the seventh century would not have known that the gate is Byzantine in design and sits above a Herodian gate of the same dimensions; the Jerusalem that lived in their imaginations was that of David and Solomon—hence Ishaq's error in describing it as a remnant of the Temple.

The poem cited by Sophronius was written by him between 614 and 630, just after the triumphant return of the Holy Cross to Jerusalem by the emperor Heraclius; it is known as the *Anacreonticon* 20; see Wilkinson (1977). Umar's disdain for too much focus on building and architecture is in a tale by Ibn Sa'd (died 845), describing what the Prophet said to his wife, Umm Salama, when he discovered she had built an extension to her room "to shut out the glances of men." The Prophet said: "O Umm Salama! Verily, the most unprofitable thing that eateth up the wealth of a Believer is building"; cited by K. A. C. Creswell, *Early Muslim Architecture*, part I (Oxford: Clarendon Press, 1932).

The Gate of the Column, *Bab al-Amud*, is also known as the Damascus Gate. It is impossible to know exactly when *Bab al-Amud* came into use as a name. Since Muslims would not have been happy with the name Saint Stephen's Gate, it is not unreasonable to assume they would have from very early on begun calling it by the name of the column that sat so conspicuously at its center. Saint Stephen's Gate today is the east-facing gate, through which Umar and Sophronius entered the city. The martyrdom of Stephen is recorded in Acts 7:54–8:1. The description of what could be found on Jerusalem's prime commercial street, the Cardo, is based on al-Muqadassi's description of his native city written in 985.

The highlight of Umar's tour, *Kanisat al-Qiyama* to Eastern Christians, or the Church of the Resurrection, is more commonly known these days as the Church of the Holy Sepulchre. The description of the fourth-century Basilica (destroyed in the eleventh by a deranged Caliph) is a montage of different Christian accounts, beginning with the Church historian Eusebius, who was an eyewitness to the construction, and including the first Christian pilgrim known to have visited the finished building, the Pilgrim of Bordeaux in 333; his description is discussed in Jeffery. Sophronius and Umar visited other churches as well; Grabar (1996) notes the importance of the New Church of the Virgin Mary, known as the *Nea,* and the Church of Zion. But the Holy Sepulchre was by far the most important of the churches visited by Umar. It has had a continuous history of use from the second quarter of the fourth century until today. The political importance of the alignment of the Church of the Resurrection on a longitudinal axis facing east, overlooking the ruins of the Temple, is highlighted by Grabar in *The Shape of the Holy* using computer-aided reconstructions of the Church in relation to the seventh-century city. Christian tradition refers to the Rotunda over the tomb of Jesus by the Greek name of *anastasis,* or resurrection; the word "rotunda," however, is ancient and was used by the pilgrim Arculf in the seventh century.

Ka'b's warning to Umar not to enter into the Church of the Resurrection is adapted from a remark made by Ka'b as cited by Al-Wasiti: "Do not come to the Church of Mary or approach the two pillars, for they are idols. Whoever goes to them, his prayers will be as naught. . . . Cursed be the Christians for not seeing the things to come. They could not find a place in which to build a church except in the valley of *Jahannam* [Hell]." The reference here is to the Church of Mary on the slopes of the Mount of Olives, and to the Church of the Ascension on the top of the same mountain, known as *Kanisat al-Tur* in Arabic; it had two pillars facing the north and south walls, according to the eighth-century pilgrim Willibald. Amikam Elad convincingly makes this connection by citing several versions of Ka'b's words in his *Medieval Jerusalem and Islamic Worship: Holy Places, Ceremonies, Pilgrimage* (Leiden: E. J. Brill, 1995).

Sophronius's comment to Umar regarding the two Jerusalems is adapted from a line by Cyril of Jerusalem in the fourth century (Grabar, 1996). Cyril proclaimed victory over Judaism with the phrase "Jerusalem crucified Christ, but that which now is worships him." The interior of the Basilica is based on the description by Bishop Eusebius of Caesarea, who was born in Palestine around 275–280 C.E.; Eusebius was an eyewitness to the construction of the Basilica, which he describes in his *Life of Constantine.* The description of the Holy City's "baptism" by rain is taken from an observation by the British pilgrim Arculf, who visited Jerusalem around 680.

The New Temple

This chapter's physical descriptions of the Church of the Holy Sepulchre are based on the reconstruction by Father Charles Cousanon in *The Church of the Holy Sepulchre in Jerusalem* (London: Oxford University Press, 1974). Sophronius quotes from John 16:33 when describing the slow death of Christ on the cross. The phrase "rock of refuge" is from Psalm 31. The famous words of Christ predicting the destruction of the Temple are found in Mark 13:1–2. Sophronius's argument regarding the founding of the church on the body of Christ, and the discussion of the transfer of the center of the world from Moriah's rock to the body of Christ, are based on the interpretations developed by McKelvey in *The New Temple*. The discussion of Sophronius concerning the end of Jewish sacrifices refers to the ending of the tradition of animal sacrifice carried out by the Sadducean priests in the Herodian Temple after Titus's destruction of it in the year 70. See Busse (1984) for the ways in which the Church of the Holy Sepulchre was seen as a successor to the old Temple.

Adam's Tomb

Saint Augustine discusses the burial place of Adam in *De Civitate Dei* (The City of God), in which he writes, "The ancients hold that because Adam was the first man, and was buried there, it was called Calvary, because it holds the head of the human race." Sophronius's sentence, "As in Adam all die, even so in Christ shall all be made alive," comes from I Corinthians 15:22. The idea that Christ's sacrifice affected the nature of death itself, as argued by Sophronius, is adapted from Saint Basil, who wrote: "Probably Noah was not ignorant of the sepulchre of our forefather and that of the first born of all mortals, and in that place, Calvary, the Lord suffered, the origin of death there being destroyed"; cited in the Reverend William Wood Seymour's *The Cross: In Tradition, History, and Art* (New York: Knickerbocker Press, 1898).

The words that Sophronius sings are a stanza from John Donne's poem entitled "Hymne to God, my God, in my sickness." John 19:17–18 refers to the meaning of Golgotha: "And carrying his cross himself he went out to the place referred to as 'of a skull,' which in Hebrew is Golgotha." The opinion attributed to Ka'b concerning the real meaning of Golgotha comes from Saint Jerome, who lived in Jerusalem and studied its local lore carefully, and who said that in his own day the places where criminals were executed were called Golgotha. See S. Gibson and J. Taylor, *Beneath the Church of the Holy Sepulchre, Jerusalem: The Archaeology and Early History of Traditional Golgotha* (Palestine

Exploration Fund Monograph, 1994). The distance between Moriah and Calvary, it should be pointed out, is under 600 meters.

The Tree of Life is known to Arabs as the heavenly tree of *Tuba.* Another tree is mentioned in the Quran (37:60), called the *Zaqqum;* it is reserved for the damned, has fruit in the form of demons, and grows in the depths of the furnaces of Hell, like the tree that Seth saw in Sophronius's story. The story of Seth, Adam, and the Tree of Life is from a fifteenth-century Dutch source, as retold by the Reverend Seymour (1898). The Muslim denial of Jesus' crucifixion is referred to in the Quran 4:157. Unlike Jews, however, Muslims hold Jesus in very high regard and argue that, if he was not crucified, someone made to resemble him probably was. The caliph al-Mahdi is said to have explained to the Catholic Timothy I that God did not allow the Jews to crucify the Messiah because He esteemed him so highly that He took him up to Heaven before the deed could be done. The description of Adam's role on the Day of Resurrection is taken from *Kitab Muthir al-Gharam li-Ziyarat al-Khalil, Alaihi al-Salam, The Book of Inciting Desire to Visit Hebron.* It was written in 1351 by Abu al-Fida Ishaq, preacher of the Hebron mosque, who died in 1429. Charles Mathews translated it as *Palestine—Mohammedan Holy Land* (Yale University Press, 1949).

The Rock of the Cross

Cousanon explains how, assuming that local memories kept alive the actual place of Jesus' crucifixion, the Bible—in particular John 19:41, cited by Ishaq—might be reconciled with what is left at or below the foundations of the Church of the Holy Sepulchre. The description of the tomb is based on the account of Photius, Patriarch of Constantinople, who wrote a detailed description sometime between 867 and 878. His account conforms in its broad outlines with what one can still see under the rotunda of the existing church. The description of the fifteen golden lamps comes from the English pilgrim Willibald, who visited Jerusalem between A.D. 724 and 730. *Kanisat al-Qiyama,* the Church of the Resurrection, is occasionally referred to in Muslim sources as *Kanisat al-Qumama,* the Church of the Dungheap. S. D. Goitein sees in this phrase a retaliation for the previous Christian desecration of the Temple site; see his "Jerusalem in the Arab Period: 638–1099," in *The Jerusalem Cathedra: Studies in the History, Archaeology, Geography and Ethnography of the Land of Israel,* edited by Lee Levine (Detroit: Wayne State University Press, 1981). There is no evidence that Ka'b was responsible for this play on words as is stated in the narrative.

Ka'b's angry assertion that the empire allowed Helena to have her way and Christianize the world is adapted from the words of Ambrose, the fourth-century Bishop of Milan, and Philostorgius (mid-fifth century), as cited in Jan Willem Drijvers, *Helena Augusta: The Mother of Constantine the Great and the Legend of Her Finding the True Cross* (Leiden: E. J. Brill, 1992).

Finding the Cross

There is no evidence that the historical Sophronius would have told the story of Helena's discovery of the true cross of Christ in quite the form that I have him telling it. The legendary versions of the story (the only ones that any Christian believed in before modern times) seem to have originated in Jerusalem shortly after the empress's death in the year 328. I have based Sophronius's account on a version known as the Judas Cyriacus legend, which originated in or around the Syrian city of Edessa sometime in the fifth century. Of the three versions of the legend identified by scholars, this was by far the most widespread; it is also the only one that is anti-Jewish, a factor which explains its considerable popularity in medieval Europe. All three versions are translated and discussed by Drijvers.

Inside the main frame of the Judas Cyriacus legend, I have made several insertions. Sophronius's description of the Jewish presence in Jerusalem on the day of the destruction of the Temple is taken from Saint Jerome's commentary on Zephaniah 1:15. A pilgrim who arrived in Jerusalem from Bordeaux in 333 informs us that Jews, although banned from the city, were still visiting the site of the Temple and anointing the rock. This Bordeaux Pilgrim, as he has become known, has provided the earliest travel account of the emerging Christian geography of the Holy Land. Some anti-Jewish passages spoken by Sophronius are from Ambrose, the Bishop of Milan. Helena's self-aggrandizing declaration of intent regarding the finding of the cross, in which she compares her role to that of Mary, is also adapted from Ambrose; his account of the discovery of the cross in 395, which is the first official account provided by the Church, is translated in Louis De Combes, *The Finding of the Cross*, vol. 10 (London: International Catholic Library, 1907). Helena's physical features are based upon a representation of the empress on a medal in the British museum, shown at the end of "The Rock of the Cross." The prayer of Judas, asking God's help and promising conversion in return, is found in Drijvers, as is the recounting of the miracle that followed. Cyril, a later Bishop of Jerusalem, claimed to witness the miraculous light that emanated from the cross. He recorded the event for posterity in a letter to the emperor in 351, believing it to be proof of divine support for the emperor and his military campaigns. Many different variations on this miracle exist in the literature. The verse containing Christ's prophecy is based on Matthew 23:37–39, 24:29–31. The discovery of the cross under a temple to the Goddess of Love, Venus, is based on *The Life of Constantine*, by the Church historian Eusebius, an eyewitness to the building of the Church who was born in Palestine at the end of the third century. The conversion of Judas and his re-christening as Judas Cyriacus is the origin of the name given to this fifth-century tale of the discovery of the cross—the Judas-Cyriacus legend.

Not long after Helena's departure, a piece of the cross was carefully mounted in a casket of pure gold and precious stones. It was placed in a silver shrine around which had been built a great mausoleum. On Good Friday of every year, the casket containing the piece of the Holy Cross would be opened. The description of the yearly display and veneration of the wood is taken almost verbatim from the fourth-century observations of Sister Egeria, who witnessed the ceremony (Wilkinson, 1971).

Finding the Rock

All sources, Muslim and Christian, agree that, when Umar came to Jerusalem, he was intent on seeing a specific site that had nothing to do with the Christian holy places. He wanted to see the place where the Jewish Temple had stood, or what the Quran (38: 20–21) refers to as David's *mihrab*, or prayer place. Both formulations amounted to the same thing. See Oleg Grabar, "The Umayyad Dome of the Rock in Jerusalem," *Ars Orientalis* 3 (1959), and Grabar, *The Shape of the Holy* (1996). It stands to reason that Umar thought of this site as the first *qibla*, or sacred axis of Islam, which he was visiting for the first time.

When Umar arrived, writes Jamal al-Din Ahmad, "There was over the Rock of the Holy City a great dungheap, which completely masked the Mihrab of David, and which the Christians had put here in order to offend the Jews, and further, even, the Christian women were wont to throw their cloths and clouts. . . . Now when Umar had come to the Holy City and conquered it, and saw how there was a dungheap over the Rock, he regarded it as horrible and ordered that it should be entirely cleared. To accomplish this they forced the Nabateans [native peasantry] of Palestine to labor without pay. On the authority of Ja'far ibn Nafir, it is related that when Umar first exposed the Rock to view by removing the dungheap, he commanded them not to pray there until three showers of heavy rain should have fallen. It is related . . . that Umar entered by the Gate of Muhammad, crawling on his hands and knees, he and all those with him, until he came up to the Court of the Sanctuary. There he looked around to right and to left, and, glorifying Allah, said: 'By Allah, verily this—by Him in whose hand is my soul!—must be the Mosque of David." (Le Strange, 1890). With the exception of the last sentence, which I attribute to Ka'b, not Umar, I have stuck closely to the spirit of this "classical" Muslim account, which, as Peters (1985) notes, "appears to embody . . . some very early Muslim perceptions about Jerusalem."

I surmise that the gate through which Umar and Sophronius would have entered the Temple Mount, the Gate of Muhammad in the *Muthir*, was the Double Gate facing Mecca on the southern edge of the sanctuary. This gate, whose construction dates to Herodian times, was blocked in the Middle Ages and has since remained useless as a means of access to the Haram. More on the gate can be found in Rosen-Ayalon (1989). Busse (1984) makes important observations on the prayers of Umar on the Temple Mount in his "Omar b. al-Hattab in Jerusalem."

On other details in this chapter: The phrase "Heaven is as close as one's sandal-straps, and so is Hell" is attributed to the Prophet, not to Umar, in the tradition. The legend of the pillars of the Temple, carried off by Titus's soldiers, weeping every year on the ninth of Ab can be found in Vilnay's *Legends of Jerusalem*. Other legends in this chapter from Vilnay are associated with the existence of a perfect heavenly counterpoint to the Temple. The description of Titus's persecution of the Jews takes from Mujir al-Din, medieval Jerusalem's Muslim historian writing in 1496. Mujir al-Din records Helena's singling out of the rock for desecration by designating it as a dumping ground for manure. The theme of desecration through sewage and waste, particularly women's menstrual cloths, is constant in Muslim sources. It should be noted that, to this day, one of the Gates to the Haram is called the Dung Gate.

Christian sources incline to the view that Umar chose the Temple Mount to build upon based on Christian advice. According to Said Bitriq, Umar said to Sophronius, "You owe me justice and a guarantee of safety. Show me where I can build my mosque" (Busse, 1984). Eutychius, the later patriarch of Alexandria who wrote toward the end of the ninth century, suggests in his account of the Muslim takeover that Sophronius persuaded Umar to build in the general area of the Jewish Temple in exchange for leaving the rest of Jerusalem free of mosques. A large area was needed, and Umar was committed by treaty to not confiscate churches; the abandoned empty space of the Temple would have been a suitable location from both parties' point of view. However, I am not convinced that this "utilitarian" approach fully resolves the religious tensions involved. In a collection of edifying tales, for instance, collected by a monk named Anastase of Sinai between 630 and 690, the archdeacon Theodore, a contemporary of Sophronius and eyewitness to the construction, tells Anastase: "Atheistic Saracens entered the Holy City of Christ our God . . . in punishment of our negligence which was considerable, and, running, they reached the place called the Capitole [the Temple Mount]. Some men they took with them by force, others with their full consent, in order to clean this place and to build this damned thing intended for their prayers which they call a mosque." From an article by Bernard Flusin, "L'Esplanade du Temple a L'Arrivee des Arabes, D'Apres Deux Recits Byzantins," in *Bayt al-Maqdis: Abd al-Malik's Jerusalem*, part I, edited by Julian Raby and Jeremy Johns (Oxford: Oxford University Press, 1992). The most intriguing glimpse into Umar's mindset, however, comes from the exchange between him and Ka'b that ends with Umar's rebuke, and the decision to build south not north of the rock. The earliest version, to whose spirit I have remained faithful (but in which Sophronius is not present) is in Tabari's *History*, vol. 12. This exchange, often interpreted as a conscious Muslim repudiation of its Jewish antecedents in the very place where it most needed doing—the site of the Temple—is the kernel from which this book was first conceived.

Facing Whose Rock?

In 670, Bishop Arculfus, a pilgrim to the Holy City, left this description of the mosque that Umar built in the location today occupied by the al-Aqsa Mosque on the Haram: "On the famous place where once stood the temple, the Saracens worship at a square house of prayer, which they have built with little art, of boards and large beams on the remains of some ruins." The travels of Arculf were recorded by Adomnan, the seventh-century Abbot of Iona, as included in Wilkinson (1977). On Umar's policies and bias toward non-Arabs, see Wilfred Madelung, *The Succession to Muhammad: A Study of the Early Caliphate* (Cambridge: Cambridge University Press, 1997). The continued expansion of Islam ended the possibility of Umar's desire for a pure, untainted Arab state. S. D. Goitein notes the shift from purely Arab dominance to the growing influence of other nationalities, especially Iranians, in his "A Turning Point in the History of the Muslim State," in *Studies in*

Islamic History and Institutions (Leiden: E. J. Brill, 1966). A fragment
of Ibn Ishaq's *Life* includes Umar's quote that, "Two religions cannot
subsist together." A passage in Muhammad al-Dhahabi's *Ta'rikh al-
Islam* (The History of Islam), tells us that Ka'b al-Ahbar helped convert
forty-two Jewish scholars, *ahbar*, to Islam during the days of Mu'awiya
who were granted subsidies and grants (Gil, 1992).

Umar's debate with Ka'b concerning the direction of prayer draws
on many Quranic verses (20:112; 42:5; 2:144; 13:37). The decisive
verses recited by the Prophet, making the change, are in Quran 2:
138–139. Ibn Ishaq's *Life* records that the change took place in the seventeenth month after Muhammad's arrival in Medina, and that it posed
an existential problem for Believers as expressed in the inquiry into the
condition of those who had died before the change took place. My
account ignores the detail preserved by tradition that has the revelation
descending on the Prophet near Medina, in a small outlying village
called al-Quba. I have translated the phrase *ahl al-qibla wa 'l-jamma'a*
into "the People of the Sacred Direction"; see *EI2* under "Ahl al-kibla."
The verses just preceding the story of Bara' come from the Quran 2:136.
I have taken the story of Bara' from Ibn Ishaq, although I have changed
the characters and eliminated a few details. Muhammad's ambiguous
response when asked to rule against Bara' is included as it appears in
Ibn Ishaq's *Life*. It is interesting to note Tabari's observation in his commentary on the Quran on the reasons for the change: "The first injunction which was abrogated in the Quran was that concerning the *qibla*.
This is because the Prophet used to prefer the Rock of the Holy House
of Jerusalem, which was the *qibla* of the Jews. The Prophet faced it for
seventeen months after the Exodus in the hope that they would believe
in him." This the Jews of Medina did not do.

The early debate in Islam over the direction of prayer is part of a
larger competition between Mecca and Jerusalem as sites of veneration
and pilgrimage. In the late seventh century many Muslims thought of
the two cities as equally holy. The poet al-Farazdaq (d. 728), for example, places them on a par in a poem. Writing in the fourteenth century,
Ibn al-Hajj al-Abdari in *Madkhal al-shar' al-Sharif* points out that there
were still Muslims who prayed from behind the rock in order to combine
the *qibla* of the rock and the *qibla* of Mecca. M. J. Kister discusses these
debates in his important article, " 'You Shall Only Set Out for Three
Mosques': A Study of an Early Tradition," in *Studies in Jahiliyya and
Early Islam* (London: Variorum Reprints, 1980).

Other details: Ka'b's statement, "those who can see lift their eyes to the heavens. . . . Those who cannot see look at the onions in the ground," is attributed to the first-century Hellenized Jewish philosopher Philo Judaeus, as cited by E. M. Forster in *Alexandria: A History and a Guide* (London: Michael Haag, 1986). The lashing of Umar's son, on his father's orders, for having a taste of wine is in Ibn Asakir's *Tarikh Dimashq*.

Growing Up in Jerusalem

The death of Umar at the hands of Abu Lu'lu'a is from Tabari's *History*. The image of oaths as screens for misdeeds is from the Quran 58: 15–18. Ka'b's "prophecy" of Umar's assassination in Tabari's *History* reads: "Ka'b al-Ahbar came and said to [Umar], 'O Commander of the Faithful, make your will, for in three days you will be dead.' 'What tells you this?' asked Umar. 'I find it in the book of the Almighty God, in the Torah.' 'What, do you find Umar ibn al-Khattab in the Torah?' 'By God, no, but I find your description and features, and behold your span is ended.' " Whereupon follows the tale of his murder.

On early bookbinding techniques in this and later chapters, I have relied on Johannes Pedersen, *The Arabic Book* (Princeton, N.J.: Princeton University Press, 1984). By the second century the illustrated papyrus scroll was replaced with the codex (book of leaves), made of parchment and later on paper. Nothing is known about Muslim practitioners of the arts of the book in the seventh century; no indisputably seventh-century Muslim manuscript has survived. By the eighth century, however, Pedersen attests, there were Muslim craftsmen of the book like Ishaq skilled enough in the arts of geometry and graphics to be enclosing sura headings in Quranic manuscripts "in a frame with the Kufic script executed in gold, surrounded by tracery, twisting lines, and geometrical patterns."

The struggle for control over the fledgling Islamic state between the Hashimites and the Umayyads is described in all the general histories. See, for instance, Madelung (1997), who also recounts the grievances against Uthman. The third Caliph's use of the Quran to justify favoring his relatives is in Ibn Sa'd's *Tabaqat*. Silwan, or Shiloah, borders the Old City of Jerusalem on its southern side. The story of Uthman setting aside the village of Silwan's gardens for the poor is from al-Muqaddasi. See S. D. Goitein's "Jerusalem in the Arab Period," in *The Jerusalem Cathedra*.

Mu'awiya, the first Umayyad Caliph, is believed to have had significant building plans for Jerusalem while a governor of Syria. In the course of archaeological excavations south and west of the Haram in the late 1960s, Professor Benjamin Mazar uncovered a group of seventh-century structures, suggesting that considerable building activity took place under the Umayyads; see Mazar, *The Mountain of the Lord* (New York: Doubleday & Company, Inc., 1975). Ka'b's anger over book illustrations was the kind of sentiment that was later developed in the *Shari'a*, Muslim holy law, into a prohibition on any kind of a representation of a living thing. An overview of the details of this law, including debate over whether the injunction applies only to animals or to trees as well, can be found in *EI2* under "Sura."

Arculf, who visited the Church of the Ascension around 680, writes: "Nowhere on the whole of the Mount of Olives is there a higher spot than the one from which it is said that the Lord ascended to heaven. A great round church stands there, which has round it three porticoes with vaulted roofs. But there is no vault or roof over the central part of the church; it is out of doors open to the sky. . . ." (Peters, 1985).

The English bishop Willibald, who visited Jerusalem between A.D. 724 and 730, describes the altar: "On the altar is a beautifully engraved brass lantern with a small candle inside. The lantern encloses the candle on all sides so that it will continue to burn, rain or shine, night and day." Then he goes on to talk about the two columns standing against the north and south walls of the church; see Wilkinson (1977). The bright light of the lamps shining from the church's upper windows comes from Arculf. The word *qindil* came to the Arabs from the Latin, *candela*, via the Aramaeans. Early Arabic poetry suggests that the lamps that illuminated churches fired the imagination of the Arabs, as they do Ishaq's.

The traditions of sacrifice mentioned by Ishaq in the course of his bitter exchange with his father are from Rubin's "The Ka'ba." Al-Fakihi is Rubin's source for the statement that the Black Stone was stained due to the blood of sacrifices. Ishaq's reference to the Torah is to Jeremiah 19:5–6: "They have built shrines to Baal, to put their children to the fire as burnt offerings to Baal—which I never commanded, never decreed, and which never came into My mind. Assuredly a time is coming—declares the Lord—when this place shall no longer be called Topheth or Valley of Hinnom, but valley of Slaughter." Hence, presumably, the name *Wadi Jahannam*, The Valley of Hell, previously discussed. The description by Ishaq of a good monk is a combination of the words of Paul in 1 Corinthians 3:16–17 and those of Gregory of Nyssa, who lived in the fourth century. (Idinopulos, 1991). The verses recited by Ishaq, the Christian overtones of which send Ka'b into a fit, are by the blind

Syrian poet Abu al-'Alaa al-Ma'arri (d. 1057), as translated by Ameen Rihani; see James Kritzeck's *Anthology of Islamic Literature* (Holt, Rinehart and Winston, 1964). Kritzeck's *Anthology* is also my source for the verses by Abu al-'Alaa inserted on p. vii. Ecclesiastes 11:10 gives us Ishaq's woeful lament that "Childhood and youth are vanity."

The Death of Ka'b

Ishaq's description of the onset of old age in Ka'b and his changing physical symptoms as he nears death borrows from Sherwin B. Nuland's book, *How We Die: Reflections on Life's Final Chapter* (New York: Vintage, 1995), and Ralph Jackson, *Doctors and Diseases in the Roman Empire* (London: British Museum Press, 1988). The description of Izrail, the Angel of Death, and his declaration to Ka'b, are adapted from the anonymous *Kitab Ahwal al-Qiyama;* see Yvonne Y. Haddad and Jane I. Smith's important book, *The Islamic Understanding of Death and Resurrection* (New York: State University of New York, 1981). The story featuring Abu Dharr, Uthman, Ka'b, Mu'awiya, and Ali ibn Abi Talib is reported in al-Mas'udi's tenth-century *Muruj al-Dhahab* (Meadows of Gold) (Beirut, 1984). Some of the details of Mas'udi's account have been changed, but the setting, characters and alliances are presented as they appear in the original. Ka'b's remarks about the uselessness of amulets and his request to be propped up and have kohl put around his eyes, are attributed to Mu'awiya in Tabari's *History*, vol. 18, *Between Civil Wars: The Caliphate of Mu'awiya.* The description of the soul slipping easily or painfully from the body is from al-Ghazali's *al-Durra al-Fakhira.* The final sentence is from the Quran 2:152.

The Wait in the Grave

A martyr's death is described in the Quran 3:164: "Count not those who were slain in God's way as dead, but rather living with their Lord. . . . No fear shall be on them, neither shall they sorrow."

Medieval Muslims believed that the dead and the living interacted in sleep. See Ibn Qayyim al-Jawziyya's fourteenth-century *Kitab al-Ruh.* Ishaq's dream is loosely based on a story taken from Mujir al-Din al-Hanbali, a fifteenth-century native of Jerusalem who wrote a history of sayings and stories about the city of his birth entitled *al-'Uns al-Jalil bi Ta'rikh al-Quds wa al-Khalil* (Marmarji, 1948). When Ishaq hears Ka'b's grave mocking him, he is citing Al-Ghazali's *al-Durra al-Fakhira.* The great ninth-century critic Al-Jahiz, in his *Kitab al-Bayan* (The Book of Proof), includes a narrative on the questioning of souls after

death by the two angels *Munkar* and *Nakir;* I have used an excerpt from
Kritzeck's *Anthology.* Abu Dharr's mocking of Ka'b is borrowed from an
image in the Quran (62:5) criticizing Jews: "The likeness of those who
have been loaded with the Torah, then they have not carried it, is as the
likeness of an ass carrying books. Evil is the likeness of the people who
have cried lies to God's signs. God guides never the people of the evil-
doers." Other passages from the Quran cited by Ishaq in his reflections
on the wait in the grave, and Ka'b's fixation on Judgment Day, are 2:172
and verses 3, 4, and 36–40 from Sura 75, "The Resurrection."

The interregnum between biological death and resurrection, known
as the *barzakh,* has received a great deal of attention in Muslim theological literature. I have relied on its comprehensive treatment in Haddad
and Smith (1981). They cite Jalal al-Din al-Suyuti's fifteenth-century
Bushra al-ka'ib bi'liqa' al-habib, upon which I have drawn. The tale of
the Prophet comforting Aisha on the subject of the "torment of the tomb"
is found in the jurist Abu Laith al-Samarqandi's tenth-century *Tanbih
al-Ghafilin* (Arousing the Heedless). See Arthur Jeffery's anthology, *A
Reader on Islam: Passages from Standard Arabic Writings Illustrative of
the Beliefs and Practices of Muslims* (Salem, N.H.: Ayer Co., 1962).

The account of the first *fitna,* civil war, that followed the murder of
Uthman follows the standard Muslim account. I have relied in particular
on Mas'udi's *Muruj.* Tabari attributes far less altruistic motives to
Hasan's renouncing of the Caliphate to Mu'awiya in his *History,* vol. 18.
That God did not intend to unite Prophethood and the Caliphate in the
House of Hashim was, according to tradition, the opinion of Hasan as
expressed on his deathbed to his brother Husayn. Ishaq's description of
the mind in sleep is adapted from a text by Gregory of Nyssa (335–395),
"On the Making of Man," found in *A Select Library of Nicene and Post-
Nicene Fathers of the Christian Church,* vol. 5, ed. Philip Schaff and
Henry Wace (Peabody, Mass.: Hendrickson, 1994).

The Footprint

Just before his death in 680, Mu'awiya adjudicated a controversy
in Jerusalem between Christians and Jews that was witnessed by the
European pilgrim Arculf; it concerned a piece of linen cloth that had
covered Christ's head and was allegedly stolen from his tomb by a Jew
in whose family it remained for six centuries. Cited in full in Peters,
Jerusalem (1985). I have adapted this story into the controversy over the
ownership of a footprint discovered on the Rock. There is no firm evidence that the story of the footprint on the Rock—alleged by different

pilgrims to be Jacob's in the twelfth century and Christ's in the year 1102—dates to the seventh century.

Mu'awiya's inauguration in Jerusalem is in both Muslim (Tabari) and Christian sources (the anonymously authored *Maronite Chronicle*). The latter states, "Many Arabs gathered in Jerusalem and made Mu'awiya king. He went up and sat in Golgotha and prayed in it. He also went to Gethsemane and went down to the Tomb of Blessed Mary and prayed in it." Cited in Robert Schick, *The Christian Communities of Palestine from Byzantine to Islamic Rule* (Princeton, N.J.: Darwin Press, 1995). On Mu'awiya's use of the title *Khalifat Allah*, "The Deputy of God," see Patricia Crone and Martin Hinds, *God's Caliph: Religious Authority in the First Centuries of Islam* (New York: Cambridge University Press, 1986). On Mu'awiya's general character, habits, and sayings, I have relied on Mas'udi's *Muruj*, Tabari's *History*, and Schroeder's *Muhammad's People*. The discussion of the softness of the rock in the time of Abraham is from the ninth-century *Kitab al-Hayawan* by al-Jahiz.

In his biography of the Prophet written in the middle of the eighth century, Muhammad ibn Ishaq ibn Yassar tells the story of the Prophet's night journey and ascent to Heaven that I have adapted and put into the words of one Yassar, a former slave like Ibn Ishaq's grandfather (see A. Guillaume's introduction to his translation of Ibn Ishaq's *Life*). Ibn Ishaq is the earliest literary source for this much elaborated upon story in Muslim tradition, which was destined to become the basis for current Muslim belief regarding why the Dome of the Rock was built—as a shrine to "the rock on which it is said that the Messenger of God put his foot when he ascended into heaven," in the words of the ninth-century traveller and geographer, al-Ya'qubi. This widely held belief is grounded in an interpretation of one verse in the Quran (17:1): "Glorified be He Who carried His servant [i.e., the Prophet] by night from the Masjid al-Haram [in Mecca] to the Masjid al-Aqsa [literally, the farthest place of worship, assumed nowadays to be a reference to Jerusalem]." The connection, however, between this verse (which is not among the inscriptions on the Dome of the Rock) and Ibn Ishaq's story has been shown by scholars to be very tenuous if we are interested in the actual historical reasons the Dome of the Rock was built. I know of no serious scholarly argument in its support. See on this Grabar (1959, 1996); F. E. Peters, "Who Built the Dome of the Rock?"; and Rabbat, "The Meaning of the Umayyad Dome of the Rock." The conclusion I have worked with in my story is that the legend of Muhammad's miraculous journey must have followed closely on the heels of the erection of the Dome, just like the legends of Helena's discovery of the cross followed the building of the Church of the Holy Sepulchre, and the fantastical accounts of Solomon's Temple so obviously followed its construction.

Ibn Ishaq, author of the earliest biography of the Prophet, confirms in an indirect way just how controversial his story must have been at the time: Did it occur during sleep, in a dream (like Jacob's)? Or was it an actual event? he asks. The Prophet is recorded as saying, "My eyes sleep while my heart is awake." Ibn Ishaq recounts the controversy and insists that, whether the Prophet was asleep or awake, the story was true and actually happened. Mu'awiya is alleged to have denied that the trip actually took place, downgrading it to a "vision." Aisha conjectured that only the Prophet's soul had risen during the trip, leaving the corporeal substance of her husband's body behind. Umm Hani, the Prophet's cousin, disputes that he left from near the Ka'ba because he was in her house: "The apostle went on no night journey except while he was in my house. He prayed the final night prayer, then he slept and we slept. A little before dawn the apostle woke us, and when we had prayed the dawn prayer he said, 'O Umm Hani, I prayed with you the last evening prayer in this valley as you saw. Then I went to Jerusalem and I prayed there.' " These opinions suggest that the story must have been contentious in Ibn Ishaq's day (the middle of the eighth century) and hardly likely to have been the reason seventh-century Muslims built the first great architectural work of their civilization.

What about Ishaq's resolution of the footprint's origin? On the authority of one Hisham ibn 'Urwa, Abd al-Malik, not Mu'awiya, is reported to have made this remarkable statement: "This is the rock upon which God had set His foot." Cited by Joseph van Ess in his important article, "Abd al-Malik and the Dome of the Rock," in *Bayt al-Maqdis*. The anthropomorphic view of God that the sentence implies became heretical in Islam but may not have been so in the seventh century. After all there were footprints in the Church of the Ascension on the Mount of Olives described by the intrepid Arculf (680) as the reason why the rotund Church was unroofed: "so as not to prevent those who pray there from seeing the way from the last place where the Lord's feet were standing when he was carried up to heaven in a cloud. At the time when they were building this church . . . it was impossible . . . to extend the paved part over the footprints of the Lord. Indeed the earth was unused to bear anything human and cast back the coverings in the face of those who were laying them. Moreover the footmarks on the dust on which God stood provides a testimony which is permanent, since his footprints are to be seen in it, and even though people flock there, and in their zeal take away the soil where the Lord stood, it never becomes less, and to this day there are marks on the earth like footprints" (Peters, 1985). If God's footprints were in evidence in the seventh century and inside a church that bore a closer resemblance to the Dome of the Rock than any other in Jerusalem, would it make sense for Muslims to accept the footprints of anyone lesser than God, like His Messenger, Muhammad?

Ishaq's image of the origin of God's transcendence in the moment after He rose to Heaven, leaving His footprint behind, is borrowed from *The Zohar*, as included in Scholem's *Major Trends in Jewish Mysticism*. There is no proof that precisely such an image was adhered to in early Islam, but the way of thinking associated with it was and later got purged out of the tradition. Al-Waqidi's *Fada'il*, citing that the rock was the place of God's ascension back into the Heavens, confirms it.

War of the Holy Cities

The account of Yazid's succession to the Caliphate in 680 and the slaying of Husayn ibn Ali on the plains of Kerbala in that same year follows the standard historical narrative of these events. I have drawn upon Tabari's *History*, vol. 19, *The Caliphate of Yazid b. Mu'awiya*, and Mas'udi's *Muruj*. The nature of Yazid's three-year reign is from *Muruj*, vol. 2. The details concerning the abuse of Husayn's severed head loosely follow Tabari; I chose to have Yazid, not his governor Ibn Ziyad, be the recipient so as to reduce the number of characters; see also the chapter entitled "The World and the Flesh" in Schroeder's *Muhammad's People*. General histories on the subject are Hodgson, *The Venture of Islam*, vol. 1, and Hugh Kennedy, *The Prophet and the Age of the Caliphates* (Longman Group Ltd., 1986). The citation that ends the account is from Sura 84 of the Quran.

The events of the second *fitna*, civil war, began with Abdallah ibn al-Zubayr's revolt against Umayyad rule in 681. Popular reaction to the death of Husayn was considerable; by Yazid's death in 683, Ibn al-Zubayr was generally considered the Caliph. This eleven-year civil war had an important bearing on the building of the first Muslim monument, the Dome of the Rock. Basing themselves on the texts of the ninth-century historian al-Ya'qubi, scholars through the first half of this century argued that Abd al-Malik "attempted to make the True Believers circumambulate the Rock at Jerusalem, in place of the Black Stone in the Ka'ba at Mecca" (Le Strange, *Palestine*). Abd al-Malik's intent, in other words, was to establish an alternative religious center in Palestine, which remained under Umayyad control throughout the troubles. Most recently this position has been defended by Amikam Elad, *Medieval Jerusalem*. However, since S. D. Goitein's short but powerful argument against this thesis in "The Historical Background of the Erection of the Dome of the Rock," *Journal of the American Oriental Society* 70:1 (1950), it has lost ground; see Peters, *Jerusalem*, and Grabar (1959, 1987). That the threat from Ibn al-Zubayr had a great deal of bearing on Abd al-Malik's decision seems to me hardly in doubt; but that the Umayyad Caliph's intent was to replace Mecca with Jerusalem seems unlikely, for reasons that Ishaq expands upon in his account.

Other sources: The Prophet named his wife Aisha, Umm Abdallah, the mother of Abdallah, because she was unable to conceive and Abdallah ibn al-Zubayr was her sister's son and the first child born a Muslim in Medina; see Abbott, *Aishah*. On Yazid's new rules of punishment, which resulted in the execution of 8,000 men in Basra, see Hadi al-Alawi, *Tarikh al-Ta'dhib fi al-Islam* (Markaz al-Abhath wa al-Dirasaat al-Ishtirakiyya fi al-'Alam al-'Arabi: Beirut). The compliment to Abd al-Malik, that he would one day rule the Arabs, was not actually uttered by Mu'awiya but by Abu Hurayra. Cited in Rabbat's "The Meaning of the Umayyad Dome of the Rock."

"He who takes revenge after forty years is in a hurry" is cited in Goitein's *A Mediterranean Society*, vol. 5. The description of Hajjaj as a "gray wolf who breakfasts poorly" is adapted from a line in a poem by Al-Shanfara Al-Azdi; see Irwin, *Night and Horses*. Al-Hajjaj's use of the sacred rite of pilgrimage as a ruse, which comes from Baladhuri and Tabari, suggests that the Syrian army had not changed the site of their canonical obligations. Why then was Abd al-Malik accused by Ya'qubi of wanting to divert pilgrims? The problem, it seems to me, is one of understanding how such an accusation actually appeared to be true to those who made it out of hostility to the Umayyads, while being false in its most extreme formulations. Details on the bombardment of the Ka'ba are from Peters's *Mecca*. Descriptions of the harsh treatment of the people of Mecca and Medina in the wake of Abdallah's defeat can be found in Tabari's *History*, vol. 22. The verses praising Abd al-Malik are from the same source; Tabari attributes them, however, to Bakr b. Wa'il, following Hajjaj's success in crushing rebellion in Iraq in the year 74 after the *hijra*.

Meeting Abd al-Malik

Abd al-Malik's connections to Jerusalem, and his conception of Solomon as a model of the ideal Muslim ruler, are discussed in Rabbat's "The Meaning of the Umayyad Dome of the Rock." On the desert swallowing up Yazid's army, see Wilferd Madelung, "Abdallah b. al-Zubayr and the Mahdi," in *Journal of Near Eastern Studies* 40:4 (1981), pp. 291–305. The phrase "Naught is as His Likeness" is from the Quran 42:9, and the mention of the Day of Resurrection, when the Heavens shall be rolled up by God with His right hand, is from Quran 39:66. The plausibility of a conversation between Abd al-Malik and Ishaq on the footprint is my extrapolation from sources that have already been discussed (Waqidi, Rabbat, Van Ess). The details of a typical day in the life of an Umayyad Caliph are from Mas'udi's description of Mu'awiya's habits in *Muruj*; Abd al-Malik would have inhabited the same palace. The Caliph's command that he not be addressed with flatteries or exhorted to righteousness is also from *Muruj*, but in a conversation with al-Sha'abi, reputed to be his only confidant.

Unlike his mentor Mu'awiya, Abd al-Malik's character comes across as very fragmented from the sources. Ibn Sa'd tells us that he witnessed the murder of Uthman as a boy of ten, suffered an attack of smallpox in his youth, was not prone to speaking much, had his teeth held together with bands of gold, and had the head of his former friend, Mus'ab ibn al-Zubayr, Abdallah's brother, stuck on a pike in order to set an example; his meanness and tendency to violence are attested to by Mas'udi; more stories of his meanness, along with his foul breath, bad teeth, and the nickname *Abu al-Dhuban*, Father of Flies, are from Baladhuri's *Ansab al-Ashraf* (Beirut, 1996). On the other hand, Baladhuri also tells us that Abd al-Malik was a very pious man before becoming Caliph and one of the four most learned men in Medina. See on this Rabbat, "The Meaning of the Umayyad Dome of the Rock." By all accounts, the man who finished building Islam's first great monument in the same year that he stoned and flattened the Ka'ba was an orthodox and observant Muslim. Putting all of this into a coherent picture required considerable license; I opted to leave the Caliph's character and motives somewhat enigmatic and mysterious.

Abd al-Malik's reference to the place of Adam's Fall are from traditions attributed to Ibn Ishaq, as edited by Newby. Adam's head poking into Paradise is in Tabari's *History*, vol. I. Al-Akhtal was a Christian Arab who was considered the most accomplished eulogist of the Umayyads. Irwin writes that the name al-Akhtal means either one "whose ears are flabby and hang down" or "one who is loquacious." Ahktal's fondness for wine is apparent in his poetry; he was the earliest poet in the Islamic period to compose a piece in its celebration. His antics at the Umayyad court, and the story of his appearance before Abd al-Malik drunk, including the exchange between the two men, I found in Jurji Zaydan's *Tarikh Aadab al-Lughah al-Arabiyya*, vol. 1, *The History of Arabic Literature* (Cairo, 1957). Both Zaydan and Irwin discuss the growth of poetry and patronage in the Umayyad court. On the truce Abd al-Malik negotiated with the Byzantine emperor, allowing him to focus resources on Ibn al-Zubayr in Mecca and building the Dome of the Rock in Jerusalem, see Khalid Yahya Blankenship's *The End of the Jihad State* (State University of New York Press, 1994).

Mecca and Jerusalem

If it was not the story of the Prophet's miraculous journey from the Rock, or inner-Islamic political rivalries, that gave rise to Abd al-Malik's decision to engage in the enormous undertaking of building the Dome—which cost him seven years of Egypt's revenue, his richest province—then why did he do it? It is impossible to read Abd al-Malik's mind from the sources. Accepting that he was an orthodox Believer suggests that underlying his decision lay deeply contentious and unresolved issues among Muslims of the seventh century having to do with the relative sanctity of Arabia versus the "Holy Land"—a phrase which often included Palestine, Lebanon, and Syria. A new religion was in the process of defining itself in relation to its earliest roots in Judaism and the overwhelming cultural and political fact of Christianity in the newly conquered territories. It would have been imperative for Abd al-Malik both personally and politically to justify himself religiously by elevating in importance the status of Jerusalem over Mecca; how he might have gone about doing so is what this chapter speculates upon.

The traditions extolling the sanctity of Jerusalem are among the oldest in the Islamic tradition; see Moshe Sharon's extremely important "The 'Praises of Jerusalem' as a Source for the Early History of Islam," *Bibliotheca Orientalis* 49:1/2 (January–March 1992). Priscilla Soucek considers "that by the end of the first century of the Islamic era the Temple area was regarded as one of the holiest places in the world." See her important article "The Temple of Solomon in Islamic Legend and Art," in J. Gutman, ed., *The Temple of Solomon* (Missoula: Scholar's Press, 1976). Al-Azraqi, the chronicler of Mecca's history, reports that Meccans were preoccupied with disproving the notion that Jerusalem was "greater than the Ka'ba, because it [Jerusalem] was the place to which the Prophets emigrate because it is the Holy Land." This kind of concern simply confirms the prevalence of the idea. Cited in Grabar, *Formation*. I have also drawn upon Busse, 1968, and H. Busse, "Jerusalem and Mecca, the Temple and the Ka'ba: An Account of Their Interrelation in Islamic Times," in *The Holy Land in History and Thought*, edited by Moshe Sharon (Leiden: E. J. Brill, 1988); S. D. Goitein, "The Sanctity of Jerusalem and Palestine in Early Islam," from his *Studies in Islamic History and Institutions* (Leiden: E. J. Brill, 1966); Abdul Aziz Duri, "Jerusalem in the Early Islamic Period: 7th–11th Centuries A.D." in *Jerusalem in History*, edited by K. J. Asali (New York: Olive Branch Press, 1990).

Other sources: Stories of Abraham's critique of his father's idolatry were in circulation in the closing centuries B.C.E; see Kugel's *The Bible as It Was*. These found their way into the Quran (19:41–50, 9:115). Other verses from the Quran relevant to the chapter are 53:38, 4:124, and 18:9. Hebron was in all likelihood designated as Abraham's burial place during the Umayyad period, not earlier. I am unaware of particular instances of how the story in Genesis (16:10–13 and 21:16–19), of two sons born of the same father but separated by jealousy, was actually used in the tradition to symbolize the relationship between Judaism and Islam; Ishaq's line of reasoning with Abd al-Malik on this matter is therefore my invention.

The relationship between weaving and geometry is explored in Joseph Rykwert's *On Adam's House in Paradise: The Idea of the Primitive Hut in Architectural History* (Cambridge, Mass.: MIT Press, 1997). On Mecca's growth around the pre-existing sanctuary of the Ka'ba, and on the Black Stone as the kernel of the Ka'ba, see Peters's *Mecca* and Rubin's "The Ka'ba." Rubin cites Ibn Jurayj, who was born in Mecca in the eighth century and had an excellent knowledge of its history; he relates that the Ka'ba was originally an *'arish*, the word by which the Arabs used to refer to the tabernacle built by the Israelites in the time of Moses (and which was the precursor to the first Jewish temple). "The report of Ibn Jurayj seems to imply," writes Rubin, "that the Ka'ba was originally built and treated like a similar sacred tabernacle, in which the dominant element was the *kiswa* [the black cloth cladding the building]." Busse also describes the relationship between Yom Kippur and the Ka'ba's annually renewed clothing of black in "Jerusalem and Mecca, the Temple and the Ka'ba." The idea of the Ka'ba being "the first sanctuary to be established on earth" is based on the Quran (22:30), which refers to the Ka'ba as "the ancient house."

Sons conspiring against their own souls is drawn from the Quran 6:123. The hand of fate is a common image in Arabic poetry, and the idea of God's Messenger raising witness against his own people is taken from Quran 2:143. On the uses of the language of wonder in Arabic literature and letters, I have benefited from Roy. P. Mottahedeh's wonderful article, "Aja'ib in the Thousand and One Nights," pp. 29–39 in *The Thousand and One Nights in Arabic Literature and Society,* edited by R. G. Hovannisian and G. Sabagh (Cambridge University Press, 1997). The embrace of the Black Stone and the Rock is one among many harmonizing traditions (the others deal with the Day of Judgment and the Dome as the heir of Solomon's Temple). I have taken this particular idea from the eleventh-century scholar and resident of Jerusalem, Abu Bakr al-Wasiti, embellishing his words with the addition of an erotic dimension present in early Jewish sources; see Sharon's article citing al-Wasiti, "The 'Praises of Jerusalem' as a Source," and Patai's *Man and Temple* for the erotic imagery.

A curious tradition attributed to Ka'b arguing how the Black Stone and the Rock are connected in the larger scheme of things appears in *Kitab Ba'ith al-Nufus ila Ziyarat al-Quds al-Mahrus* (The Book of Arousing Souls to Visit Jerusalem's Holy Walls) by Burhan al-Din ibn Firka al-Fazari, born in Damascus in the thirteenth century. It reads: "Verily, the Kaaba is in an equivalent position to the Frequented House in the Seventh Heaven, to which the angels of Allah make pilgrimage. And if rocks fell from it, they would have fallen on the place of the Rock of the Temple of Mecca [i.e., the Black Stone]. And, indeed, Paradise is in the Seventh Heaven in an equivalent position to the Holy Temple (in Jerusalem) and the Rock; and if a rock had fallen from it, it would have fallen upon the place of the Rock there. And for this cause the city is called *Urushalim,* and Paradise is called *Dar al-Salam,* the House of Peace." Translated by Mathews (1949).

One of the compilers of these early traditions in praise of Jerusalem, Ibn al-Murajja, who wrote his *Kitab Fada'il Bayt al-Maqdis* in the first half of the eleventh century, cites a prophecy which he attributes to Ka'b al-Ahbar: "It is written in some holy books: I [God] will send to *Aryusalaim,* which means Jerusalem, and the Rock which is called the *haykal* [Temple] my servant Abd al-Malik, who will build you and adorn you. I shall surely restore to Bayt al-Maqdis its first kingdom, and I shall crown it with gold and silver and gems. And I shall surely send to you my creatures. And I shall surely invest my throne of glory upon the Rock, since I am the sovereign God, and David is the King of the Children of Israel." Cited by Elad, *Medieval Jerusalem.*

A Moment of Decision

Whatever the reasons for building the Dome of the Rock, just like its great predecessor the Temple of Solomon, the project would have been controversial in a Muslim–Arab context that was still simple and pure in its habits and ways. David had after all positively ached to build the Temple but was unable to do so, perhaps because building a Canaanite–Baal temple—which is what Solomon built—was perceived by a majority of the Israelites at the time as a concession to the despotic systems of kingship they were ideologically against. Direct evidence for this tension at the heart of the whole Solomonic enterprise is in the Bible (2 Samuel 7: 5–7). "Go tell my servant David," says God, speaking to David's seer and counselor, Nathan, "would you build a house for me to dwell in? I have never dwelt in a house [before] but have been moving about in a tent as a dwelling." What is this if not an argument against kingship of the sort Umar ibn al-Khattab would have felt completely at home with? Both Solomon and Abd al-Malik did not agree, and for much the same reasons, although perhaps Solomon had his doubts (I Kings 8:27), which are cited by Ishaq as he struggles with his own doubts over the idea of building over the Rock.

It is worth noting, in view of the origin of Solomon's Temple in the tentlike structure of the ancient tabernacle used by the ancient Israelites, that Abd al-Malik decided to build his temple in the shape of a *qubba*, which today means "dome," or "cupola," in Arabic, and by extension has become a reference to the whole building. But in the seventh century, *qubba* meant "tent," or some variety of a temporary covering like the Ka'ba's covering of black cloth, the *kiswa*. The use of the word *qubba* in the inscription on the outer face of the octagon of Abd al-Malik's building is, as Grabar puts it in *The Shape of the Holy* (p. 64), "the first example of a new usage for a traditional Arabic word." With these comments in mind, it is interesting to return to the image of the destruction of the Temple of Solomon in al-Biruni's fourteenth-century manuscript (shown in "Finding of the Rock"). The Muslim illustrator has, it is worth noting, imagined Solomon's Temple as a tented dome modelled after the Dome of the Rock.

The diameter of Abd al-Malik's *qubba*, as K. A. C. Creswell has measured it, is "within less than half a metre" of that of the dome of the Church of the Holy Sepulchre, strongly suggesting that the Dome of the Rock, in addition to all its other meanings, had to rival the Church of the Resurrection; see Creswell, "The Origin of the Plan of the Dome of the Rock," *British School of Archaeology in Jerusalem*, Supplementary Papers no. 2 (1924). When al-Muqaddasi, a resident of Jerusalem, asked his uncle why Abd al-Malik's successor, his son Walid, spent so much money building the mosque of Damascus, his uncle replied: "O my little son, thou hast not understanding. Verily al-Walid was right, and he was prompted to a worthy work. For he beheld Syria to be a country that had long been occupied by the Christians, and he noted there the beautiful churches still belonging to them, so enchantingly fair, and so renowned for their splendor, as are the Church of the Holy Sepulchre, and the Churches of Lydda and Edessa. So he sought to build for the Muslims a mosque that should be unique and a wonder to the world. And in like manner is it not evident that Abd al-Malik, seeing the greatness of the martyrium [*qubbah*] of the Holy Sepulchre and its magnificence, was moved lest it should dazzle the minds of the Muslims and hence erected above the Rock the Dome which is now there." Cited in Grabar, *The Formation of Islamic Art*.

On the importance of books as artifacts, see the delightful story of the Holy Scroll in al-Mahalla, a provincial capital in the Nile delta, in Goitein's *A Mediterranean Society*, vol. 5.

The Father and the Son

There are only two, nonexclusive ways that the Jewish symbolism of the Rock could be appropriated for Muslim purposes and used to rebut Christian religious claims to Jerusalem: through the Rock's association with God and his center of Creation, and through its association with the "Friend of God" and the first Muslim, Abraham, a prophet who was the ancestor of the Arabs and in the Muslim view, neither a Christian nor a Jew. The hypothesis that the latter might have been the case was powerfully put forth in the seminal essay by Grabar, "The Umayyad Dome of the Rock." But between the story of Abraham's trial as told in Genesis (22:16–18), and the Muslim version in the Quran (37:99–110), an important change had taken place. The son, who is not identified by name in the Quran and whom the majority of early traditionalists thought of as Isaac (Ishaq), became an active participant in his own sacrifice. "My father, do as thou art bidden," he tells Abraham in the Quran, "thou shalt find me, God willing, one of the steadfast." The interregnum was of course filled with the enormous influence of Christianity and the example of the supreme sacrifice of the Christian Messiah on Golgotha. Judaism had to confront the same influence long before Islam, the difference being that Muslims found the figure of Christ admirable and attractive, whereas Jews did not. And still the pressure to prove one's own foundational act of sacrifice to be at least equal to that of Christ remained great. Shalom Spiegal's translation and marvelous 140-page commentary on a twelfth-century poem by Rabbi Ephraim of Bonn, which retells the story of the *Akedah,* provided me with my inspiration for the writing of this chapter: See his *The Last Trial: On the Legends of Lore of the Command to Abraham to Offer Isaac as a Sacrifice* (New York: Schocken Books, 1969). Spiegal argues that the requirement of blood for expiation of sins is a Talmudic teaching that predates Christ. Certainly that was also true of the Arabs before Islam, as the story of Abd al-Muttalib's sacrifice from Ibn Ishaq's *Life* demonstrates. Two other books were helpful: Jon Levenson's treatment in *The Death and Resurrection of the Beloved Son;* and Frederic Mann, ed., *The Sacrifice of Isaac in the Three Monotheistic Traditions* (Jerusalem: Franciscan Printing Press, 1995). The words of the son of Abraham cited in the last paragraph were attributed to him by Ibn Ishaq, the eighth-century biographer of the Prophet, as edited by Newby.

The Importance of Eight

In "The Origin of the Plan of the Dome of the Rock," published in the *British School of Archaeology in Jerusalem,* Supplementary Papers no. 2 (1924), K. A. C. Creswell shows that the design of the Dome of the Rock was arrived at working from the inside out, as I have Ishaq working it out, and he argues that the all-critical diameter of the Dome, and its height off the ground, were the governing factors in the design. In both the Church of the Resurrection and the Dome of the Rock, "the height of the top edge of the drum from the ground is equal to its diameter." This observation accords well with al-Muqaddasi's previously cited explanation for why the Dome of the Rock was built. However, while the Church of the Resurrection was the monument that Abd al-Malik's new Dome had to overshadow, the round (or octagonal) Church of the Ascension on the Mount of Olives was more likely to have had an influence on its general form. The Cathedral at Bosra in Syria, built in the sixth century, another annular building, was set out in much the same way as the Dome of the Rock; it may also have influenced the design. Ishaq's drawings in the sand follow Creswell's line of reasoning closely.

In Anastase of Sinai's seventh-century collection of edifying tales, the story is told of the archdeacon John, who incurred the wrath of Sophronius in the year of the Muslim conquest. John was a marble setter or a stonemason by trade who was "very good with his hands." But he "let himself be seduced by the Saracens," according to Anastase. He started to work on Umar's mosque "for a dishonest gain." When Sophronius found out, "he made John come, and asked him, like a father . . . not to profane his hands, and to keep away from such an abominable enterprise." Sophronius also promised John alternative work at double the wages. "Only, disobey not my will. Do not do harm unto yourself and do not be for others the cause of their loss, while working on the construction of the place which Christ has damned." Two days later John was discovered working on Umar's mosque "in secrecy," whereupon Sophronius had him excommunicated. A few days later, John fell off a ladder, was disabled, and died in agony from gangrene. I have based the character of Nicholas on this tale, reprinted in full in Flusin. The moral of Anastase's story is a line attributed to Jesus (Matthew 16:19) and cited in the chapter "Building on the Rock": "What you bind on earth will be bound in the heavens, and what you unbind on earth will be unbound in the heavens."

The association of the number eight with Paradise is one that has persisted across the ages; it is discussed in Annemarie Schimmel's chapter on "The Auspicious Number" in the *The Mystery of Numbers* (New York: Oxford University Press, 1993). A famous saying of the Prophet speaks of the eight gateways to Paradise. The Islamic Paradise, *Janna*, is a garden in Muslim thought and imagery, more prominently so than in Christianity or Judaism, from which derives the custom common to Iran and Muslim India of dividing gardens into eight parts. This Garden is lavishly built with bricks of silver and gold and furnished with seats made from precious stones. See more on this in *Images of Paradise in Islamic Art*, edited by Sheila Blair and Jonathan M. Bloom (Hanover, N.H.: Hood Museum, Dartmouth College of Art, 1991), and the article on "Djanna" in *EI2*. The lote tree is mentioned in the Quran 53:14. Other descriptions of Paradise used in this chapter are from Quran 15:45, 47:15, and 64:9. On the association of Rightness with Truth and Right, see the delightful essay by Elaine Scarry, *On Beauty and Being Just* (Princeton, N.J.: Princeton University Press, 1999).

Finally, the Dome's relation to the Ka'ba with which this chapter ends is a figment of my imagination; it works nicely if the tradition of the Ka'ba's "union" with the Dome of the Rock (which is not an invention), told at the end of the chapter on Mecca and Jerusalem, was in circulation at the time. Otherwise, there is no evidence that the builders of the Dome of the Rock had such an idea in mind, nor has anyone previously suggested it.

Stone into Light

The plans of the ninth-century mosque of Ibn Tulun in Cairo were drawn on animal skins, according to Creswell (1932). Regarding the Dome of the Rock, al-Muqaddasi suggests that a model was made for the benefit of the Caliph. It stood somewhere in the Haram court. Scholars have suggested that another very old Umayyad structure on the Haram, due east of the Dome of the Rock, *Qubbat al-Silsila*, the Dome of the Chain, may very well have been that model. See Rosen-Ayalon, *Early Islamic Monuments* and Grabar, *The Shape of the Holy*. Ishaq's reply to Abd al-Malik, "To Him belongs the sublime similitude," comes from the Quran 16:61.

In his *Muruj*, al-Mas'udi identifies the Temple of Solomon as one of the three most important monuments of ancient times. According to Soucek, citing Ibn al-Faqih and Wahb ibn Munabbih, the edifice itself was imagined as encrusted with jewels and precious stones. "It shone in the darkness of a moonless night like a brilliant lamp because of the quantities of jewels and gold used in its construction," writes the ninth-century chronicler al-Dinawari. Moreover the Temple was surrounded by a miraculous garden in which trees grew spontaneously overnight and artificial trees made of gold bore real fruit. On these and other elaborations, undoubtedly of Jewish origin, see Soucek's "The Temple of Solomon."

Raja' ibn Haywa and Yazid ibn Sallam are the only two names mentioned in the sources who clearly had something to do with the building of the Dome of the Rock. The information I have provided about Raja' is true to what little is known about him. That he was considered an expert on the Holy City is a point made by Nasser Rabbat in "The Dome of the Rock Revisited: Some Remarks on al-Wasiti's Accounts," *Muqarnas*, vol. 10 (1993). Yazid ibn Sallam was a local Jerusalemite and less important than Raja'.

On the issue of light and the design of the Dome, which Ishaq and Raja' argue about, there is reason to believe that the fifty-six windows in the edifice let in much more light before Sultan Sulayman changed all the marble grilles in the sixteenth century. Transparency, brightness, and vividness of color are central features of the design that must have

made this building stand out dramatically from all its Christian predecessors in the seventh century. Although we can only guess at the design
of the exterior mosaics on the eight octagonal walls, because they too
were replaced in the sixteenth century, it is known that a great deal of
color was deployed. As Grabar puts it in *The Shape of the Holy,* "such
external decoration in color is virtually unknown before Umayyad
times." The twenty-fourth Sura from the Quran that so moved Ishaq
(verses 35–37 are cited) is called "Light," and is often used in association with glass lamps hung in mosques to symbolize the divine presence. The conversation about the origin of the use of calligraphy in
Muslim religious architecture is an invention. Words on walls, however,
became prominent in Muslim architecture in place of images. The
Dome of the Rock stands at the forefront of an aesthetic revolution in the
use of calligraphy as decoration. Grabar, who has written extensively
about the inscriptions, considers applied calligraphy on this scale an
invention inspired by Islam; its manipulation on buildings is compara-
ble to the ways in which images were used in Christianity. A great deal
of aesthetic energy and symbolic meaning was invested in the act of
writing itself, as well as in all that accompanied or made writing on a
surface possible; see Grabar (1987, 1996).

Building on the Rock

The reference to a visit by Abd al-Malik to Jerusalem during the
rebellion of Mus'ab ibn al-Zubayr in Iraq (687–90) during the construction of the Dome of the Rock has been transmitted on the authority
of Raja' ibn Haywa. See on this Elad, *Medieval Jerusalem.* The platform
upon which the Dome sits today has eight sets of stairs, not four, and is
an irregular trapezoid in shape. Sources tell us nothing about its appearance in early Umayyad times. Following Grabar, I have assumed that it
had four sets of stairs opposite the four entrances to the Dome. See *The
Shape of the Holy.* The use of flour instead of plaster because it is an
"emblem of fertility" is an anecdote I took from Creswell (1932); it
relates in the original to a different building and Caliph. According to
the sources, the labor force on the site was Egyptian and Nabataean
peasants, the remnants of the Aramaic-speaking population of Syria and
Iraq. On all matters of construction methods and details, I have relied
on Creswell's *Early Muslim Architecture.* The ceiling of "expressed
structure" described by Ishaq is not what one sees today, because all
structural elements were covered up with false ceilings in later centuries. The pilgrim John of Wurzberg reported seeing the "most beauti-

fully adorned beams . . . supporting the roof itself." On the strength of this description, Creswell (1932) believes that there was no false ceiling at the outset, "and that the beams of the roof were visible from within." The effect would have undoubtedly been to make the building feel lighter and more impressive. Marguerite Van Berchem, in her essay on "The Mosaics of the Dome of the Rock" included in Creswell's *Early Muslim Architecture*, cites a mosaic worker during the reign of al-Walid, Abd al-Malik's son, who says of a different building "we have made it [the decorations] according to what we know of the forms of the trees and mansions of Paradise." And Rosen-Ayalon, in *Early Islamic Monuments*, relates the whole iconographic scheme in the Dome to the theme of Paradise. Finally, Abd al-Malik's concluding comment "Not for the sake of God did your friend meet his end but for the sake of money," is adapted from a report in Tabari's *History*, vol. 21, *The Victory of the Marwanids*.

All Is Vanity

The writings of al-Muqaddasi confirm how deep and pervasive Christian influence on Muslims in Jerusalem remained through the tenth century. See also Goitein, "Jerusalem in the Arab Period." Grabar, in *Formation of Islamic Art* and his other writings, sees in the use of crowns, diadems, breastplates, and other imperial ornaments of the Byzantine and Persian princes on the surfaces of Abd al-Malik's Dome "a conscious use of symbols belonging to the subdued or to the still active opponents of the Muslim state." Soucek has argued the connection between the mosaic decoration of the interior of the Dome and the memory of the decoration of Solomon's Temple as retained in the Muslim literary tradition; see "The Temple of Solomon." The craftsmanship of the glass mosaic work above the arches on the outer face of the octagonal arcade is still the original of thirteen centuries ago. The mosaics are of outstanding quality, and rank, as Rosen-Ayalon has written, "among the most beautiful" and largest preserved walled surfaces of mosaic in the seventh century. With the exception of the dedication of the building, the inscriptions are taken from the Quran (4:169–71 and 3:16–17 are cited). As Grabar has stressed, these Quranic passages "precede by more than two centuries any other dated or datable quotation of any length from the Holy Book including pages from manuscripts"; see *The Shape of the Holy*. On the words that were left out of one verse by mistake, presumably because of a miscalculation, see Grabar, "The Umayyad Dome of the Rock." It is an irony that the cru-

sading order of the Knights of the Temple, ferocious fighters who took
the Temple Mount area as their headquarters in Jerusalem during the
Crusades, mistook the Dome of the Rock for Solomon's Temple. They
converted this Muslim building celebrating a Jewish Rock into a Christian Church called *Templum Domini*, the Temple of our Lord Jesus. Staring in the face of the Christian knights every day for eighty-eight years
were inscriptions asserting the importance of Muhammad, and impa-
tiently demanding of Christians that they submit to his faith; it was for-
tunate for the ensuing history of Islamic art and architecture that the
good knights appear not to have had anyone in their company who could
read Arabic.

Abd al-Malik's appointment of Jewish Servants of the Haram,
known as the *akhmas,* and the extremely important ritual ceremonies
held on the Haram during the days of Abd al-Malik, are cited in Sibt
ibn al-Jawzi's thirteenth-century *Mir'at al-Zaman.* Al-Jawzi bases his
account on the earlier ninth-century writings of al-Waqidi. The relevant
several pages of Sibt ibn al-Jawzi, upon which I have based my account,
are translated in full and exhaustively analyzed in Elad, *Medieval
Jerusalem.* S. D. Goitein, in "Jerusalem in the Arab Period," says the
practice of having foreigners serve in temples was not all that unusual in
ancient times (see Ezekiel 44:9–10). The tradition of employing Jews to
light the lamps in the Dome of the Rock seems to have continued until
the reign of Umar ibn Abd al-'Aziz (717–720). The significance of the
cleansing and purifying rituals being performed on Mondays and Thursday, as cited by Sibt ibn al-Jawzi, is that these are the days Jews read
the Torah. Julian Raby, in "In Vitro Veritas: Glass pilgrim vessels from
seventh-century Jerusalem," has shown that a first century Jewish tradition of making glass vessels for ceremonial and religious purposes during the days of the second Temple was restarted by Abd al-Malik in the
seventh century; see his article in *Bayt al-Maqdis: Jerusalem and Early
Islam,* part 2, edited by Jeremy Johns (Oxford: Oxford University Press,
1999). See the same source on the coins issued by Abd al-Malik, probably in Jerusalem, showing a branched candlestick that looks like a
menorah. The sum total of all of these activities must have been viewed
by the Christians of Jerusalem as deeply threatening; certainly, according to Anastase of Sinai, they seemed to have interpreted Abd al-Malik's
actions as building "the Temple of God." Elad in "Why Did Abd
al-Malik Build the Dome of the Rock?" in *Bayt al-Maqdis*, part 1, cites
a Kharijite sermon denouncing Abd al-Malik in these words: "He
destroyed the sacred house of God, and revived the way of the ignoble

people [the Jews]. Then he gave the Rock a form like that of the Place [the Ka'ba], to it the rough Arabs of Syria go on pilgrimage." Finally, while there is no direct written testimony confirming that the Umayyads considered Jerusalem to be their capital during this period, Elad convincingly shows in his article that the scale of their human and material investment in the city was such as to leave no doubt that this was the case.

Other details: On the significance of the passage from the Book of Revelation cited by the hair-shirted leader of the group that intended to destroy Abd al-Malik's Dome (a fictional incident), see Norman Cohn's *The Pursuit of the Millennium* (New York: Oxford University Press, 1970). The imagery that Ishaq conjures up comparing the Dome to a beautiful woman bedecked with ornaments is adapted from Lamentations 4. I have adapted the early traditions relating to the merits of Mecca versus Jerusalem from the examples cited in Kister's "You Shall Only Set Out for Three Mosques." On the smells of Paradise, see the Quran 83:23–28, 76:5–22, and 52:19.

Grabar, in *Formation*, tells a wonderful story taken from the tenth-century geographer Ibn Rusta on the origins of the extremely elaborate uses that various kinds of incense and perfumes were put to in the Dome of the Rock. One day a certain Uthman ibn Maz'un spat in the covered part of the court of the Prophet's mosque in Medina. "It made him so sad that his wife enquired about the reason for his unhappiness. He answered, 'I spat in the *qibla* while praying. But I did then go back there to wash it, then I made a paste with saffron and covered it with it." Ibn Rustah comments: "It is thus this particular Uthman who was the first one to cover the *qibla* with perfume." Grabar goes on to make a very important observation: "The very nature of the story, its incidental and accidental character personalized through some otherwise little known individual, illustrates the point that, in the Muslim view of Islam and of its growth, there was no preconceived, theoretical notion of a holy place but an accretion of unique and at times trivial events that became accepted. It is as though the culture were psychologically reluctant to interpret abstractly the physical reality of its Muslim life."

Finally, the title of this chapter comes from the line in Ecclesiastes 1:2, "Vanity of vanities, saith the Preacher, vanity of vanities; all is vanity," and the last citation "The eyes attain Him not, but He attains the eyes," is from the Quran 6:103.

The Rock of Judgment

The correspondence of the ancient Egyptian words for "south" and "north" with "face" and "back of the head" is from Henri Frankfurt, *Before Philosophy: The Intellectual Adventure of Ancient Man* (Penguin Books, 1949). Umar ibn al-Khattab is reported to have said that he would not have kissed the Black Stone had he not seen the Prophet doing it. On Zion's "foundation stone," Ishaq is citing Isaiah 28:16. The Jerusalem-born historian and geographer al-Muqaddasi wrote: "The Holy Land is truly a mine of profit both for This World and the Next." (Le Strange, 1890). Ka'b's denunciation of building is a combination of Isaiah 14 and a saying by the famous preacher, Hasan al-Basri, who died in 728. See *EI2* under "Hasan al-Basri." Desert monks used the expression "to work the earth of the heart"; see Norris. Abraham is referred to in the Quran 4:124 as the "friend of God." Ishaq's ruminations on true faith versus good works is adapted from a conversation between the great ninth-century Sufi teacher Dhu 'l-Nun and his disciples. See Tor Andrae, *In the Garden of Myrtles* (Albany, N.Y.: State University of New York Press, 1987). The passage from the Quran cited just before the end of the chapter is 2:130.

In the Name of God . . .

At the heart of the prophet Muhammad's message lay the conviction that the last day, the day of judgment and retribution, was about to strike. The Quran speaks of it in the present tense. Different natural catastrophes will usher it in—the signs described by Ishaq. On this matter, see Tor Andrae, *Mohammed: The Man and His Faith* (Harper & Row, 1960). As a consequence the set of beliefs in *al-sa'a*, the last hour, *al-fana' al-mutlaq*, the complete annihilation, *yawm al-qiyama*, the day of resurrection, and *yawm al-din*, the day of judgment, became essential in Islam. The disappearance of the Ka'ba and the evaporation of all words from the pages of scripture are signs according to al-Ghazzali (1058–1111). See Haddad and Smith (1981) for a comprehensive discussion. The parallels in Jewish messianic thought are discussed in G. Scholem, "Towards an Understanding of the Messianic Idea," in *The Messianic Idea in Judaism* (New York: Schocken Books, 1971). Passages from the Quran that are integrated into the text or cited are, in the order of their occurrence: 54:2; 54:1; 69: 13–16, 81:1–14; and 82:17.

Ishaq's description of the *al-mahdi*, or rightly guided restorer of true religion and justice who, according to a widely held belief among Muslims, will rule before the end of the world, is actually attributed in the tradition to his father, Ka'b. See *EI2*, vol. 5, under "al-Mahdi," where much of my material on the Divinely Guided One originates. The three things that catch men unawares, a found article, a scorpion and "the coming of the Divinely Guided One," or the *mahdi*, is from a third-century Talmudic teacher cited in Scholem, *The Messianic Idea in Judaism*. The image of redemption breaking like a dawn on the horizon is from a story in the Mishna cited in the same source. Scholem notes that, by medieval times, it is no longer easy to tell whether it is Jewish messianic ideas that are being incorporated into Muslim ones or the other way around.

Was the Dome of the Rock, and the Haram complex of which it is a part, conceived with the Day of Judgment in mind? Concluding a chain of careful argument from site planning considerations to the decorative scheme of the Dome, Rosen-Ayalon (1989) thinks that it was. She cites this revealing passage from al-Wasiti, author of *Fada'il al-Quds* (The Merits of Jerusalem): "the Dome of the Rock is the Temple . . . the throne of the Day of Judgment will stand on the Rock, and there will all congregate. . . ." This congregation, *wuquf,* which I have called "the Standing," follows the gathering, *hashr,* and bears a strong resemblance to a pilgrim's experience of God during the Meccan pilgrimage, the high point of which is standing before a small protuberance of rock on *Jabal al-Rahma*, the Mountain of Mercy, in the plain of Arafat in Mecca. For a powerful literary evocation of this scene, see Elias Canetti, *Crowds and Power* (New York: Farrar, Straus and Giroux, 1995). The "King of Absolute Sovereignty, the Avenger, the Dominator, the All-Powerful, the Abaser, the Exalter" are attributes and names of God according to al-Ghazzali. The idea of terror being "the ruling principle of the sublime" is from the essay by Edmund Burke, *A Philosophical Enquiry into the Origin of Our Ideas of the Sublime and the Beautiful* (University of Notre Dame Press, 1968).

Illustrations

p. iii   The Temple of Solomon. Drawing of floor mosaic in the Theotokos Chapel, Church of Mount Nebo, Jordan, early sixth century. The Holy of Holies is at the center with the great altar just below it shown in flames with an offering. Dan Bahat and Shalom Sabar, *Jerusalem: Stone and Spirit* (Rizzoli International Publications, 1998). For a photograph of the original mosaic, see Michele Piccirillo, *The Mosaics of Jordan* (Amman, Jordan, 1993).

p. vii   The Rock from the apex of the Dome. Photograph by David Harris.

p. 7   Granite sculpture by Ronald Rae, entitled *War Veteran*, 1997. Regents Park, London.

p. 13   Mount Hor, or *Jabal al-Nabi Harun* (the Mount of the Prophet Aaron) as seen from the cliffs surrounding Petra. Pilgrimages were being made to this mountain, venerated by Muslim and Jew alike as the site of Aaron's death, until modern times. Lithograph by David Roberts, *The Holy Land, Syria, Idumea, Egypt, Nubia*, vol. 3 (London, 1849). By permission of the Kufa Library, London.

p. 19   The World According to Ka'b, showing the Ka'ba and the Black Stone in the south; Mount Zion and the Rock in the north; the bird of Paradise to the east; and the Tree of Life to the west. © Zeynep Yurekli.

p. 29   Muhammad preaching his farewell sermon. From al-Biruni's *al-Athar al-Baqiya* (Surviving Traces of Ancient Nations). Al-Biruni died in 1048. The illustration is from an early-fourteenth-century edition of his manuscript produced in Tabriz. By permission of Edinburgh University Library (Ms. 161, fol. 6v).

p. 36   The Prophet David. From Qazwini's *Wonders of Creation*, which contains all the important prophets within medallions. The flame enveloping the Prophet symbolizes the fire of the love of God emanating upward toward His Divine presence. Baghdad, seventeenth century. Gouache on paper. © Jewish National and University Library, Jerusalem (Yah. Ms. Ar. 8 1113).

p. 54   Photograph of a twelve-foot-high rock of red granite known as the Rock of Moses in Sinai. Local Arabs believe this to be the actual rock struck by Moses to quench the thirst of the Israelites. Photographer unknown. Scanned from an edition of *The Holy Land* by David Roberts, published by Studio Editions (London, 1989). Courtesy of the Kufa Library, London.

p. 58   The Prophet solving a dispute between the tribes of Mecca by having them join in replacing the Black Stone into the southeastern wall of the Ka'ba. From the *World History* of Rashid al-Din. By permission of Edinburgh University Library (Ms. 20, fol. 45r).

p. 61   The Black Stone inside its silver frame. Excerpted from a postcard printed in Saudi Arabia.

p. 68   Jerusalem from the Mount of Olives. © Zeynep Yurekli.

p. 76   Abraham, Isaac, and the Angel. Limestone relief, 20¾ inches by 15½ by 2 inches. Coptic, fifth century. © National Museum of Antiquities, Leiden, The Netherlands.

p. 92   Mosaic icon of Saint John Chrysostom (344–407), one of the founding fathers of the eastern Church. By permission of the Byzantine Collection, Dumbarton Oaks, Washington, D.C.

p. 96   The city of Jerusalem in the seventh century. © Zeynep Yurekli.

p. 101   The Gate of the Column in the seventh century. © Zeynep Yurekli.

p. 104   The Church of the Holy Sepulchre, or the Church of the Resurrection as it is known in Arabic. © Zeynep Yurekli.

p. 106   A reconstruction of Byzantine Jerusalem based on the Madaba map in Jordan. The domed Church of the Holy Sepulchre is shown in the foreground. A cross is believed to have sat on top of the column at the Gate of the Column for a century or so into the Muslim conquest. Courtesy of the Tower of David Museum, Jerusalem.

p. III   Inside the rotunda of the Church of the Holy Sepulchre. From Corneille Le Bruyn, *Voyage au Levant*, vol. 2 (Paris, 1725). Courtesy of the Kufa Library, London.

p. 118   Photograph of what remains of the Rock of Calvary, seen here encased in a glass box on the floor. Photographer unknown. See M. T. Petrozzi, *Dal Calvario Al S. Sepolcro* (Jerusalem: Franciscan Printing Press, 1972).

p. 123   Byzantine gold coin depicting a portrait of the Empress Helena. © The British Museum.

p. 128   Three woodcut engravings from J. Veldener's illustrated *History of the Cross*, first published in Dutch in 1483 and then reissued as a facsimile in 1863. The woodcut to the left depicts Judas being lowered into a well as Helena and her retinue look on. The central woodcut shows his repentance, and the woodcut on the far right shows him digging "with might and main, To find the Holy Cross again." By permission of Widener Library, Harvard University.

p. 138   The Destruction by fire of the Temple of Jerusalem as depicted in al-Biruni's *Al-Athar al-Baqiyah*. The illustration is from an early-fourteenth-century edition of his manuscript produced in Tabriz. The standing figure on the right is Nebuchadnezzar, and the Temple is shown as a large domed structure supported by a circular colonnade and enclosed by a wall. A white inscription at the base of the Dome reads, "*Bayt al-Maqdis,*" which derives from the Hebrew *Bet ha-Miqdash*, or Temple. The imagined form of this first Jewish Temple is clearly modelled on the Dome of the Rock. Notice that the first Temple is also imagined as a tentlike structure, an allusion, however indirect, to the origins of both the Temple and the Dome of the Rock in tent construction. By permission of Edinburgh University Library (Ms. 161, fol. 134v).

p. 139   Architectural ruins. From Charles W. Wilson, *Picturesque Palestine, Sinai and Egypt*, vol. 2 (London, 1882). Courtesy of the Kufa Library, London.

p. 156   The Church of the Ascension. Loosely based on a description left by the pilgrim Arculf in 660. © Zeynep Yurekli.

p. 178   The Prophet's Footprint. Photograph of a relic. By permission of the Topkapi Palace Museum, Istanbul.

p. 181 Muhammad riding his extraordinary steed, Buraq, traditionally represented in Islamic art as a composite of mule and camel with a woman's face. From a manuscript of the *Miraj Nameh*, produced in the workshops of Herat, Khurasan, in the fifteenth century. The text is decorated with sixty-one illuminations that tell the story of the Prophet's ascent to Heaven. By permission of the Bibliothèque Nationale de France, Paris.

p. 183 Muhammad negotiating with Moses the number of daily prayers he should enjoin upon his followers. Plate 35 of the fifteenth-century *Miraj Nameh*, produced in Herat. By permission of the Bibliothèque Nationale de France, Paris.

p. 200 A possible representation of the Caliph Abd al-Malik shown grasping a sword with his left hand. It is thought to have been issued during his reign on a coin known in the literature as The Mihrab and 'Anaza bust. See Luke Treadwell, "The 'Orans' Drachms of Bishr ibn Marwan and the Figural Coinage of the Early Marwanid Period" in *Bayt Al-Maqdis: Jerusalem and Early Islam*, edited by Jeremy Johns (Oxford: Oxford University Press, 1999). By permission of the Bibliothèque Nationale de France, Paris.

p. 207 Abraham and Sara with Isaac (Ishaq) dispatching Ishmael (Isma'il), the ancestor of the Arabs, into the desert. From a manuscript produced in Constantinople in the twelfth century, known as the *Codex Graecus* 746, folio 80 recto. © Biblioteca Apostolica Vaticana.

p. 209 The city of Mecca growing around the Ka'ba. © Zeynep Yurekli.

pp. 227, 228, 231 Sequence of geometrical diagrams showing the derivation of the plan of the Dome of the Rock and culminating in an axonometric drawing showing how Ishaq imagined the Ka'ba fitting into the Dome. The axonometric is based upon a drawing in Creswell, *Early Islamic Architecture*, and the portrayal of the fusion between the Ka'ba and the Dome borrows a drawing of the Ka'ba developed by Zeynep Yurekli.

p. 237 The Rock and its Dome. Photograph by Garo Nalbandian.

p. 244 Vegetal decoration arising from jewelled vase. Photograph of interior mosaic in the Dome of the Rock. © 1992 Said Nusseibah Photography. San Francisco.

p. 247   Holy Rock, Summit of Mount Moriah. Jerusalem, 1891. Watercolor by Carl Haag. © Christie's Images, London.

p. 250   Jewelled crown inlaid with mother-of-pearl amid lush vegetation. Photograph of interior mosaic in the Dome of the Rock. © 1992 Said Nusseibah Photography. San Francisco.

p. 253   Two sides of a copper coin with a menorah-styled candlestick and the inscription "Muhammad Messenger of God" on the reverse. Issued in Jerusalem by Abd al-Malik as the Dome of the Rock was nearing completion. Numismatic Collection, Yale University.

Acknowledgments

For reading and commenting on this manuscript in one or more of its multiple transfigurations, Ali Allawi, Pamela Berger, Patricia Crone, Musa Farhi, Rena Fonseca, Mai Ghoussoub, Margaret Makiya, Mary Ann Mcgrail, Hassan Mneimneh, Afsaneh Najmabadi, Anne Marie Oliver, Rend Rahim, Emmanuel Sivan, Naghmeh Sohrabi, Daniel Terris, and my dear friend, Emmanuel Farjoun, who first walked the streets of the Old City with me.

For historical research that went far beyond the call of duty, Chris Berdik, Jonathan Stern, and Rashid Khayoon. For sharing with me the index cards of his research as they related to Ka'b, Nasser Rabbat. For research into images and photographs of relics, Lara Tohme, Kris Manjapra, and Anne Marie Oliver. For sharing with me the heartache of constructing images allied to this book in their spirit, and then making them, Zeynep Yurekli. For countless hours spent teaching me the intricacies of Photoshop and Minicad, Walid al-Khazraji. For tracking down copyright owners and pursuing picture permissions Kris Manjapra and Keramet Reiter. For going over my transliterations, Bruce Fudge. For fact checking and completing and reorganizing my scattered sources, Jennifer Meier and Kathryn Hinkle.

Finally for being the kind of editor that most writers only get to dream about, Dan Frank. And for introducing me to Dan, and being there when I needed him, Toby Eady.

To all of them, my deepest gratitude.

About the Author

Born in Baghdad, Kanan Makiya is the author of *Republic of Fear, Post-Islamic Classicism, The Monument,* and *Cruelty and Silence,* which was awarded the Lionel Gelber Prize for the best book on international relations published in English in 1993. He has also written articles for *The New York Times, The New York Review of Books, The Independent, The Times* (London), and *The Times* (London) Literary Supplement. A trained architect, he is a founding director of The Iraq Foundation, a Washington-based nonprofit organization that facilitates research toward a democratic Iraq. He has collaborated on two films for television, one of which was shown in the United States under the title *Saddam's Killing Fields,* and he received the Edward R. Murrow Award for Best Television Documentary on Foreign Affairs in 1992. Kanan Makiya is currently directing the Iraq Research and Documentation Project at Harvard University, and teaches at Brandeis University.